BOOK II

A Fury of Wolves:
The Continuing Exploits of Ranger Sergeant Jacob Clarke

BOOK II

A Time of Wolves

The Legendary Exploits of
Rangi, Seream, Jacob Clark

BOOK II

A Fury of Wolves:
The Continuing Exploits of Ranger Sergeant Jacob Clarke

By
Erick W. Nason

Strategic Book Publishing and Rights Co.

Copyright © 2019 Erick W. Nason. All rights reserved.

No part of this book may be reproduced or transmitted in any form or by any means, graphic, electronic, or mechanical, including photocopying, recording, taping, or by any information storage retrieval system, without the permission, in writing, of the publisher. For more information, email support@sbpra.net, Attention: Subsidiary Rights.

Strategic Book Publishing & Rights Co., LLC
USA | Singapore
www.sbpra.com

For information about special discounts for bulk purchases, please contact Strategic Book Publishing and Rights Co. Special Sales, at bookorder@sbpra.net.

ISBN: 978-1-949483-16-1

This book is dedicated to my fellow Rangers, those who led the way in the first battalions of the Second World War, to those who fought in small companies in the mountains of Korea and the steamy jungles of Vietnam, to the modern Rangers of the Regiment, who live by the motto
"Sua Sponte"

I want to recognize and thank Sheila Nason once more for being my second pair of eyes, whose editing organized my thoughts and help tell this story. I also want to thank Bryant White of White Historic Art for the cover, and Gary Zaboly for his detailed sketches of Fort Edward and Rogers Island.

TABLE OF CONTENTS

PROLOGUE		xxiii
CHAPTER 1	JANUARY 1758: FORT EDWARD	1
CHAPTER 2	FORT EDWARD: SETTING THE CONDITIONS	23
CHAPTER 3	FORT CARILLON AND THE BATTLE ON SNOWSHOES	42
CHAPTER 4	FORT EDWARD AND THE GATHERING STORM	64
CHAPTER 5	JULY 1758: THE CAMPAIGN BEGINS	85
CHAPTER 6	BATTLE FOR FORT CARILLON	112
CHAPTER 7	ANOTHER MASSACRE	135
CHAPTER 8	HONOR AND REMEMBRANCE	167
CHAPTER 9	REVENGE OF THE 44TH	176
CHAPTER 10	NEW MISSIONS AND RESPONSIBILITIES	200
CHAPTER 11	RECRUITING DUTY	217
CHAPTER 12	THE MOHAWK TRAIL	233
CHAPTER 13	TO THE RESCUE ONCE AGAIN	252
CHAPTER 14	BACK ON THE ROAD	276
CHAPTER 15	FINAL LEG OF THE JOURNEY	301
CHAPTER 16	1759: THE NEW WINTER CAMPAIGN	316
CHAPTER 17	A CHANGE OF SCENERY	352
CHAPTER 18	THE RIVER CAMPAIGN	376
EPILOGUE		384

Major Robert Rogers Rules of Ranging:

1. All Rangers are to be subject to the rules and articles of war; to appear at roll-call every evening, on their own parade, equipped, each with a Firelock, sixty rounds of powder and ball, and a hatchet, at which time an officer from each company is to inspect the same, to see they are in order, so as to be ready on any emergency to march at a minute's warning; and before they are dismissed, the necessary guards are to be draughted, and scouts for the next day appointed.
2. Whenever you are ordered out to the enemies' forts or frontiers for discoveries, if your number be small, march in a single file, keeping at such a distance from each other as to prevent one shot from killing two men, sending one man, or more, forward, and the like on each side, at the distance of twenty yards from the main body, if the ground you march over will admit of it, to give the signal to the officer of the approach of an enemy, and of their number,
3. If you march over marshes or soft ground, change your position, and march abreast of each other to prevent the enemy from tracking you (as they would do if you marched in a single file) till you get over such ground, and then resume your former order, and march till it is quite dark before you encamp, which do, if possible, on a piece of ground that may afford your sentries the advantage of seeing or hearing the

enemy at some considerable distance, keeping one half of your whole party awake alternately through the night.

4. Sometime before you come to the place you would reconnoiter, make a stand, and send one or two men in whom you can confide, to look out the best ground for making your observations.

5. If you have the good fortune to take any prisoners, keep them separate, till they are examined, and in your return take a different route from that in which you went out, that you may the better discover any party in your rear, and have an opportunity, if their strength be superior to yours, to alter your course, or disperse, as circumstances may require.

6. If you march in a large body of three or four hundred, with a design to attack the enemy, divide your party into three columns, each headed by a proper officer, and let those columns march in single files, the columns to the right and left keeping at twenty yards distance or more from that of the center, if the ground will admit, and let proper guards be kept in the front and rear, and suitable flanking parties at a due distance as before directed, with orders to halt on all eminences, to take a view of the surrounding ground, to prevent your being ambuscaded, and to notify the approach or retreat of the enemy, that proper dispositions may be made for attacking, defending, And if the enemy approach in your front on level ground, form a front of your three columns or main body with the advanced guard, keeping out your flanking parties, as if you were marching under the command of trusty officers, to prevent the enemy from pressing hard on either of your wings, or surrounding you, which is the usual method of the savages, if their number will admit of it, and be careful likewise to support and strengthen your rear-guard.

7. If you are obliged to receive the enemy's fire, fall, or squat down, till it is over; then rise and discharge at them. If their main body is equal to yours, extend yourselves occasionally; but if superior, be careful to support and strengthen your flanking parties, to make them equal to theirs, that if possible you may repulse them to their main body, in which case push upon them with the greatest resolution with equal force in each flank and in the center, observing to keep at a due distance from each other, and advance from tree to tree, with one half of the party before the other ten or twelve yards. If the enemy push upon you, let your front fire and fall down, and then let your rear advance thro' them and do the like, by which time those who before were in front will be ready to discharge again, and repeat the same alternately, as occasion shall require; by this means you will keep up such a constant fire, that the enemy will not be able easily to break your order, or gain your ground.
8. If you oblige the enemy to retreat, be careful, in your pursuit of them, to keep out your flanking parties, and prevent them from gaining eminences, or rising grounds, in which case they would perhaps be able to rally and repulse you in their turn.
9. If you are obliged to retreat, let the front of your whole party fire and fall back, till the rear hath done the same, making for the best ground you can; by this means you will oblige the enemy to pursue you, if they do it at all, in the face of a constant fire.
10. If the enemy is so superior that you are in danger of being surrounded by them, let the whole body disperse, and every one take a different road to the place of rendezvous appointed for that evening, which must every morning be altered and fixed for the evening ensuing, in order to bring the whole party,

or as many of them as possible, together, after any separation that may happen in the day; but if you should happen to be actually surrounded, form yourselves into a square, or if in the woods, a circle is best, and, if possible, make a stand till the darkness of the night favours your escape.

11. If your rear is attacked, the main body and flankers must face about to the right or left, as occasion shall require, and form themselves to oppose the enemy, as before directed; and the same method must be observed, if attacked in either of your flanks, by which means you will always make a rear of one of your flank-guards.
12. If you determine to rally after a retreat, in order to make a fresh stand against the enemy, by all means endeavour to do it on the most rising ground you come at, which will give you greatly the advantage in point of situation, and enable you to repulse superior numbers.
13. In general, when pushed upon by the enemy, reserve your fire till they approach very near, which will then put them into the greatest surprise and consternation, and give you an opportunity of rushing upon them with your hatchets and cutlasses to the better advantage.
14. When you encamp at night, fix your sentries in such a manner as not to be relieved from the main body till morning, profound secrecy and silence being often of the highest importance in these cases. Each sentry therefore should consist of six men, two of whom must be constantly alert, and when relieved by their fellows, it should be done without noise; and in case those on duty see or hear anything, which alarms them, they are not to speak, but one of them is silently to retreat, and acquaint the commanding officer thereof, that proper dispositions may be made; and all occasional sentries should be fixed in like manner.

15. At the first dawn of day, awake your whole detachment; that being the time when the savages choose to fall upon their enemies, you should by all means be in readiness to receive them.
16. If the enemy should be discovered by your detachments in the morning, and their numbers are superior to yours, and a victory doubtful, you should not attack them till the evening, as then they will not know your numbers, and if you are repulsed, your retreat will be favoured by the darkness of the night.
17. Before you leave your encampment, send out small parties to scout round it, to see if there be any appearance or track of an enemy that might have been near you during the night.
18. When you stop for refreshment, choose some spring or rivulet if you can, and dispose your party so as not to be surprised, posting proper guards and sentries at a due distance, and let a small party waylay the path you came in, lest the enemy should be pursuing.
19. If, in your return, you have to cross rivers, avoid the usual fords as much as possible, lest the enemy should have discovered, and be there expecting you.
20. If you have to pass by lakes, keep at some distance from the edge of the water, lest, in case of an ambuscade or an attack from the enemy, when in that situation, your retreat should be cut off.
21. If the enemy pursue your rear, take a circle till you come to your own tracks, and there form an ambush to receive them, and give them the first fire.
22. When you return from a scout, and come near our forts, avoid the usual roads and avenues thereto, lest the enemy should have headed you, and lay in ambush to receive you, when almost exhausted with fatigues.

23. When you pursue any party that has been near our forts or encampments, follow not directly in their tracks, lest they should be discovered by their rear guards, who, at such a time, would be most alert; but endeavour, by a different route, to head and meet them in some narrow pass, or lay in ambush to receive them when and where they least expect it.
24. If you are to embark in canoes, bateaus, or otherwise, by water, choose the evening for the time of your embarkation, as you will then have the whole night before you, to pass undiscovered by any parties of the enemy, on hills, or other places, which command a prospect of the lake or river you are upon.
25. In paddling or rowing, give orders that the boat or canoe next the sternmost, wait for her, and the third for the second, and the fourth for the third, and so on, to prevent separation, and that you may be ready to assist each other on any emergency.
26. Appoint one man in each boat to look out for fires, on the adjacent shores, from the numbers and size of which you may form some judgment of the number that kindled them, and whether you are able to attack them or not.
27. If you find the enemy encamped near the banks of a river or lake, which you imagine they will attempt to cross for their security upon being attacked, leave a detachment of your party on the opposite shore to receive them, while, with the remainder, you surprise them, having them between you and the lake or river.
28. If you cannot satisfy yourself as to the enemy's number and strength, from their fire, conceal your boats at some distance, and ascertain their number by a reconnoitering party, when they embark, or march, in the morning, marking the course they steer, when you may pursue, ambush, and attack them, or let them pass, as prudence shall direct you. In general,

however, that you may not be discovered by the enemy upon the lakes and rivers at a great distance, it is safest to lay by, with your boats and party concealed all day, without noise or shew; and to pursue your intended route by night; and whether you go by land or water, give out parole and countersigns, in order to know one another in the dark, and likewise appoint a station every man to repair to, in case of any accident that may separate you.

Erick W. Nason

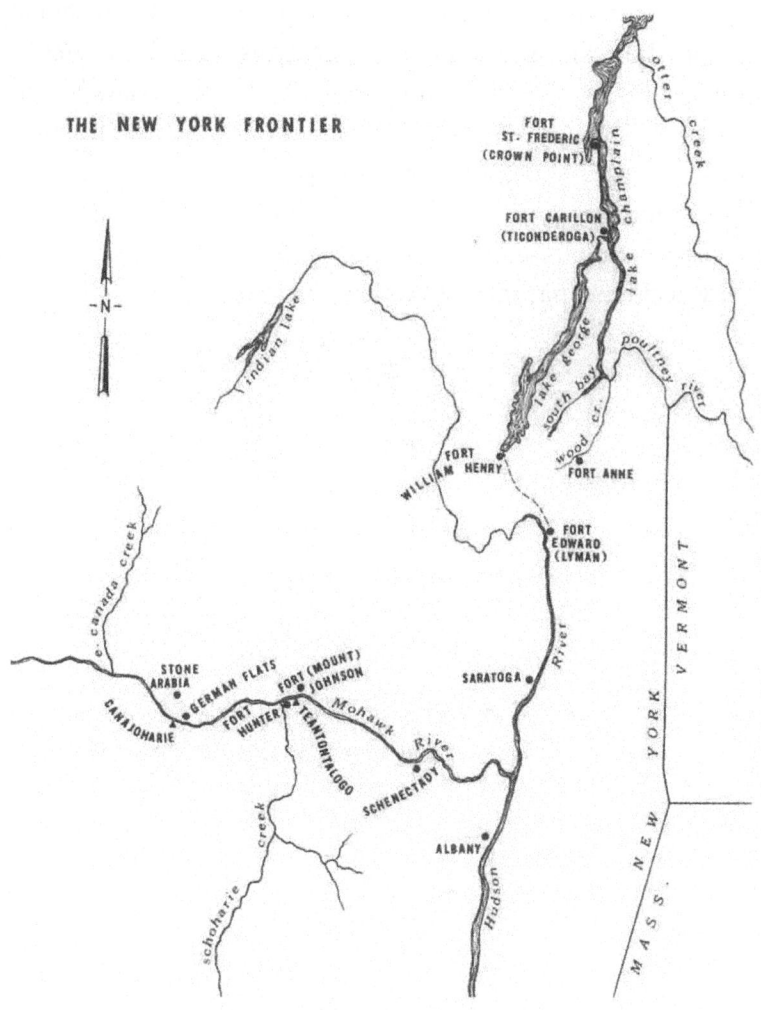

Theater of operations: New York

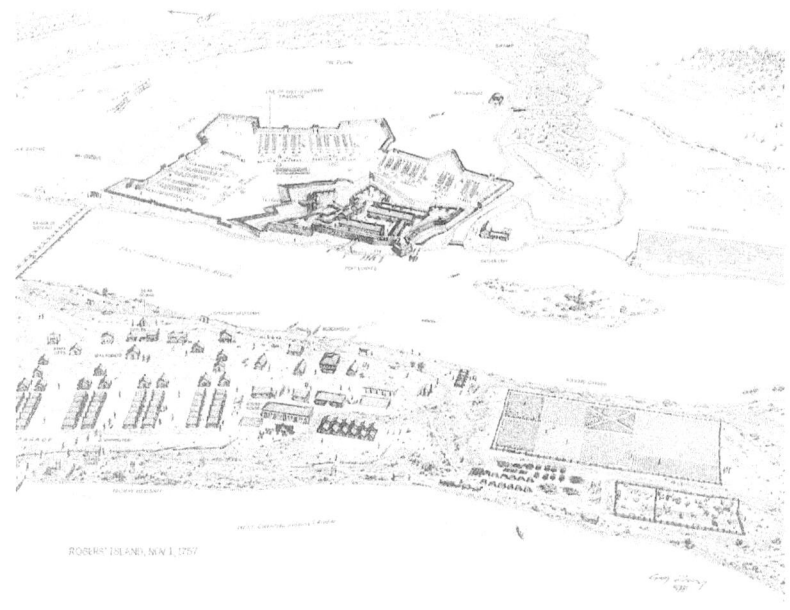

Fort Edward and Roger's Island November 1757
(Sketch provided by Gary Zaboly and Timothy J. Todish's The
Annotated and Illustrated Journals of Major Robert Rogers)

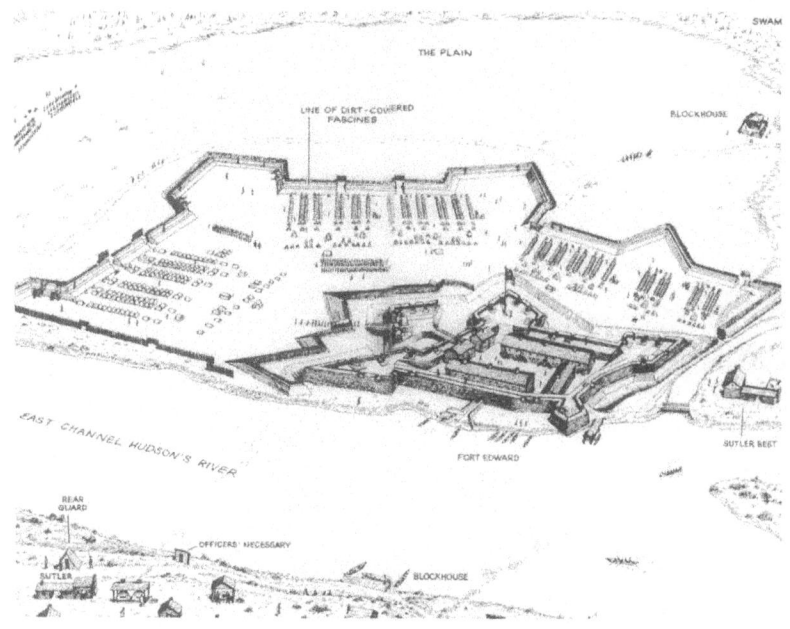

Detail of Fort Edward and Mr. Best's Sutler Shop
(Sketch provided by Gary Zaboly and Timothy J. Todish's The
Annotated and Illustrated Journals of Major Robert Rogers)

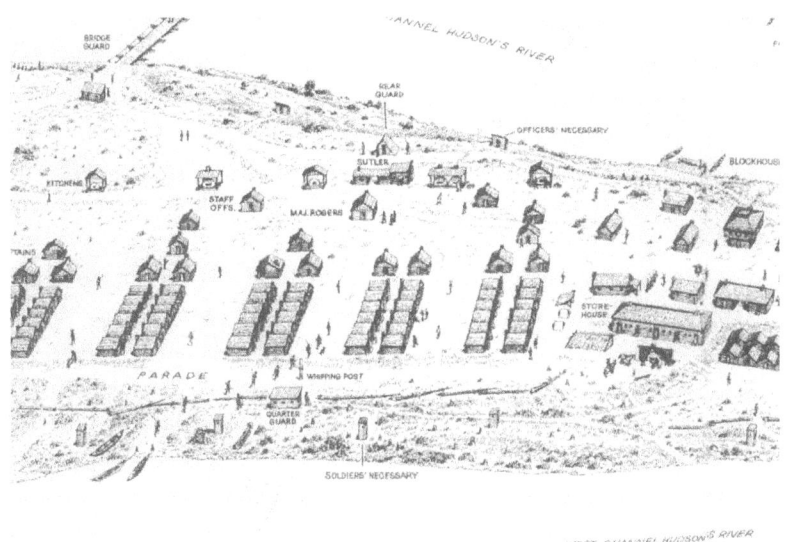

ROGERS' ISLAND, NOV. 1, 1757

Details of the Ranger Camp and Major Roger's Hut
(Sketch provided by Gary Zaboly and Timothy J. Todish's The
Annotated and Illustrated Journals of Major Robert Rogers)

Erick W. Nason

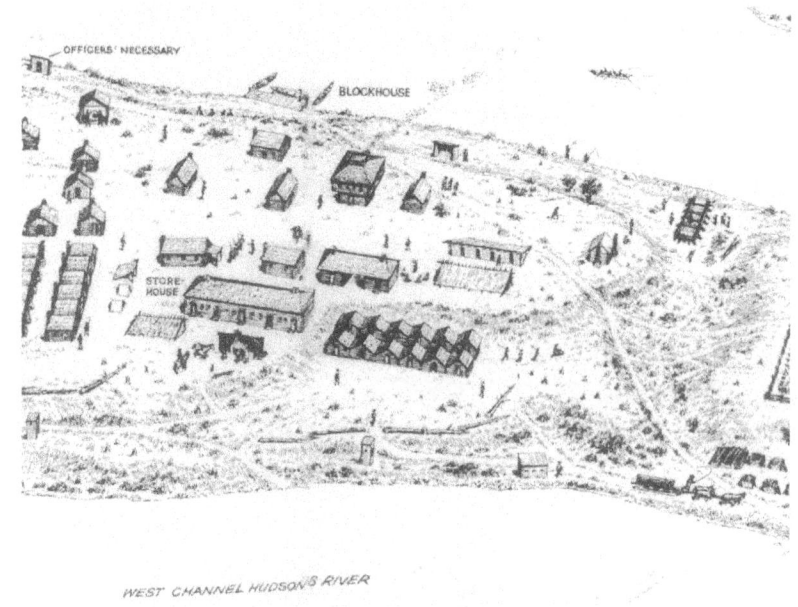

Detail of the Smallpox Hospital and Gardens
(Sketch provided by Gary Zaboly and Timothy J. Todish's The Annotated and Illustrated Journals of Major Robert Rogers)

PROLOGUE

The giant, weathered and quiet grey sentinels of the mountains gazed down into the valley below, the warming sun bathing their sides and and turning their thick white cloaks from the winter of 1757 into gold. Below in the valley, snow and ice stubbornly held their ground, a constant battle between Mother Nature and Old Man Winter for supremacy and control of the valley. In the swampy area at the southern end of Lake George, as the British had named it, or Lac du Saint-Sacrament, as the French who had discovered it named it, another battle raged between two great powers for control of the valley and its surrounding territory.

A large grey and brown wolf sniffed around a disturbed area, where blackened timbers rose from the snow like ribs of a dead giant. This giant was formally known as Fort William Henry, the northern bastion and line for the British in the war against their hated foes, the French. At the northern end of the same lake, the French had built their bastion and southern line, Fort Carillon, at a place the local natives called Ticonderoga.

The lake was a no-man's land, and numerous skeletons had been absorbed back into the earth from the many skirmishes between these two combatants. The French, along with their Canadian and Indian allies, stalked and hunted the British, who with their Provincials and their own Indian allies, in turn hunted the French. It had been a bloody and deadly game for the last couple of years with no signs of letting up. But there was some quiet during the winter as both sides rested, waiting to renew their fight in the spring.

Fort William Henry had been the scene of bloody battle, as the French, under their commander, the Marquis de Montcalm, had laid siege to the fort to open the way south into the heart of New York and his objective, Albany. The fort had been reduced by superior firepower, completely surrounded and cut off. The fort's commander, Colonel Monroe, having learned there would be no relief from the next British position at Fort Edward, had been forced to surrender in order to save the lives of his men and the families who had accompanied them to the fort.

While the French had observed the honors of war, their allies from the Abenaki, Huron, and Ottawa Indian tribes had had other thoughts. For reasons unknown, either due to great quantities of alcohol or the promise of scalps, pillage, and prisoners, they had ambushed and attacked the defenseless British column that had been marching away to the south. The ensuing carnage had stained the ground with the blood of the helpless, many adding their bones to the earth.

The only saving grace for the English was that the French had halted their advance, though the door was now open to their next objective, Fort Edward. The French had burned the remains of Fort William Henry and the surrounding buildings before returning north to Fort Carillon. That had been some months now, but to the wolves and other animals that crossed this area, the ground never smelled the same; it had a bad scent. With a frustrated look, the wolf stopped sniffing and padded off back into the quiet forest.

Like the great bears from the surrounding mountains who slumbered in their dens, Great Britain and France were stirring and waking from their winter camps, looking to their next military offensive in the spring. This conflict was a continuation of many between these two global superpowers. The genisis for this warfare, as with all of the conflicts in the New World, lay in Europe.

The first of the wars that would be fought both in Europe and in the colonies had been known as Queen Anne's War in the colonies. This war had been followed by King George's War, when France began raiding English settlements in New England. In New York, Fort Anne had been laid under siege, the Town of Saratoga had been raided and burned, and the Town of Schenectady had been raided. The French and their Indian allies had made it so terrible that all of the settlements north of Albany were abandoned. The war came to an end, and for the colonies, there had been nothing gained; the borders remained the same, but the losses were heavy. With the conclusion of the fighting, both sides licked their wounds, and the tension between them simmered.

The tension would once again come to a boil and begin the current conflict, known in Europe as the Seven Years War. In the colonies, it became mostly known as the French and Indian War for the two main combatants were once again the English and the French, both using their Indian allies and colonists. While the Seven Years War was a World War, for the colonies in the new world, it was just a continuing conflict that had begun when both nations placed their settlers on the continent's shore.

The conflict had begun in 1754 with a dispute in the Ohio Valley as the French began encroching on the English terriroy. The tension had popped and the bullets had flown when a Lieutenant Colonel George Washington of the Virginia Blues engaged the French. Both sides had used this as an excuse to begin hostilities all over again. It seemed they had been waiting for an excuse to restart their fighting, and this was enough.

1755 saw the English and their Provincials under General Braddock soundly defeated near the French Fort Duquesne. The fighting in the colonies was greatly different from the fighting in the same conflict over in Europe. While great armies maneuvered and fought using linear tactics that were the mainstay of all modern armies, this tactic would not work in the great forests of the frontier wilderness in the colonies.

These conditions required a new style of combat and a new style of soldier. While most of the English and French regulars were involved in the fighting in Europe, these nations would have to rely on their colonies' Provincial soldiers and militias to do most of the fighting, augmented by some regular soldiers. The geography would also require the experts at fighting in the wilderness, Native Americans and their style of irregular warfare.

To meet this need for specialized men who understood how to fight in the wilderness and survive, a man from Connecticut named Robert Rogers had formed a specialized company of backwoodsmen, who were already experts on tracking and wilderness skills, and turned them into Rangers. These men were to become a new breed of soldier, a force which used irregular warfare, having learned this style of fighting mostly from their connections and integration with local Indian tribes like the Mohawks and the Iroquois.

These Rangers would serve as the eyes and ears for the English army in the northern colonies, as well as take the fight to the French and counter the French irregulars. France too recruited specialized Canadians who, like the Rangers of New England, were experts on wilderness fighting and survival. Like their British counterparts, they served as eyes and ears for the French, and they would lead raids deep into English territory.

It was in 1755 that a young Jacob Clarke, a long hunter from the northern Massachusetts colony, which would later become known as Maine, had heard about the need for specialized men. So Jacob, along with his Stockbridge Mohican friend, Konkapot, had joined Rogers's Rangers and begun their baptism by fire when they arrived at Fort Lyman in northern New York.

Jacob had quickly learned the hard, brutal lessons of irregular warfare, personally understanding the cost on the local populace caught in the middle. Jacob's own father had been killed during an Indian raid on their home, and his younger brother had been taken as a prisoner, which eventually had caused his mother to die of a broken heart.

After some small actions, Jacob and his fellow Rangers had participated in General Johnson's campaign against the French. Moving north from Fort Lyman, which would later be renamed Fort Edward, Jacob and his fellow Rangers had fought against a French expedition under the command of French General Baron Jean Erdman Dieskau. General Johnson had built a camp at the southern end of Lake Sacrament, a name which he would later change to Lake George. There had been heavy fighting in the woods and in an area that would later be called Bloody Pond, but the French had been defeated and the English had begun consolidating their hold by constructing Fort William Henry.

The British had suffered through 1756 as the Marquis de Montcalm arrived and took command of the French forces. Instead of striking south towards the new Fort William Henry, Montcalm had struck westward near Oswego, destroying or capturing three British forts in western New York. Jacob and his fellow Rangers kept a constant eye on the French to the north to keep the English commanders as well as the Provincial leaders informed of French activities.

During the winter, while on an expedition with Captain Rogers, Jacob and his Rangers had fought a hard battle against the French irregulars and had been pushed back, giving Rogers one of his numerous defeats at the hands of the French and Canadian irregulars. Rogers and his Rangers were effective fighters, but so were their French and Canadian counterparts. With both sides evenly matched and brutal in their effectiveness, the fighting was violent and bloody..

The year 1757 was no better for the British, who had always thought they were the paramount nation in the ways of conducting war. Perhaps so on the open battlefields of Europe, but in the dense forests and mountains of the colonies, the French were the masters and were maintaining the upper hand. Montcalm, riding on the wave of his string of victories, had launched the campaign to take Fort William Henry, to be followed by Fort Edward, and, if his luck held, he would push all the way to Albany.

Rogers with Jacob and his Rangers had conducted a successful raid against the French at Carillon that Christmas, to remind them that the English were still there and were not giving up.

In response to the British disasters, the British Government had appointed Lord Loudon as the new overall commander for the His Majesty's forces in the colonies, who had developed a strategy to defeat their French rivals. Lord Loudon's plan had involved three major campaigns: to send overwhelming forces into the Ohio River Valley and the Lake Champlain Valley and to take the great French fortress of Louisburg, which guarded the approach to the St. Lawrence River, which in turn led to Quebec. Once these three critical areas were secured, the final objective would be to seize Montreal and remove the French dominance from Canada. Jacob and the Rangers would support the campaign through the Champlain Valley.

To meet these objectives, Great Britain had authorized the movement of regular British regiments to the colonies, who would be supported by the colonial militias and Provincial soldiers. To meet the need, a fast fleet had been gathered and over twleve thousand men were assembled under General Amherst to sail to the colonies. Prime Minster Pitt also knew that the Royal Navy would have to support the operations in the colonies, choking French commerce and trade from Canada to Europe. The colonies had been tasked by Lord Loudon to gather their Provincial and militia regiments to support the coming operations. While the regulars were supposed to do most of the fighting, the Provincials and the militia would have to guard the frontier.

While Great Britain had no issue with sending regulars to reinforce its army in the colonies, the French Government was more reluctant. Canada received the lion's share of reinforcements, and Montcalm had to rely on his Canadian Militia and Provincials and their Indian allies. King Louis of France was more concerned about their operations in the West Indies and in Europe, and he sent the majority of the French regulars there. Montcalm reasoned that once the snow and ice thawed and the campaign season began, the British would have to take Fort Carillon in order to move northward. After wintering in Montreal and Quebec, Montcalm had began moving his army of over four thousand back to their position at Ticonderoga.

Newly promoted Major Rogers had been busy while the great military leaders planned and prepared for the upcoming campaign. Grudgingly, some of the regular British officers were beginning to realize there was a need for these specialized Ranger units to fight in the wilderness. Rogers, with help from Jacob and his men, had run a Ranger School so the regular British officers could learn their tactics.

While some dug their heels into the earth and refused to learn from Provincials, others were beginning to understand the need to adapt. A small number of the regular British battalions began to adopt the shorter coat and hats of the Rangers so they could move more easily through the thick forests. In the fall of 1757, Rogershad organized a Company of Cadets who, along with learning the academics of the Ranger mission, had participated in a practical application of Rogers's lessons by taking part in scouting missions.

One of the biggest supporters of the Ranger tactics was Lord Loudon himself. While the school and cadet company was able to train some of the men, Lord Loudon wanted Ranger tactics and best practices distributed thoughout the entire army. So Major Rogers had begun writing down his Rules of Ranging to be published and distributed across the army. Rogers wrote his rules seated in his hut located on what would become known as "Rogers's Island," an island in the Hudson River across from Fort Edward, connected by a wooden bridge.

On the island were rows of wooden huts where the Rangers lived during the winter. They were arranged in rows with the officers at the top of the street and the men's huts lined up behind their officer's hut. With the outbreak of small pox, a hospital had been built on the opposite end of the island from the Rangers' camp. Some believed the hospital had been built on the island on purpose because of the tension between the British regulars and both the Rangers and the other Provincials.

Fort Edward was steadily growing into one of the largest communities in the colonies. Following the fall of Fort William Henry, it was now the front line against the French. The great Union Jack flew from the center of the fort, and around the walls was a sea of white canvas tents, arranged in neat, orderly rows of company streets. The number of tents had grown as more British regulars arrived at the fort. There were two large gardens, one on the island and one near the Fort to augment the food rations from Albany and what the Rangers could procure through hunting and fishing.

With the growing number of mouths to feed, the quartermasters were busy. Near the fort, numerous small stores were beginning to be established, centered on the main two-story log house/store of Mr. Frederick Best. Here, Provincials, militiamen, and British regulars could buy what they needed from soldiering items, to rum and beer, to extra food or other supplies.

The need for Rangers was growing, and Rogers was responsible for nearly a battalion of eight companies of Rangers, which included a company of Stockbridge Indians. Most of the men who served in these companies were from New Hampshire, Massachusetts, and New York, but Rogers did not accept any average men. He had strict criteria for what these men needed to have for wilderness skills before he would accept them.

Along with the need for more Rangers, there was a need for officers to lead them, and on several occasions Major Rogers, along with Captains Stark and Putnam, had worked on Jacob to accept a promotion to lieutenant. While honored, Jacob wanted to remain a sergeant and to lead his men. Jacob suspected that the coming campaign year would be another bloody one, and he wanted to remain with the men he trusted. Rogers accepted that, seeing Jacob had saved his hide on several occasions while scouting around the French positions at Ticonderoga and Crown Point.

There was a growing tension between the regular British soldiers, and especially their officers, and the Provincial officers and men. They especially chaffed at Rogers's Independent Command, which made his men exempt from British discipline. Rogers had done much to mold a group of normally fiercely independent long hunters and trappers into a battalion of closely-knit men who would follow him loyally into hell itself, if required.

While most British officers still looked at the Rangers as a group of malcontents and rabble, who would never achieve the rigid discipline and parade ground lockstep performance of the regular British soldiers, the desertion rate of the Rangers was lower than that of any Provincial or British regiment. Tension between the British and the Rangers had nearly come to a head when there was a mutiny on Rogers Island by Rangers angered over draconian British discipline of some of their men, despite their exempt status. It took Rogers's skillful diplomacy with the British higher command authorities and his own men to resolve the situation.

The tension still remained, and as hard as Rogers worked with the British regular commanders, he made little to no headway with them. His saving grace was the support he received from Lord Loudon, who not only believed in the Rangers, but also relied on them to do the jobs his very own units, including the 60th Regiment known as the Royal Americans, could not do. Lord Loudon had wanted to raise two Ranger companies to be added to each of his British regiments in the colony, but this was untenable.

Instead, Thomas Gage of the 44th Regiment of Foot, having learned the Ranger tactics himself, stated he would form a five-hundred-man unit of Light Infantry to become known as the 80th Regiment of Foot, which he would personally pay the bill for. The core cadre of the 80th would be graduates from Rogers's Ranger School. With the financial strain of organizing for the coming campaign, the Provincial Government of the colonies could only field five Ranger companies and one company of Stockbridge Indians under Rogers's command.

The winter refused to leave easily, momentarily winning its tug-of-war with Mother Nature and the cold snow once again gripped the men in the fort and on the island. The ice jams that clogged the river caused flooding, and the Rangers had had to clean the mud and silt from their huts and rebuild their latrines, which had been carried off by the floodwaters. The only signs of the flood now were the piles of ice chunks still lining the shore. But then the sun had disappeared, and the cold bitter snow and wind returned.

The great silent sentinels of the mountains with their thick winter cloaks sat and waited, time meaningless to them. Only the passage of the seasons was noticed, and even the great mountains wanted the warmth of the sun to return. The valley sat and waited, almost holding its breath to see what would happen when spring arrived and the two armies once more took to the field to wage their war upon one another.

CHAPTER 1

JANUARY 1758: FORT EDWARD

The sun had briefly shown itself in the morning, bright and golden, but it didn't last. Old Man Winter still had a firm grip on the northern frontier, and the thick grey clouds quickly overwhelmed and blocked out the sun. A cold breeze soon turned into a stinging wind that blew in from the north, down through the mountains and valley, chilling the men on Rogers's Island. Large fluffy snowflakes began to dance about the wind, harbingers of another cold day to come.

This winter had been a tough one for the men stationed at Fort Edward, limiting their activities to local scouts and hunting expeditions. Still, the island was a hive of activity as Rangers continued the clean up after the flood that had briefly covered their island. Men were out in the company streets with shovels, removing mud and debris.

The shock from the slaughter at Fort William Henry still hung about the shoulders of the men, who were now the farthest line drawn in the frontier to halt the French.

The Ranger huts were small, log-cabin types, just big enough to hold the six to eight men that occupied each one. The spaces between the logs were well chinked with mud and straw to keep the cold wind out, the roof shingled with wooden slats. At the end of each hut was a stone chimney, from which numerous grey columns of smoke rose from the island to be lost in the grey of the beginning snow storm. The company street was arranged so that the first hut was for the officer, either a lieutenant or a captain, and the door faced the eastern side of the island.

Behind the officers' huts were the enlisted men, sergeants, corporals, and privates. Rangers' huts had doors that faced into the center of the street. It made sense in a way; the messenger would come for the officer at the end of the street, who would in turn and go down his street to gather his men. It also followed regulations on how a military camp was to be established, but instead of tents, they had huts. The Rangers mostly occupied the huts in the fall to early spring, choosing to sleep under the stars or in lean-tos during the hot summers to avoid the close quarters that led to unbearable smells and sickness. Most of the time in the spring and summer, the Rangers were out scouting the enemy or on other missions.

Jacob's hut was just like all of the others. His was located on Captain Putnam's street, which happened to be very close to Major Rogers's hut. This seemed appropriate; Jacob was often called to Major Rogers's hut for an assignment. A thick, wool blanker hung in the door frame, their door having been torn off and carried off by the flood. Jacob decided that if winter was going to hang in there, they were going to have to replace their door.

Jacob was a stout man, chiseled from the harsh life of growing up on the frontier and being a Ranger now for three years. He had grown up outside of the Town of York where his father had ran a trading post. It was there that he became a long hunter and met Konkapot as he went on hunting expeditions with the Mohicans. It was after the raid that killed his father, took his brother, and basically caused his mother to waste away, that Jacob moved away and went to live with the Mohicans in Stockbridge. It was from there that he and Konkapot had left to join the Rangers.

Both Jacob and Konkapot had been young men, full of the energy of youth and excited for the adventure to come when they first joined, but now the nearly three years of fighting had matured and hardened Jacob to the rigors of frontier fighting. This was reflected in the large scars on his face from injuries suffered in battle, and from time to time, in the far-off look in his eyes as he recalled the carnage and the loss of his friends.

Jacob had felt many losses during his time with the Rangers. First was his sergeant, Patrick McKinney, from whom he had learned much, building his skills as a frontiersmen and hunter into those of a Ranger. Other members from his original section, William Halley and Robert Blakefield, were all lost to fighting the French. Other men replaced the fallen Rangers, stepping in to take their places, and eventually falling as well.

His greatest loss had been Maggie, a young woman he had met through Mr. Frederick Best, a local merchant who had a shop at the fort. Maggie and her sister Audrey had been indentured servents, and Frederick had purchased their contracts to get them away from the cruel city and to have them work for him on the frontier. He treated them more like daughters than servants, and it was through the shop that Jacob had met Maggie. She had filled a void in his life that had been emptied by the death of his family and his need to harden himself for fighting this war.

It was an unfortunate circumstance that led Jacob into a conflict with Captain Archibald Reynolds of the 48th Regiment of Foot and his trusted Sergeant-Major Lovewell. The sergeant-major had a sadistic streak in him, taking pleasure in harshly disciplining men on behalf of Captain Reynolds, especially Provincials and Rangers. There was no love lost between the sergeant-major and Jacob, which led to the unfortunate event that had changed his life.

In a druken rage, the sergeant-major stalked and attacked Maggie as she was out cutting wood in the nearby forest. To make the situation worse, the Canadians and Indians had launched a raid against the fort at the same time. In the midst of the fighting, Jacob had arrived in time to prevent the sergeant-major from completing his lustful attack, only to watch him drive his knife into Maggie's back just as Jacob's ball found his forehead. Maggie died in his arms, and at that moment, a part of Jacob's soul died as well.

Jacob reflected as he recalled the friends and Rangers he had lost fighting the war, and wondered if it had been worth it. The British wanted the Rangers to go out and find and kill their enemies while threy treated them poorly. In some instances, Jacob felt more of a kinship with the Canadian irregulars he fought against. At least he knew where he stood with them, kill or be killed in a strangely honorable way. Jacob had no problem killing. He never really reflected about it; it just was. Either he killed his enemies, or they killed him. In Jacob's mind, it was as simple as that.

Why did he still fight? Jacob stopped and mused on it for a second or two, then looking around the cabin saw the easy answer. He did his duty to stop the French, and in a way avenge his parents, who had died to Indians allied to the French. Reality was more simple, as he looked at the faces of his section; he fought and killed to keep them alive and hopefully see them home again once this war, like the others, came to an end,

As the cold wind pounded the hut causing the temporary wool door to dance, Jacob was drawn out of his thoughts and back to the present. He was sitting on his bunk and sewing up a tear in his thick green overcoat. He looked around and observed what was going on in the hut. His best and longest friend Konkapot was over at the fireplace, melting lead in a small pot to be ladled into his bullet molds. So far, he had been spared any grievous injuries from the war, though he still wore minor scars from when he had been captured during the siege of Fort William Henry, and Jacob along with the other Rangers of his section had rescued him.

To Jacob, Konkapot was more than just a friend; he was a brother, filling the void that had been the family he had lost. Konkapot and his family took Jacob in and taught him their ways, and in a sense, he had became one of them. Konkapot and Jacob had hunted together, traveling to and spending time with the Mohawks to the west, meeting other members of the Iroquois and Indians from other nations to the south. Jacob learned their language and their ways, forming him into the tough, competent young man who had joined the Rangers.

While Konkapot had been spared from any grevious injuries, this could not be said of the man next to Konkapot at the fire, Samuel Penny from Connecticut. The top of his head was bald, almost like a Franciscan Monk of old. Only this had not been of his own choosing, but from a scalping that he had been fortunate enough to survive. Samuel was busy making Johnnycakes on a shovel that had been placed over some of the fire's coals.

Samuel had joined the section as a replacement for one of their fallen and had quickly fit right in. Jacob had to admit he liked Samuel, though he had an odd sense of humor and a different view on life in general. On numerous occasions, Samuel would say or do something that would take edge off the harshness of the day, even joking about surviving his scalping. In fact, he seemed to use it to his advantage, especially when he met some of the youger women from the Mohawks or Mohicans, who wanted to touch his head.

"Samuel, you did remove the dirt and mud from the shovel before you started making those, right?" asked Jacob.

Samuel looked over his shoulder at Jacob, gave a wry smile, nodded, and replied, "Mostly."

Jacob snorted and continued to look around the room. The bunk beds, flat boards with straw on them for bedding, were along the sides of the hut, keeping the center open. Hanging near each bunk were the Rangers' shooting bags, powder horns, and haversacks, while their rifles leaned against the walls.

They hung their gear along the back of the hut, packs, snowshoes and ice skates, great coats, and other items. The floor of the hut was packed earth, and Peter Fisch was busy scrapping up the last of the accumulated silt and mud from the flood, and dumping it outside in the street. Peter was a Bavarian, who had migrated over to the colonies and eventually joined the Rangers. He had been a Jaeger, a hunter, and he had experience with the East India Company.

Peter and Konkapot were the sole survivors of the original Ranger section that Jacob had joined. Jacob liked Peter for his different view on life in general and his easy attitude and calm deamonor, his constant pipe wreathing his head in a halo of grey smoke. He joked and laughed with the rest of them, though Jacob sometimes never really understood what Peter was talking about. In the forest though, Peter was a professional who was deadly with his rifle.

The last two men of the section were James Cooke and Charles Matthews. Both had been seasoned scouts from New York when they joined the Rangers, and they had knowledge of the extensive wilderness in which they were operating. As the newest members in Jacob's section, they had earned their places and had become key members, sharing their knowledge of the area. Each had earned the other's respect, and they would do anything for each other, if needed. They had proved this numerous times in battle, and even back in garrison, they always had each other's backs.

Nodding to himself, Jacob confirmed in his mind his reason for continuing the fight against their enemies: these men here before him. It was still a tight-knit group of men within the Ranger Companies, and their resepctive sections within the companies. It was no different for these men, who were more than just mere comrades and fellow Rangers. They were his friends, and Jacob would do everything in his power to see them safely through this war.

Sharing their hut were three large wolves that Jacob and his men had found as pups returning from a scouting expedition against Fort Carillon. Jacob's own large grayish-white wolf named Smoke was curled up under his bunk, his tail covering his nose but his golden eyes taking in the activity, especially the cooking near the fire. A large, darker wolf had been adopted by Konkapot, who had named her Raven. She was sitting near Konkapot chewing on some deer leather. The third wolf, Otto, belonged to Samuel. He sat expectantly near the fireplace as Samuel cooked.

It did make for tight quarters, and during the winter it smelled rather rough in the hut, with sweaty, unwashed men, smoke, wolves, and the sulfurous odor of the black powder they used. Jacob was looking forward to spring when it would get warmer and they could move out of the hut and to the other side of the island where they lived in their lean-tos.

Jacob and his Rangers were spending the day repairing and sewing up holes in their thick winter coats, fixing snow shoes, and, as always, keeping their rifles in tip-top condition. Even in the thickest of winters in the North, the French and their Indian allies had been known to launch raids against British forts or villages, so they must always be prepared. The call of "turn out Rangers," as the drummers in the fort beat the long roll, always snapped the Rangers into action, and they grabbed their gear and rifles and turned out to meet the threat.

While the Rangers were busy on the island, Major Rogers had been passing his winter months writing down his best ideas of Ranger tactics. He was constantly being asked to train the regular British forces and with the creation of the 80th Light Infantry, Rogers knew he couldn't train them all in his school. There was a war to fight, and he didn't sign up to train soldiers.

Leaning back in his chair and resting his quill on his small table, Rogers picked up his pages of good ideas, and tried to come up with a name for it, other than "Rogers's Good Ideas." As he sat, puffing on his pipe, Jacob entered the hut to report that he and his men were departing for a daily scout around the valley.

"Jacob," Rogers asked, "seeing you are here, look at this and tell me your thoughts." Rogers handed Jacob his stack of papers, and he quickly thumbed through them.

"Oh, I see you wrote your rules down," Jacob said. "Good. I get tired of trying to answer questions from the recruits, and I sometimes don't use the same words you do. Makes sense." Jacob handed the stack back to Rogers.

Rogers accepted the stack back from Jacob. "Well," Rogers murmured from around his pipe stem, "the old memory isn't as good as it used to be. Can't hurt to be safe." After Jacob departed for his scout, Rogers sat and puffed on his pipe, then dipped his quill in his ink pot, and wrote a title on the top sheet.

"Major Rogers Rules for Ranging," he read aloud, "sounds good to me." A few days later, Rogers, having had an orderly copy a few extras for the island, brought one of the copies with him as he traveled to Albany and New York to plan the next campaign.

In the City of New York, Rogers meet with Lord Loudon to discuss his plans to increase the size of the Ranger Corps, as well as a daring plan for a winter attack against both Fort Carillon at Ticonderoga and Fort Saint Frederic at Crown Point. Lord Loudon agreed that there should be more Rangers, but instead of the thousand-man corps which Rogers wanted, Loudon only authorized the raising of five new companies, which would give Rogers a total of nine, plus the company of Stockbridge Indians.

As Rogers waited for the commission papers for the officers who would command these new companies, he spent some time with Lord Loudon, explaining his plan to take the two main French positions to the north, which would open the way for them to advance on Montreal and Quebec. He believed the French had only about fifty men garrisoning Fort Carillon in the winter, with only a hundred and fifty at Fort Saint Frederic. The time was ripe for a surprise attack that could take these positions without the long and bloody siege that he recommended avoiding entirely.

Rogers, to prove the feasibility of his plan, recalled his ruse to lure the French out a few months earlier, just before Christmas, which had almost worked, so he planned to use a similar ruse again. Rogers's plan was simple. He would lead four hundred of his men along the backside of the mountains bypassing Carillon, set an ambush between Carillon and Saint Frederic, and intercept the French supply sleighs. He would dress some of his men in the captured clothing, putting his French-speaking Rangers in front.

They would travel to Saint Frederic and, while the rest of his men remained hidden in the woods, get the commander to open the gates to the fort so they could enter. Once inside, his men would subdue the guards at the gate, and the rest of the Rangers would move in and take the fort. Taking Crown Point would cut off the supplies to Fort Carillon, making it vulnerable to siege.

Lord Loudon listened intently to Rogers's plan and nodded his head in understanding. Unfortunately for Rogers, Loudon had his own plans for a winter attack on the French at Carillon and Saint Frederic. Lord Loudon had not been a successful military leader so far, and he knew Rogers's plan would probably work, denying him the glory and honor of a victory. So Lord Loudon said Rogers would have to secure approval from General Abercrombie in Albany before he could authorize this expedition.

With a heavy sigh, Rogers acknowledged the instructions and traveled north from New York to Albany to speak with General Abercrombie. Both General Abercrombie and his nephew listened intently and liked Rogers's daring plan. However, after they dismissed Rogers so they could confer, they took the core of Rogers's plan and submitted their proposal for the raid except with them leading it, not Rogers. The following morning, a dispatch rider took their plan to New York, and it was presented to Lord Loudon. Not wanting to ruffle any feathers between Major Rogers, whose Rangers he needed, and his subordinate, General Abercrombie, he decided to disapprove both plans.

By the end of January, a disgruntled Major Rogers returned to his island at Fort Edward. Rogers's frustration with the British command grew, as he watched the politics and subterfuge between these lords and generals affect their military operations. "Damn bloody fools are failing to see reason, and we're going to have a rough go at this campaign season if they don't see true," grumbled Rogers. "We're in for a tough one, sure enough."

Jacob and his men were out on another scout when Rogers arrived back on the island. To Jacob, it was another cold winter's day, just like many previous and many to come. He and his men wore their thick, green coats to protect them from the cold, thick leather leggings to protect their legs, and warm, fur-lined hats to cover their heads. They even had special gloves with a hole for their trigger fingers so they could shoot their rifles while wearing them and keep their fingers inside their gloves when they weren't shooting. The snow was deep, and so they all wore snowshoes that they had made so they could walk on top of the snow, rather than sinking up to their knees or deeper.

Konkapot led the scout with his wolf Raven ranging ahead like a silent shadow. Peter was just behind and to his right, followed by Jacob and Samuel, then Charles and James. Jacob's wolf Smoke and Samuel's Otto were also following along, one on each side of the section as they moved through the woods, their sharp noses, eyes, and ears looking for any sign of the enemy. Jacob had learned to use their wolf senses to his own benefit, and he took them whenever he could. Not to mention the sheer terror they could cause the enemy when they attacked!

The Rangers moved slowly to try and make as little noise as possible except for the soft crunching of the snow under their snowshoes. They were spaced out about ten feet apart and staggered, each Ranger scanning to his left and right, always looking for signs of the enemy in the area.

Today's scout was out towards Old Fort Anne, an old stockade and blockhouse that had been used during previous conflicts, but that now sat abandoned. It was used by both sides as a landmark, and Jacob was out to see if there had been any enemy scouting activity in the area. When they arrived at the old fort, its dilapidated vine-covered walls were thick with snow and ice, the cold wind whistling through the old blockhouse. With the exception of some animal tracks, there was no sign that anyone had been at or near the old fort since the last snowstorm.

Jacob pointed for Konkapot to follow the perimeter of the walls and head northwest towards Lake George. The woods were thick and grey, without sunlight due to the dark clouds that were threatening another snowstorm.

"Hopefully it doesn't cause the ice to build up and flood the island once more," thought Jacob as he continued their scout of the area.

***

To the north of Jacob's scout, Sergeant Shankland was not having a good day. Another ball whizzed just past his ear and smacked into a tree. Shankland had led a four-man scout of Ticonderoga, where they had successfully ambushed and eliminated a French patrol. As they were returning to Fort Edward, they were themselves attacked by a large French and Indian force that had been sent after them, and he had been in a running gunfight for the past twenty miles or so.

It was just himself and Private Goodenough now, the other two having fallen to enemy fire. They were well past exhaustion. Every time they stopped to catch their breaths, Sergeant Shankland had to shake Goodenough awake. Their muscles screamed, their minds were operating automatically, and he hoped Lady Luck would just return to them once more.

Lady Luck must have listened because Jacob and his men heard the sound of musket fire to their north. Jacob ordered his Rangers to quickly spread out as the sound of the running fight came closer. They moved forward, their wolves loping alongside of them. As the fight drew near, Jacob and his men took up good firing positions, each two-man team covering one another, and waited to see who would appear. The wolves sank to the ground, coiled tight like springs.

Soon they could hear the labored breathing as two men dressed in Ranger clothing burst through the trees. Quickly jumping up, Jacob yelled out and waved, "Rangers, this way!"

Shankland stopped and saw Jacob and altered their path towards the Rangers. For the first time since this ordeal had started, Shankland began to have hope. He giggled out of pure exhaustion and joy at finding not only a friendly face, but Sergeant Jacob Clarke! Dragging Goodenough with him, Shankland veered over towards Jacob's position and ran past the Rangers. Jacob and his men looked down their rifles and waited for the enemy to arrive, their faces set in hard determination. "Keep going, we have you covered!" Jacob yelled and resumed his shooting position.

Not too far behind Shankland, the first of the white and blue thick coats of the French and Canadians burst from the woods, hot on Shankland's trail and unaware of the ambush awaiting them. Konkapot, Jacob, and Charles pulled the triggers of their rifles, and the first three enemies fell, the sound of the rifles echoing off the trees. As they began to reload, Peter, Samuel, and James covered and fired at the next three enemies who emerged from the trees, but then the French and Canadians skidded to a halt.

The enemy had just lost six men quickly when they, the hunters, had thought they were about to bag their prize. The French and Canadians moved cautiously forward once again to be greeted by three more accurate rifle shots, dropping three more men, as well as by three large, snarling wolves that charged into them. Two more fell to the ground as Raven and Otto attacked one, and Smoke pulled the second to the ground and began tearing into the man's arm with his sharp teeth.

That was enough for the enemy. The easy quarry was no more, and now they were being pressed by these demonic-possessed wolves and the devils firing on them from the trees. The rest turned, deciding the hunt was over, and they ran back northward. After making sure the enemy was gone, Jacob and his Rangers cautiously moved forward towards the fallen men. Believing they were safe, they searched the bodies for any information and trinkets, and then took their scalps. The Colony of New York paid them a bounty for every enemy scalp they brought in, and Jacob and his men were going to collect. Once their grisly task was over, they went over to help the exhausted men, Shankland and Goodenough, who had collapsed not far behind their position.

When they returned to their camp on the island, Jacob passed the rescued Rangers off at the command line of huts, Sergeant Shankland shaking his hand and thanking him and his Rangers. Samuel, who had what they had found on the dead enemies, dropped them off at the company's orderly hut, and then Jacob and his men, followed by their wolves, went to their hut, dropped off their gear, and began cleaning their rifles.

Once they were finished, they took their fresh scalps and headed over to the fort to get their bounty. The wolves decided that they had had enough excitement for the day and remained behind, curled up on the floor in front of the crackling fire in the fireplace.

After crossing over the wooden footbridge and entering the gate of Fort Edward, they ran into Captain Reynolds, the fort's appointed provost, and the hand-picked goons he always had with him. Captain Reynolds, in his immaculate red British officer's uniform, was in the process of dressing down a Provincial soldier for improper wearing of his uniform and for not shaving.

Jacob did not like this man. He had never liked him, beginning the first day Reynolds had arrived at the fort. He was a short man, who openly disliked anything Provincial or non-British. Jacob also hated the man for what he truly was, a coward with a short-man's inferiority complex. It always seemed to Jacob that Captain Reynolds went out of his way to try and find something wrong with them so he could take pleasure in bringing them up on charges and then seeing to their punishment.

"You bloody uneducated Provincials better get your act together or you will feel the sting of the cat," Reynolds screamed up at the Provincial soldier who stood a good six inches taller than he. "Two days in the stockade. Sergeant, take him away!"

One of Reynolds' goons grabbed the poor Provincial soldier and led him to the stockade. Captain Reynolds had a satisfied smirk on his face when he spotted Jacob and his men enter the fort.

"You there, stop!" ordered Captain Reynolds as he pointed his walking stick at Jacob.

Jacob stopped and took a deep breath, while Samuel muttered under his breath, "Ah damn. Here we go again." Captain Reynolds strutted up to Jacob, feeling confident with his goon section backing him up. Jacob looked at these men; the bottom of the barrel of his most Royal Majesty's Army. Their eyes showed they enjoyed their power to harass under the command of the provost; they were simply thugs wearing uniforms.

"What are you slovenly dressed men doing in this fort looking like… that? You're a disgrace; I have half a mind to flog the entire lot of you. What is your business here?" Reynolds demanded.

Jacob shrugged his shoulders, reached down and opened a bag he was carrying over his shoulder, and pulled out a handful of scalps. "We've come to get our bounties."

Reynolds' face quickly changed from a smirk to revulsion as he backed away from the horror of these scalps, not wanting anything to possibly drip onto his uniform. Jacob knew the captain had a fear of blood, especially his own, and he had surprisingly avoided any combat action for the past couple of years he had been assigned to Fort Edward. Jacob stepped forward towards

Captain Reynolds, who continued to step backwards until he bumped into his men.

In a low, icy voice, staring down at the captain, Jacob simply said, "Do you really want to try and flog us, knowing full well you don't have the authority over independent companies and you would have Major Rogers's wrath coming squarely down on you?"

Captain Reynolds quickly turned and pushed through his men, moving away. The provost goons stood there dumbfounded. They did the intimidating, not the other way around. Jacob walked up to the corporal and stared him dead in the eyes.

"You going to do something, corporal?" asked Jacob in the same quiet, icy voice.

The corporal felt he was looking into the eyes of blue frozen death and decided he should go check on Captain Reynolds. Suppressing grins as the goon section turned to follow after Captain Reynolds, Jacob and his men continued over to the quartermaster for their bounty. As they moved through the fort, the Provincials smiled and nodded their heads in approval, while some of the British regulars also nodded in respect. It seemed they all had common ground in the general dislike of Captain Reynolds.

While Jacob and his Rangers continued with the business of getting paid and securing supplies from the quartermaster, messages and orders had begun arriving at Fort Edward from Lord Loudon instructing the troops to begin preparations for a winter attack on the French. After reading the orders, Major Rogers was livid. It was clear from the colorful language coming from his hut that he had read Lord Loudon's instructions.

"That damned man is using my idea!" could be heard coming from Rogers in his hut. Jacob and his men, having returned with their bounties, heard Major Rogers growling and sputtering from his hut and what sounded like wood splintering as if he had kicked something.

"That doesn't sound good," said James, and everyone nodded as they made their way past Rogers's hut towards theirs. Something was afoot, which meant they would soon be back out on scouts. This became evident a few days later as supply sleds with barrels of food, boxes of equipment and stores, and artillery shot began arriving at the fort.

Knowing they would have to use the lake to move supplies, Major Rogers instructed Captain Stark to scout the lake to see if it was frozen thick enough to handle the heavy sleds supporting the attack. Personally leading the scout and the assessment of the lake, Stark departed with some of his Rangers.

Jacob and his men wished them luck and safe journey. They had received a good bounty for their scalps and were heading over to Mr. Best's sutlery for some celebrating. Once there, they sat on the porch of the sutlery, enjoying mugs of ale and watching the large sleds of supplies from Albany being pulled by oxen through the snow and into the fort. It was something different to watch, and in a strange way, it entertained them.

***

Unknown to Jacob, other sets of eyes were also watching the sleds, but from afar. The French partisan leader Jean-Baptiste Langy had been able to move his force of over a hundred French regulars, Canadians, and Indians undetected to within sight of Fort Edward. Major Rogers's greatest rival in unconventional warfare, Langy observed the activity around the fort, concerned about the large sleds of supplies and the tracks other sleds had made on the road from Albany.

Langy had come looking for some revenge against Rogers, whose bold Christmas raid had bothered him. Now it was his turn to show Rogers how it was done. The fort itself was too strong, too well-defended to make a move directly against it, so Langy would use the tactics that had worked well for him in the past. He would wait for a work detail to leave the fort and ambush them once they were in the woods outside of the range of the fort's protective cannons.

Scanning the area with a telescope, he spotted the wood-cutting area away from the fort. Numerous trees had been cut down and were in different stages of being sawed and stacked for movement into the fort. Langy nodded and decided that that would be where he would place his ambush position. Putting his telescope away, Langy quietly moved his men to a place where they could spend the night, waiting for the morning when they would move to their ambush position.

They didn't need to wait long. The following morning, Langy spotted a group of men leaving the fort and heading towards the wood-cutting area. He observed only a small detail of British regulars as a security element and a large number of unarmed regulars and Provincials dragging sleds with their axes. Langy was disappointed that there were no Rangers with them.

"Still enough of a message to be given, though it would have been sweeter if they had been Rangers," thought Langy. "Or even Rogers himself. Ah, someday, soon perhaps."

Using his hands, he signaled for his men to follow him to their ambush position, Langy looking forward to dealing out some sweet revenge against his foes.

He deployed his men to both sides of the trail leading to the wood-cutting area. Langy was surprised to see that none of the approaching party was wearing snowshoes and that they traveled instead on a well-used trail on which all of the snow had been flattened. Langy waited until they were deep into his arch of fire before giving the command to shoot. Then, the woods erupted into a thunderous roar as a hundred rifles and muskets fired at once, followed by the air splitting war cries of the Indians as they charged into the shocked mass of wood cutters.

The security party was immediately eliminated. Of the twenty-five men, thirteen were killed outright, five were wounded, four quickly captured by the charging Indians, and the others fled.

The woodcutters, who had no snowshoes, were at the mercy of the Indians, who showed none. They turned but quickly sank into the deep snow and became mired in the drifts. The charging Indians crashed into the helpless woodcutters, brutally attacking with tomahawks and knives, churning the white snow into shades of red.

***

In the fort, the long roll was beating the call to arms, while on the island Major Rogers ran out yelling, "Rangers turn out!" Jacob and his men quickly grabbed their rifles and shooting bags and assembled on the company street. Rogers was concerned that he did not have many men, with Stark's scout supposed to be returning that day. Rogers ordered his men to go grab their snowshoes and meet him at the southwest corner of the fort. Jacob and his men raced back to their hut, quickly grabbed their snowshoes, and then ran across the bridge to meet with a fuming Rogers. The large cannons on the fort began to fire at the French attack in the distance.

"Damn fools won't leave the fort to go rescue their own people!" Rogers exclaimed.

From the sound of the shooting, Rogers could determine that it was a large enemy force, and the fact they were able to sneak in undetected meant that it had to be either Langy or one of the other partisan leaders. He looked at his assembled men, maybe forty strong with snowshoes, and knew it was not enough to fight that many French. They would have to wait for the Provincials and regulars to assemble enough men to move against the enemy.

Making a snap decision, Rogers turned to Jacob.

"Take charge of these men. I want you to lead them towards the lake and support Captain Stark. I don't want him to run into these attackers after they're done chopping up our men."

Jacob instructed his impromptu platoon to put on their snowshoes. He had Konkapot lead them out as they headed north away from the fight while Rogers continued to kick snow and spit and sputter about "these damn bloody fools who call themselves officers and commanders."

Jacob's platoon moved quickly, even on snowshoes, and soon arrived at Halfway Brook, so named because it was halfway between Fort Edward and the old ruins of Fort William Henry. Jacob placed his platoon into a defensive circle, to intercept Captain Stark, and they did not have long to wait. One of his pickets had spotted Captain Stark's approach and signed to them as they turned towards Jacob's position. In the center, Captain Stark met with Jacob, who quickly told him what had happened at the fort.

Now reinforced, Stark decided they would try to get in front of the French as they headed back north towards safety and see if they could ambush them. Stark led the way, followed by Jacob and his platoon as they moved northeastward, believing that would be the route the French would take back towards Fort Carillon.

They had reached an area near South Bay when they found the tracks of the French raiding party. They heard the sound of men approaching, and Stark deployed their force into a large ambush line. But instead of the French, it was Major Rogers leading a tracking force. Stark and Jacob stood up, waved to the approaching force of Rangers and Major Rogers. They must have just missed the French, and once more Major Rogers began kicking the snow, spitting and sputtering about being too damned slow.

Jacob and the other Rangers understood his frustration; they felt it too. Acknowledging that the French had won this one, the Rangers turned and returned to Fort Edward. "Enjoy it now while you can," growled Rogers as he faced towards the north. "I am going to make sure it's your last!" Then he turned and led his Rangers back to Fort Edward.

Erick W. Nason

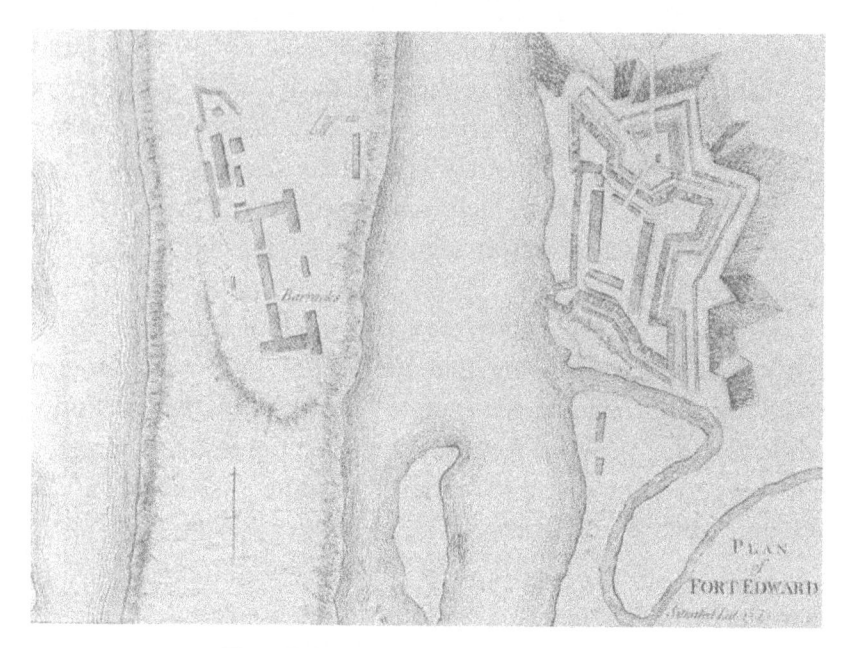

Fort Edward and Rogers's Island

CHAPTER 2

FORT EDWARD: SETTING THE CONDITIONS

On the nights following the raid, Jacob and the other Rangers sat around fires in groups, mugs in hand, discussing their thoughts with one another. Many were feeling the same frustration that was dogging Major Rogers: They always seemed to be one step behind the French, who were more successful than both the Rangers and the pride of the British Army.

The discussion among Jacob's men was continuing one day in their hut as they worked on various maintenance chores. "I mean I know the Canadians are good," griped Samuel, "but they cannot be as good as us, can they?"

Peter pulled his pipe from his mouth and responded, "Don't underestimate your enemies; dat has been a major failing back in the home country. Dese men live like us here, yes? Tough life, tough men, all fighting for wat they believe in, just like us." Peter returned the stem of his pipe to his mouth and pulled, blowing a long stream of smoke. "So to answer the question, yes," he concluded.

Sitting on his bunk, Jacob, who was sewing up another tear in his clothing, nodded in agreement, just as Samuel and the others did. It made sense, which meant it was going to continue to be a tough fight if their enemies were as good as they were. Jacob hoped their enemies were not better.

He held up his shirt to look at his stitching; his shirt was more stitches and patches than the original fabric. He hoped that with the coming spring and this talk of a new offensive, perhaps new uniforms would arrive. Jacob looked up as the sound of the long roll began over at the fort, quickly followed by the cry, "Rangers turn out!" which echoed through the camp.

"Not again," groaned Samuel as they dropped what they were doing, grabbed their rifles and shooting bags, and once more headed out to the company street.

As usual, Rogers was already there pacing, and as they approached, he simply said, "Follow me." He led them across the bridge at a trot and around the southwest bastion of the fort. Jacob was surprised not to hear the sound of firing or fighting, but he still remained tightly coiled like a spring, ready to fight. The reason for the call out soon became apparent. Across the field was a group of French regulars under a flag of truce.

"Now this should be interesting," said Peter.

***

It was a group of sixteen French regulars, drawn up properly in a military formation, their muskets at their shoulders. The group was under the command of Captain Wolfe, who had been instructed by the Marquis de Montcalm to proceed to Fort Edward. Using the guise of negotiating the return of French prisoners, Captain Wolfe's real mission, unbeknownst to the British and the Rangers, was to confirm Langy's report that Fort Edward was preparing for an upcoming attack.

From his position outside the fort's walls, Wolfe could see neither heavy artillery nor piles of supplies that were obvious signs of preparation, but perhaps the English commander had hidden his supplies from view. Perhaps the commander would be gullible enough to allow him to enter the fort to talk, which was the usual practice during a prisoner exchange negotiation.

"Sir," one of his lieutenants called to Captain Wolfe, pointing. "Men approaching from around the bastion on the right."

Wolfe turned to see a large group of armed, green-clad men come trotting around the corner and began deploying into a line. Perhaps these were the infamous Rangers he had heard about. Perhaps he could meet this famous Major Robert Rogers, who had been the bane to his commander's operations.

To make sure his intent was clear; Captain Wolfe had his men sling their muskets so their muzzles were pointing towards the ground, and he made sure the flag of truce could be clearly seen. Soon, a party of English officers came around the same corner of the fort, and Captain Wolfe could see many men observing them from along the top of the fort's wall. One of the British officers conferred briefly with one of the Rangers before the group of English officers marched out of the fort towards them, followed by the Rangers.

The two groups met in the middle of the field, and Captain Wolfe presented himself to the lead British officer, who was Colonel Alexander, the acting commander for Fort Edward. They began discussing the reason for his presence. Bowing deeply in the proper fashion and removing his tricorn, Wolfe began, "Sir, I am honored to present my commander's best wishes and regards, and I am here under his direction to secure the release of French prisoners whom I believe are under your direct care."

Colonel Alexander retuned the bow, though not as formally, and removed his tricorn before replying. "It is a pleasure to make your acquaintance; however you must forgive me if I don't return the regards of your commander, having witnessed his honorable ways at Fort William Henry."

Colonel Alexander stared at Captain Wolfe with a flat expression, waiting to see how Wolfe reacted to his comment. He was pleased to see Captain Wolfe's expression change as he wrestled mentally with this statement.

Captain Wolfe was startled by the less-than-civil response from this English officer, as the English were known for their professionalism and decorum. What occurred at Fort William Henry were simply the fortunes of war. Could he not see this? Then there was this line of green-clad men who seemed to be on the verge of striking out at him and his men. Perhaps this subterfuge would not be as simple as he had thought.

Having followed the party forward, just standing behind Colonel Alexander and his staff, Major Rogers with Jacob and the rest of the Rangers were lined up. Leaning on their rifles instead of standing in a crisp military formation, they stared at the French with open hostility, glaring at them with blood in their eyes. Samuel was picking his nails with his fighting knife while staring at the French regulars.

"I must confer with my staff," Colonel Alexander excused himself. "Please remain here so I may quickly return with our answer to your request." Quickly bowing and returning his tricorn to his head, Colonel Alexander turned and walked back to the fort.

After Colonel Alexander left, and Captain Wolfe was left standing apart from his men, Rogers could not pass up this opportunity. He approached Captain Wolfe, with Jacob coming along. Rogers nodded to Captain Wolfe, greeted him, and asked, "Did his Excellency the Marquis, receive our receipt for the fine oxen that we enjoyed last Christmas?"

Captain Wolfe stared at this man who must be the infamous Major Robert Rogers he had heard so many stories about. So this was the boogey man who had vexed the Marquis and others in his upper chain of command. Rogers, smiling, continued his so far one-way conversation with Captain Wolfe.

"If you wouldn't mind," continued Rogers, "please convey my personal thanks to his Excellency." Rogers turned to face the Rangers who were making "yummy" noises about the oxen, rubbing their stomachs. "Oh yes," Rogers continued as he turned back to face Captain Wolfe. "Pass along the thanks from my men."

Captain Wolfe coldly stared ahead at Rogers who stood there with a slight smile on his face. He had thought earlier about the fortunes of war, and now he also recalled how fickle fortune could be. Rogers's raid and daring display of roasting some of the oxen, then eating them in plain view of Fort Carillon and the French lines was a knife in the eye of the French.

Bowing his head slightly, Wolfe gave a small smirk before replying, "I would be careful if I were you the next time we meet. You may not be so lucky next time."

Rogers replied, "I guess that's why I am not you." Slowly stepping closer to Captain Wolfe, Rogers remarked, "I am looking forward until we meet again, out there." Rogers pointed behind Wolfe towards the frontier. Hearing the approaching steps of Colonel Alexander, Rogers winked, turned, and went back to his Rangers.

Colonel Alexander returned, bowed, and stated, "I am sorry but I am not in a position to speak about freeing French prisoners, and there will be no negotiations. Only my superior has that authority, and he is in Albany. You are welcome to remain here and await his return, which should be in a few days."

Captain Wolfe nodded, surprised at his underestimation of the English commander. He realized their ploy to gather information would not work. Bowing, Captain Wolfe said, "I will inform my commander." He turned his men around and began to march away.

"We'll see you all soon enough," Rogers called out. Then to add more insults to the situation, Rogers and his Rangers smiled and waved farewell to the departing Frenchmen, before returning to the island.

"Damn that was fun," remarked Samuel, and the other Rangers joined in laughing, Rogers as well. All of their pent-up frustration was slightly released as the Rangers marched out to their island laughing, and they drew some odd stares from the British and Provincials watching from the wall.

Jacob and his men returned to their hut, wiped the moisture from their rifles, and picked up their dropped tasks of mending their clothes and repairing their gear.

"Now that was rather strange," said Peter. "Have they ever done that before?"

Jacob put his sewing down and thought about it.

"No, no, they haven't done it since I have been here," he replied. Samuel looked up from his sewing. "Do you think they were up to something?"

Jacob nodded. "They're always up to something, so we'd better be on our guard. I have a feeling we're going to have some business soon enough."

Everyone nodded and went back to checking and repairing gear, paying closer attention to their work.

The next morning after the roll call and morning formation, Jacob and his men were back inside their hut inspecting their snowshoes and repairing what was needed. The weather was cold and grey, the wind again tugging at their makeshift door, making it flap and flutter. As Jacob was working, a messenger stuck his head through the door and said, "Sergeant Jacob, Major Rogers would like to see you."

Jacob acknowledged with a nod, set his snowshoe down, and stood up.

Samuel looked up and asked, "You think we're heading to Carillon or somewhere new in this fine weather?"

Peter stopped his repair of his winter moccasins and replied, "Of course, we always go out when the weather turns bad, and seeing the British have been turned back a couple times now by the weather, we must be going."

Jacob shrugged as he placed his green bonnet on his head, and headed out the door. Jacob nodded to a few other sergeants who were also heading to the hut for the meeting. He joined them on the company street. "Messenger was busy this morning," Jacob mused. After ducking inside and taking off his bonnet, Jacob could see that the entire command had been called for this one.

In the center of the large room was a table with maps. Major Rogers was flanked on either side by the company commanders: Captains John Stark, Israel Putnam, Charles Bulkeley, Joseph Hopkins, the newly promoted Joseph Waite, who had been Jacob's platoon leader in the beginning when he had first joined, and Chief Naunauphtaunk, who led the company of Stockbridge Indians.

The company commanders were all hunched over the map as Rogers was pointing and explaining what was coming up. Jacob took a place along the wall with the other sergeants and some of the lieutenants. He leaned over and whispered to the Ranger next to him, "Any word yet on where we are we going?"

The Ranger shrugged, and they waited for the meeting to begin. Almost immediately, Rogers looked around the room to make sure everyone that he needed was there, and then he began.

"Gentlemen, as you all are quite aware; the winter seems to have a strong grip on us." Pointing over towards Captain Stark, Rogers said, "Our scout with the royal engineer confirmed that the King's Highway up to Lake George is buried under four to five feet of snow, and the lake itself is buried under almost two feet of snow. Lord Loudon has been attempting to send expeditions north to see what our French friends have been up to, but the weather sent them all back with nothing. Captain Putnam's recent expedition also did not turn up any worthwhile news.

Rogers paused as he scanned the assembled Ranger leaders. "Now for the really bad news." Rogers observed the reactions of his men. "I'm sure you have all learned that I have been planning a major expedition north, as we always do in the winter, knowing the French greatly reduce the size of their garrisons in winter."

Looking at his men, Rogers continued, "After I went to secure permission for my plan from General Abercrombie, I was told 'no.' Recently, I learned that a version of my plan had been stolen by our illustrious leaders in Albany, and I also just learned that Colonel Haviland decided to make the plan publically known."

As he expected, the Ranger leaders groaned at the news. Colonel William Haviland was the new Commander of the 27th Regiment of Foot, as well as the newly appointed commander of Fort Edward. He had not been a strong supporter of the Rangers, restricting the number of volunteers Rogers could accept, even as an independent formation.

There was a shocked murmur around the hut, and Rogers waited a few moments for it to subside.

"I have also recently learned that just about every British soldier has been informed of my plan, and we all know they can't keep their bloody traps shut about operational matters. Four days ago, a sutlers' convoy traveling from Albany and escorted by British regulars was attacked and a couple of the regulars were taken."

Rogers paused as his men murmured amongst themselves. "So you can probably guess. Because every British soldier knows of my plan, then our friends up north probably know everything by now from the captives."

"I still intend to continue with my planned expedition, only now we have to assume there is no surprise or secrecy, and our enemies may be well aware that we are heading north."

In a way, this didn't surprise Jacob, given the way the British seemed to be handling this war. With everything he had recently observed, from the shoddy defense of Fort William Henry to the success the French and the Canadians had been having on their raids, Jacob was really beginning to wonder if the British high command had a clue about how to fight and win this war.

"Captains Putnam, Stark, Buckley, and Naunauphtaunk," Rogers continued, and Jacob refocused his attention on what Rogers was saying. "You will provide me with able-bodied men ready to depart in two days, equipped for a long trek north. Captain Hopkins, you are in charge here on the island and will support the fort as necessary. Captain Waite, you are the detail company. I want you to do local scouts to see if there are any enemy eyes in the area and hunt when you can."

"The expedition will depart from here and travel to the southern end of the lake, and then we will travel along the western side and scout out the French near Carillon and report what we observe. Lord Loudon still wants to invest in Carillon, and he needs updated information on their strengths."

Looking around the room at his gathered Rangers, he said, "That's it. Commanders, get your companies ready, issue rations, and make sure everyone has at least sixty rounds of shot and powder – I would recommend bringing more – and cooked rations for at least a week."

After speaking briefly with Captain Putnam, Jacob headed back to his hut to brief his men. They were already waiting and after chewing on a warm Johnnycake, Jacob briefed them on their expedition to Fort Carillon. They all nodded their acceptance and as they had on numerous other occasions, they began the ritual of preparing to head out.

Jacob, Peter, and Samuel went over to the fort to draw the extra rations they would need for the journey. While at the fort, Jacob spotted Captain Reynolds typically skulking about, performing his duties as provost with his regular zeal, seeming to delight in his duty. New arrivals of British regulars were not spared from the scrutiny of Captain Reynolds, though it did seem that he was trying to avoid the Rangers more than he had before.

After securing what they needed from the quartermaster, Jacob and his men returned to the island with the sacks of food, containing salt pork and salt beef, flour, corn meal, potatoes, ginger, salt, onions, and chocolate. They cheerfully greeted other Rangers they passed either going to the fort or like they, returning, bantering back and forth about the coming scout.

They headed over to the field kitchen, a large trench dug into the ground with large fire holes built into one side and with a hole through the top serving as a chimney, and they joined the other Ranger sections that were beginning to cook their rations. Rangers were sitting on old logs to keep them off the wet ground or on ground clothes along the lip of the cooking trench, their cooking implements scattered around them.

Konkapot, James, and Charles had cleaned the snow out of the section of the trench they occupied and had three fires burning hotly. James and Charles took the sacks of food, dumping the salt beef and pork into buckets of water to soak, while Samuel and Peter began making ash cakes and Johnnycakes, and Konkapot and Jacob used bacon to make grease to cook the onions and potatoes.

More Rangers began heading over to the field kitchen to begin their own preparations. The three wolves had come along to supervise the cooking along with some of the other Ranger sections' own dogs, ready to do their part by eating the scraps the men didn't cook. As Jacob sat on a log, smoking his pipe, he observed that if the enemy were watching the cooking activity on the island, it would be a key indicator that they were preparing to march.

Puffing on his pipe, Jacob knew it couldn't be helped now, and with what Rogers had said about the plan's being released to everyone, it was a safe bet the enemy already knew. Jacob looked around the field kitchen, Samuel and Peter joking with some Rangers, while Charles and James appeared to be swapping cooking ideas with some other Rangers.

As he did with other missions, Jacob began the horrible contemplation of who wouldn't be coming home. In his mind, his men would make it no matter what, and he would see to it, if possible. He hated this thought though, especially when they knew the enemy had a good idea they were coming, and they could expect a tough fight ahead.

As Jacob watched his men and the other Rangers laugh and joke, he took strength in knowing these were good men, well-trained, and hardened. There were no soft green troopers anymore, and he hoped it would be enough. Looking over at the Ranger graveyard where too many of his friends were laid, Jacob made a commitment not to add any of his men to the growing ranks.

Taking turns at cooking, maintaining the fire, and tossing scraps to the wolves, Jacob and the others also worked on checking their snowshoes and ice creepers, which more than likely would be needed on this trip. Konkapot melted lead in a small pot, and they all took turns making bullets. Since each Ranger had his own unique mold, each one made his own balls, clipping the excess lead off and then using a file to smooth the balls before adding them to his bag.

James had taken their powder horns over to the fort and filled them, bringing back some extra horns just in case, and he handed horns to Jacob, Konkapot, and Samuel. As they prepared, the Rangers sat and talked, bathed in the sweet smell of cooking meat and fire smoke. Jacob finally finished mending his great coat; it would probably be needed on this trip.

"Make sure you all check your clothes, hats, and gloves before tomorrow," Jacob instructed. "Don't need to freeze anything important on this trip."

By evening, all the food was cooked and distributed to the section, each man wrapping his rations in leather and placing them in his haversack or pack. Once everything was packed, and they had wished everyone a good night and luck, the Rangers wandered back to their huts for the night.

The following morning, Jacob and his men, who had no duties for the day, traveled over to the fort and then headed to Mr. Best's sutler shop. While there were now smaller and closer sutlers on their island, they had made friends with Mr. Best and only shopped there.

Mr. Best looked up from some of the Provincials who were shopping and went over to greet Jacob and his Rangers warmly. They shared a kinship in a way, having met Frederick Best and his family when they first arrived at the fort. The relationship had grown stronger as Maggie and Jacob's romance bloomed before its tragic end. In that tragedy, the Best family and Jacob and his Rangers grew even closer, welded by their shared pain into a big family, which had helped Jacob through the mourning of his loss.

Wiping his hands on his work apron, Mr. Best took Jacob's hand, followed by each of his Rangers, welcoming them all to the shop.

"Good to see ya, lads. Come for some items you'll need on the trip?"

Jacob raised his eyebrows at that.

"Guess the major was right about no one keeping a secret around here."

"Well…yes," Frederick stuttered. "The news has been bouncing around for days, but I would never tell a soul," he said.

Audrey, Maggie's sister, who still worked for Mr. Best, came over and gave Jacob a hug and asked if he was doing OK. Jacob replied that he was getting by. There was still pain behind Jacob's eyes, just like hers, dealing with Maggie's loss the best way they could. Smiling, Audrey gave Jacob's arm a squeeze before heading back to serving the customers.

Audrey had married a Provincial soldier from the local area and settled down to a decent life there at the fort. The shop had been doing extremely well since Frederick first started in a couple of tents back in 1755. Now there was a large, two-story log house, stocked with just about everything a soldier would need on the frontier. Along with the Rangers, men from the local and other colony militias, the Mohicans, the Mohawks, and the British regulars were all frequent customers.

Tension still continued to smolder and grow between the Provincials and the British regulars, and this strain sometimes became apparent here in the shop. Provincials would usually leave when the British regulars arrived to prevent any incidents, having been instructed like the Rangers by their commanders not to cause any more problems. It also seemed that the regulars knew this and went out of their way to constantly be over in the shop, irritating the Provincials. Mrs. Best helped to keep order with a stout club that she carried with her, and actually, Captain Reynolds helped by driving the soldiers out and back to duty.

The day of departure arrived, cold and blustery with snowflakes once again dancing in the wind. A heavy freeze arrived during the night, and the ground crunched under the feet of the assembling Rangers. The expedition formed on the parade ground there on the island, some two hundred men with their weapons and kit, standing before Major Rogers.

After the officers accounted for everyone, inspecting their men and equipment, Rogers led the Rangers across their icy footbridge and out into the grey gloom of the wintery forest. Jacob and his men left their wolves behind on this trip, and the Rangers staying behind would see that they were taken care of.

They had guests accompanying them on this scout. Along with the Rangers were eight British regular volunteers from the 27th Regiment of Foot, who were coming along to observe. Having strapped their snowshoes to the winter moccasins on their feet, the Rangers plodded through the woods carefully, always scanning their surroundings. Once they crossed the valley and entered the woods, they were in no-man's land, and the enemy just like them, frequently sent scouts into this territory.

The Rangers carefully moved along the general route of the military road that had connected Fort Edward and Fort William Henry. What little sunlight that broke through the clouds showed how cold the night before had been. The trees and the tall grass along the old road appeared to be sheathed in glass, a thick coating of ice covering everything. The Rangers and their snowshoes didn't sink in the snow because a thick layer of ice coated the top of the snow.

While they frequented these woods often, the Rangers would not be complacent and get caught unaware by their enemies like the fort had been in the attack on the woodcutters. Jacob wore a wool and fur-lined hat on his head, just covering the top of his ears so he could listen to the sounds of the forest to detect the presence of enemies nearby. All he heard was the wind, the creaking of the trees, the occasional sound of snow falling to the ground from the trees with a soft "thump," and the creaking of the ice that coated everything. Wisps of steam leaked from the covered faces of the Rangers, and the accompanying men from the 27th, who wrapped scarves around their bright red noses and ears.

The long Ranger column was well spaced out, each Ranger scanning to his left and right while his snowshoes made soft crunching noises in the snow. The volunteers from the 27th were kept in the middle of the column so the Rangers could keep an eye on them. After some falls, the volunteers soon got the hang of walking in snowshoes. Their stumbles provided entertainment to the Rangers as they watched the men from the 27th try to learn how to operate in the frozen woods.

As they moved north, they came across one lonely mountain that they used as a navigation point, because it was close to Bloody Pond, the site of the ambush a few years ago that was the first battle fought at the southern end of Lake George. Some of the Rangers even named their navigation point, "French Mountain," for only the French owned it now, not they. Perhaps soon they would completely regain control of this valley, and they would have to come up with a new name.

It was nearly nightfall when the head of the column broke from the woods and out onto the open plain of the southern shore of Lake George. Rogers led the column over towards what little remained of the walls from Fort William Henry, ugly black ribs poking up from the snow. Off to the east was the high ground where they had stopped Baron Dieskau and built the first encampment, now barren with snow covering anything that had been left of their destroyed camp.

They stopped and listened for sounds of the enemy, and a few Rangers conducted a quick circular scout to make sure they were alone. The Rangers then took turns digging out some of the snow from around the old logs of the wall to make sleeping shelters while the other Rangers were posted as sentries before the rotation for the guard watch began. Already concerned about the French knowing they were coming, Rogers instructed no fires, and the Rangers settled in for a very cold night, wrapped in their thick blankets and eating their cold rations.

During the evening, Rogers came around and informed Jacob and the other Ranger leaders that the snow was still too deep to travel overland, so they would head out onto the frozen lake where it was less deep. Jacob nodded as Rogers smiled, clasped his shoulder, and continued around the perimeter.

Each section kept one man up on watch while the others tried to get some rest. Jacob noticed the volunteers were having a tough go at sleeping on the frozen ground, and he showed them how to wrap themselves in blankets to stay warm and to lie on pine branches instead of the frozen earth.

The shivering regulars had no problem accepting advice from Jacob and the other Rangers, anything to ease their suffering, wondering why they had volunteered for this scout. They had wanted to see how these Rangers fought, but now they were just happy to learn how not to freeze.

The night passed quiet and cold, the stars in fact finally coming out as the clouds moved on for a change, but this made it feel even colder. Before dawn, as was their practice, all of the Rangers were up, packed, and observing the woods for any signs of the enemy. After they tried to remove all signs that they had been there, Rogers agreed that all was well and led the column down to the shore, which was hard to identify with so much snow. There, the Rangers took off their snowshoes, tying them to their packs, and put on their ice creepers, metal jaws/spikes that they tied to the bottoms of their winter moccasins to get traction on the ice.

While it was easier traveling along the ice where the snow was not as deep, the Rangers advanced with extra caution for they were out in the open and could easily be seen. Speed would have to be their security, as the enemy would sometimes use the frozen lake to move instead of traveling in the deep snow of the forests. They moved quickly, constantly scanning the shore line, which was half a mile away.

As they moved across the frozen landscape, Jacob tried to keep his mind focused on the job at hand, but it was so damned cold. Despite how much time he had spent here on the frontier, it always shocked him how cold it would sometimes become, and he thought how odd it was for people in their right minds to be out in it, let alone waging war in it. Jacob could now understand why most armies either went home in winter or went into winter quarters instead of fighting.

Jacob had seen first-hand numerous men, even hardy hunters and Rangers, who lost fingers, ears, and noses to the frost, the body parts turning black and either falling or breaking off, or the surgeons removing them once the men returned to their camps. It was cold, a burning cold that delved deep into your bones and would kill you quickly if you didn't respect it. Jacob had found on a few occasions men who had become lost in a blizzard and were discovered frozen in place where they had sat or lay down and fallen asleep, never to awake.

At least they were moving, which helped them to stay warm, but it was still cold. Jacob wondered if perhaps in the future he would go somewhere else where it was warm, like to the south. Samuel, who had been working with merchants before the war, spoke of warm areas he called "the Carolinas," where it could be unbearably hot. As cold as it was now, Jacob thought unbearably hot sounded better than frozen.

They made good time and soon came to an area of the lake known as the narrows, where Rogers decided it would be best to head back towards the shore and make camp. The Rangers moved into a thicket that provided concealment, but still Rogers ordered no fires. Once in the thicket, Rogers sent a scouting expedition ahead to see if they were still alone. The scouts returned and confirmed that there were no signs of anyone near them.

The Rangers maintained their nightly watch, and time passed quietly with no sign of the enemy. As Jacob took his frozen watch, he wondered where the enemy was. They were getting close to the French position at Fort Carillon, and the French should have scouts out. The night still passed uneventful but cold, and they were up before dawn, with Rogers sending out another quick scout around their perimeter to make sure all was clear.

The column returned to the ice and continued their northward trek. They had only moved about three miles when the column was halted, and everyone knelt down. A dog had been spotted out on the lake well in front of them, which normally meant there was a patrol nearby. The Rangers quickly formed a perimeter, kneeling or lying in the snow drifts, rifles and muskets at the ready, watching. After some time nothing had happened, and Rogers ordered the column up to continue moving north, but now everyone was scanning the woods and shoreline with a keener sense of urgency.

Rogers no longer wanted to chance traveling in the open, and he directed the column to head straight for the western shore and make for the woods. After changing back into their snowshoes, the men continued their march north until they could see a mountain they used for a landmark and had named, "Bald Mountain or Old Baldy." Spotting the mountain meant they were nearly at the end of the lake and close to the French lines at Ticonderoga.

The Rangers found a suitable area to make camp and sent out a scouting party to make sure there was no one near them.

They then settled down for another cold night, while Jacob, the other sergeants, and the officers were called into the center for a quick meeting with Rogers.

While some sunlight remained, Rogers drew in the snow his plan for the following day's scout of Fort Carillon. It would be similar to the expedition Jacob had participated in a few months ago when Rogers had led them up to the walls of the fort and had tried to lure the garrison out in an attempt to take the fort. The French hadn't taken the bait, and the Rangers settled for the destruction of the French oxen grazing nearby.

Rogers laid out his plan, which sounded simple enough. They would scout around the perimeter of the French lines, determine any improvements or weaknesses, and then set up an ambush to take prisoners for more sources of information. The French were normally sending out daily patrols from Carillon, so the Rangers thought they should get lucky.

Jacob returned to his men, told them what they were doing in the morning, and settled down to chew on his cold rations. During his rotation on watch, Jacob watched the woods around them in the inky black night. The clouds had returned, and there were no moon or stars for light, just the black cold veil of the night. There were no sounds, no night animals yet, and thank the Lord, no bugs. They would be back soon enough; the bugs and black flies could be bad enough to drive a man crazy during the summer.

In the morning, they would go into action against their enemies, and Jacob wondered how bloody this campaign year would be. His thoughts returned to hoping that none of his men would join the growing ranks in the Ranger Cemetery on the island, though if they did go there, they would be in good company. Shaking the thoughts away, Jacob steeled himself to focus on the job in the morning, to strike hard, strike fast, and bring his men home.

CHAPTER 3

FORT CARILLON AND THE BATTLE ON SNOWSHOES

The snow still clung stubbornly to Fort Carillon, covering the ramparts, all of the buildings, and construction materials in multiple mounds of snow and ice. Long icicles hung from the fort, like great talons reaching for the ground. The reinforcements and supplies that Montcalm had ordered had begun to arrive. Work details were moving about the fort and the French encampment, unburying supplies and construction materials and moving them to new areas to make room for the arriving equipment and men.

Ensign Sieur de La Durantaye of the Compagnies de la Marine arrived with thirty French soldiers and two hundred Indians from Montreal. While Montcalm himself was not yet at the Fort, Langy, the French partisan leader, welcomed Durantaye and his men and invited Durantaye inside for a hot breakfast. Accompanying Langy was Captain Wolfe, who had recently returned from his trip to Fort Edward. Shaking the snow from his overcoat, Durantaye graciously accepted and entered the fort.

***

That same morning to the south, Atecouando was relieving himself, steam rising from his stream as his six Abenaki warriors were rising from the ground, the snow falling from their blankets and hides as they prepared to continue their march north to Carillon. Atecouando had just finished a scout of the English at Fort Edward and was looking forward to returning to the encampment where they'd feast and drink brandy with their French friends. At least he could warm up from this venture.

While he had not seen all that much activity around the English fort, Atecouando could always exaggerate a little to make sure that he and his warriors received perhaps an extra ration or two of French brandy or other spirits. Morale among his warriors was high, even after spending the last week out in this cold. Atecouando looked forward to the coming spring and warmth, the next fighting season against the English, and their promised plunder.

As they journeyed north across the frozen lake, Atecouando's mind had wandered to warmth, food, and women, but was quickly snapped back to reality as his two lead warriors stopped, knelt down, and began looking at the snow and moving it with their fingers. Atecouando moved quickly up to his men, wanting to see what they had found.

"What is it?" asked Atecouando, but he too saw once he reached the two warriors. Just under a small dusting of snow was the sign that many men using ice creepers had carved paths on the lake ice. Nodding, Atecouando had his men circle out to find more signs that had been left behind.

As Atecouando's men spread out, they could see the scrapings and markings that indicated that hundreds of men had just recently passed this way, heading north. The Abenakis gathered together to discuss what this meant. No other Indian or French party was supposed to be down here, which meant this could only be the English, or even those bold men called Rangers, who had raided Carillon a few months back.

Atecouando's mood brightened. The Great Spirit had presented him this gift, and he must quickly get the information back to Carillon so he could receive his reward, probably an even bigger reward than he had anticipated. His warriors agreed about the need for speed, and they picked up the pace, moving as quickly as they could over the frozen lake.

***

As the Abenakis were making their way northward, inside Fort Carillon in one of the larger rooms where a fire crackled at one end, Durantaye pulled apart some warm, fresh bread, inhaled the sweet aroma of its steam, then lathered some honey onto a piece before stuffing it into his mouth and chewing blissfully.

"So, what news of our English friends to the south?" asked Durantaye between mouthfuls of bread.

Langy, who was sipping a mug of steaming tea, explained that there had been no recent activity since the raid by the Rangers back in December. Durantaye nodded as he took another bite of his honeyed bread.

"Was it true this Rogers left a receipt for the oxen he killed?" Wolfe asked.

Langy snorted and nodded.

"He even asked me about it when I was recently down at Fort Edward, arrogant English bastard."

Durantaye raised his eyebrows.

"Did you say anything to him?"

Wolfe nodded. "I warned him to take care the next time he visited," and all three men began to chuckle.

"Still, I am becoming concerned about the lack of activity," said Langy. "Last night, one of the elder shamans of the Abenaki proclaimed that he had had a vision of Englishmen moving along the ice towards us here."

As a partisan leader who relied on his Indian allies, Langy understood the importance of village shamans and the power they wielded over their warriors.

"Any reactions from the Abenaki?" asked Durantaye.

Langy shrugged while Wolfe reported that the warriors were excited at the prospect, since these visions carried great weight, and they were all looking for a fight.

All three nodded and continued to enjoy their breakfast, Durantaye telling of the political intrigue and maneuvering currently going on in Montreal and Quebec. Langy was in the process of describing what had occurred at Carillon for the past couple of months when an orderly ran into the room and said one of their scouting parties was returning up the lake and moving fast.

Understanding that this usually meant news, all three men quickly stood from the table and hurried out of the fort and down towards the shore. With no vegetation yet on the trees and brush, only snow, it was easy to see the approaching scouting party of seven warriors moving fast, throwing up plumes of snow as they raced towards the encampment.

Other Indian warriors were on the shore, letting out war whoops for the approaching scouts, who were drawing the attention of both the warriors and the Canadians, who were starting to arrive at the shoreline as well. There was a crowd of Indian warriors, French, and Canadians waiting when Atecouando and his warriors arrived at the shore line, panting for air.

Seeing Langy, Atecouando approached him while his six warriors were trying to catch their breath, bent over and hands on their knees. Between gulps of air, Atecouando explained what they had found on the lake, the trail of several hundred men moving towards them.

Langy, knowing there were no large scouts going on right now by their men, realized these had to be English. Perhaps Rogers himself had come out to play.

Grasping Atecouando's shoulder and stating, "Well done," Langy turned and started heading back towards the fort.

"Duty drummer, sound assembly!"

The long roll of the drum began to sound and echo off the fort's walls and buildings, which led to a rising chorus of war cries as Abenaki and other Indian warriors, grabbed their tomahawks and the rest of their weapons and began to gather. Canadians and French regulars began spilling out of their huts and barracks, pulling cartridge boxes over their great coats and blanket coats, and they too began to assemble. Finally some action had arrived to break up the boredom.

Langy and Wolfe moved quickly back inside the fort, gathering their gear and weapons. Durantaye was ready to go, since he had just recently arrived and was eager to get into some action. Pulling him over to a map on the wall, Langy pointed out a stream/trail intersection southwest of the fort.

"You will take your men along with some of my Canadians and Abenakis and move to this location," Langy pointed to the map and Durantaye nodded, smiling. "Myself and Captain Wolfe will bring up the rest of the force. You will pin them in place and we'll seal their doom."

Excited to be heading off to action, Durantaye nodded and, with one of Langy's sergeants as a guide, ran outside where he met up with his men and an assembled force of some two hundred Indian warriors and Canadians, who were all ready to march. They were feeding off one another's energy, jumping around in the excitement of going to battle against their hated foes, waving their muskets and tomahawks, yelling their war whoops, and working themselves into a bloody frenzy.

They calmed only for a quick second as Durantaye ran up and gave a simple command, "Follow me." The war party charged out of the encampment and headed into the woods.

Durantaye had only been gone for a few minutes when Langy and Wolfe exited the fort and stood in front of the rest of the assembled French and Canadians. Another two hundred men stood in a loose square, composed of French regulars, Marines, Canadian fighters, and more Indians, who had not charged out with the first group.

As Langy finished settling his shooting bag across his shoulders and taking his rifle from Wolfe, he called the formation to attention.

"Men, there is a good chance our old friend Major Rogers and his Rangers may be heading here," boomed Langy. "We will not allow a repeat of what he did back in December!"

Langy pulled a folded piece of paper out of his haversack. "I want to personally shove Rogers's receipt up his ass!"

The assembled men roared in approval, raising their weapons over their heads, and followed Langy and Wolfe, who led them out of the encampment and into the woods in the direction from which they believed Rogers would be approaching.

***

As Langy and Durantaye led their men from the fort, the Rangers to the south did not suspect that their enemy was moving towards them. They began their morning ritual of rising from their sleeping holes in the snow and preparing for the coming day.

Jacob woke his men for stand-to and finished rolling up his blanket and waterproofing skins and tying them on to his pack. Jacob knelt down next to a tree, observing his men behind cover and also facing out, watching the woods. The night had shifted to pre-dawn grey and cold, and Jacob involuntarily shivered. The dawn grey was slowly becoming lighter as the sun clawed its way up into the cold morning air.

Once satisfied all was well, Rogers ordered the column to assemble and continue on their march towards Carillon. They should reach it today, do their scout, and if their luck held, perhaps grab a prisoner or two for information before heading back to Fort Edward. Moving out of the thick draw, the Ranger column began to spread out and stagger left and right in their line of march, the Rangers automatically taking up their scanning fields.

The snow was deep and required the Rangers to put on their snowshoes, or men would sink up to their knees or deeper as some of the volunteers from the British regulars found out. The Rangers moved quietly yet purposefully through the snow towards the mountain they called "Baldy."

The sun finally crested over the mountains and bathed the valley in a rich glow, but it did nothing to warm the frigid air. It was going to be one of those clear, crisp, and cold northern days. Jacob was beginning to dislike the cold, which made his injuries from earlier fighting ache.

By mid-morning, Rogers called a halt and gathered his officers and sergeants into the middle of their perimeter.

"We're going to start fishing early today gentlemen, as we close on Carillon," Rogers began,. "There is a chance we could catch one of their patrols coming out of the fort and bag them first, and then conduct the scout. Buckley, you will lead the column; send a screening party ahead of the main column. Stark your company will bring up the rear. Place out a rear scouting party to make sure no one catches us from the rear. Putnam, send out flankers to screen the column. Everyone understands?"

Everyone nodded and returned to their companies. Putnam grabbed Jacob's coat sleeve.

"I want you to be the flanker to the west, watch our backs."

Jacob nodded and told his men their responsibility. At least they were out on their own and not caught up in the gaggle of the large column. They shouldered their packs, Jacob swimming his shoulders in the straps to get them settled. He led his men out and moved towards the west, crossing a frozen stream before turning northeast to parallel the route of the column.

"Peter, keep your eye on the column. Don't lose them," Jacob instructed.

Jacob signaled his men to move forward, and Konkapot and Samuel took the lead, Peter and James on the right side and Jacob and Charles on the left, creating an open wedge. The column was moving slowly enough that it was rather easy for Peter to keep an eye on them and not lose them in the forest. Jacob's wedge moved through the trees and brush, thankful that they were not yet thick with leaves.

***

Crunching through the snow, Ranger Ensign McDonald and two other Rangers were the lead scouts who had been sent ahead of the column from Captain Buckley's Company. McDonald noticed it was quiet, almost too quiet, like a tomb. Normally the woods were alive with sounds, but today there was nothing, as if the world was holding its collective breath. There wasn't even a breeze.

McDonald spotted a large snow-covered boulder, and he pointed over to it so they could take a break. Leaning against the boulder, the three Rangers caught their breath from the tiring work of breaking trail through the snow. They had only been sitting for a few minutes when one of the Rangers spotted movement down slope and across an open field to their front. An Indian broke from the woods, followed quickly by a second, then a few more. All three Rangers spun and flattened themselves into the ground, wiggling into the shadow of the boulder.

The clearing was beginning to fill with several Indians and men wearing blue and white capotes, a leader pulling everyone together and held a quick meeting. The group included Durantaye, a few of the Canadian scouts, and the Abenakis, who were quickly scanning the woods to their front, not noticing the high ground to their left where McDonald and his men were concealed.

Durantaye pointed towards a frozen stream heading in the general direction from which they believed the Rangers were approaching.

"That will allow us to move faster than fighting through this maddening snow," commented Durantaye, and everyone nodded in agreement, taking up their arms and heading towards the steam.

***

After observing that the meeting was over and the area clear, Ranger McDonald and his men slowly stood up and took a knee. They never noticed the cold or wetness of the snow; they were too concerned about what they had observed. They quickly turned and began to move as fast as their snowshoes would allow them along their own trail, which had packed down the snow.

They stayed to the high ground, masking them from the French and Indians, who were traveling on the lower ground along the frozen stream. Churning the snow into a white powdery mist, McDonald and his two men huffed and puffed and their legs began to burn as they charged through the snow, their breaths trailing behind them in lines of steam. They broke through the woods, and the column halted as they called out, "Rangers coming in!"

As the column went into a quick perimeter, McDonald, gasping for air, told Rogers what they had just seen.

"Could you tell how many there were?" asked Rogers.

McDonald shook his head no.

"Only…saw…a small…group," he panted. "But there…was movement…in the woods…a lot of movement…coming our way."

Rogers nodded.

"Buckley, send out another scout in force to determine the enemy's strength."

Buckley nodded and moved up to his company, dispatching a scouting party.

"Prepare for action!" Rogers called out, and the Rangers began to reform, bringing their packs and bedrolls and piling them up in the middle of the perimeter and returning to their spots on the line. Jacob and his men were set out as flank security to make sure the enemy didn't try to get around them.

Buckley's scouts came back, reporting they had observed about a hundred, mostly Indians, moving through the woods towards them. Rogers rubbed his hands together in anticipation. They still had the numbers on their side if the scouts were accurate.

Rogers moved the column forward to a depression immediately behind the thirty-foot embankment overlooking the frozen stream the Indians were using. Rogers in a crouch moved along the line, telling everyone to hold their fire and wait. He would initiate the ambush and then the Rangers would stand and fire.

"We need to be ready to bag the whole lot of them," whispered Rogers as he moved along the forming line. "Wait for my command!"

The Rangers positioned themselves as best they could, using boulders, dips, and trees for cover. Rogers's ambush line was over a hundred yards long, looking down into a clear and open killing field which should be a turkey shoot for his men. They were all silent, grimly looking down the barrels of their rifles and muskets, waiting for the enemy to enter the open killing ground. Jacob and his men were still out on the flank of the ambush line to make sure they were not themselves flanked by an unseen enemy.

Jacob quickly looked to make sure his men were all in the best position they could find, then over his shoulder to make sure he could see the ambush line. The excitement began to build inside Jacob in anticipation of the looming fight. Any doubts or fears were quickly pushed away as Jacob concentrated on watching for the enemy and picking his targets when he saw them.

Soon, a lone Indian broke out into the clearing and stopped after moving only a few feet. All of the Rangers watched and waited as the muzzles of their muskets and rifles slowly shifted over to where the Indian had come from the woods.

The Indian had knelt down to adjust his snowshoe when from the left side of the ambush line, there was a thundering crack as a single Ranger, disobeying Rogers's instruction, pulled the trigger. To add insult to injury, he missed, but the crack caused other Rangers, coiled up like tight springs, to open fire. As luck would have it, a group of Indians broke from the woods just as the muskets and some rifles fired.

The balls screamed through the air, some smacking into flesh with wet impacts while others hit the trees with dull thuds, causing white geysers of snow to fly up. Some of the Indians, warned by the first musket shot, dived for cover behind trees, which took most of the balls, sparing them. Others who had been too caught up in the run to take cover were hit. Many twisted and spun, blood spraying out in crimson arcs as they fell to the snow.

Seeing his well-set ambush blown, Rogers jumped up and yelled, "Buckley, head 'em!"

The Rangers rose up and yelling their own war cries, charged down the hill towards the Indians to prevent them from fading back into the woods. Brandishing knives and tomahawks, the Rangers crashed into the stunned survivors of the first small volley. A brutal close and quick combat ensued as knives and tomahawks flashed. Rangers fired at fleeing Indians who were fading away into the woods. Some of the Rangers paused to scalp the dead, as others ploughed into the forest in pursuit.

As the pursuing Rangers came around a bend, they were confronted with a shocking sight. They had caught up with the running Indians, but now also faced a wall of two hundred White and Blue Capotes with Langy, who gave the order to fire. The Rangers tried to skid to a halt, but their momentum carried them forward on the slippery snow and ice into the murderous fire, and the French and Canadian balls tore into them.

The devastating volley dropped nearly fifty Rangers, many never to rise again. Dozens more, who were hit hard tried to run, limp, or crawl back towards Rogers and safety. Many would not make it as the Indians fell upon them like eagles, savagely taking their lives. Such was the brutal fighting and quick turn of events in frontier warfare.

The other groups of Indians and Canadians had been moving so fast that they actually had passed Rogers's position. Drawn to the sound of fighting, they angled back towards the firing. Langy and Wolfe moved forward with their men, coming upon a shaken Durantaye, who had been leading the initial group that had been caught in the opening musketry. He was uninjured, but the shock of being caught in the open had shaken him. Now, the shock was wearing off.

***

Around them, the Indians were killing any surviving Rangers and scalping them. Langy checked on Durantaye who waved and nodded that he was OK and then stood up. Langy directed Durantaye to lead his war party and circle to the left. Captain Wolfe would go up the center, and he would lead a war party to the right, encircling their foes and finally eliminating them.

"Today I will bag that pompous ass, Rogers!" growled Langy as he led his group off to the right side of the fighting.

***

From the sound of the fighting, Jacob knew everything had gone wrong. They had heard the first shot, followed by the second volley before Rogers gave the order to head them off. Next there was the sporadic firing, and then the thunderous volley away from their position.

"Ah damn, that's not us," thought Jacob.

"Do we go see what's happening?" asked James, but Jacob shook his head "no" as he continued to watch the woods near them.

Instead of joining the pursuit, Jacob and his men held their position on the flank. It wasn't long before they saw the line of white and blue capotes moving through the woods towards them, and there were a lot more of them than they had thought. They were greatly outnumbered, and Jacob decided it would be better to run than to fight.

"Fall back to the main position!" ordered Jacob, and they all spun around and ran towards the ambush line. They arrived just in time to see some of the Rangers staggering out of the woods. This proved that Jacob had been right; something had gone wrong, again.

"They're coming right behind us yelled Jacob as his men took cover in ditches and behind rocks, facing the way they had just come. Rogers nodded and started yelling for some of the Rangers to face the direction from which Jacob had just arrived.

Jacob took up his rifle and sighted along the barrel at an approaching Canadian in his blue capote.

"Fire by sections, commence firing!" yelled Rogers, and Jacob squeezed the trigger, feeling the secure buck of the rifle against his shoulder. Through the smoke, he saw his target fall.

Automatically, Jacob and his men took turns in pairs, one firing while the other covered as he loaded, and then they switched. Jacob and his Rangers began a steady rhythmic discharge of their rifles, which was quickly responded to by the Canadians and Indians who sought cover and fired back.

Balls whined and whizzed overhead, and among the Rangers, bouncing off trees and boulders or flying harmlessly by. Some were not harmless, however, striking Rangers with resounding smacks.

In between firing, some of the Rangers hurled insults back at their French adversaries. Jacob noticed one Ranger, a big man with a beard from Captain Hopkin's Company bellow out curses and insults while he loaded from behind cover. He turned and fired and then returned to load while continuing his verbal assault against French, Canadians, and Indians alike.

Jacob was impressed that this Ranger maintained the steady rhythm of loading and firing, without breaking stride in his constant verbal assault against the enemy. He must have gotten their attention. As he broke cover to fire once more, three bullets hit him squarely, killing him before he hit the ground. Jacob shook his head before he returned to aim and fire once more at an approaching Indian.

Jacob was feeling the heat. This was one hell of a fight. As he brought his rifle up to aim at a running Abenaki, he felt a burning sensation as a ball creased his right shoulder and chipped the stock of his rifle, which at least deflected the bullet away instead of letting it continue on its path into his neck. But the ball hitting his shoulder threw his aim off, and he missed his target.

"Damn, Jacob," shouted Samuel who had seen him miss. "You getting old or something? You never miss." In spite of his injury, Jacob had to laugh and shake his head as he began reloading. Samuel's timing always seemed perfect for changing the situation and shifting the mood.

As he was loading, Jacob heard James grunt when he took a ball through his arm. Charles went over to him quickly, checked him, and helped him tie some cloth around it for a bandage.

"Just through the meat. Didn't hit any bone," yelled Charles. James nodded and returned to the fight, a grim and determined look on his face.

However, as Charles turned to return to his firing position, he was knocked over as a ball skimmed his head, knocking off his hat. Pushing himself up to his knees, Charles reached up, touched the wound, found it was minor, shrugged, and then reached out, grabbed his hat, knocked the snow off, and placed it back on his head.

Jacob's wound stung but didn't really stop him, and his next shot was true. Concern was creeping like the cold into his mind. Almost half of his section had been hit, but their luck had held so far with minor injuries. Around him though, Jacob was seeing other Rangers getting hit, some rising back up while others did not. The situation was beginning to look grim, and a question about whether they would get out of this one alive rose its ugly head, but Jacob pushed the thought back down.

There was no shortage of targets; the woods seemed full of either the white and blue capotes of the French and Canadians or Abenaki and other Indian warriors. The fighting produced a constant roar, and the woods were filling with the grey smoke of hundreds of rifles and muskets. Rangers and Canadians exchanged insults, bullets whizzed and banged off trees, and men screamed or groaned in pain from being hit.

Jacob's rifle was becoming hot from all of the firing, and he was glad he had brought extra powder and shot. He had just returned his rammer and was priming his rifle when another close call occurred. A ball ricocheted off the boulder he was using for cover, and rock splinters hit the left side of his face and his left eye.

Dropping lower to the ground, Jacob shook his head and after pulling his glove off, rubbed his face and eye to clear his vision. It did return, and Jacob whispered thanks to the spirits for not being blind, the rock chips having missed anything vital. Eventually, the gunfire subsided to a low roar.

Like two fighters, both sides seemed to stop firing to catch their collective breaths, but they still circled and watched one another. Rogers had pulled everyone into a tight perimeter that was being squeezed in from three sides by the enemy.

Rogers had to grudgingly accept that he might be in deep trouble on this one. Every time one of his Rangers tried to rise to fire, three or four bullets hit him or hit around him. They were picking off his men one by one. Rogers knew he had many wounded, and the prospect of surviving was quickly diminishing.

A group of Rangers that had charged down in pursuit of the running Indians, had been surrounded and captured, and they were led out to where they could be seen by Rogers and his Rangers. Jacob and his men watched as they were tied to a tree after having their weapons taken away. Durantaye called up for Rogers to surrender or he would kill these prisoners.

"Like hell I will!" yelled Rogers who brought his own rifle up to his shoulder and fired. Jacob and his men opened fire on the Indians below them.

***

Durantaye ducked as a Canadian in front of him fell back, bullets striking him and whizzing about him. Some of the Indians buried their tomahawks into some of the tied Rangers, while others fell from the Ranger fire. Durantaye and those who had not been hit fell back into the woods, leaving the Rangers who had not been tomahawked tied to the trees. Rogers knew he was helpless to try and rescue these men, and they were as good as dead anyway.

Both Langy and Rogers saw that the sun was starting to set, and time was running out to determine who would be the victor and who would be the vanquished. Rogers wordlessly hoped the sun would set fast and bath them in darkness so they could make their escape. Langy was wordlessly hoping the sun would stay up longer so he could secure his victory against the Rangers. It was so close that he could taste sweet victory over Rogers!

Rogers took stock of his situation. He had only around sixty men left alive. They could not last long against a determined assault; the numbers had shifted to his enemy's favor.

"If they attack us in strength," Rogers instructed, "I'll give the word to break for it. Break up and head back towards the lake where we had our last camp or Fort Edward the best you can. Good luck!"

All the Rangers understood and grimly nodded their heads. Jacob looked at his men, while Charles and James, like himself, were injured, they could all move. "I'll bloody well get out of this place one way or the other!" growled Jacob, Konkapot and the others nodding their heads in agreement, a determined expression on their faces as they waited to see what would happen next.

As the sun was getting closer to setting, Langy decided to try one more final throw of the dice. He would try and bag Rogers and his surviving Rangers by "coup de main," charging with everyone, and by sheer numbers, overwhelm and finally put this boogey man and his Rangers to rest. Pulling Durantaye and Wolfe close, he quickly pointed out which way he wanted them to go before raising his fusil over his head and giving the command to "Charge!"

With a great surge, the human wave of Indians, Canadians, and Frenchmen broke from the woods and charged up the hill with shouts and yells, some stopping to fire at the Rangers in the purplish grey of the setting sun.

"Every man for themselves. Run for it!" yelled Rogers, as it seemed the very gates of hell itself had opened and released these screaming demons and hellhounds charging up the hill at them.

Breaking up into two- and three-man groups, the Rangers scattered into the growing darkness. Some fell to the accurate French and Canadian fire. The wounded tried to move as best they could, but were quickly overtaken and killed by the charging Indians.

Jacob, Konkapot, and Samuel broke one way, and Peter, Charles, and James another, each praying for the best for the others as they crashed into the darkening woods, branches slapping at them as they went. Adrenaline helped to push already tired legs to carry them through the woods as quickly as they could move over the snow. They were all headed to where they had left the lake and had hidden some hand sleds and extra equipment.

Through the night, Jacob, Konkapot, and Samuel moved, having slowed from their initial sprint. Now they moved quickly and cautiously, listening for any pursuit. While they could hear lone musket shots in the distance, it did not sound like there was anyone pursuing them. Keeping Baldy in view, bathed white by the moon in a clear sky, Jacob and the others vectored towards their camp from the night before.

Near midnight, they carefully approached the old campsite, calling out, "Rangers coming in." In return they heard a welcoming, "Come in Rangers." Rogers had just arrived before them, with a few other Rangers. Peter, James and Charles quickly came in, and they shook hands in joy at finding everyone still alive.

"Jacob, after you and your men rest up, I want you to head to the fort and warn them. Have them bring sleds and supplies and meet us along the way. I will wait here for the others and start down the lake in the morning." Jacob nodded, and after a brief rest, they headed down to the lake, put on their ice creepers, and began their journey back to Fort Edward.

As they tied on their creepers, Jacob felt relief and joy in seeing that all of his men were there, alive and not in tough shape. Jacob had felt a growing fear that he along with his men would die in that lonely spot in the woods, that all would have been over. They had prevailed, and that feeling of joy added some spring to his exhausted legs as they made their way to the south.

Jacob kept a good pace, moving for about an hour, and then taking a quick break to catch their breaths. The sun rose and Jacob kept moving. His legs burned, the constant exertion over the past several days having taken their toll. Driven by their desire to get to the fort, they all "Rangered-on," with only quick rest breaks, chewing on some jerky or hard tack for energy. They drank water from their canteens whenever possible as they trotted along on the frozen lake.

The weather cooperated, and they reached Fort Edward in good time, reporting to Colonel Haviland and Captain Waite. Waite gathered several large horse-drawn sleighs and loaded them with blankets and food. Bringing one of the regimental surgeons with him and his company, he led his relief party out of the fort and headed towards the lake, hoping to reach Rogers and the survivors quickly. Since they were spent from the rapid trip south, Waite told Jacob and his men to head to their hut and thanked them for their service and the warning.

They crossed the bridge to the island and moved to their hut. Their wolves were so happy to see them that they charged out and knocked down the three tired Rangers as James and Charles chuckled and began working to get a fire started in their fireplace. Pushing Smoke off him and throwing him a large chunk of jerky, Jacob shrugged out of his gear, hung everything on the pegs, and sat on his bed, enjoying the warmth of the fire that James and Charles were feeding.

Everyone got out of their wet outer clothes, hung their equipment, and began to clean their rifles. As he withdrew the rammer with the rag, he saw that Peter was helping to lift James' legs onto his bunk since he had fallen asleep and tumbled over. Samuel had leaned back against the hut wall and was snoring, mouth open and head back, his rifle across his lap.

Removing the rag from his ramrod, Jacob reloaded his rifle and leaned it up against the wall next to his bunk. Smoke was curled up underneath, content that his master was back. Jacob helped Peter put the rest of the loose gear away, lean rifles up against the walls, and make sure everyone was set.

Peter checked Jacob's shoulder, where there was a long bloody crease but nothing serious. Konkapot was lying on his back, hands behind his head. As Jacob walked by, he commented, "That was a close one. Too close."

Jacob nodded, and said, "We live to fight another day."

Konkapot nodded and folding his arms against his chest, closed his eyes, rolled onto his side, and was quickly asleep. Jacob looked at Charles. The bloody crease along his head was also minor. Jacob made a mental note that they should go see the surgeon in the morning to be safe. Satisfied all was in order, Jacob lay down on his bunk and finally surrendered to exhaustion, quickly falling into a deep sleep.

***

Waite and his relief column met up with Rogers and the survivors six miles north of the ruins of Fort William Henry. Waite was surprised at the low number of survivors. Rogers had waited until morning before starting out. Along with the company commanders who had started out with the column, only about fifty men had survived.

None of the volunteers from the British regulars had made it back; they had all been either killed or captured by the French. Langy controlled the field, and had camped there, understanding it would be folly to chase after an enemy in the darkness.

***

In the morning, Langy's men scoured the field. The commander of Fort Carillon had dispatched sleds to move the wounded and living prisoners back to the fort. Atecouando, who had decided fighting was better than brandy, approached Langy. He presented a well-tailored green coat with silver buttons on it.

"What's this?" asked Langy.

"War chief of the Rangers' coat," Atecouando replied, and he stood with his chest puffed out. "I killed him."

Langy accepted the coat, not sure if he could believe that Rogers was dead. They found documents in the pockets that indicated it was in fact Rogers's coat. The documents included Rogers's commission, which he would never have left behind willingly.

Atecouando strutted and boasted he had killed the fleeing Rogers and taken his coat. He was surrounded by his Abenakis and other Indians, who whooped their pleasure and shook their tomahawks in the air.

Langy carried the coat, looking at it carefully; there were no blood stains on it or in it. Perhaps it was true; perhaps it was not. Only time would tell. Still he had wanted to be the one who finally caught and killed Rogers. Langy pulled the folded receipt Rogers had written and stuck it into one of the pockets.

Well, it wasn't as good as stuffing it up his ass, but he had done it; he had solidly defeated Rogers at his own game, again. He hoped that Rogers was still alive, so he could kill him himself. Nodding and muttering that only time would tell, Langy turned and began heading back towards Fort Carillon as the French and Canadians collected fallen Rangers' items and the dead.

CHAPTER 4

FORT EDWARD AND THE GATHERING STORM

The Rangers had been devastated by what they would call the disastrous Battle on Snowshoes as it would come to be called. Jacob and his men remained at the fort, surprised at how lucky they had been to have survived with only minor injuries. It took a while for them to thaw out and return to health after the arduous fight and travel.

In their hut, sitting around the fire wrapped in wool blankets, they reflected on how close it had been. "Will I ever warm up?" grumbled Samuel as he sat near their fire, his face the only part exposed from under the blanket. The wolves, who watched with their golden eyes, tried not to be judgmental as they sat hunched over towards the fire.

"This isn't that cold," remarked Peter, who sat wrapped in his blanket, his pipe in his mouth. He added, "Been through a lot colder back home." Samuel gave Peter a dirty look, but all he received back was a wink. "Maybe I live somewhere where it's warm more than cold when this is over," Peter said.

Samuel nodded and pulled the blanket tighter around him. "Think this war will ever end?" Jacob had to think about that one, running his finger over his fresh wounds from this last fight and pondering the very same question. "Don't know," answered

Peter as he puffed on his pipe, and then coughed. "Even when this one ends, a new one starts."

Jacob sat and watched his men banter back and forth as he continued to run his fingers over the puckered fresh wounds and to reflect on how close this fight had come to being their last one. Yet, they sat, joked, and were still alive.

Smoke padded over and rested his head on Jacob's lap, perhaps sensing his master's thoughts. Taking a deep breath and scratching Smoke behind his ears, Jacob nodded and concluded that they would make it. He decided not to dwell on it, to look forward, not back.

As they rested and recuperated, Rogers traveled to Albany to speak with General Howe, the new commander on the New York Front, as General Abercrombie had been recently promoted to take over Lord Loudon's position as Commander-in-Chief.

When Rogers returned to the island, he went straight to work reorganizing his smashed companies to bring the battalion of Rangers back to full strength. Rogers was smarting from his defeat at the hands of the French, and he began planning the next raid, looking for some payback. It wasn't very long before a messenger arrived for Jacob to report to Major Rogers for a mission. Having been part of this unit now for a couple of years, Jacob and his men could usually expect a runner to arrive once Rogers had begun planning an expedition.

When Jacob arrived at Rogers's cabin, Captain Naunauphtaunk of the Stockbridge Company of Rangers was already there. Jacob greeted the captain warmly by grasping forearms and speaking to him in his native tongue.

"Thus, why I called for you, Jacob," said Rogers as he looked up from his map. "I know you two can operate together."

Both Naunauphtaunk and Jacob nodded and looked to Rogers for their instructions.

"Gentlemen, I want you here," said Rogers, pointing at his map with the stem of his pipe. "Jacob, with your experience in this region, I want you to go with the captain here on a scout of the French around Carillon. As you know, the British generals want to invest in that position and want more information."

Rogers looked up from his map again and looked sternly in Jacob's and the captain's eyes.

"I also want prisoners, but don't hesitate to kill some of the French or Canadians. I want them to know we're still here and that they may have won the last one, but we're not done yet!"

Jacob nodded and looked at the spot on the map where Rogers was pointing. On the map, the mountain was named "Rattlesnake Hill," and it was at a very narrow section of the lake, directly across from the fort. Their scout would be from Rattlesnake on the eastern shore of the lake to determine the strength of Fort Carillon.

Rogers showed them on the map where four other Ranger sections had been sent for their scouts so they wouldn't blunder into one another. Most of the other sections were Stockbridge Indians, the only company of Rangers at just about full strength.

Once they both understood what was expected of them, Jacob and the captain left to get their men ready to depart in the morning. When Jacob arrived at his cabin, the men were already preparing their gear, and Konkapot simply asked, "Are we heading to Carillon or Saint Frederick?"

Jacob filled them in on the plan and told them to draw rations and extra powder.

"At least we're never bored to death," said Samuel. "Just likely to be frozen to death!"

Jacob's men were by now well-seasoned veterans, and they automatically knew who would draw the rations and who would cook while the others molded bullets and filled powder horns.

They were happy they were going out with the Stockbridge Indians with whom they felt a kinship, especially Jacob and Konkapot.

Once all was ready in the morning, Jacob took up his trusty rifle and led his men over to where they were to meet the Stockbridge Company with Captain Naunauphtaunk. He was waiting there with around eighteen other Rangers, and Jacob and his men went over to greet them.

One of the Stockbridge Indians took off Samuel's hat, and they all lined up to rub the bald spot from the scalping, believing it was good luck to rub the man who had survived such a brutal attack, and in a way, to show him honor. Samuel had become used to it and simply lowered his head until the warriors all had had their chance to rub his head for good luck.

Both Jacob and Captain Naunauphtaunk smiled, and then the captain ordered his men to lead out. Jacob's men would trail them and watch their rear.

Instead of traveling to the southern shore of Lake George, Captain Naunauphtaunk led them to the ruins of old Fort Anne to the northeast, and from there they traveled past South Bay along trails east of the lake until they closed in on Fort Carillon.

They traveled for several days. Some were warm as if spring had won its wrestling match with Old Man Winter, but others were filled with cold, drizzly spring rains. They saw or heard no indicators of French or their Indian allies in the area before they arrived at the high ground that Rogers had indicated. The only sounds were the songs of birds and the rustle of squirrels in the leaves.

They climbed the slopes and came out in a thick field of wild grass, brush, and trees. Below them stretched the lake and, in the distance, Fort Carillon. Rattlesnake was a valuable observation point, standing a good two hundred feet high. It was slightly over a mile long, with two prominent peaks from which to observe the French and the fort.

Jacob sat under a tree behind a bush with his rifle resting across his knees, and he was impressed by how much work the French and Canadians had accomplished since they had first started scouting them. Jacob had to acknowledge his foes' ability to build strong positions.

"I'm surprised they haven't done anything over here," whispered Jacob to Konkapot. "This would be a great position to support the fort and stop men like us from constantly observing it."

Konkapot nodded, and then replied, "Let's hope they don't figure that out. It would make our jobs harder."

Jacob and his men rotated scouting duties with the Stockbridge Rangers as they clover-leafed around the high ground to get better views of the French works. Where the British relied on thick wooden walls, the French had chosen thick stone walls, similar to Fort Saint Frederick up north. This made better sense to Jacob; stone would be stronger for withstanding artillery fire versus wooden walls like those that had been breached in William Henry.

What they also saw from their vantage point were the long lines of white tents of the French regulars, the numerous bateaux along the shore, storehouses, and what appeared to be earthworks opposite the fort facing the landward side of the peninsula the fort was built on.

Jacob and Captain Naunauphtaunk were comparing notes on the morning of their fourth day of the scout, when Peter came over and told them they had movement coming their way. Jacob and Captain Naunauphtaunk followed Peter back to his position, Jacob pulling out his telescope.

While it was a foggy morning, they could see three bateaux loaded with woodcutters leaving the shore next to the fort. Jacob looked up and down the boat for anyone armed, and he spotted only axes and saws, no muskets. Jacob passed his telescope to Captain Naunauphtaunk, who looked at the approaching target of opportunity.

"Do you think Major Rogers would accept some of them as prisoners?" Captain Naunauphtaunk asked.

Jacob, who took his telescope back, nodded in the affirmative. "He wasn't specific on the *who* part, just prisoners," he said, and Captain Naunauphtaunk nodded, smiled, and called everyone together. He and Jacob quickly came up with a plan to ambush the woodcutters from the shore. Everyone nodded, and the excitement intensified as Captain Naunauphtaunk led them forward down the slope to the shore where the bateaux were heading.

Moving as fast as shadowy wraiths through the woods, the Rangers came to a clearing along the shore where they waited for the boats to approach. They could hear the sound of voices and oars, but could see only the grey wispy fog beginning to turn gold as the sun rose higher. It was a small landing area; big enough for only one boat, but it was where they were heading.

Jacob took his men to the right while the Stockbridge went left, everyone taking up a good but concealed hasty firing position. Twenty-four rifles and muskets were slowing tracking and converging as the lead boat began to appear as a grey shape in the fog closing in on the shore. Everyone held his breath. Jacob sighted along his rifle and began to slowly take in the slack of the trigger.

There was a scraping and a bumping noise as the boat's keel struck the rocky shore, and the French and Canadian woodcutters jumped into the water with a splash to walk onto the shore. When about half of the woodcutters were on the shore, helping to steady the boat or standing idly by waiting for the next group,

Captain Naunauphtaunk rose up and gave a war cry, at which all of the Ranger rifles and muskets barked as one. Bullets slammed into the boat, sending wood chips and splinters flying. Some hit the water causing small geysers, while most hit their targets with a wet thud as blood and brain matter splattered against the boat, the lake, and the other men.

Through the smoke, the Rangers rushed out with tomahawks and knives. They quickly captured ten of the woodcutters, who had dropped their woodcutting tools immediately and had thrown their hands up. Those who had resisted were cut down.

Jacob approached, and one of the stunned woodcutters, blood running from a bullet wound in his abdomen, swung his axe at him. Jacob ducked and blocked the axe with his tomahawk. Following through, Jacob's knife smoothly sliced the poor man's throat, his blood spraying out in a red fan. As the woodcutter dropped to his knees, Jacob grabbed the top of his hair and in a swift clean motion, scalped the dying man.

Jacob felt the thrill of the fight and the kill course through him, like a jolt. Pent-up feelings of anger and frustration from the numerous times his enemy had nearly killed him and his men, as well as anger from the loss of other Rangers he knew, rushed through him, and Jacob allowed himself to be caught up in the emotion of the moment, and the moment felt good.

Jacob held up the bloody scalp for the other boats to see and gave a blood-curdling war cry as the other Stockbridge held up their grisly prizes. Their war whoops and victory cries echoed off the trees and through the fog, rising and falling. Jacob felt good to let all of this pent up energy loose. Not reflecting on the man he had just killed, he just savored and relished the victory.

The other two boats, hearing the war cries and fighting, were quickly turning around and heading back towards Carillon. Leaving the dead where they had fallen and chopping a hole in the bateaux to sink it, the Rangers departed with their prisoners and headed back to Fort Edward. Jacob turned once more towards his enemies at Carillon, raised his rifle up over his head, and gave a parting war cry, which was taken up by the rest of his men and some of the Stockbridge, before they turned around and headed back into the woods.

"That should a send a message to our friends," Jacob remarked looking one last time across the lake at the fort. "Hopefully, it's what the major wanted."

The return trip was also uneventful, and the Rangers arrived at Fort Edward with their prisoners, which they handed over to Major Rogers. He was happy to get them, smiling from around his pipe stem. He became even more pleased when Jacob and Captain Naunauphtaunk recounted what they had done with the rest of the woodcutters. They were sure the French were now well aware that the Rangers were still there and they still had some fight in them.

Jacob and Captain Naunauphtaunk were still with Rogers when Ensign Etowaukaum from the Stockbridge Company stumbled into the cabin, head bloody from a wound. He reported that his section had been six miles from Fort Carillon on the western side when they had been hit by Canadians and Indians. They had been ambushed, and only he and half of his men had escaped, while the other half had been either killed or captured. Rogers nodded.

"You win some, and you lose some, the fickleness of war," he commented. "See to your injuries."

The warm days of spring had melted away the snow and firmed up the dirt roads. The trees and plants bloomed, beginning to add some color once more to the dreary, barren fields. The forests became alive with the sounds of life, and like hibernating bears, the garrison and families at Fort Edward ventured from their barracks and huts and began their spring cleaning.

The island was a hive of activity. The Rangers were cleaning their company areas, and the sound of axes and hammers added to the din, as new construction was begun now that the snow had mostly melted away. Perhaps as a sign of things to come, a large, two-story log barracks was begun.

Jacob and some of the Rangers watched as workers began dragging the logs into place, after they were floated across the river from the fort's side. "Is that for us?" asked Samuel, but Jacob shook his head "no."

"From what Major Rogers told me, that's for the British regulars that will be coming," reported Jacob. Then he thought, "Perhaps it is also a way to better place us under their thumbs."

Calculating the size of the barracks based on what the engineers had traced out, Samuel whistled. "Sure going to be a lot of soldiers in there. We're going to have a busy campaign season for sure."

At Fort Edward, dispatches arrived ordering that the fort be prepared to support the gathering of General Abercrombie's army, which was traveling from New England to arrive there to assemble for the campaign against Fort Carillon. Within days of the dispatch rider's arrival, wagon trains of supplies began coming in to be added to the growing stockpiles that had been started in the winter. More troops began to arrive, including both regular British and Provincial regiments.

Jacob and his men were just returning from an uneventful scout when they observed a line of blue-coated Massachusetts Provincials marching towards the fort. They also observed in the column a brown-uniformed regiment of soldiers whose uniforms looked almost identical to theirs. Jacob shrugged and they angled over to try to identify this new unit.

As they approached, they saw two red-coated officers. One was Captain Reynolds in his immaculate red uniform and gold braid, and the other was an officer in a plain, cut-down, red-faced coat. What drew Jacob's attention was how Captain Reynolds was standing ramrod straight as the other man was talking to him.

This new man's hair was cut short, no powdered wig, and his hat brim had been cut short. His coat was void of any lace, and the tails had been removed. Looking closer, Jacob remembered the face of the man, and realized it was General Howe himself, who had learned the Ranger ways from Major Rogers and Jacob, and who had adapted to the teachings of their Ranger school.

"That explains why Captain Reynolds is all smiles and ramrod stiff," thought Jacob as they closed in on the pair. Captain Reynold's eyes caught Jacob's approach and his expression began to turn frosty.

When Jacob approached the pair, he could see Captain Reynolds begin to say something to him, but General Howe quickly ordered, "That is all, captain. You are dismissed."

After opening and closing his mouth silently for a few seconds, Captain Reynolds saluted and spun on his heels, stalking away. Jacob and his Rangers stopped and actually saluted Lord Howe, one of the few English officers that had earned their respect because he respected them. After acknowledging their salute, Lord Howe approached and shook their hands, and then pointed to the men in the dark-brown uniforms.

"So what do you think?" he asked just as Major Rogers arrived. "Ah, Major Rogers, so good to see you!" Major Rogers shook Lord Howe's hand, and then turned to look at the brown-uniformed men passing by. "Gentlemen, let me introduce you to the men of the 80th Regiment of Light Armed Foot."

Rogers nodded in approval, and Jacob recognized numerous sergeants and captains in the ranks whom they had trained in the Ranger school. It was a ray of sunshine in the gloomy world of professional ignorance. At least one lord and one regiment understood what Major Rogers had been explaining for so long about what was required to fight and win in the wilderness. Here was finally a success story.

After Rogers reviewed the 80th and shook a bunch of hands, Lord Howe and the 80th resumed their march to the fort and their campsite, and the Rangers returned to their island. Over the next couple of days, numerous other regiments arrived, including one which was led by the sound of screeching bagpipes. The 42nd Royal Highlanders, the Black Watch in their kilts, had arrived.

The sound of the bagpipes and the odd uniforms of the 42nd drew a lot of attention, especially from the Indians, who gathered to watch the regiment pass by and move off towards their camp. Jacob and the other Rangers exchanged raised eyebrows at this odd unit, Samuel commenting, "This is new. We're going to scare them to death, or at least that ghastly sound will chase the Frenchies away."

Over the next couple of days, more regiments arrived with their carts and wagons. The 55th Regiment of Foot and the 44th Regiment of Foot also marched in, their regimental colors flapping in the breeze. Jacob was leading his men out on a scout as they passed these long columns of men and equipment. "Looks like this is going to be another big one," said Konkapot.

In a column of both British regulars and New York Provincials marching to Fort Edward from Albany, there were three men in civilian attire. One was well-dressed and was constantly fanning a handkerchief to his nose due to the dust and odors, another rode next to him in dark but functional civilian clothes, and a third, a brutish-looking individual, simply followed behind them in regular workman's clothes.

The man in the fancy clothes was Robert Aislabie, newly appointed to the South Sea Company, having arrived from

England to establish and maintain trade, support the British expedition's logistical needs, and establish firm trade routes. Once the French were destroyed, he was also expected to set up new trading posts to fill in the gaps left by the defeated French.

His main goal was to become a wealthy Baron, even in this God-forsaken frontier and backwoods colony. Because his family had recently disinherited him due to his excessive drinking and gambling, he needed riches to maintain his lifestyle. He acted a dandy to throw suspicion off his true goal, which was to own as much of the new territories as he could swindle or steal.

Next to Robert was William Maclane, who was the liaison between the South Sea Company and Sir William Johnson, Superintendent of Indian Affairs. What Robert and Sir William Johnson did not know was that William was also a captain in the British Army and a spy assigned to observe and report on the colonial activities in New York. He was also playing his own game. Like Robert he wanted to be wealthy, and he didn't care who paid him. To William, loyalties could be bought and sold, and, if need be, this fop Robert was expendable. He had seen how much wealth Sir William Johnson was gaining and thought it shouldn't be too difficult to replicate his success.

Following behind William was Joshua Harper, who went by "Big Harpe" since he was over six feet tall and solidly built. He also had a younger brother known as "Little Harpe," and both were employed by the captain. His job was simple: he was the muscle. All he had to do was keep his mouth shut and his eyes and his ears open and act like a servant. His reward: the captain allowed him to silence, remove, or make disappear, anyone the captain didn't want around. This was a great job for Big Harpe; he got a thrill from the kills, especially innocents, and if he did his job right, he would have a free run of all the killing he would want.

His butt sore from the saddle, Robert Aislabie moaned, "Oh the humanity in this. I shan't be able to sit for weeks!" As he had been doing for the entire trip, Robert waved his handkerchief to try and wave the dust away.

"Not much further, your lordship," William responded. "The fort should just be ahead."

"Oh, I do hope they have an inn and a bath. It will take days for me to wash this dust off of me," replied Robert. William just shook his head, and Big Harpe chuckled to himself, thankful he was behind them so they couldn't see his expression.

"Ah soon, we shall get down to business," breathed Robert, and both William and Big Harpe agreed, though their definitions might be different on what "business" meant. The column marched in and joined the growing army around Fort Edward, and all three were thinking of what they would do next.

General Abercrombie arrived a few days later and instructed Major Rogers to scout the northern end of Lake George and to map roads and enemy fortifications, both the terrain around Fort Carillon and the terrain where General Abercrombie wanted to land his force.

Following the meeting with the General, Rogers called together a group of his leaders, and, as in times past, Jacob was one of the men summoned to receive instructions on their next mission. Rogers explained that this mission would be to scout the northern shore to prepare the way for the army to follow. The force, which would be led by Rogers himself, included Rangers from Stark's and Putnam's companies and the Stockbridge Indians. Captain Putnam was not present as he had been dispatched by Major Rogers on a recruiting detail to replenish their depleted ranks.

They were to prepare a week's worth of rations and be ready to move in two days. Jacob returned to his men, and they fell to work automatically, Konkapot and Peter getting the fires ready over in the field kitchen and Jacob, Samuel, and James drawing the rations while Charles secured extra lead and powder. The wolves were there to sample the cooked rations and to help clean up any leftovers. As their rations cooked, the Rangers made final spot checks on their gear and weapons to be sure everything was in working order and their blades were sharp and rust-free. Jacob also made sure they rested when they could, to build their strength up before this next trip.

On the morning of their departure, Rogers formed the men, numbering roughly about fifty, and Jacob was pained by seeing so many of his fellow Rangers gone. It would take some time to replenish the ranks, because it was tougher for the Rangers than it was for the other Provincials, who would accept anyone. The Rangers were very selective about whom they allowed to join their ranks, Major Rogers making sure they maintained the same standards on recruitment that Jacob had been held to when he first joined.

Still, Jacob couldn't help but feel the loss at the empty spaces on the field, which used to be full of Rangers. The war was creating a harsh attrition in their ranks, but hopefully the field would soon be full once again of green-uniformed men instead of barely a company's worth, which they now had for this expedition. After inspecting the men, Rogers marched them off the island and up towards Lake George.

Jacob and the others looked for and spotted their quiet, lonely friend as they marched pass French Mountain. As they moved past the bald, rocky face of the mountain, Jacob wondered how many times they had been through here and how many more times it would be for them. When they arrived at the ruins of Fort William Henry, the area was already active with men clearing and preparing the old fields, with piles of supplies growing steadily, and with some tents already going up.

Waiting for Rogers was a wagon train of whale boats brought over from Massachusetts. They would be going via the lake on this trip, instead of through the woods. Jacob and his men were now experienced boatmen, having conducted several amphibious operations with or for Rogers. He led his men to their assigned boat, and they began loading their gear.

Samuel stood in the bow looking around as if something was amiss.

"What's wrong Samuel?" Jacob asked.

"I miss our old boat," pouted Samuel.

Shaking his head, Jacob replied "No, you miss that old swivel gun."

Samuel turned and smiled. "Yes, that's what I meant."

As his men continued to load, Jacob went up to the wagon train. After a short while, he returned with a bundle.

Samuel's eyes lit up when he spotted Jacob heading back towards their boat, carrying what appeared to be a giant version of a blunderbuss.

"Sorry Samuel, they didn't have a swivel gun," Jacob grunted as he lowered the gun into the boat. "But they did have one of these."

It was a wall gun, which was a large version of the stubby blunderbuss with a five-inch-wide bore. Like a child opening a Christmas present, Samuel giggled in glee as he took charge of the gun and its shooting bag, positioning it on the bow of their boat.

"Yeah, bring me someone to shoot at!" growled Samuel as he hefted his new weapon, "Watch out Frenchies. Here comes your destruction!"

Jacob shook his head and wondered if he had created a monster. Still, Samuel had been very good with that swivel gun, and it had helped them tremendously during some of their fights with the French and their Indian Allies.

Once all of the boats were loaded, manned, and ready, Rogers gave the signal to launch and head up the lake. It may have been a while, but Jacob and his men quickly got back into the swing of rowing as a team while Samuel and his wall gun scanned the area to their front. He was all serious now, watching for any sign of their foes.

It was a cool, crisp morning, blue sky over a mirror-flat lake. As Jacob took his turn pulling on the oars, his mind drifted again back to earlier times on this lake. They passed the eastern shore bay where Jacob and his men had rescued Rogers and his survivors with their boat after he had been squarely beaten by the Canadians and their Indian allies.

As Jacob got into the steady rhythm of pulling, lifting, pushing, lifting the oars, he just stopped thinking, letting his mind drift to the sound of the oars squeaking and the paddles dropping into the water. For a time, it was peaceful so Jacob just closed his mind down except for the mission-focused part. He automatically bent to the repetition of the rowing and did not dwell on the future or on whether they would survive. He was, just was for the moment, a part of the team.

They passed Sabbath Day Point, and Jacob recalled the bloody scene there when an expedition of Provincials had been nearly wiped out by a well-placed Indian ambush. They did not see anyone else on the lake, and they continued northward until Rogers pointed to the shore where he wanted them to make their landing.

Rogers had decided to land in the vicinity of the old French advanced position at Coutre Coer on the east side of the Ticonderoga River. Jacob and his men would join a guard detail under Captain Naunauphtaunk to hold the beach, Lieutenant Porter and ten men would scout the French at Fort Carillon, and Major Rogers with three others would climb a mountain that overlooked the valley so they could map it.

Jacob moved his boat so the bow and its deadly wall gun could cover the likely approach of any Frenchman or Indian from Carillon. Samuel really liked the wall gun, because he did not have to keep a linstock lit all the time as he had for the swivel gun; he just had to pull the trigger.

While the two scouting parties were out, Captain Naunauphtaunk had Jacob and his Stockbridge Indians spread out in a fan just in the woodline while Samuel and a few others stayed with the boats.

Most of the morning went by peacefully with no sign or sound of enemies in the area. Jacob didn't like it. They were in the French's back yard and they had not seen anyone. Just the sound of birds and the creak of the trees were heard, and it bothered Jacob,

"Keep your eyes and ears open. I don't like this," whispered Jacob to Konkapot and to the others. Konkapot, not taking his eyes off the woods, nodded. Something was bothering Konkapot, and he couldn't put his finger on it. Perhaps it was a premonition. Jacob didn't know, and it bothered him.

***

As Jacob pondered his apprehension, Captain Wolfe, their old adversary from the Battle on Snowshoes, was moving along the woods with fifty Canadians and Indians. They spotted the trail made by Lieutenant Porter and his men, pausing to look at the trail and to track where it had come from.

Crouched over, Wolfe and his men quietly moved through the trees and when they could barely see the clearing on the shoreline, they spotted a Stockbridge Ranger. Using his arms and hands only, Wolfe pointed for half of his men to split right and the others to split left. When all were in position, he signaled for them to move forward, and just before they could be spotted, they opened fire on the Rangers.

***

Jacob heard a snap of a branch and without thinking, flattened himself on the ground as the woods around them erupted in smoke and flames. The forest filled with Indian war whoops and cries, as the Rangers returned fire. Balls were flying around Jacob and his men, striking trees or hitting the ground around them. Working in pairs, Jacob and his men began firing at a sustained rate, knowing from the sound of the enemy fire that they were outnumbered once again.

Captain Naunauphtaunk ordered his men to fall back and in a un-Rangerly fashion, they all turned and ran. Jacob and the Rangers from Putnam's and Stark's Companies began falling back in two-man teams. One moved while the other fired, and then he leapfrogged so that they never lost their volume of fire and could move back in an orderly fashion.

Konkapot ran past Jacob, who lowered his rifle barrel to aim at an Abenaki warrior and fired, hitting his target squarely in the head. Then Jacob turned, already beginning the loading process and ran past Konkapot, who was in a firing position, waiting for Jacob to pass.

As Jacob and his men continued to fire and bound back towards the boats, there was a roar like a small cannon from their right. Samuel had fired the wall gun at the woodline. Samuel's bullets shredded trees and enemies alike. As Jacob finished priming his rifle and shutting his pan, he had to shake his head and smile. Samuel was really good at using those big guns.

Then Jacob got back down to business, sighted along his rifle, and squeezed his trigger to drop a Canadian in the woodline.

"Let's go!" commanded Captain Naunauphtaunk, at which Jacob turned, and they began loading into their boat as balls splashed around them.

Once loaded, they had begun to pull away when Samuel spotted Rogers further down the shore. "Major Rogers is just over there!" yelled Samuel as he pointed towards the shore to their right. Jacob headed the boat that way. As they closed on Rogers, Samuel let loose with his wall gun to cover Rogers and his men, who jumped into their boat.

"Damn, Jacob, you and your boatload of privateers including your mad gunner up there …," Rogers remarked as Samuel fired while yelling a war whoop, "… keep pulling my bacon out of the fire. Thanks."

Jacob nodded and simply replied, "Always glad to be of service!" As the oars slapped the water, Jacob looked to Rogers, "Anywhere in particular?" Rogers just waved behind them towards the southern end of the lake. Jacob's boat withdrew out into the lake as the enemy continued to fire on them, which drew Samuel's attention and he fired his wall gun at their puffs of smoke from the woods.

Rogers led them back to the southern shore of the lake, and he and the other Rangers returned to Fort Edward to report on what they had observed and on their fight with the French.

Jacob looked at a saddened Samuel as he turned the wall gun back over to the quartermaster. "It's too damn heavy to carry in the woods," said Jacob, and Samuel sighed, shrugged his shoulders, and nodded.

"Yeah, but boy it does a great job!" Shaking his head, Jacob put his arm around Samuel's shoulders and led them back towards their campsite to grab their gear and begin their journey back to Fort Edward.

At the fort, General Abercrombie thanked Rogers for his scout and the information he had gathered, including the details of the fight at the shore. Lord Howe instructed that Rogers and all available men were to proceed with him to Lake George to stage for the upcoming attack. Only the sick and the invalids would remain to manage the camp there at Fort Edward.

When everything was in order, Lord Howe led three thousand regulars and Provincials while Rogers brought most of his Rangers to the now growing camp at and around the ruins of their old encampment and Fort William Henry. Lieutenant Porter had also arrived at the lake, having traveled south from the scouting expedition when he heard all of the firing. He had thought Rogers and all of his men had been killed and was greatly relieved that he had been wrong.

Major Rogers had brought as many of his men as he could, seven understrength companies to support this campaign against the French. Rogers personally commanded four reduced companies, including Jacob's, since Captain Putnam was still away on recruiting duty. Captain Stark and Captain Waite led their companies, and Captain Naunauphtaunk commanded two companies of Stockbridge.

A new company had just arrived, Captain Moses Brewer and his Mohicans from the Connecticut, Rhode Island, and Massachusetts regions.

Each company was at only about half-strength, and Rogers reported this to General Abercrombie, who instructed Rogers to recruit from the Provincial regiments there at the lake. Though strict on their selection criteria, Rogers was able to get enough Provincials with woodsman skills to volunteer to join, and all seven companies filled up to one hundred men each. Rogers told his veterans that he was relying on them to quickly school these new volunteers on their tactics before they began this campaign.

"It's not what I wanted," he explained. "But it's what we must do to have our strength replenished. Still, we only took those Provincials who demonstrated a better understanding of tactics and a grasp of our style of fighting."

Along with the thousands of men and the supplies to support and feed them, hundreds of wagons transported whale boats and bateaux to the lake to move the army to the northern shore. They would use the lake instead of trying to hack their way through the woods. It would be faster going on the lake than through the woods, and they were less likely to be ambushed there by their enemies.

Jacob and his men worked around the encampment, helping to make rifle and musket balls, filling powder horns, and moving artillery pieces while some of the other Rangers continued to scout to the north. They even ran a crash course on Ranger tactics for the new Provincials, Jacob hoping it would be enough to see them through the coming fight.

Major Rogers was concerned when one of the scouts who had taken boats northward did not return. What Rogers never learned was that all twenty Rangers had been captured by an overwhelming force in the second narrows by none other than his old foe, Langy, with his Canadians and Indians.

When Jacob heard the news about the missing scout, he asked Rogers if they should be concerned that the enemy knew they were coming for sure now.

Rogers only shrugged. "It's always safer to bet they know we're coming," he said. "And this army is marching whether the French know it or not."

CHAPTER 5

JULY 1758: THE CAMPAIGN BEGINS

The southern end of Lake George was overrun with supplies, artillery, and men. The largest army ever assembled in the colonies was now gathered at the lake. Almost seventeen thousand men were assembled and organized for the upcoming campaign.

In the main command area, in large marquee tents, Robert Aislabie and William Maclane along with the quartermasters and other civilian traders, met with General Abercrombie and Lord Howe, discussing the flow of supplies and anything else the army needed for the upcoming campaign. The generals spoke of food and powder, general supplies to last an army on the march, and the transportation needed to keep the supplies moving from Albany to the army.

Using a large map, Abercrombie pointed out the best routes for moving supplies, mostly the road to the southern camp there on Lake George, then via barges and boats up the lake to their northern staging base.

"The woods and terrain on either side of the lake are too treacherous for the construction of roads, too time consuming," explained Abercrombie. With a sigh, he added, "And full of enemy and Indians." They went over timetables. They didn't have much time to assemble the army and begin the march.

"My lord, the South Sea Company is happy to provide boats, barges, crews, anything you need for this campaign," Robert Aislabie spoke up to the assembled traders and officers.

General Abercrombie looked around, and none of the other traders were offering. "Is this true? Can your company handle this?"

With a flourish, even from his stool, Robert Aislabie smiled, and answered "Why but of course your Lordship. The company is always ready to help the Crown Forces." William Maclane just stood behind Robert, a stoic and unreadable expression on his face.

Satisfied and seeing that none of the other traders were counter-offering, Abercrombie stood up, clasped his hands together. "Right. Quartermaster-General, make the arrangements."

Once the meeting was over, Robert and William returned to their tent, which also served as their office, and when they were sure no one was within earshot, Robert danced for joy. "Excellent, most excellent. Your plan worked marvelously!"

Robert simply shrugged, poured himself a drink, and handed another to a prancing Robert, who took it and raised it in a toast.

"Amazing that there is no competition," said Robert, looking over his cup at William. "Your doing?"

Sipping from his cup, William shrugged. "My man can be very persuasive."

Robert smiled as their tent flap opened, and Big Harpe entered, carrying a large leather satchel. "Speaking of the devil" was all he said.

Big Harpe froze with a, "Huh," but William waved him to never mind, and Harpe dropped the satchel on their table, with a clink. William opened the bag and poured out the several leather coin purses that spilled out and across the table.

"Hmm, what's all this?" Robert asked as he picked up and began tossing a purse in his hand.

"Part of your cut" replied William, as he divided the contents into three piles, most going to Robert, a slightly smaller one going to himself, and the rest to Harpe. "I have secured application fees for all of the boat and barge suppliers in New York that will now support the company's contract with the army."

Robert smiled, looking at the small pile of purses in front of him. William continued, "Additionally, we'll get another ten percent in company dues and a five percent security fee from each of the companies providing the boats."

"Well, well...well indeed!" Robert rejoiced. At least he wasn't asking any more questions, thought William. He had known that as soon as Robert saw the bags of coins, he would allow his greed to take over.

There was a simple reason there had been no competition. He had turned Harpe loose on anyone capable of competing with them. With such a large army in a dangerous land, no one seemed to notice that a few tradesmen had disappeared. Raising his cup, he saluted Harpe, who winked and pocketed his few bags of coins. He was just happy to exercise his thrill of the kill, which was payment enough. The look of terror as he squeezed the life out of these men was all he needed.

"Ah finally, I can purchase a bathing tub and another wagon to make this less miserable," said Robert as he continued to skip around the tent, tossing a bag of clinking coins. William looked at Harpe, who simply shrugged and left. This will work out in the end, thought William as he watched Robert. Perhaps I can kill two birds with one stone, "Or one Harpe," he said out loud, but Robert did not hear him; he was too wrapped up in his celebrations.

The fruit of the arrangements that William had put in motion began to arrive, as hundreds of whale boats, bateaux, and large rafts arrived and were assembled at the lake. The cantonment area contained regular British regiments assembled into three brigades, the Provincials included the Massachusetts, Connecticut, and New Hampshire regiments, and there was a New York, New Jersey, and Rhode Island regiments in a second brigade.

As the army grew and prepared, Jacob and his men continued to run a Ranger mini-school to train the new men and any others interested in learning their way of fighting. For some, it was an easy transition from one style of fighting to the other. Many of the men had grown up on the frontier, and they already had a basic knowledge of woodsman skills and hunting.

During one of the training scouts around the southern area of the lake, Jacob was leading a group through the tall grass. Their only companions were grasshoppers taking flight as they strode through the warm morning. He had angled the scout towards the swampy area, when he detected the strong smell of a dead body. He raised his fist to halt, and the trainees automatically took a knee and faced out as they had been taught. Konkapot and Samuel came up and knelt next to Jacob, looking around them.

"What is it?" whispered Samuel, and then Konkapot wrinkled his nose and looked at Jacob.

"There is a dead body close," Konkapot whispered back, and Jacob nodded, and then Samuel caught the smell and nodded as well.

"Let's see what it is," Jacob said as he stood up and began following the smell. Soon the trainees, a mixed group of Provincials and some regulars, picked up the distinct smell of a dead body.

Jacob, who was leading, came across a trail, and then in one of the marshy areas of the swamp, they found the dead body. The smell was pungent, and Jacob heard a few gagging and retching sounds from the trainees. Steeling himself, Jacob rolled over the dead body, and stared at the dark, bloated face of a trader.

"He has his hair. Don't see any wounds," Jacob commented, and then looked around the area for any tracks. "Doesn't look like a war party," he continued, and then scratched his chin. "This is very strange."

"Could he have been out for a walk, and, you know, died?" Samuel asked. Jacob continued to look at the corpse and shook his head.

"Don't know, but this is something we need to report," Jacob responded. He then had the trainees build a travois, and they brought the corpse to the camp. Jacob reported to the officer of the day, a Major Tompkins, what they had found. To his dismay, the officer called for the Provost, Captain Reynolds.

Big Harpe was watching from behind a stack of boxes. He was dressed as a common worker, and no one seemed to pay any attention to him. He was concerned that his handiwork had been discovered. He would have to do a better job of hiding his hobby. He was still watching when Captain Reynolds arrived.

"Come to turn yourself in?' Reynolds sneered as he saw Jacob standing with the Officer of the Day. "Confess, and I'll see to a quick hanging."

Major Tompkins cleared his throat, and Captain Reynolds put on his business face.

"Captain, this Ranger found this civilian dead outside of the camp, the camp that you are responsible for safeguarding. If you would spend more of your time seeing to this camp's safety instead of worrying about uniform infractions, perhaps we wouldn't have this issue. What is your plan?"

Captain Reynold's face fell at the Major's critique of his services. "Ah, yes sir," Reynolds stammered. "I'll see to it immediately!" Then without changing stride, he faced Jacob.

"How do we know who killed this good man? Perhaps it was savages," Reynolds demanded, facing Jacob. "Or perhaps even this Provincial savage murdered this loyal subject of the Crown."

Jacob's blood boiled, and without thinking, he grabbed Reynolds by the arm and pulled him over to the corpse on the travois and ripped off the ground cloth that was covering the body. Reynolds blanched; dry heaved, and actually turned green when he saw the corpse.

"If a war party did this, he would have been scalped and the body mutilated," growled Jacob. He continued, "And if I killed him, why would I bring you the corpse?"

Reynolds stood, his mouth opening and closing but no words coming out. "Captain, this man has better things to do than listen to your ridiculous notions," rebuked the Major, who turned to Jacob. "You may return to your camp. Thank you for bringing this to our attention."

Big Harpe watched the British captain and this big Ranger with sadistic glee, especially the venomous looks the captain gave the Ranger as he left. "I see a great opportunity here," Harpe whispered to himself. "A great opportunity for fun."

As Jacob and his men ran the new recruits through their training, observers from the British regulars made comments. Some pointed and scoffed at the style of drill Jacob was leading the new men through, while others observed and nodded in understanding. Some heated debates grew between observers on the merits of the Rangers' tactics, but Jacob ignored them to focus on the training at hand.

As he watched the new men follow Samuel and the others who demonstrated the drill, Jacob again began to wonder how bad this next fight would be, how many more faces would disappear from the formations. Jacob wondered for how many of these new recruits, this would be their first and only fight. The war was taking a heavy toll on men, Rangers, Provincials, and regulars alike. Still, he decided not to dwell on it and refocused on the task at hand. Once finished for the day, the Rangers returned to their encampment.

Major Rogers had sited the Ranger's camp in a separate area away from the British regiments and the Provincials. Jacob had never seen so many men, supplies, and artillery all assembled in one area. Looking at the sheer size of their force, Jacob felt confident that this time they would outnumber the French for a change and give them a pounding to make up for all of the defeats at their hands.

General Abercrombie held a council of war, which Major Rogers attended, and placed his plan in motion. Lord Howe would lead the expedition in the morning and make for Sabbath Day Point. From there, the army would move to the landing area on the northern shore of the lake. The men and supplies would be loaded into the whale boats and bateaux, while the forty-four pieces of artillery would be loaded onto the large barges.

***

As the army prepared for the coming campaign, William Maclane was sitting comfortably in a tavern in Saratoga, on business both for the army and for himself. No one seemed to pay him any mind, just another trader in a sea of traders doing business. The door opened, and a lone tradesman entering and looking around, spotted Maclane. Observing the tradesman at the door, Maclane nodded and motioned to the chair across from him, where a tankard was already waiting.

Speaking in a low voice to hide his French/Canadian accent, Pierre du Mons sat and raised the tankard in salute to Maclane. "To you my friend, may your endeavors be profitable."

Returning the salute, Maclane raised his tankard and said, "and to yours as well."

Looking around slowly, wiping his mouth on his arm, Pierre made sure no one was close enough to overhear. "So my friend, is business going well? I hear you cornered the market for water transportation?"

Maclane smiled briefly and responded, "Yes, it's been a profitable venture. You? I heard you have done the same, something about the river traffic from Quebec to Montreal to …" Maclane left the statement hanging.

"Carillon, yes. I too have entered the water transport business. The governor and generals are fighting amongst one another in Quebec, but everyone needs to eat, so my barges and boats are doing well." Pierre took a sip from his tankard.

"At Carillon, do they need so much food?" Maclane asked.

Pierre scoffed, "Oh no my friend, my business is mostly with Quebec. That's where the most people are, not so much in Carillon. Still trading is good along the lake between Montreal and the outposts to Carillon. My coffers are full."

Pierre stopped and looked at Maclane. "Shall we stop with the pleasantries and get down to business?" Maclane smiled and nodded. "Where is your army?" Pierre asked, pulling out a leather purse that clinked and handing it to Maclane.

After hefting the bag in his hand, weighing it to determine how much he would say, Maclane answered, "They are heading to Carillon. With what I saw and supplied, we should own it and Saint Frederic soon enough. I see a potential of over forty-five percent profit for your transport requirements, or more, if your government officials and generals panic enough and need quick supply and movement."

Pierre thought about what he had heard and nodded. "Yes that would definitely drive supply and demand up, seeing I own all water transportation and have a cut with our Navy, since they are lacking transports. Very profitable indeed."

Maclane raised his eyebrow, and asked, "So Pierre, what do you have for me?"

"Our people are not as fore thinking like yours," Pierre replied. "They are caught in personal squabbles right now, and they are using the army and navy as pawns in their game. Most of the army is at Montreal, and the navy at Quebec, and both are being used as bargaining chips. So that's where most of my business is at."

Maclane nodded, pulled a bag from his coat, and handed it to Pierre, who also weighed it in his hand before putting it in his coat. "How many at Carillon?"

Pierre scoffed once again. "Not many; that's for sure," he replied. "You are correct, my friend. I think your grand army, if it's as big as you say, then you will own Carillon and Saint Fredric soon enough."

Maclane thought about it and nodded. Then he ordered two more tankards, and the two tradesmen discussed prices and demands, and what was big in the markets in Canada. "You know my friend," Maclane said, raising his tankard in salute once more. "If we play our cards right, you and I could own all of this; you in Canada and I here, establishing a good trade once all of this foolishness is over."

Pierre raised his tankard and clanked it with Maclane's in a toast. "No matter which side wins," Pierre added.

"No matter which sides win," Maclane confirmed. "It's only business of course, nothing personal."

***

Back up at the southern end of Lake George, Lord Howe instructed Major Rogers that his Rangers would lead the way and be the advance guard for the army. Once the council of war broke up, Rogers called his men together, told them of the plan for the morning, and ordered them to do their final prep. The campaign to take Fort Carillon had officially begun. Jacob and his men, after finishing their final checks, tried to get some sleep.

At night, thousands of men moved about the encampment. Some were in their orderly lines of white tents while others like the Rangers just slept on the ground in the cover of the trees. Hundreds of fires were dotted across the camps. Jacob and his men leaned back on their gear, smoking their pipes and taking in the whole scene.

The evening air was still enough that they could hear different sounds from all around the camp. In one area, a group of soldiers was singing, while in another, there was laughter and conversation, while a violin played in the distance. Watching over the entire scene was the star-lit sky, the moon staring down passively over the camp and the men. It was an impressive sight to behold.

It was difficult, even for the veterans, to fall asleep with so much going on, and for Jacob, so much running through his mind. He leaned against his gear, the glow of his pipe illuminating his face, as he sat in deep thought. Finally with a sigh, he realized there wasn't a whole lot he could do, but just take care of his men and make it out alive. Tapping out his pipe, he closed his eyes and was surprised at how quickly he fell asleep.

Morning arrived sooner than they expected, bright and shiny with a clear blue sky. Up as they always were before dawn, Rogers and his Rangers moved to the shore and began loading their fifty whaleboats, Samuel lugging the wall gun and placing it in the bow of Jacob's boat.

Once all of the boats were loaded with Rangers and their gear, Rogers moved them out away from the shore to allow the next group of boats to load. The Rangers floated in their boats off shore, some lowering fishing lines while waiting for the flotilla to build. It took several hours before Lord Howe gave Rogers the signal to proceed. The Rangers manned their oars, and the boats began to move forward like great water bugs, their wakes churning the crystal blue water of the lake.

Jacob manned the tiller for this portion of the trip, and looking to the rear he was impressed by what he saw. The flotilla literally filled the mile-wide breadth of the lake, and it was almost twelve miles from their position in the lead to the barges bringing up the rear.

As the Rangers pulled on their oars, the other boats began raising white sails to help move the heavy loads through the water. Jacob could see the brown uniforms of the 80th Regiment near them, the center of the flotilla contained the regular British regiments, the Provincials split to both sides, and the supplies with the artillery were coming up last.

There was a strong enough breeze that Jacob elected to raise their sail. They had just reached some of the smaller islands when Samuel yelled out that he spotted canoes up ahead. Passing the tiller to Peter, Jacob pulled out his telescope and sure enough, spotted several canoes with Indians and Canadians just ahead of them beginning to turn around.

"Damn!" growled Jacob. "Man the oars. We need to catch them!"

Jacob yelled over to Rogers that they had seen canoes and were going after them. Rogers nodded and began issuing orders to pursue.

With the sail assisting them, Jacob and his men pulled hard on the oars, the bow cutting a frothing white wake as the boat knifed through the water. Peter stayed on the tiller, guiding them after the fleeing canoes. Jacob's breath was labored as he pulled on his oars, but he soon knew the enemy would get away. Their canoes were much faster than the British boats.

By the time they entered the narrows and the numerous small islands found there, none of the canoes could be seen. Jacob ordered a halt, and his men pulled their oars in while breathing heavily from the exertion.

Rogers caught up with them and saw that the canoes had gotten away. Jacob shook his head and pounded his fist on the bench. There was no doubt now that the French would know they were coming. Still, they had a huge force. Maybe it was to their advantage that the French knew how big they were, but Jacob had his doubts.

Being so far ahead because of the pursuit, Rogers led his Rangers onto the shore at Sabbath Day Point. The Rangers splashed into the lake, their rifles and shooting bags held over their heads, and secured the beach. With Samuel covering the beach with his wall gun, Jacob and the others fanned out into the woods line to make sure it was clear of any enemy.

After doing a quick scout, Jacob halted his men to listen for a while to see if they could hear what they couldn't see. All they could hear was the breeze in the trees shaking leaves and the sound of jays and finches. No sound indicated any French, Canadians, or Indians in the area.

Satisfied, Jacob returned to the beach where the flotilla had begun to arrive and the British regulars were beginning to splash into the water and make their way to shore. As the army started to make its camp, Rogers, who had placed his Rangers in the woodline, instructed Jacob to take his men and their boat and scout the northern shore as soon as it was dark.

Moving their boat well away from the rest of the army, Jacob and his men built a small fire on the beach to cook their meals and to provide the soot they would need later. They wrapped leather and cloth around their oars to muffle the noise, and once finished, rested in the shade until the sun began to sink.

Jacob watched the activity around them and wondered if the ghosts from the massacre that had taken place there watched them, some wishing them success, others perhaps hoping they were going to their doom. Shaking his head, Jacob chased the thought away and focused on their preparations. Fate would determine what happened to them, more powerful then he, but he would make every effort to bring his men home and not join the ranks of the dead.

Once the sun was so low it was barely seen behind the mountains, Jacob nodded his head as he tapped out his pipe and placed it away in his haversack. They extinguished their fire, but took some of the burnt wood and twisted the soot off into their hands, then smeared the soot on their faces, arms and hands. As they were placing the muffled oars in the oarlocks, Major Rogers stopped by to see them off. Jacob shook Rogers's hand. He could see that the entire beach was cramped with the hundreds of fires of the huge encampment.

"Be safe, but confirm if the enemy is at the landing site or not and get back here before morning," Rogers whispered.

Jacob nodded, climbed into the boat, and shoved off. With only a soft creak, the boat moved quietly through the dark night, the moonlight reflecting and dancing off the wake as they traveled northward. They stayed close to shore to blend in with the long shadows of the landscape.

As they closed in on the northern shore, they spotted their old familiar landmarks, Old Baldy and the other mountains along the shore, their dark silhouettes welcoming the Rangers. Jacob whispered that they were to pull the oars and allow the boat to simply drift silently forward. The men stayed low in the boat, Jacob in the bow with Samuel.

Sure enough, on the shore they had recently scouted, there were fires dotting the beach. There was someone there, either French or Canadians, but it didn't appear to be a large number.

"Well, looks like we'll have some excitement in the morning," whispered Jacob to Samuel, who nodded and patted his wall gun. Smiling, Jacob quietly instructed the men to slip oars; they were heading back to Sabbath Day Point.

***

Langy was concerned. His garrison at Fort Carillon was not very impressive. Between his Canadians and the French regulars, he had only eight battalions, around four thousand men. During the spring, the Indians had all departed, upset over the lack of activity and opportunities for plunder. Langy knew he would need them, but none of the tribes had answered his call for battle.

Then there was this report of the massive British Army, which had been spotted heading their way by a scouting expedition at the southern end of the lake. Langy dispatched more scouts to observe both sides of the lake, and he sent men to secure beaches at the northern end, specifically where they had fought the British a few months before.

As Langy and Captain Wolfe walked around the ramparts of Fort Carillon, Langy felt secure that they could hold out. Still, if the reports were true, there could be a hard fight coming.

"Captain Wolfe, tell the engineers to gather men from the regiments and to begin building abatis in front of their earthworks."

The abatis, trees chopped down but still connected to their trunks, their limbs sharpened, made a difficult obstacle to move through. Captain Wolfe saluted and took off to get the work started. Langy looked over the field in front of their works, the most likely avenue the enemy would take. He kicked at a tuft of grass and dirt. "Damn in-fighting," he grumbled. "The Generals are playing politics and holding men, and I have to hold this place against a superior force. Why me?"

***

Jacob arrived back at Sabbath Day Point and informed Rogers of what they had seen at the northern shore. Rogers thanked him, told him to go catch what sleep he could, and went to see Lord Howe. Lord Howe nodded his head and instructed that Rogers would lead out again in the morning, show the way to the landing site, and if need be, take the landing site from the enemy.

After stand-to, the Rangers went to their boats, loaded their gear, and pushed off towards the northern shore as the rest of the army began to assemble and load their boats. It was a beautiful morning, but Jacob could only enjoy the moment for a few brief minutes before they went into action.

A thick grey fog hung just above the water, bathed in golden hues as the morning sun rose. All fifty boats made their way northward and by mid-morning, the landing site came into view. Major Rogers stood up in his boat and waved his hand forward, pointing to the shore.

All fifty boats picked up speed. Six Rangers in the bows of each boat with rifles ready would be the first to land on the beach while covered by swivel guns and wall guns mounted in the bows of their boats. The boats, which were lined up abreast, closed on the shore like wraiths from the fog, their bows ploughing through the water. They could see a few Canadians, who quickly turned and fled into the woods.

As soon as the keel of the boats scraped on the rocks and sand of the shore, the first six Rangers from each boat went over the side and ran onto the beach, while a couple Rangers held the boats in place. Jacob, Konkapot, Peter and Charles were among the first Rangers from their boat who splashed into the water and began running, the water being only calf deep. They passed several smoldering cooking fires and other signs that men had been camping on the beach, but none could be found now. Jacob and the others moved into the woods, but saw no one. It seemed the Canadians had decided it was better to run and live to fight another day.

Jacob left the woods and reported to Major Rogers that his area was clear, and then he returned to watch the woods with his men. Rogers waved his hat towards the lake as the lead elements of the 80th Regiment approached, followed by the rest of the army.

Jacob led his men deeper into the woods on a scout to make sure the area was, in fact, clear of enemies. They had moved about a mile or so from the beach as part of their sweep when they spied smoke and moved towards it to investigate. They found the remains of a large encampment where in their haste, either a Frenchman or Canadian had knocked over their meal of bacon. The grease had caught fire and was spreading around the camp.

When Jacob returned to report, Major Rogers was receiving a report from the scout who had covered the west side, and his squad also had found an abandoned encampment. It seemed all of the French and Canadians had been pulled back to Fort Carillon. General Abercrombie and Lord Howe were pleased with their unopposed landing, and they began to build their encampment, which was now only a couple of miles from their objective.

Jacob and his Rangers rotated scouting duties while the army assembled its camp. Jacob was still concerned. The Canadians might have withdrawn, but that didn't mean they were running away.

He also thought that this was not going to be as easy as the generals believed. From what he saw, Fort Carillon was in a strong position and could withstand an attack. They would have to lay siege and starve them out. Any assault would be bloody. Still, they did have a lot of men, but he didn't want to be simply a number in the task of wearing down the enemy through attrition.

Jacob and his men returned to their camp area, and quickly Peter and Konkapot built a fire.

"What's for dinner tonight?" Jacob asked.

Samuel pulled out some nice-sized fish he had caught in the lake, James pulled some of their Johnnycakes and bacon from his haversack, and Charles pulled onions and potatoes from his pack. Jacob nodded and pulled some salt pork from his pack to add to the feast.

General Abercrombie, Lord Howe, and the other regimental commanders held a council of war to plan their next step. Abercrombie was overjoyed at the ease of their operation so far, and he was also pleased that he was the only commander to have made it in force here to the northern shore. Soon he would bag Fort Carillon, then sweep north and take Saint Frederic, and if everything went well, Canada could be his.

Lord Howe suggested that they press their advantage and march on the La Chute River, securing it and the saw mills, thus trapping the French on the Ticonderoga Peninsula. General Abercrombie agreed and began issuing orders that in the morning, the army would form three columns. The Massachusetts Provincials would be on the left, the center would be composed of the 44th, 55th, 46th, and the 42nd Regiments, and the third column on the right would be composed of the 27th, the 4th, and the 60th Regiments.

To support their advance, Lord Howe would employ his own light infantry, and Major Rogers and his Rangers would screen the advance and secure key locations *en route* to Carillon. Lord Howe would lead some of the Rangers and Provincials from Connecticut, New Jersey, and New York. Major Rogers and some of the 80th would scout ahead and secure the Bernetz Brook for the army to cross.

"We must move quickly and quietly, secure the crossing, and keep the enemy both blind and deaf to our actions," Lord Howe instructed the gathered officers, including Major Rogers. "Rogers, you will be key in holding the crossing. That could be a tight wicket if the enemy controls it."

Having received these instructions, Major Rogers returned and called his officers and sergeants to give them their directives. Jacob listened to the major's plan and understood what he was to do. Acknowledging their tasks, the officers all returned to their men to explain their role in the morning, and they all tried to get some rest.

"So, we're leading the way and hunting the Frenchies?" Samuel asked as he chewed on a Johnnycake, leaning on his elbow., "sounds just about the same we always do, easy."

Jacob thought about it for a moment, chewing on his Johnnycake, "Don't get too confident my friend," Jacob warned, "we're on their soil, their home, and we've seen the fort, it could be a tough one."

Samuel nodded, swallowed his bite, "they're all tough ones, this is just another day, another walk in the woods." Samuel took another bite, and then winked at Jacob.

Jacob shook his head, "I hope you're right, I hope they heard about the scalped one and his monster gun, and run away screaming!" They all laughed and Samuel saluted with his cake, "That's all correct!"

In the morning, the Rangers followed their tradition of stand-to. It still amazed them that the army did nothing like that, even this close to the enemy. The French and their Indian Allies loved to attack at early dawn, hoping to catch their enemies just waking up or eating breakfast. Perhaps they thought the Rangers would alert them to the enemy if they attacked in the early morning.

The Rangers packed their gear and checked their powder, shot, and weapons. Jacob and his men would accompany Major Rogers, who would lead an early morning scout and then meet the rest of the force at the brook. The Rangers were traveling light, with just their weapons, shooting bags, powder horns, knives, tomahawks, rifles, canteens, and haversacks. They were going to move quickly and quietly, green and brown shadows slipping through the trees.

Rogers and the Rangers moved along the route the army would take, crossed over Bernetz Brook, and continued on towards Fort Carillon. They were less than a mile from the fort when they first smelled the smoke and cooking bacon, and then spotted a large French and Canadian encampment. Rogers halted his Rangers and quickly gave whispered commands to separate into three groups

Jacob would lead his men around to the right, Rogers would observe the center, and Sergeant Wade would head to the left. Jacob nodded and with a jerk of his head, led his men off to the right to carefully circle around and observe the encampment. Jacob angled them away from the camp so as not to parallel it and give themselves away. When Jacob felt they were in the right position, they approached the encampment in a straight line, moving at a slow and low crouch. They were just to the southeast of the camp where they stopped in a thicket to observe.

Jacob used his telescope to see the good-sized camp.

"That's odd," whispered Jacob as he looked through his telescope.

"What is?" asked Konkapot.

"There are no Indians, no Abenakis, none of them in the camp. There are just French and Canadians that I can see."

Konkapot thought about it and agreed that this was strange news.

"Perhaps there is finally some bad blood between the French and their Indian friends," remarked Konkapot. "Perhaps the French did something to insult them."

If true, would be some good news to report. If the Indians didn't fight for the French, it would give the British an advantage. Putting his telescope away, Jacob said that they needed to report back to Major Rogers with this news. When they met with Rogers and Sergeant Wade, they said that they too had observed no Indians with the French and Canadians, and they thought that was rather strange. Rogers led them back to the brook to wait for the columns to arrive.

***

Also tramping out in the woods was French Captain Trepezec's three hundred and fifty man scouting party, which had become hopelessly lost. Without their Indian guides, they were having a difficult time finding their way around, having recently arrived and not familiar with this area.

"Mon dieu," exhaled Trepezec as he took his tricorn hat off and wiped his brow, "here we learn that the enemy is on the move, and what do I do, I can't find my way towards them." Lieutenant de Monts nodding, also not liking the situation. "There is a massive army wearing red coats, and I can't find them."

After wandering around the woods for most of the day, they arrived at the La Chute River and met with a scouting party being led by Langy, who had wanted to see with his own eyes the size of this English Army. Trepezec joined with Langy and they headed towards the beach by following the Bernetz Brook, happy to find someone who knew their way around.

***

Rogers had just arrived at the brook and concealed his men in the woods while waiting for the column. Lord Howe's column arrived. Howe dispersed his men into the woods while he listened to Rogers report about the French encampment and the lack of Indians.

***

As Langy was leading his column along the brook, he spotted someone in the woods who was wearing dark blue. Not sure who it could be hidden in the shadows, Langy called out in French and asked, "Who goes there?" The man answered in bad French and said "the French."

Not being fooled, Langy ordered his men to open fire, not knowing that just a few hundred yards away were Lord Howe and the large columns heading to the brook. Hearing the musketry, Jacob and his men reacted quickly and dove for cover as the balls began flying around the brook. They quickly took up supporting firing positions and began to shoot back.

***

Lord Howe and Major Rogers arrived quickly and ordered the men forward to drive the French away. The main body of the army under Abercrombie would be arriving soon, and they had to clear the French out.

Jacob brought his men on line, "Fire by sections, and advance!" Jacob and the Rangers began advancing by moving from tree to tree, only stopping when they had a clear target to shoot. The woods were thick, and they were concerned that they could shoot at one of their own or at Provincials by mistake.

The ground around the brook began to open up and generally slope upward. The French reacted well, maintained order and fell back by moving from tree to tree, stopping once in a while to shoot back. Rogers was directing his Rangers to sweep to the right as Lord Howe and his men were sweeping up from the left. Between the two forces, they were trying to catch the Frenchmen in a vice and squeeze them dead.

Moving through the thick brush, Jacob ignored the sting of a branching snapping him in the face, shook it off as he brought his rifle up, aimed and dropped a French soldier in front of him. As he loaded, Konkapot was covering until Jacob finished, where he yelled, "Loaded" then Konkapot advanced as Jacob covered.

The intensity of the fight was growing, the sound of battle filling the air, the whistling balls and the screams of anger, hatred or being hit. Jacob was also looking to the sides, making sure they made contact with their own elements, and not get too far ahead. The woods were thick, and he didn't want to be fired upon by their soldiers by mistake.

The encirclement was beginning to close on the French and Lord Howe moved to the top of the hill in order to see the battle better. As he was giving directions, his body snapped back and fell to the ground. A French bullet had hit him square in the chest, tearing out his heart, lungs and backbone. Lord Howe crumbled to the ground, eyes staring open and skyward, only his hand twitching and then going still.

Jacob and his Rangers had no idea that Lord Howe had been killed, having been caught up in the fierce fighting in the woods. It was chaotic, Frenchmen popping out of seemingly nowhere in the thick trees, firing, and fading away. Jacob had several close calls as balls snapped by his head, but he maintained his cool, aimed calmly, and took out another Frenchman.

The French were breaking up; the pressure of the British attack was taking a heavy toll. Through the woods, Jacob could see the La Chute River in the distance, and he drove his men on to cut the French off before they reached the river.

However, the Frenchmen were running too fast, and as Jacob and the other Rangers broke from the tree line into the open and began firing on the fleeing Frenchman, the French reached the river. Some had thrown down their muskets and were trying to swim across; others who could not swim tried to make a stand of it. Jacob and his men were caught up in the blood fury of the fight and went after the Frenchmen who were trying to make a stand.

Jacob took a knee and aimed along his rifle, leading a running Frenchman before pulling his trigger. The bullet caught the man in the center of the back and propelled him into the river with a splash. As Jacob began to load, Konkapot ran up and also fired on another running Frenchmen, dropping him into the river.

Jacob and his men stopped in a short, ragged line and were picking off Frenchman one by one, when a company of French grenadiers emerged from the woods across the river from them and prepared to fire a volley. Jacob watched their muskets lower, and seeing that he and his men were out in the open, he grabbed Konkapot who was next to him. While pulling him down, Jacob yelled to take cover just as the volley thundered from across the lake. James had just turned to see what was going on when a ball tore through his throat and another tore through his chest. He was dead before he hit the ground.

Squeezing eyes shut in despair, then looking at the rest of his men, Jacob and the others remained prone on the ground as the grenadiers continued to fire volleys to cover their retreating men. The sun was beginning to set, and the French grenadiers finally withdrew and allowed Jacob and his men to gather up James. They knelt around James, Charles volunteering to carry his body back to the encampment.

It was a somber moment. They had been lucky so far, but now they had lost one of their own. They formed a wedge around Charles who carried James over his shoulder, and they began their journey through the woods towards camp. It was dark and gloomy in the woods, the sun going down and the shadows stretching long.

They could still hear movement and orders. The British columns were in the woods and close by. There was still some sporadic firing, but nothing near them. As they moved cautiously through the woods, they were coming up out of a dip when they saw the red coats and white breeches of the British just to their front.

"At least it wasn't the French," thought Jacob.

Just on the other side of the dip, a second line of men appeared, but they were obscured by the diminishing light and growing shadows of the evening. Looking up at the British line to their front, Jacob heard the command of present, and their muskets lowered to aim at the second line in the gloom. Jacob spun around to warn his men to take cover when the British line erupted in a sheet of fire and smoke.

Jacob felt a burning sensation along his neck and felt like he had been hit with an axe in the back, falling forward. Charles, who had been struggling up the slope with James across his back, had enough time to look up and mutter "damn" before four balls shattered his chest and abdomen. He fell to the ground, entangled with the body of James, and was no more.

Konkapot and Samuel rushed over to look at Jacob while Peter and the others yelled and waved their arms at the British line that had just fired and were loading, yelling "cease fire, we're friends!" Konkapot and Samuel helped Jacob who was having a hard time breathing, the wind having been knocked out of him.

In the confusion and the smoke, other voices could be heard, yelling the same but in a more colorful way and with heavy

Scottish accents. "Bloody damn fools, open your bloody eyes!" was heard just to the right of the Rangers. More angry voices were heard, going back and forth along with "cease fire" commands.

Konkapot and Samuel grabbed under Jacob's arms and helped him to sit up. Samuel checked Jacob's back. The bullet had just hit him the upper back, but luckily the powder must have burned poorly and only slammed into Jacob, but not tearing into flesh.

Jacob was in shock, having been just hit and having lost another Ranger, to a mistaken identity no less, or so he thought. Jacob heard men approaching and then a familiar voice.

"Bloody sorry about that; hard to see in the woods you know."

Jacob looked up to see a short man, and the unmistakable smirk of Captain Reynolds. Jacob's blood began to boil, and he was attempting to stand and pull his tomahawk when he heard a booming Scottish voice yelling, "You there, are you the bloody fool who ordered that volley?"

It was Lord John Murray, commander of the 42nd Highlanders. Captain Reynolds' smirk quickly vanished, and he began to stammer his apologies and to explain how hard it was to see men in the woods.

"Are you bloody telling me that you can't see," screamed Lord Murray as he grabbed Reynolds and turned him towards his men and their distinct kilts and bonnets that could easily be seen, even in the darkness. "That's my men over there!"

As Lord Murray tore into Captain Reynolds, Konkapot and some other Rangers who happened to be passing by helped Jacob to his feet and held him tight as was trying to get after Captain Reynolds. "Not now, not now" Peter spoke to Jacob who finally relented and allowed them to help him to walk to the camp, while others helped to carry the bodies of James and Charles. Jacob, his gear taken by Konkapot, was taken to the surgery by Samuel to have his wounds looked at.

109

There were many injured, bleeding men at the surgery, some of them the very highlanders that Captain Reynolds' foolish volley had wounded along with Jacob and his Rangers. Jacob was still in shock when the orderly arrived to work on his shoulder. He had lost two men, one because of a stupid mistake. Or had it been a mistake? Did Captain Reynolds mistake the other unit for French in the dusk? He was after all completely inexperienced at fighting.

But that smirk, that smirk spoke volumes. Had he actually used the dusk as an opportunity to try and kill Jacob? Gritting his teeth until his jaw ached, Jacob growled "That's it, one way or the other; this will end with that ass of a man!"

The orderly finished closing the wound with a couple of stitches, poured some alcohol over it, mumbled about trying to keep it clean, and continued down the line. Jacob, in his rage, actually forgot about the orderly, mumbled his thanks and left the surgery.

Jacob returned to their camp, and soon Major Rogers sought him out. Rogers passed his condolences to the loss of James and Charles, which Jacob thanked him for. He then told Major Rogers what he thought happened, that Captain Reynolds had used the encounter as an opportunity to either get him directly, or his men.

"He has bloody well had it in for all of us," growled Jacob, anger seething, "It wouldn't surprise me in the least."

Major Rogers nodded his head in agreement. He knew there was no love lost between the two and he knew the circumstances of Maggie's death at the hands of Captain Reynolds' old sergeant-major.

"These are strong accusations, against an officer of the crown," Rogers remarked, "do you want to present charges?"

Jacob thought about it then looked at Rogers, "I wouldn't have a snowball's chance in hell seeing that man in a court-martial, do I?"

Rogers shook his head, as much as he hated the man, though probably not as much as Jacob did, he knew the reality of a Provincial, even a Ranger like them, successfully brining charges against a commissioned British officer.

"Are you still able to fight?" asked Rogers, and Jacob nodded.

"You men stand down tonight and get some rest; we're going back in tomorrow."

Jacob nodded again, and Major Rogers departed. Jacob sat back and sighed, this was the Ranger way, live free, and fight hard, then get up and do it again. Sometimes Rangers died and that's the hard truth. Jacob swallowed his anger and his grief. There would be time to grieve later. As for Captain Reynolds, two can play this game, and Jacob was a better player.

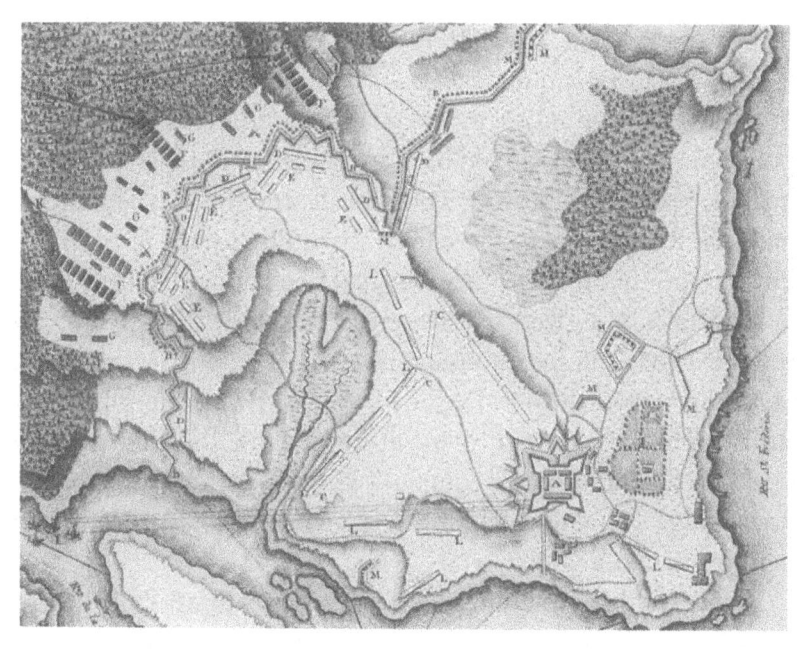

Map of Abercrombie's attack on Fort Carillon

CHAPTER 6

BATTLE FOR FORT CARILLON

The loss of Lord Howe threw the whole army into a spin, and the fact that a small band of Frenchmen had been able to cause utter chaos and stop the advance of the entire army bothered General Abercrombie.

Still, he had an objective to take, and in the morning after a ceremony to remember the fallen, the army got back into the war. Abercrombie called for a quick council of war to discuss what their next move should be. After some furious debate, it was finally agreed that the army would head straight for the military road that led directly to the enemy sawmills instead of trying to skirt around them via the brook as had been done the day before.

The task was given to Lieutenant Colonel Bradstreet, who was entrusted with five thousand men to accomplish it. His force was composed of the 44th Regiment, the 1st Battalion of the 60th, and two Massachusetts Provincial Regiments. Leading the way would be Captain Stark's company of Rangers and some of the Stockbridge Indians. Two pieces of artillery would accompany them for support.

Jacob and his remaining men stayed in camp to bury James and Charles after bundling their gear or giving some of it to Rangers who needed it. They wished their fellow Rangers luck as they watched them leave the encampment.

Then they went over to a shady spot and dug graves for their friends. After burying them, they placed two wooden crosses over their graves, placed their Ranger bonnets on the crosses, and then each man said his farewell and returned to the camp.

There were no sounds of gunfire in the distance, which they hoped meant everything was going well. There was a steady flow of messengers coming into or out of the camp. By the afternoon, word had spread around camp that the expedition had been successful and had secured the sawmills.

General Abercrombie ordered the rest of the army to advance, including Rogers and his Rangers. Jacob and his men shouldered their gear, fell into their columns, and marched with the Rangers to the next objective.

***

The Marquis de Montcalm had arrived finally at Fort Carillon and was immediately briefed on the situation by Langy. Understanding immediately, having been kept abreast of the reports of the large English Army assembling at the southern end of the lake, Montcalm jumped into action.

He instructed the La Reine, Guyenne, and Bearn Battalions to build earthworks and fortifications to block the military road from the sawmills. He sent the La Sarre, Royal-Roussillon, and Languedoc Battalions to support the reinforcement of the abatis and fortifications, which Montcalm himself would oversee.

For a small reserve, a battalion was stationed just outside the fort, and the last battalion was stationed inside the fort. Some of the Canadian Provincials and metropolitan companies had trickled in, but there had been no major reinforcements. It seemed they would have to defend this position with what they had. Some reinforcements did arrive just in the nick of time, however, as Montcalm's favorite second-in-command, General Levis, arrived with four hundred French regulars.

Montcalm stood with Langy, over watching the field full of the sound of axes ringing, trees falling and voices as they army built and sharpened the abatis. "You saw them, did you not?" Montcalm asked Langy, who nodded. "Oui mon general, I saw them at the brook."

Montcalm nodded, "Was it as many as we have been told?" Again Langy nodded. "I believe so, though I did not see the whole army, but I could tell from the amount of fire we were overwhelmed. I believe they do outnumber us, two maybe three to one."

Montcalm thought about it, and then looked to Langy. "I have received from a reliable source that it is a large army, perhaps the largest we have ever faced here." Langy looked concerned with the news.

Looking over the field, Montcalm told Langy "We may have to rely on your unique skills my friend. If we can't stop them here, then we must slow them so we can build our defenses at Saint Frederic, or Montreal."

Langy nodded as Montcalm continued, "You must make them pay for every mile, for every inch. Make them fear the woods once more. Make them move slow and unsure, then we'll finish them."

Nodding, Langy thought that this did not bode well for them. The enemy had the superiority in numbers, and they did not. "Then it's in God's hands. We must fight them hard and to the last man here," Langy answered as the sound of axes continued to ring across the field and from the woods.

***

General Abercrombie quickly had entrenchments thrown up around the army's encampment, now less than a mile from the French positions. As the men built their defenses, Abercrombie sent engineers forward to scout out and determine the strength of the French fortifications.

Jacob and his Rangers escorted some of the engineers forward to a vantage point, a thickly covered knoll that overlooked some French entrenchments. The engineers crept as close as they could while Jacob and the others watched the surrounding woods. They could hear axes in the distance, but not many.

The engineers moved forward and found some unfinished earthworks, and in hushed whispers, discussed their findings. Jacob looked around, and something was nagging him. Something wasn't right.

"You have dat look, Jacob," Peter whispered, which caused both Samuel and Konkapot to look over at Jacob. His faced was creased as he thought about what was laid before them. He pulled out his telescope and looked, then lowered it and shook his head.

"Something's not right," Jacob whispered back. "We saw how many there were at the brook. This can't be all of them. We've seen the fort from across the river and the number of tents, so this can't be their entrenchments."

"Perhaps they are staying in the fort, behind the walls," commented Samuel, but Peter shook his head. "Not how these fights go," he said. "The French won't let the British get close and bring their artillery, like the French did at William Henry. No Jacob, I think you're right, something is wrong."

When the engineers returned, they said they believed the defense to be negligible. "They must have withdrawn to the fort after the fight at the brook, feeling safer behind the thick walls. There are no outer works." Jacob still didn't like it, but his job was to see to the engineers' safety, and he did, returning them without incident to the camp.

The engineers provided their assessment to Abercrombie. What the engineers and Jacob had failed to detect, however, was that the French, concerned that the British would use the high ground to scout their positions, actually had camouflaged the completed earthworks, fortifications, and abatis with fir trees and shrubs, effectively concealing them from the engineers.

After the engineers reported, General Abercrombie was ecstatic, and he called for a council of war, but he invited only the regular British officers and none of the Provincial commanders. Passing on the reports the engineers had presented, Abercrombie said, "We have achieved our initial objective and have the initiative. The engineers report no obstacles; therefore we must maintain this advantage!"

The general started writing his orders for the attack. After he put his quill down, he held the orders up and read them aloud to the assembled officers, including a few Provincial officers whom runners had found and brought back to the council.

"The light infantry, the right wing of the Provincials, are ordered to march immediately to the vicinity of the enemy works, but are instructed to stay out of enemy artillery range. They will deploy in line, securing their flanks to the lakes and allowing the rest of the army to form behind their screen.

"To the rear of the skirmish line will be the Massachusetts Provincials. Colonel Haviland, your brigade will form to the left; Colonel Donaldson, your brigade will form the center, and Colonel Grant, your brigade will form the right. The Connecticut and New Jersey regiments will form the rear guard. I intend to do this assault without waiting for the artillery to catch up. Any questions? Then see to your men. We march within the hour!"

Jacob, who had been walking back from the quartermaster, saw the activity and the gathering of regular officers, and he went to find Major Rogers. He was surprised to see that Major Rogers was having a conversation with Captain Stark.

"There is something afoot," Jacob warned. "Saw a large meeting over near the general's marquee and seeing you're not there makes me even more sure something is brewing."

Rogers stood up, saying, "Damn these bloody fools!" He sent his orderly to gather the company commanders and as fate would have it, as soon as the company commanders arrived, so did a messenger from the general with instructions for the Rangers.

Major Rogers read his instructions, and cursed once more. He realized he had only enough time to yell, "Rangers turn out!" while grabbing his own weapons and gear. The Rangers quickly formed, and Rogers informed them that the General had decided to attack this very day and that they would be leading the way.

"In his infinite wisdom, his lordship, without including any of us in his council, has decided to launch the attack against the French right now," Rogers told the assembled men of the Ranger companies. His frustration showing on his face, he turned to Jacob.

"You were with the engineers. What did you see?" he asked and then looked sternly at Jacob. "What does your uncanny gut tell you?"

Feeling everyone's eyes on him, Jacob spoke truthfully. "It didn't sit right with me. While I didn't see the French positions, I have seen the fort and its garrison numerous times from across the lake, and I think there is something wrong here."

The Rangers looked to one another, murmuring. "And your gut?" Rogers asked, to which Jacob replied, "We're in for a bad one. My gut is telling me we're going to have a rough go of it."

To Jacob's relief, Rogers nodded and concurred. "I have the same feeling," he said, looking at the Rangers. "I don't think our illustrious commanders have any idea of what or who we're facing, and to be honest, with the loss of General Howe, no one over there has a clue. But we do! Take care, cover each other, and show these regulars how Rangers fight! Commanders, see to your men."

As they were making their final checks, a cheer went up from the Provincials as a rider leading a large group of Mohawks entered the camp. Sir William Johnson had returned once again, and the few Rangers like Jacob who had been at the original Battle of Lake George greeted their old commander with yells and bonnets waving in the air.

Johnson looked over, and when he saw the Rangers and the New York and Massachusetts Provincials, he waved and saluted back to the cheering men. Jacob, Konkapot, and some of the Stockbridge Company gave Mohawk war cries and salutes, which welcomed the passing warriors, who smiled and gave war whoops back in return.

At the very end of the column strode Robert Aislabie, William Maclane, and Big Harpe, with some supplies they had accompanied from the southern shore. "Well, seems the game is afoot here," remarked Robert. "How exciting!"

William just looked around, as he calculated how much revenue he would acquire once the battle was over, and they secured Carillon. The advantage of being a spy, even a double-agent, is that you have a leg up on your competition. As long as he kept this flop Robert as the front man for their trading endeavors and he remained in the shadows, he would always have a ready scapegoat and plausible denial for himself.

Big Harpe looked with greedy eyes, though he didn't see any of the camp followers and prostitutes he had been playing with down near the fort, no soft flesh here. He did see the coming battle, the marching corpses, and the loot he could secure if he volunteered to help gather the injured so he could relish their pain.

After Johnson passed, the Rangers formed up and began to move forward to join with the 80th Regiment. General Abercrombie was there, and he personally gave the command to advance. The Rangers split to the left to form their line, and the 80th Regiment went to the right. Captain Stark's company was first in line and centered, followed by Rogers bringing the rest of the Rangers. Jacob, Konkapot, Samuel, and Peter had been assigned to Stark's company for the attack.

The Rangers and the men of the 80th advanced slowly, cautiously, quietly towards the French lines. Between the dark green of the Rangers and dark brown of the 80th, the men blended in with the trees and brush as they moved forward. The only sound was the wind whistling through the tree tops and a woodpecker knocking in the distance.

Jacob scanned the woods, trying to pierce the veil that hid the truth from him. His gut feeling was that they were being watched by unfriendly eyes. Straining to hear or see anything, he detected only the sound of their legs swishing through the grass and brush. Jacob was wondering where the enemy pickets were. Even if they had garrisoned the fort, there still would be early warning pickets out, since the French knew they were there.

They were closing in on what they thought were the French lines when the woods in front of them exploded in fire and smoke. Having waited for the Rangers and the 80th to draw near so their fire would be more accurate, the French advanced position fired on the approaching and unaware Rangers and light infantry of the 80th.

Bullets whizzing by, Jacob and his men found cover behind trees, and then spun around and took the enemy under fire. They worked as teams, Jacob with Konkapot, and Samuel with Peter, one firing while the other covered. Hearing the firing, Rogers angled his line more to the right and rushed up to support Stark.

"Contact to the right, form line and advance!" was heard, and the men of the 80th reacted to their drill, forming into their sections and advancing towards the enemy fire. The Rangers employed their tactics of moving in smaller sections, reducing their size as a target. The 80th began to fire in platoon volleys, each section firing and advancing, similar to how the Rangers employed a two-man covering and firing element.

The volume of fire the Rangers were pouring into the French was more than the French were returning, and when Rogers joined Stark, the Frenchmen turned and retreated. Jacob was ramming a ball down the barrel as he watched the Frenchmen turn and disappear. Returning his rammer, he finished priming, closed his pan, and was ready to engage.

Jacob looked to his left and right, saw Konkapot, Samuel, and Peter as the grey smoke of the musketry settled like a fog on the ground. Turning, he watched the 80th advance, and then the green uniformed Rangers were lined up, Rogers and Stark waving the line forward.

Rising up, Jacob and his men moved forward, passing from the thick woods into a more open woods that was getting brighter where some of the shrubs had been cut down and removed. Jacob quickly stopped and looked down at the ground, the freshly cut stumps of small trees poking up from the grass. It almost looked as if the French had cleared the ground for an open field of fire. Jacob stood up and moved to catch up with the advancing Rangers.

Trotting up to Captain Stark, Jacob pointed out the numerous tree stumps mingled in with the bushes and standing trees. "Looks like our friends were busy" Jacob pointed to the stumps and Stark nodded, "Thought so myself."

Jacob returned to his section as Stark issued "Be cautious lads, our friends have been busy!" The woods continued to thin out and through the trees, an open field with thick brush could be seen.

They came across a French position, having spotted a couple of dead, white-uniformed Frenchmen. Jacob stopped to look at the uniforms, French regulars with dark blue cuffs and facings and a well-formed cocked hat. As Jacob looked up, two more Frenchmen jumped out from behind a bush and fired, both balls flying high and wide. Samuel and Konkapot fired nearly at the same time and struck both men as they turned to flee. Jacob and Peter covered them as Samuel and Konkapot reloaded, before continuing their move forward.

All around them was the sound of fighting, echoing off the trees and orders being yelled in both English and French, as well as insults that the two sides were hurling at one another. Again, Jacob and his men were surprised to see no Indians in this fight, and in a way, they were relieved.

The Rangers continued to move forward. The New York Provincials were moving up and to the left of the Rangers when the woods erupted again from another French advanced guard position. The New Yorkers turned and faced their attackers, and began to fire by company volleys. Then the New Yorkers charged into the woods and drove their enemy away with a loud "Huzzah!"

The New Yorkers, feeling the enemy was on the run, started after them in pursuit, moving up behind the Rangers and the 80th, which were still advancing. Colonel Haviland, leading his

27th Regiment of Foot and the 1st Battalion of the 60th Regiment, heard the firing from his right, then the loud shouts and huzzahs of the New Yorkers in the distance.

"The Provincials have them on the run, forward men!" Haviland ordered and the brigade surged ahead.

Seeing no French before them, Haviland waved his sword over his head and they continued their charge forward until they ran into the hidden and camouflaged abatis. The downed trees and sharpened limbs began to channel Haviland's men, whose formation completely broke up with most forming into single files as they tried to climb over or around the obstacles.

The Rangers also ran into the obstacles as they moved through the thinning woods, and more into the field. As the Rangers advanced, they began running into limbs laced as tangle foot, while Jacob and his men continued to move forward in small sections, constantly running into abatis, but seeing nothing that looked like the French earthworks.

"Where's the enemy's line?" wondered Jacob, who ducked quickly as a Frenchman appeared from around a tree and took a shot at him. As the Frenchman turned, Jacob's ball tore through his back and then his front. As Jacob was reloading, another Frenchman appeared. He raised his musket but never got the chance to fire as Konkapot took him.

Along with the smell of smoke, the smell of fresh-cut wood and sap was everywhere. This was a new position, only recently built. They could hear the firing all around them, the yells and screams of the wounded, and officers giving orders. Jacob and his men moved forward and found the reason for the fresh-cut smell. Piles of fir trees and bushes were interlaced, which the French had used to camouflage their positions.

"Well this explains everything," observed Peter. "The scouts missed it."

Jacob looked at the hard work, and as much as he hated to admit, was impressed with the field work.

The sound of battle was beginning to increase as more of the British and Provincial units broke from the woods and began crossing the field, trying to maintain their lines of battle, but were being broken up by the tangle foot and obstacles.

Advancing at a crouch, the Rangers moved in open order, not allowing the obstacle to stop them, but flowed around them like water. The field was rolling with dips and small hills, which made it difficult to spot the enemy.

Cresting a small rise, Jacob and his men occupied a fence line, and finally found the true French positions as they observed across from them a long log wall and earthworks, which were located on high ground overlooking an extensive abatis along their front.

Jacob and the Rangers knelt down, using the fence and what few trees that were standing for some cover and Samuel whistled looking at the French fieldworks. "They've been busy as beavers!" The Rangers had a good position to watch the beginning of the battle unfold as the blue lines of the Provincials and the red line of the British battalions, advancing into the killing fields in front of the enemy earthworks, and into the abatis.

"Ah damn!" yelled Peter as the log wall opened a murderous fire on the Provincials and British regulars alike. From their elevated strong position, the French began pouring fire into the massed British regulars of the 27th, forcing many of them to seek cover on the ground. When they tried to climb over or around the abatis, they were hit, causing some to fall on the sharpened limbs, impaling themselves.

The Rangers and the 80th, having moved along the flank of the advancing line, were spared from the murderous fire that the French were beginning to pour into the British and

Provincial lines. The command of "Froward" was given, and both the Rangers and the 80th began to move and find supporting positions to fire on the enemy and perhaps save the regulars.

Jacob and the Rangers took up positions within the abatis and used them to their advantage as cover and stable firing platforms. It was still no cake walk, as balls continued to whizz and ping off of limbs and trees. Jacob with Konkapot, Samuel with Peter worked as teams firing on the French to their front, moving low and slow forward.

Resting his rifle on a trunk, Konkapot was taking aim as Jacob covered him. The French were well entrenched; only their heads were visible over the log wall, and many of them were rising up to shoot down at an angle at the British and Provincials. Konkapot waited and when a Frenchmen rose up to shoot, Konkapot fired. As he loaded, Jacob took up a good firing position and waited for his shot.

"You know, if it wasn't for all of this firing at us, this could be rather fun," quipped Konkapot.

Jacob looked over at his friend, who was chuckling to himself. Laughing to himself, Jacob shook his head and took up his shooting position. Just then, there were large booms from the French line as artillery began to fire on the trapped regulars and Provincials. Jacob and Konkapot both ducked as a cannon ball came screaming and bouncing through the trees, throwing splinters and wood fragments along their paths. Some caught people, tearing them in half and spraying the abatis and their comrades with blood and body parts.

"Is it still fun now?" asked Jacob. He looked over at Konkapot, who rapidly shook his head no.

Jacob and his men wound their way through the abatis, bending and ducking around the obstacles, and when the opportunity presented itself, took careful and waited for an enemy's head to rise up before they took their shot. It was slow movement, though the obstacles at least shielded them from most of the enemy fire. Instinctively, they flattened themselves when they heard the boom of enemy cannon, then waited for the bouncing cannon ball to come sailing through.

Marching up behind Jacob and his Rangers was the combined grenadier battalion under Colonel Haldimand, formed by taking the grenadier companies from each of the regiments and combining them into one grenadier battalion to serve as shock troops. They pushed forward but gained nothing except becoming entangled in the abatis and drawing murderous fire from the French. They continued trying to push through the tangled branches, some climbing over while others strained to go under. The tall grenadier caps were getting caught in the numerous branches, and some were being shot off the heads of their owners.

Jacob shook his head in amazement at the stubbornness of the British regiments, refusing to seek alternatives, but blindly charging ahead. The orderly line of the grenadiers had been broken up by the obstacles.

"Give them support!" shouted Jacob, and he fired at the French in the distance.

Most of the French fire was focusing on the British instead of the Rangers, which made it easier for them to aim and pick off their targets while the British were being shot like fish in a barrel. The center brigade of the 44th and 55th Regiments arrived and attempted to support the grenadiers, while the 46th and the 42nd Highlanders moved towards the left to begin their attack through the abatis.

As the 55th began fighting their way through the abatis, Jacob looked over to see none other than Captain Reynolds himself. Jacob noticed the look of utter terror on his face, his haughty expression gone. Jacob watched as he gingerly moved forward, but behind his men instead of leading from the front as other officers were doing. His once immaculate uniform looked dingy and torn in some places.

Captain Reynolds's company became entangled in the abatis, and cohesion began to break down. Instead of trying to reorganize his men, he stayed behind them crouched low, trying to avoid any enemy fire.

A rage took over Jacob, and seeing an opportunity, he turned his rifle towards Captain Reynolds and began to take aim at the stumbling, cowardly officer. Calmness came over Jacob as he was taking in the slack of his trigger, but he held his fire. Gritting his teeth, and for some unknown reason, Jacob did not pull the trigger.

There was a loud boom, and a French cannon ball arched over and struck a tree, shattering limbs and hurling off a large splinter that sank itself into Captain Reynolds's shoulder. Screaming in a high-pitched voice, Reynolds collapsed to his knees, trying to pull the splinter out, but it was in too deep. Rising, Reynolds turned to head back towards the rear, never seeing the second cannon ball that cleanly took his head off.

As Reynold's head spun a few times on the ground, sightless eyes staring in an expression of shock, Jacob lowered his rifle with a grim satisfaction. "At least I didn't have to waste a ball on him," Jacob muttered to himself, then turned back to the fight at hand.

Ducking under a limb, Jacob sided up next to Samuel. "Guess who is worm dirt," Jacob yelled, and Samuel looked over curiously. "Our dear old friend Captain Reynolds." Samuel raised his eyebrows as Jacob recounted how he had lost his head to a cannon shot.

"That's still too good for the likes of him," yelled back Samuel. "He deserved a slow and painful death, or drowning in a privy. But I'll accept it. Good riddance!" The two smiled and got back to work, choosing their targets while trying not to get hit by the hundreds of enemy balls flying around them.

A new sound joined the growing symphony of battle; in the distance the large guns of Fort Carillon begin firing, not at the British ensnared in the abatis, but out towards the lake. Unbeknownst to Jacob and the men fighting through the abatis, a small flotilla of barges with artillery and men was trying to move up the La Chute River to flank the French.

The large balls were very effective, sinking one barge right away and then a second one before the flotilla decided to turn around and retreat. It would be up to the infantry to try and win the day.

The 27th and the grenadiers fell back to reorganize themselves, as the 44th and 55th went back into action, but in the same place, trying to fight through the same abatis. Under the leadership of the regimental officers, they blindly charged back into the carnage of the fallen and bloody remains of the previous assault.

"Where the hell is the bloody general?" yelled Samuel. "Why is he not giving orders or something? This is insane!"

For a moment, it felt that time had decelerated, the sound of battle becoming muffled as Jacob took in the fighting around him. It seemed everything slowed. Men were pushing forward in slow motion, fighting with the limbs of the cut trees while others, having been hit by musket and cannon balls, spun as their life spilled upon the ground.

Jacob's senses were becoming overloaded with the aroma of fresh-cut pine sap mixed with the smoke of battle and the smell of torn bodies and blood everywhere. The sound was becoming muffled, almost a constant roar of shot and muskets, pierced from time to time by shouts of orders or the screams of the wounded.

Jacob saw a wounded British soldier, having lost his left arm to a cannon ball, pick it up with his right, and try to shuffle to the rear before he collapsed on the ground. Balls flew and ricocheted, wood splinters flying in all directions. Men were hacking at the limbs with hatchets and axes, trying to clear a path through the thick obstacles, nearly blinded by the choking grey smoke of the battle.

It was as if Jacob had stepped away from the fight, a spectator to the carnage all about him. He barely noticed the cannon ball that bounced off a log in front of him and flew just over his head. But then reality slowly returned, and the sights and sounds of battle returned to normal.

Jacob shrugged and shook his head as he loaded his rifle. This was pure insanity, and these brave, foolish men were plunging forward to their unnecessary deaths. The fighting continued well into the afternoon, the British regiments falling back, regrouping, and re-attacking the same sections of the abatis.

Jacob was becoming concerned that they were getting low on ammunition. But there was no shortage of muskets and cartridge boxes lying around. They could always take up a Brown Bess and keep firing, he thought.

Finding a small depression to rest in, Jacob checked on his men. They'd been extremely lucky so far, suffering mostly cuts and bruises from flying splinters. Like the regulars and Provincials, the Ranger sections had broken up, but they had joined with other Rangers and continued to fight as small groups and to help where they could.

"How are we set for powder and ball?" Jacob asked, while wiping down his lock.

"Getting low," replied Konkapot. Peter and Samuel nodded.

"Salvage what you can from the dead. Use their muskets if you run out."

Jacob looked around at the battlefield covered in the thick grey fog of smoke from the constant fighting. Then a new scent caught his attention. Samuel and the others lifted their noses and smelled it too, the smell of wood burning. The abatis had caught fire in some places, and the flames were racing along the dried out wood and branches.

"Ah damn, the place is catching on fire!" yelled Samuel.

Jacob yelled over, "See if you can help any of the wounded! Get them away from the flames!"

Placing his rifle next to Konkapot, who nodded and covered him, Jacob began to squirm and crawl through the abatis, checking on the fallen around them. Many were dead, eyes staring blankly into nothing, covered in blood. Jacob could see the fire now. It was beginning to grow and move towards them, leaping from limb to limb.

Using his elbows to move through the abatis, Jacob winced as he called through the entrails of a British soldier who had been cut in half by a cannon shot. Clenching his teeth tightly, Jacob kept crawling, looking for anyone who could be saved, ignoring his surroundings.

Jacob came across a British soldier, who was trying to move, but his leg had been impaled on a sharpened limb. Crawling quickly, he made it to the struggling soldier.

"Hold still!" commanded Jacob who drew his tomahawk and in a quick motion, cut the branch at the tree, freeing the man. While the branch was still stuck in his leg, Jacob helped drag the wounded soldier away from the creeping flames.

Jacob, Konkapot, Samuel, and Peter all took turns searching among the dead to find any wounded who could be helped. They had to keep moving to stay ahead of the fire, which was burning itself out in some places. Many of the wounded caught out in the middle screamed for help, their screams rising in a crescendo before abruptly stopping as they burned to death. No one was able to reach them because of the heavy enemy fire.

Eventually they did run out of ammunition, having fired over sixty rounds each. The Rangers slung their rifles over their shoulders and picked up the heavy Brown Bess muskets, stripped the dead of their cartridges, and continued firing at the French while helping the wounded when and where they could. The Besses were a lot different from their rifles, heavier and more cumbersome.

The Rangers adapted and continued to fire at the French, except now their shots weren't as accurate. The area around them was still filled with smoke from the burning abatis and from the musketry.

Through this Dante's Hell marched the brave men of the 42nd Highlanders, with the sound of their screeching bagpipes, and the reformed grenadiers. Moving to Jacob's left, the column smashed into the abatis and began to claw their way through. At least they were trying to move around to a flank, rather than the unsuccessful approach through the center and right. Still, Jacob was surprised that there was no sign of the commanding general or anyone taking charge.

Through pure force of will, the Highlanders pressed onward, and Jacob was amazed by their pure tenacity. Caught up in the moment, Jacob and the others began to cheer on the Highlanders, hoping they could finally break through. But they did not fare any better than those who had tried earlier, and soon their losses began to mount.

Some of the Highlanders were able to break through the abatis and began assaulting the French works, but there were too few of them. The French now had the advantage in numbers, and that began to have a telling effect. Finally, the order arrived from Abercrombie to retreat, and the Highlanders and the Rangers were the last to leave the field, covering the retreat and helping to move the wounded or the dead if they could, not wanting to leave their fallen comrades behind.

As night fell, the broken army limped back into the encampment, the victorious shouts and hurled insults from the

French finally fading in the distance. The Rangers had been lucky. Only three men from the entire Ranger force had died during the attack. The regulars did not fare as well. The Highlanders alone lost over half of their men.

From a safe position watching over the battlefield, strewn in red and blue uniformed broken and dead bodies, Rogers, Jacob, and the other Rangers watched the field in case the French decided to take advantage of the situation. Soon, work details arrived from the encampment to begin moving the dead or looking for wounded, though none moved close to the French position. Rogers and his Rangers stayed on the battlefield until it was too dark to see, and then the Rangers returned to the encampment.

General Abercrombie, pride broken, ordered a general retreat back to the southern end of the lake. In all, Abercrombie lost nearly two thousand men. Even so, the British still outnumbered the French. Many thought the loss of Lord Howe and the brutal mauling at the abatis had been enough to break Abercrombie's spirit and his will to continue.

Jacob and his men were sent out as scouts to watch the battlefield to make sure the French would not try to attack now when the army was at its most vulnerable. The night was ghastly, the cries and moans of the wounded echoing over the battlefield. The smell of the burned and in some cases still burning, fires filled the air, along with the smells of death, torn bodies, blood, and entrails.

This was a new hell on Earth that Jacob and his men witnessed as they watched over the broken and scorched battlefield. For the first time since he began this fight, Jacob faced a new feeling, doubt. He began to really question if they would win this fight. They had had superior numbers this time, even if the French had had a good position. A good leader should have prevailed. While it wouldn't have been easy, the numbers were on their side for a change; this should have been the victory they needed.

Jacob mused this over in his mind, watching out over the glowing, ember-dancing field of the dead. He answered his own question; good leaders seemed to be in short supply. Why did Lord Howe have to been killed? He would have made the right decisions, and they would be inside the walls of the fort, victors, instead of out on the field, trying to save as many of the wounded as they could in the dark. Fate it seemed could be very fickle. The good leaders died, the poor ones lived to make bad decisions, and then more men died.

The wounded were still trickling in, some on their own and others being helped by search parties. There was nothing they could do for the wounded that were too close to the French lines, where the abatis were thickest and where most of the regulars had fallen.

Jacob felt a tap on his shoulder as Peter passed him a small flask. He pulled the cork with his teeth, took a long pull of rum, placed the cork back, and thanked him. Peter patted his back and moved over to share his flask with Samuel and Konkapot. The rum warmed Jacob's stomach but couldn't take the edge off of losing two friends and witnessing the horrible slaughter of another failed attack.

***

Rolling a dead body over, once an officer by his fine cut of a coat, but missing a head, Big Harpe went through the pockets and bags, shoving coins and trinkets into his own bag, before dragging the headless body towards a growing pile of dead. He had wormed his way onto the work detail to gather as much loot as he could while performing a service for the King, even if it meant that when he found a wounded soldier, he silenced his cries and took the pain away, relishing the thrill of the kill, justifying it as a mercy killing.

Big Harpe's bag was bulging. "May need to get another bag. Business is good," he mumbled to nobody, then looked around at the many dead still needing to be dragged out. "Going to be good business indeed." He lifted the headless corpse, and trudged on to the pile of the dead.

As he dropped the headless body onto the pile, Harpe could see a group of those Rangers. He thought he recognized the shape of the big Ranger that he had seen at the southern end of the lake, and then he looked down at the headless body. Seeing the fine uniform, Harpe wondered, "Hmm. Is this the captain that was giving those Rangers such a hard time? Interesting twist of fate."

***

As Harpe shuffled off to continue his looting of the dead, Jacob and his men were relieved by other Rangers, and Jacob led his men back to the encampment where they lay out on top of the blankets and tried to get some sleep.

In the morning, the Rangers conducted their stand-to, concerned the French would try to attack their position. The French were too exhausted to attack, however, and they remained behind their entrenchments and allowed the British to retreat unmolested.

Major Rogers checked on his men, once again gave his condolences to Jacob and his men over the loss of Charles and James in the earlier fight and then continued on his rounds. They packed all of their gear and loaded it into the boats before heading out to the perimeter of the camp.

The Rangers provided security while the army broke down the camp and began loading the boats. Supplies and the wounded were loaded first, followed by the regulars, the Provincials, and the Rangers last.

"First in, last out," sighed Samuel as they watched the army limp back down the lake.

Jacob nodded and let out a soft grunt. "That's our life."

As they were about to load their boat, Jacob and his men stopped over at Charles' and James' graves and wished them an undisturbed rest in peace. They loaded their boat and took up their oars, rowing back to the southern end of the lake. It was a quiet trip, each man caught up in his own thoughts.

At least the weather was decent and spared the retreating army any rain or thunderstorms. The Rangers rotated their turns on the oars and used the sail when they could. They didn't stop at Sabbath Day Point, instead continuing straight on until they arrived at the southern shore.

Once they arrived at the lake, Rogers formed the command, and they went into their camp area to rest, Rogers instructing them to draw rations and get a warm meal while he continued on back to Fort Edward. They were to follow in the morning under Captain Stark.

Jacob and his men went over and drew rations of beef and venison, along with some rum and ale, and returned to their camp to enjoy their meal while watching the army reorganize and some of the units begin their move south. The four men sat on the ground on their blankets, leaned against their packs and bags, and sipped on mugs of rum, which they had drawn from the quartermaster.

"Here's to James!" toasted Samuel, and then they slurped their drinks.

"Here's to Charles, Prost!" toasted Peter, and they all drank.

"Here's to all our friends who have gone on before us," toasted Jacob. "And here's to hoping this war is over soon," which they all drank to.

CHAPTER 7

ANOTHER MASSACRE

A dark and depressed state enveloped the men at Fort Edward with the exception of Major Rogers and his Rangers. The loss of Lord Howe and the hard trouncing the expedition had taken from a much smaller French Army had placed the encampment into a gloomy funk. Rogers and his Rangers, who had suffered only minor losses compared to the rest of the army, were determined to get back into the fight, the rest of the army be damned, though they did mourn the loss of Lord Howe whom they considered to be one of them.

Jacob, Samuel, Konkapot, and Peter, along with a few other Rangers, headed over to Mr. Best's shop for some ale and rum to help take off the edge of their loss. As they stepped into the shop, they encountered two men, one fairly big and another who seemed to be doing all of the talking. They appeared to have angered both Mr. and Mrs. Best.

Maclane, with Harpe looming behind him, was speaking to an angry Mr. Best. "It would benefit you greatly to join the South Sea Company. It would be a shame if something happened to your shop. Accidents do happen, fires break out, and the company would see to your safety and well-being."

Both Mr. and Mrs. Best shook their heads, frowning. "Accidents! What are you implying, sir?" Mr. Best growled back.

"We've had no problem since we've been here without the likes of you!"

Harpe growled back, "If you know what's good for you," then sneering at Mrs. Best, "or your family, you will listen and sign on, or else."

Mr. Best looked defiantly back. "Or else what?"

As Harpe began to reach out for Mr. Best, Maclane spotted Jacob and the other Rangers, who had just stepped into the shop, and grabbed his arm.

"Is there a problem here Mr. Best?" Jacob asked as the Rangers fanned out behind Jacob, facing Maclane and Harpe, their eyes locking onto the two who were threatening their friends.

"No, Jacob, these men were just leaving, weren't you?" Mr. Best stared back at Maclane and Harpe. Maclane nodded and headed towards the door. Jacob never dropped his gaze from either Maclane or Harpe as they approached the door that the Rangers were blocking.

"Be careful not to involve yourself in business that is not yours," warned Maclane. Harpe sneered at Jacob, who didn't move, which forced the two to stop.

"I can make it my business if you like," Jacob replied softly, his steely gaze not faltering. "As I heard you say, accidents do happen." Jacob moved nose to nose with Maclane, and pointed over his shoulders out the door.

"Many accidents can happen out there, remember that." Jacob stared a few seconds more, and then moved to the side and allowed Maclane and Harpe to exit. All of the Rangers glowered at the two, concerned that they had threatened the Bests. Even Samuel offered a parting comment.

"Yes, accidents do happen out there." Samuel winked at Maclane, who walked by. "Especially in the dark."

Jacob watched as Maclane and Harpe left before turning back to Mr. Best, who already had his friendly face on, though Mrs. Best still looked worried, if relieved.

"What was that all about?" Jacob asked.

"Pah!" Mr. Best responded. "Just business. This character is trying to get everyone to join his company, and I won't have it! Been doing my own business since I've been here, and that's the way it's going to stay!"

Then he looked at the Rangers and Jacob. "But you're not here to here talk about business. How can I assist you fine lads this day?" Jacob and the Rangers secured rum and ale, toasted to Mr. and Mrs. Best's health, and got down to the business of swapping stories.

***

Maclane and Harpe headed back towards their office in the fort, Harpe looking over his shoulder at the shop and the Rangers inside. "May have to do something about that. Not good having hold outs," said Maclane.

Harpe smiled. "Just say the word, and I'll do what I do best."

Maclane looked back at the shop, and then turned around and continued heading into the fort. "You're going to have to be careful," Maclane warned Harpe. "That's the same big Ranger who found your plaything back at the lake. He also looks like someone who can't be intimidated or scared."

Harpe looked over his shoulder at the shop, and then shrugged. "Then I'll just kill him or find someone he is close to and kill them. Either way, it's going to be fun."

***

The new garrison commander of Fort Edward, Colonel James Montressor, had been tasked by General Abercrombie to keep the new position at the southern end of Lake George well-supplied. As the British and the Provincials maintained the supply line to Lake George, Jacob and his Rangers were out scouting, knowing full well that the French would sit back and bask in their victory. The Rangers were going to capitalize on it.

Jacob, Konkapot, Peter, and Samuel had joined with Major Rogers and a few other Rangers to scout the area east of the southern end of Lake George, near South Bay. Jacob, his men, and their wolves, along with the other Rangers, moved silently through the thick forest, sweat beading along their foreheads and soaking their frock shirts. Only the wolves seemed to be unaffected by the heat and humidity.

The summer temperatures up in these mountains could be just as bad as the ice and snow in the winter. The forest was still, no air moving, and the heat caught under the great boughs of the trees, baking the men as they concentrated on their scout.

As Jacob mopped the sweat from his forehead during a breather, he looked over at Samuel, and in a whisper said, "If I recall, didn't we say it would be better warmer than colder a few months back?"

Samuel looked up, and with a grimace nodded. "Yes, but we were freezing then. I think I have a change-of-heart on it now."

In addition to the heat, during the night the dreaded black flies and the smaller "no-see-ums" had pestered the resting Rangers, draining their strength just as the day's heat was doing. But Jacob and his men were veterans, and they Rangered on, well aware of what Mother Nature could throw at them. They were on their second day out of the encampment at Lake George when Jacob and Konkapot, who were leading, spotted signs of many feet moving through the area.

A Fury of Wolves

It was a large group of footprints, with numerous broken pieces of grass and bushes marking the trail. The path was wide, and it indicated a large group that was not worrying about being detected. Jacob knelt, looking at the width of the path. "What do you think?" asked Samuel. "Could it be a trap, being this obvious, wanting us to follow?"

Jacob and Rogers looked up with knowing expressions, and both men studied the direction from which the trail had come, South Bay. The French had been using the area to avoid and bypass the encampment at Lake George, which meant they had been heading either for Fort Edward or south. The wolves lay alongside of them, ears perked and noses sniffing the air.

"We need to get this back to Edward," whispered Rogers.

Jacob nodded and turned and whistled for his men to fall in, and they began to trot back towards the encampment at Lake George. Rogers kept a good pace, and Jacob found himself huffing and puffing a little as the weight of the hot, thick, humid air made it difficult to breathe. The Rangers kept going, knowing the importance of getting word back about a large war party in the area.

Rogers led the scout into the encampment and checked in with the commander there while Jacob and his men caught their breath and drank from their canteens. They barely had time to refill the canteens and swallow their rum rations, which had been doled out to them by the quartermaster, before Rogers came out and began to lead them towards Fort Edward.

Samuel moaned, "No rest for the wicked," then hitched his straps up and established the ground-eating pace back to the fort. The wolves, sitting on their haunches, tongues hanging out the side of their mouths, perked up and trotted alongside.

It was after noon and the heat hung on as the Rangers moved along the trail, sweat once again drenching their shirts. As they jogged along the trail, they begin to hear the sound of musketry in the distance.

As they got closer they could hear that heavy firing was occurring ahead. Someone was having a terrible day, and it probably involved the large war party whose trail they had spotted. The Rangers picked up their pace, adrenaline coursing through their veins in anticipation of battle with their detested enemies, the weariness from the pace they had set quickly dissipating. The wolves joined in on the hunt, keeping a silent pace with the Rangers.

The woods began to fill with smoke, held low in the trees by the high humidity, as the Rangers and their wolves spread out into a line and approached the sound of the battle. Firing was lessening, indicating that the fighting was coming to the end.

Jacob's section continued to move forward, eyes peering through the smoke to identify the enemy. They burst out of the woods and into the open field at Halfway Brook, and Jacob spotted an Abenaki warrior standing over a New York Provincial, beginning to take his scalp.

Raising his rifle, Jacob aimed and fired quickly, taking the warrior before he could finish scalping the soldier. As Jacob began to reload, Konkapot ran past him and fired on another Abenaki who was trying to run into the woods, knocking him forward so that he sprawled dead in the soft earth. The three wolves charged into the war party as grey, snapping blurs, pulling the Indians from their feet or knocking them over.

As he finished priming his rifle, Jacob advanced towards the wooden stockade that had recently been erected at Halfway Brook. He was flanked by Konkapot, Samuel, and Peter. It was a site of pure carnage, broken and scalped men lying everywhere, all wearing the blue uniforms of New York Provincials.

Major Rogers found a wounded sergeant and asked him what had happened as Jacob and the other Rangers moved around the site of battle, helping the injured as best they could.

"They waited as we relieved the company and then attacked from all sides," wheezed the injured sergeant. "We barely got the gate closed before the savages were upon us, doing frightful damage to the poor souls caught outside. We had no choice; we had to close the gate."

Jacob's section helped to gather three dead officers, twenty dead and scalped enlisted men, and another twenty or more wounded. The attack had been very specific and very well executed. The wolves returned their mouths bloody, but with satisfied looks on their faces.

Jacob's section was sent forward to Fort Edward to get carts to help move the wounded back as Rogers and the other Rangers remained with the New York men. The four Rangers made good time back to Edward, and the garrison sent out more New York Provincials and wagons to retrieve the wounded at Halfway Brook.

While at the fort, they spotted a large wall tent that had boxes and bales with planks across being used as tables. While it was just another sutler, what drew Jacob's attention was that he spotted Maclane and Harpe, having learned their names and their South Sea Company, leave the tent. "Was that who we think it was?" asked Samuel, and Jacob nodded.

"Perhaps we need to go see what is going on," said Konkapot, and they all nodded and then headed over to the new sutler. There were a few Provincials standing around the makeshift tables, speaking with the owner, a Mr. Pommery. Jacob and the Rangers leaned on their rifles while looking at the business being conducted.

"Step up, step up, don't be shy," Mr. Pommery called out to the Provincials, and to the standing Rangers. "Only the finest wares that the company can provide!" Jacob looked at Konkapot and then Samuel, and then asked, "Which company is that?"

Mr. Pommery looked over and smiled, "Why the South Sea Company of course! The best wares for our hard-fighting men on the frontier, from across the seas and now here, only the best for the best, by the best!"

Not seeing anything they couldn't get from any shop around the fort, Jacob hefted his rifle and turned towards the island. The others simply shook their heads and followed Jacob. Konkapot remarked, "Thought so. A company man."

Jacob nodded. "Guess that's why we saw our two favorite company men there."

While cradling his rifle in his arm, Jacob looked back at Mr. Pommery, who was busy doing business with the Provincials. "We may want to keep an eye on him and the other company men, …" Jacob remarked as he turned back towards the island, "… in case an accident happens with Mr. Best."

Jacob led them across the bridge, and they returned to the island to clean their weapons and gear, then to get something to eat. Later that evening Major Rogers returned with the rest of the survivors, who were being escorted back to Fort Edward by the New Yorkers. Jacob and Konkapot were sitting on a log, smoking their pipes when Rogers came over, sitting down on the log next to them. Konkapot handed a leather tobacco pouch to Major Rogers, who filled his pipe, and Jacob handed him a mug of rum, which Rogers drank, nodding his thanks.

"What's on your mind sir?" asked Jacob. "What got you all worked up?"

Rogers looked up with a smile, "You know me that well?" he asked, and then shook his head as he drew on his pipe, the grey smoke circling around his head.

"These bloody Englishmen just sit on their hands, not wanting to see the obvious," Rogers began as he blew out a puff of smoke. "The French are getting bolder, and all this Abercrombie wants to do is keep the supply lines open to the lake. We have to deny the French freedom of movement. We're letting them pick their battles just like last year when they kept beating us at our own game. It has to stop!"

Jacob and Konkapot nodded, and the three just sat, smoking their pipes and listening to the night calls of whippoorwills in the distance. With a big sigh, Rogers stood up and tapped out the bowl of his pipe on the log.

"Thanks boys. I needed to get that off my chest," Rogers said.
"Anytime sir," replied Jacob. "We understand, and we're with you. It's only going to get uglier if things don't change soon."

That ugliness arrived two days later. Jacob and Samuel had gone over to the fort to pick up some new rifle flints and lead to make balls when they observed a large wagon train being assembled just outside of the fort on the road to the lake. There were over a hundred ox carts and wagons full of supplies. What bothered Jacob and Samuel even more was several dozen women and girls mixed in with the sutlers and the quartermaster personnel. Jacob grabbed a Provincial walking by and asked what was with the wagons.

"Supply column heading to the lake. The women and girls are volunteers to serve as nurses to help the wounded from Fort Carillon."

Jacob nodded his head in thanks and looked at Samuel.

"Not a whole lot of escort appears to be going out with them," Samuel said, pointing to only a dozen or so Provincials lounging next to the wagons.

Jacob turned and started for the orderly room of the fort, climbing the wooden stairs two at a time. Raising his eyebrows,

Samuel followed Jacob up the stairs into the orderly room. Sitting behind a desk, the officer of the day was Major Gabriel Christie of the 44th Regiment of Foot. Also present was Captain Charles Lee, whose arm was still in a sling from injuries he suffered at Carillon.

Jacob stopped in front of the desk, but the major was too busy writing dispatches to notice a Provincial. Jacob cleared his throat, which attracted Captain Lee, but not the major. After a little while, the scratching sound of the major's quill stopped as he finished his document and handed it out so Captain Lee could grab it.

He finally noticed Jacob, who had been standing there for some time. Shaking his head, Major Christie looked back down and began writing another dispatch, saying haughtily, "Captain, see to this Provincial outside of the orderly room."

Captain Lee moved over and nodded to Jacob to follow him outside. Jacob stared darkly at the top of the major's head before turning and following Captain Lee outside.

"What can I do for you Ranger?" asked Captain Lee.

"Sergeant Clarke, Sir. I have concerns about that line of wagons on the road. We just had the outpost at Halfway Brook attacked only a couple of days ago by a large war party. There needs to be more of an escort to protect the wagons."

Captain Lee nodded, replying, "We had been waiting for reinforcements from the Hampshires but they haven't arrived yet. The General wants those supplies to the lake at all costs."

Jacob looked at Captain Lee and asked in a quiet voice, "What is the cost if you lose those wagons and supplies?" He turned and pointed at the women and girls sitting on the supplies in the wagons, adding, "And those people if the French or the Indians take them?"

"I see your point, but the General's orders were specific. We must make do with what we have," Captain Lee replied before turning to carry the Major's dispatches. "Fortunes of war and all."

"Damned bloody fools!" growled Jacob, who took off down the stairs and headed out to the island, Samuel racing to keep up. The wagons were leaving, their wheels squeaking in loud protests as Jacob and Samuel crossed over on the footbridge. He understood how Major Rogers got his blood boiling with these officers.

"Samuel, get Peter and Konkapot and tell them to grab their gear. We're heading out. I am going to go speak with the major," instructed Jacob as he rushed towards Rogers's hut.

Jacob stuck his head in the hut and saw that Major Rogers was there reading a document. Rogers looked up as he entered.

"What's on your mind Ranger Clarke?" asked Rogers.

"Did you see that line of wagons heading towards the lake?" asked Jacob.

Rogers stood up. "What wagons?" he asked, and Jacob waved for Rogers to follow him.

Jacob led Rogers over to the shoreline and pointed out the long, snaking column of wagons heading north.

"Where in the hell are they going?" Rogers asked. "Don't they know we were attacked only two days ago?"

Jacob explained how he had been summarily dismissed by Major Christie, his concerns ignored, and he recounted his conversation with Captain Lee.

"Just wanted to let you know I am taking my men out to shadow the wagons, just in case," Jacob informed Rogers, who nodded in agreement.

"I'll warn the men here to be ready to move quickly if something happens."

Jacob nodded and ran over to a waiting Konkapot, Peter, and Samuel, who had Jacob's rifle and shooting bag already out, along with his tomahawk. As he put his bag over his shoulder and seated the tomahawk in the small of his back, Jacob explained his concern about the juicy target that had just left the fort with little escort.

"We're going to keep pace with the wagons, and hope for an uneventful trip to the lake," Jacob explained. "But we all know that is too good of an opportunity to let go, and that war party may still be around."

They all nodded and checked their gear as Jacob grabbed his full canteen, and led them out at the trot and into the woods, the three wolves falling in alongside.

***

Abigail shifted around on the bale of leggings on which she was sitting in the wagon, trying to get comfortable. In Saratoga, she had heard from her friends about the need for nurses at the English encampment at the lake, and she had agreed to volunteer with her friends. While she did feel slightly patriotic in doing her duty, she mostly did it to anger her father and mother, who were trying to arrange a marriage between her and the son of one of the more prosperous merchants in town.

While the marriage would bring position and wealth for her family, she found the man to be fat, ugly, and uncouth. Her friends, Sally and Margaret, who had volunteered with her, were giggling and whispering about all of those lonely men at the encampment who were in need of companionship. The irony was that they were staring at the officers in their fine uniforms and gold braid, not the average soldiers.

Abigail was jostled as the wagon hit a root and bounced her out of her comfortable position, which forced her to wiggle her butt more into the bundle to get re-comfortable. Still, it was nice to be out of the house and out in the wilderness, surrounded by danger and excitement. She breathed in the air; her adventure was beginning.

Oh, how she craved excitement; anything other than the dull, boring life she led in Saratoga. She attended her lessons on being a lady and went to the numerous parties and dances her father used for business opportunities, but Abigail longed for something more. While she had been to Albany, she had never been to the deep frontier here in the north, defined in her mind by stories of Indians and brave woodsmen fighting bravely for the cause.

She looked at the great trees, the sky, the white, wispy clouds, and the hawks circling on the wind on high. Turning, she looked at the teamsters, who were dark from being out in the sun all the time and ugly. She looked at a few of the Provincial soldiers who were walking alongside of the wagons. Some were old, some were young, but none was what she envisioned as the hero of the tales she had heard, like the scouts, or Rangers she guessed they were called. They sounded like the true heroes she had read about in school, with chivalry and knights, and rescuing poor damsels in distress.

***

Watching the wagons from a distance was a woodsman, but not a hero fit for Abigail's tale. La Corne, a Canadian partisan leader had led an expedition of six hundred Canadians, Abenakis, Caughnawagas, and Ottawas a week earlier from Fort Carillon. They had passed through South Bay and had successfully raided the stockade between Fort Edward and the lake, as well as several isolated farms to the west of Fort Edward.

Now below him, moving slowly through the woods was the easiest and greatest target he had seen in a long time, a large line of wagons with minimal escort. La Corne looked over at his war chiefs, painted in their black and red, and nodded his head in the affirmative, signaling that they would attack this easy target. The war chiefs returned to their warriors as La Corne went over to his Canadians and waved them forward towards their target. It was all too easy.

***

Jacob moved with a determined, but steady pace, eyes constantly scanning for any signs of enemies nearby. Konkapot, Samuel, and Peter did the same, watching the woods around them while covering each other's back. Jacob froze as the sounds of the forest suddenly stopped; the other three Rangers quickly froze as well, straining to hear any sign of the presence that had spooked the woodland animals into silence.

Then there was a great roar as the sound of musketry and hundreds of war cries echoed through the trees. The wagons had been attacked, and they hadn't even reached Halfway Brook. From the sound of the fighting, the four Rangers would be no match, and Jacob decided stealth would be best before blundering into an enemy with superior numbers. The four Rangers crouched low and, staying in the shadows of the trees, advanced cautiously towards the sound of the battle.

Jacob and his men arrived at the tree line where they could watch the horrible disaster of the fight, or rather, another massacre. From their positions, Jacob and his men could see that hundreds of Indians and some Canadians had caught the column of wagons that looked as if it had stopped for lunch from the evidence of food and other items scattered around. As he stared at the bloody fight, his mind recalled the scene when the survivors from Fort William Henry were fallen upon and attacked as they were walking back to Fort Edward.

Jacob looked over at Samuel, Konkapot, and Peter, the three wolves looking back at him in anticipation. The other men's eyes showed the same growing anger that was quickly creeping up in Jacob, his blood beginning to boil and the desire for vengeance pouring in. "Not again," he growled in a low whisper.

The small contingent of Provincials was trying to defend the wagons. Some of the sutlers were trying to run away, but they were being gunned downed. Some of the wagon drivers were trying to cut their horses away and ride back towards Fort Edward, only to be brought down by the enemy.

Jacob and his men were about a hundred yards away from the brutal carnage. He looked at his men once more, and they nodded that they were ready, steely determination in their eyes and faces.

"Help where you can, pick your shots, cover each other, and maybe some of them can escape," he whispered as he brought his rifle up. The others nodded again. They knew they couldn't save them all, but perhaps some.

***

Abigail had crawled under the wagon in which she had been riding, and she had closed her eyes and covered her ears to block out the screaming and the shooting. Her two friends were under the wagon as well, holding onto one another and screaming from terror.

Abigail opened her eyes just to see one of the Provincial soldiers get hit by a musket ball that exploded out the back of his head, which burst like an overripe melon, spraying the wagon in red goo. She saw their driver cut the reins away on the horse, vault up on its back, and begin to turn the horse around towards Fort Edward.

"No…wait!" yelled Abigail, but it was too late as several musket balls hit the driver and he was knocked off the horse, falling in front of where Abigail was cowering, his eyes staring blankly at her.

Abigail could hear balls smashing against the side of the wagon or see them skipping along the ground. She tried to make herself smaller by wriggling into the ground, all the while holding her hands over her ears.

***

La Corne was pleased by how the ambush had been so easily begun. The slow-moving wagons had stopped for a meal and were stationary when he gave the command to attack. Now the accurate firing of his troops and the Indians was eliminating the escort and creating panic, which was what he wanted, pure terror.

Now was the time to attack in force, and La Corne waved and yelled for the war chiefs to close on the enemy and take their rewards. The Indian warriors, drawing their knives and tomahawks, burst from the woods and closed on the helpless survivors around the wagons, their excited war whoops echoing.

Nodding his approval, knowing that this would seal these warriors to him, La Corne moved forward to take part in the plunder of the wagons, looking to enjoy the spoils of war. Like a tidal wave, the Indians ran around, through or over the wagons, grabbing prisoners, taking scalps, and opening the boxes and bundles, tossing most of the contents onto the dusty road.

La Corne moved along the line of wagons, stopping now and then to look at what the warriors had found. Boxes and musical instruments were being tossed around or crushed under feet as the Indians moved about in search of plunder. Many of them located barrels of wine and brandy, and the Indians began drinking directly from the cask's spigots, or cracking them open with their tomahawks.

Then La Corne spotted a strong box and using his tomahawk, broke open the lock. Inside the strong box there were sacks of coins. He had struck a payroll box. Smiling to himself, La Corne knelt down and began to load his pockets and his haversacks with enemy coins, and then he called for his Canadians so they too could take some coins.

As he stood, La Corne observed the carnage around him where his Ottawa and Abenaki warriors were scalping the dead and the living. They slit the throats of hundreds of oxen while some of the surviving men and women sprinted into the woods, now that the Indians were distracted by the wine and rum they had found.

La Corne shook his head, mumbled "a pity," and continued to gather coins. Then grabbing a fallen mug, he went over to one of the open rum casks and took a drink.

***

Abigail was shaking from terror, her mind racing at what she saw. Her wagon had been near the end, and so far they had been spared the worst of the massacre, but the violence was moving their way.

Abigail saw a little girl run past as fast as her little legs could go, on her face a look of pure terror. She saw the darkly painted Indian warriors start grabbing some of the young women volunteers and stripping their clothes off with their knives. Some of the Indians tied ropes around the women's necks and began to lead them off; others grabbed the naked girls and dragged them into the woods.

Others began to cut and stab the women, and the high-pitched screams of those being murdered made something inside Abigail snap. She had to run and get away. She looked over and saw that both of her friends were still hugging and screaming, curled up under the wagon.

"Get up…get up, you fools and run!" screamed Abigail.

As her friends opened their eyes to look at her, several dark arms grabbed them and pulled them from under the wagon.

Then a pair of strong arms grabbed Abigail, hands like vices, and pulled her from under the wagon and stood her on her feet. There before her was a black-and-red-painted Ottawa warrior, eyes red and bloodshot, staring down at her as he placed his knife against her chest.

With an evil sneer, made worse by the war paint and the blood already splattered across his face and chest, the warrior had begun to cut away the strings of her bodice when the front of his face exploded, spraying her with warm blood as he toppled forward, tearing her bodice away but releasing her at the same time.

Fear and adrenaline pumping through her veins, Abigail turned and began to run as fast as her legs could carry her towards the woods, her heart racing and thumping in her ears as she sucked in air through her mouth and pumped her arms.

***

Jacob lowered his rifle and began to load, watching the Indian who had just grabbed a woman pitch forward. Konkapot covered Jacob as he loaded, watching the woman take off in a dead sprint towards the woods, towards them. Two Indians also spotted her and were hooting a war cry, charging in pursuit.

They were closing fast on Jacob and Konkapot, who were alone. Peter and Samuel had run off to rescue a young child who had run from the wagons. Jacob knew he would not finish loading before the Indians overtook the woman.

"Take him," Jacob commanded as he dropped his half-loaded rifle and began to rise up, pulling his tomahawk from his belt. At the same time, the three wolves exploded from the crouch and charged towards the Ottawas.

***

Abigail was pumping her arms and running as fast as she could go, tears streaming along her blood-smeared cheek, hearing her two pursuers gaining on her. Her foot caught on her skirt and she fell to the ground hard, which knocked the wind out of her as she sprawled face first into the dirt. She heard a whistling noise followed by a wet smack just above her.

She was still trying to take in air to her strained lungs when she felt a gust of wind as something grey jumped over her and another set of strong hands grabbed her. Terror gripped her, and, determined not to let these demons take her, she began to struggle. All she heard next was a wet thud, quickly followed by a second crashing sound, and the strong hands released her.

Sparkles still swimming before her eyes, Abigail began to look up when she heard, "Miss, are you all right?"

Abigail's vision cleared, she took in a shallow breath, and looked up into the face of Jacob, who was reaching down to help her up, a bloody tomahawk in his right hand.

Jacob hadn't been able to believe his luck when the woman had tripped and fallen, giving him a clear angle to attack one warrior while the three wolves took down the other. Making quick work of the warrior, Jacob helped Abigail up to her feet and led her into the woods where Konkapot handed Jacob his rifle, simply stating, "It's loaded."

Jacob nodded his thanks and returned his tomahawk to the small of his back. They both spun around at the sound of movement in the woods. Samuel came through the brush, followed by Peter holding a little girl, the one they had seen running from the wagon line. They all knelt down, and the little girl was passed to Abigail for safekeeping. Peter put his finger to his lips and said "shh," then winked and joined the others observing the massacre. It was utter bedlam as the Indians were now liquored up, shooting wildly into the air if they weren't killing the oxen, scalping, or murdering.

"They're occupied. Now is the time to move," commanded Jacob, and they all nodded.

Jacob reached down and helped Abigail to her feet, the young girl clutching fiercely to her.

"We'll get you safely home miss, don't worry," whispered Jacob. "Just be quiet, stay with us, and follow our orders."

Abigail nodded quickly and fell in line with Jacob as Konkapot led out, Peter on the left and Samuel on the right, creating a protective triangle with the three wolves ranging in front and to the sides. They had only moved about a quarter mile when they came upon Captain Burbank leading about forty-five Rangers, followed by a Colonel Hart with four hundred Provincials.

Jacob quickly told them what had happened and the number of enemy that was to their front. While Captain Burbank understood what it meant, Colonel Hart clapped his hands together in glee, saying, "The game is afoot. We'll bag the lot of them if they are as drunk as you say they are!" Captain Burbank simply rolled his eyes and shook his head.

Turning, Colonel Hart waved his men forward and they jogged towards the site of the ambush. Waiting for the Provincials to move, Captain Burbank turned to Jacob.

"Sergeant, get these two to safety and report to Rogers. Tell him what happened."

Jacob nodded. Captain Burbank smiled and clasped Jacob on the shoulder, and then led his Rangers after Colonel Hart.

Nodding to their comrades as they jogged by, Jacob pointed for Konkapot to lead them on to the fort. Neither Abigail nor the little girl said a word, their minds trying to adjust to what they had witnessed, the shock holding onto them tightly. After some time, they came out of the woods and into the valley with Fort Edward in the distance, as the sun began to set, casting long shadows across the fields.

Some of the survivors had already reached the fort, which was all abuzz with activity as the garrison assembled, the drums beating out the long roll. Jacob bent down and told Abigail, "I'm taking you to someone who will take care of you." She nodded numbly, stumbling along.

Frederic Best was standing on the porch of his shop, watching all of the activity when he spotted Jacob heading towards them with a blood-covered woman and a young child.

Calling for his wife, Frederic met Jacob as he came up to the shop. Jacob said, "Those bloody fools let that supply column go out with little escort, and they paid for it. Look after these survivors will you?"

"Aye, laddie, that we'll do," Mr. Best assured Jacob as Mrs. Best placed her motherly arms around Abigail and the little girl and began to lead them into their house.

"Wait, what's your name?" called Abigail to Jacob as he turned to walk away. Jacob turned back and replied, "Clarke, Ranger Jacob Clarke." He nodded, turned, and began to trot out towards the footbridge for the island. Peter waved at the little girl and joined Samuel and Konkapot, following after Jacob with the wolves right behind them.

Rogers had all of the Rangers assembled as Jacob reported what he had observed. Rogers shook his head. "Damnable, bloody fools. This could have been prevented!" he growled.

He turned and looked at Jacob. "You were right, as usual Jacob. I am damn glad to have you around."

As night had fallen, Rogers dismissed the Rangers, but told them to be ready to move at a moment's notice. As the formation broke up, Rogers called over to Jacob, who stopped.

Rogers walked up to him and looked straight at him. "Is there any way I can convince you to become a lieutenant? I need good leaders, and you're one of the best with that uncanny sense of premonition of yours. I have lost count of how many times you have pulled my bacon out of the fire."

Rogers looked seriously into Jacob's eyes. "I could really use a leader like you. You've seen what we're up against, and who are leading us. Think on it."

Jacob nodded that he would, and Rogers instructed Jacob to see to his men and get some rest and food, but not to go far, because they might be heading out soon. Jacob, Konkapot, Samuel, and Peter were surrounded by other Rangers as they sat around a fire, cooking their food and telling what had happened to the wagons. Their rifles and shooting bags were close at hand.

The hardened Rangers shook their heads, and some comments of "bloody animals" could be heard from around the fire. Jacob, sitting up against a log, fell asleep as the day's wear on him finally caught up. He was quickly followed by the others.

It was past midnight when they were all awakened by Rogers, who informed them that the General wanted them to pursue these attackers and finish them. The story of the massacre had

A Fury of Wolves

spread like wildfire, and all seven hundred Rangers were thirsting for some revenge.

"We're going to be moving fast to get ahead of them," commanded Rogers. "We're moving in light order. Make sure everyone has at least sixty rounds and powder, water, and some food."

It was around two in the morning when Rogers led his Rangers from the island, and they moved quickly to the lake. There, just before sunrise, the Rangers piled into bateaux and moved at a steady, mile-eating pace to Sabbath Day Point. Believing the enemy to be weighed down with plunder, prisoners, and drink, Rogers pushed his Rangers hard to make up time and distance to get ahead of their quarry, and using the lake would help in this endeavor.

Once on shore, the Rangers moved overland and through the mountains to get to the narrows, where Rogers planned to ambush the enemy. However, when they arrived at the narrows, the Rangers spotted tracks showing that the enemy had already passed. They had just missed them.

Grabbing his bonnet and kicking the dirt, Rogers shook his head and swore, cursing his hated enemies. Looking at his tired Rangers who had kept up a tough pace, Rogers told them, "We'll get them next time, I promise you," and he instructed his men to load their boats and head back to the encampment on the southern shore, where they could rest.

While at the encampment, Rogers had begun sending out scouting patrols when a messenger from Fort Edward arrived. General Abercrombie had received word of fresh enemy tracks near the fort, indicating another enemy force. The general instructed Rogers to find and eliminate this threat.

Since some of his Rangers were still worn-out from the forced march, Rogers split his force with the newly promoted

Major Putnam leading an ambush to South Bay while Rogers led another ambush to East Bay and Wood Creek. Both ambushes had no luck, and Rogers decided to regroup his Rangers and head back to Fort Edward.

Fuming from constantly missing his quarry, Rogers received permission to conduct a sweep in force to find the elusive enemy. The Rangers were issued ten days of rations, and their strength was augmented by about a hundred British regulars, a hundred and fifty of the good British light infantry, and some Provincials. General Abercrombie agreed with Rogers and wanted this new threat found. It was interfering with his logistics to the lake.

Jacob and his small section would follow Rogers; it seemed they were becoming his personal detail or security force. "Maybe he just likes having us around," Samuel remarked as he finished packing his haversack. Peter responded, "Ya, especially when he gets into trouble."

The combined force departed the fort in the early morning, and continued to scout around the area, but other than seeing some canoes on the lake, there were no enemies sighted. The force camped at the ruins of old Fort Anne, and, believing they were safe, Rogers accepted a challenge from an officer of the 80th Light Infantry to see who the better shot was.

Jacob leaned against a log with a dumfounded look on his face as he watched Rogers prep his rifle for the shooting match. "Is he really going to do this, on a scout?" Konkapot asked. "This violates everything he has pounded into us."

Jacob grimaced and shook his head. "No, this doesn't sit well with me either." Rising to his feet, Jacob approached Rogers and whispered, "This is not a good idea, sir."

Rogers just looked at Jacob as he checked the priming in his rifle. "I believe I know what is safe and what is not, and seeing we haven't heard or sighted any enemy, why not?" Rogers stared at Jacob with a steady gaze.

"It's your decision, if you feel it's safe," Jacob responded, knowing he wasn't going to change Rogers's mind, and he returned to sit against a tree with Samuel, Konkapot, and Peter. Samuel looked at Jacob in disbelief as he slid down the tree and sat next to them.

"He's doing it? He's really violating his own rules?" stammered Samuel, and Jacob nodded, concerned. "Perhaps everything is taking a toll, even on the major," answered Jacob. "Maybe Rogers has lost his mind."

***

The sound of rifles and cheers could be heard, but the force was not as safe as they had thought they were. Also hearing the sound of the marksmanship challenge was one of Rogers's old nemesis, Joseph Martin, who had recently returned and was leading a raiding party of fifty French regulars, a hundred Canadians, and over a hundred and fifty Abenaki and Ottawa warriors.

It had been the Rangers' tracks that had been spotted earlier, yet Martin had not been able to locate them. Smiling to himself, Martin suspected that it might be the Rangers he was hearing. As he crept closer to observe old Fort Anne, his suspicion was confirmed. So Rogers had survived the fight on snowshoes! Martin felt relieved that he would have another chance to kill Rogers himself.

Moving his force quietly, Martin established a crescent-shaped ambush not far from Fort Anne and began the waiting game.

"So my old friend, what are you up to?" Martin mused. "Why are you doing this very obvious thing? Are you setting a trap for me, I wonder?"

***

Jacob and his men had a restless night, wondering if they were being set up. While Rogers did win the shooting contest, Jacob was wondering at what price. After they did their stand-to prior to sunup, Rogers motioned the column to head out and head toward the fort.

***

Martin's patience paid off as he watched the advance party of Rogers's column walk into the center of his trap. In the low light of the dawn, he could see an officer leading the party, and Martin rubbed his hands in anticipation. Waiting until they were almost on top of them, Martin and some of his men quickly and quietly subdued the officer, and a lieutenant, and three privates and dragged them into the woods. Martin was disappointed that he had not got Rogers himself, but he had caught Major Putnam instead.

As Putnam and the others were being dragged off, the main body came into the trap, and Martin ordered his men to open fire. The terrain was thick, and he used it to his advantage to channel the Rangers and the regulars, making it easier for his men to shoot them and harder for them to shoot back. The front of the column took the brunt of the fire, with many men falling broken and shattered to the forest floor.

"You bloody well were right!" yelled Samuel as he dove for cover behind a tree when the ambush was sprung, "I hate it when you're right!"

Reacting to the sound of gunfire, Rogers, followed by Jacob and the other Rangers, charged forward into the grey smoke and chaos of the ambush. Rogers began giving directions and shoring up some of the shaken men who were on the verge of running. Jacob, Konkapot, Samuel, and Peter moved to Rogers's left and found cover behind a large fallen tree, where they began to engage the attackers.

Jacob's anger again boiled over. He was frustrated that this ambush could have been prevented had they followed the rules. Aiming at a Canadian, Jacob waited for him to look around a tree before firing, the ball taking him at the bridge of his nose. "Damn fool," growled Jacob as he loaded his rifle.

Rangers began to spread out, and, having fought through the thick underbrush, they began to take the enemy under fire. Some of the Canadians appeared to turn and run. Most of the Indians stayed and, challenging the Rangers with their war cries, gave as good as they got with their muskets and rifles. The Rangers challenged back with their own war cries as their rifles barked.

The British regulars and light infantry were moving up and in true British fashion, began firing in volleys at the enemy who ducked or dropped low just before the command to fire was given.

Jacob watched as into the middle of this maelstrom of fire and smoke jumped an Ottawa War Chief, who stood a good six feet four inches tall. Landing on a log, he killed two British regulars outright with his tomahawk.

Their captain reacted by swinging his musket and hitting the huge war chief in the head with the butt of his musket. It didn't seem to stun or slow him down, other than causing his head to bleed. He simply turned and buried his tomahawk into the head of the British captain who had hit him with the musket.

Raising his blood-caked tomahawk, the chief gave a great war cry, which was quickly stopped short when Rogers ran up, yelling his own war cry, and shot the war chief in the head at point-blank range. That finally toppled him. Rogers jumped up on the tree and yelled, "Come up you French dogs … like men!" Rogers's challenge echoed off the trees and around the battle.

Seeing Rogers exposing himself, Samuel again muttered, "He has lost his mind!" Jacob shook his head. "Come on lads, he'll need our help," and started towards Rogers.

With the French attacking the right, Rogers saw Jacob approach and commanded him to lead a hundred men and secure a small hill on their right to stop the French. Jacob nodded, turned, and with a commanding, "Rangers follow me," led a company to a small hill where they met a group of charging French regulars.

Both sides yelling at the top of their lungs paused and opened fire on one another at close range. Jacob heard the balls snapping past his ears and head as he knelt down and fired at a French officer. The musket and rifle balls were thick as bees, snapping and buzzing, sending splinters in all directions. Jacob was in the process of ramming his next ball down his rifle when the French launched a bayonet attack against them.

Quickly pulling his rammer out, Jacob fired from the hip without returning his rammer, knocking an attacking Frenchman back into his comrade, guts spilling all around them tangling their feet. Dropping his rifle, Jacob pulled his tomahawk and knife just in time to block a bayonet thrust to his mid-section.

The Frenchman's charge had the momentum and knocked Jacob over on his back. The Frenchman began a new thrust with his bayonet. Jacob was trying to untangle himself from a fallen log and get his tomahawk up when the Frenchman's head exploded; Konkapot had fired at point-blank range.

Reaching down, Konkapot helped Jacob to his feet.

"Thanks," Jacob said as Konkapot smiled and nodded.

Then his chest exploded outward as a French ball tore through and pulled Konkapot's life from his body. As Konkapot began to fall, Jacob grabbed his rifle and seeing the Frenchman who had just shot Konkapot, quickly aimed and killed the man who had just killed his friend.

Jacob snapped inside. All of the rage, pain, frustration, and remorse he had been carrying inside exploded out all at once. Dropping the empty rifle, Jacob picked up his tomahawk and charged forward into the attacking French. His vision was red as his anger boiled, racing forward with no concern at his own safety, a berserker rage taking over.

Another Frenchman thrust his bayonet, but Jacob simply brushed it aside with his left hand and buried his tomahawk in the soldier's head. Spinning around the falling Frenchman, Jacob flashed his tomahawk once more, severing the arm of one attacking Frenchman as a second fired blindly, the ball passing through Jacob's clothes and digging a bloody gouge along his left ribs.

Jacob was oblivious to the pain; he became a killing machine, spinning, and chopping, rending lives from his enemies. He became a moving nightmare, a whirling, death-dealing devil covered in the blood of his enemies as he charged forward deeper into the French forces.

"Samuel!" Peter yelled as he pointed at Jacob and the fallen Konkapot.

"Ah, damn!" yelled Samuel as he joined Peter to go after Jacob, who seemed to have gone mad. Jacob had moved into the middle of a group of French regulars, tomahawk flashing and rending.

Samuel took a quick site and fired at a Frenchman who was about to stab Jacob in the back. Peter aimed and took another Frenchman who was aiming at Jacob. Peter and Samuel were trying to move through the thick brush and fallen logs, which were slowing their advance.

From their right, a group of Ottawa warriors burst out and collided with Peter. There was a loud, snapping sound as Peter turned. As the Indians ran into him, he had gotten his leg caught on a fallen log, the force snapping the bone. Peter screamed in pain as Samuel fired, taking out one of the Indians. Dropping his rifle, Samuel picked up a French musket with a bayonet and stabbed the other Indian who was raising his war club to smash an injured Peter.

Retaking his rifle, Samuel moved to Peter, helped to get his leg free, and began to help him to safety, hoping Jacob didn't get himself killed. The terrifying visage of a blood-soaked Jacob, eyes maddened and tomahawk dripping, was enough to break the spirits of the attacking Frenchmen, who turned and began to run away.

Jacob, tomahawk and knife at his side, blood dripping, finally collapsed to his knees from exhaustion, screaming, tears running down his face, swinging his tomahawk at anyone who came near him. Kneeling on the ground, surrounded by several dead French and Indian warriors, Jacob sobbed as the pain within his soul finally rushed out, the loss of his friend being the final straw.

Soon, Jacob's vision cleared, his breathing returned to normal, and he shakily stood up. Moving back, he looked at his bloody knife, then knelt down and wiped the blade on a dead Frenchman. He picked up his rifle and rammer, loaded, looked at Konkapot's broken body, and then turned to join the rest of the Rangers on top of the small hill.

Rogers was organizing a defense, having his men stack logs into breastworks in case the enemy returned. All the Rangers, Rogers included, stopped and stared at the blood-smeared and splattered Jacob with Konkapot's body over his shoulder, and Samuel, who was supporting a limping Peter, when he entered the perimeter. Jacob laid Konkapot's body with the others in the center, then moved over and joined the other Rangers, who nodded their heads, and returned to work.

Jacob helped finish their breast works and then went to check on Samuel and Peter, who had been sent with the wounded to another defensive position nearby. Samuel's shoulder was bloody and bandaged. A French musket ball had just missed him, but it caused great splinters, which had pierced his shoulders. Peter's left leg was broken and splinted.

Both men looked at Jacob and nodded, understanding his grief for the loss of Konkapot. Jacob went back to the breastworks, Rogers watching him with concern in his eyes. Rogers realized he had violated his own rules, and now his men were paying the price.

Rogers wanted to approach and say something to Jacob, but that demonic look in Jacob's eyes made Rogers change his mind. "Well, if he kills me, I can't blame him," Rogers commented to himself. "He warned me, and I ignored it."

Jacob's expression was stoic, though his eyes spoke volumes. Rogers was grooming Jacob to be an officer, and now this had happened. "He won't trust me," Rogers shook his head. "He has lost his friend, and it's because of me. I wonder if I lost him, too."

Rangers stood at the ready, waiting to see if the enemy would attack again. Martin, satisfied he had hurt them badly and had captured several of the Rangers, including Major Putnam, had ordered his men to break up into small groups and return to Fort Carillon.

As the night fell, the only sound was that of the whippoorwills and night insects. The Rangers waited but soon felt the enemy was gone. Rogers looked over and saw Jacob sitting next to the body of Konkapot, and he shook his head. This had been a heavy butcher's bill for a stupid marksmanship challenge.

"Damn, bloody damn," Rogers muttered. Perhaps the war was dulling his senses. But he had thought they were safe. Still, he had lost too many good men, including Major Putnam, who was missing and believed captured.

In the morning, the Rangers and the regulars bundled up their injured and their dead and began to move back to Fort Edward. Jacob, having made a travois, pulled Konkapot's body as Samuel helped Peter limp along on his broken leg. Along the way, the column met with reinforcements who helped to carry the wounded. But Jacob refused help and pulled his burden silently, walking slowly until they arrived at Fort Edward later that day.

CHAPTER 8

HONOR AND REMEMBRANCE

Instead of taking Konkapot to the Rangers' cemetery, Jacob pulled the travois to the camp of the Stockbridge Indians. As Jacob passed by Mr. Best's shop, Abigail spotted him and was about to run out when Mr. Best took her by the arm and shook his head, "no."

"Now's not the time lassie. It's best to wait for a bit," counseled Mr. Best.

Abigail looked at Mr. Best in confusion.

"That man on the travois, don't you remember him from the other day?"

Abigail stared at Jacob's back as he continued on towards the Stockbridge camp.

"That was his best friend there, the same man that helped to save you."

Mrs. Best came up to see what they were looking at and saw the travois.

"Oh no, not again. Not to that poor man," whispered Mrs. Best.

Abigail looked at Mrs. Best and asked what had happened to Jacob. Both Mr. and Mrs. Best told Jacob's story, recounting all of the friends he had lost, the woman he had loved who was lost, all of the pain that Jacob had suffered while serving on the frontier.

Abigail turned and stared at the shrinking size of Jacob and his burden, a small tear of sympathy beginning to travel down along her cheek.

When Jacob arrived at the Stockbridge Camp, he was met by Chief Naunauphtaunk, who had called for the shamans. The Stockbridge Indians began to line up as Jacob moved towards the camp silently, escorted by Chief Naunauphtaunk. The warriors began to give an undulating war cry in honor of Konkapot and Jacob.

The shamans met them and took charge of the travois, moving Konkapot to be prepared for a Mohican burial. Resting his hands on Jacob's shoulder, Chief Naunauphtaunk nodded and told Jacob they would prepare him and they would honor Konkapot that night. Jacob nodded his head in thanks and turned to return to the island.

On the island, Jacob went over to check on Peter and Samuel, who were in the surgery. Jacob told them about honoring Konkapot that night and both agreed they would be there no matter what the surgeons said.

When Jacob returned to the hut, the wolves took their places near him. They too felt the somber loss of Konkapot, especially Raven, who after a while departed on her own.

Jacob cleaned his rifle, Konkapot's, and even Peter's and Samuel's, leaning them up against the wall. The routine activity helped him to cope, though he did keep looking at Konkapot's empty bunk. Then he sat in his quiet hut, alone except for the memories of all who had been lost. Jacob walked over to the cemetery and visited the grave of Patrick, his first section leader, who had been killed during the battle at the lake back in 1755.

"Well, you old Mic. They're all slowly joining you, my old friend. Soon you'll have your own squad of Rangers."

Then he went over to Maggie's grave and stood for a bit.

"Take care of her also, you old Mic. Watch over them all until I can join you."

As Jacob stood, he heard someone walk up to him. He turned and looked at Major Rogers, who stood next to Jacob, looking at the rows of the fallen. After a moment of silence, Rogers turned and looked at Jacob.

"I am truly sorry, Jacob," Rogers began. "I know it may not sit well with you, but I am truly sorry for what happened to your friend."

It was a hard stare that Jacob gave Rogers, fighting the different emotions that still boiled within him. While he knew it wasn't Rogers who pulled the trigger, his actions were just as guilty for the lost of his friend. Jacob also knew, though he would be angry and morn his friend, it would not bring him back from the dead.

Jacob nodded, and then looked at Rogers. "You didn't kill him. The French killed him."

Then Jacob stared directly into Rogers's eyes, and boldly stated, "You did violate your own rules, and for what? It was a heavy price for pride or bragging rights." Rogers nodded, and Jacob continued, "Remember this lesson. Don't make this mistake again."

Stepping back and letting out a heavy sigh, Jacob held his hand out to Rogers who slowly took it. "I don't blame you sir, but we need to make those bastards pay and pay hard." Rogers nodded, turned, and returned to his hut.

Satisfied, Jacob began to move over to the Stockbridge Camp, along with several of the Rangers who wanted to honor Konkapot. There was a loud screeching sound as several Rangers were helping Samuel push an old cart with Peter propped up inside.

"Told you we would not miss it," commented Peter at which Jacob even broke out in a smile.

The Rangers joined the Stockbridge Indians in a patch of woods near the river, where a burial plot had been prepared with field stones piled nearby. Konkapot had been cleaned and dressed in a mix of Mohican and Ranger clothing. Lying next to the grave was Raven, watching over Konkapot one last time, honoring him in her own wolfish way.

The shamans chanted and sang, burning tobacco and calling to the Great Spirit to accept Konkapot. Warriors and Rangers passed, leaving trinkets in the grave with Konkapot, items he would need in the afterlife. Jacob approached and knelt down and looked at his longtime friend one last time. He drew his knife and placed it on Konkapot's chest. Laying his hand on his friend, Jacob said farewell and moved on.

As they covered Konkapot's grave with fieldstones, the Stockbridge Indians began to chant, wishing him a safe journey and a warm welcome from the Great Spirit. Jacob took up the chant as well. Watching from a distance, Abigail and Mr. Best observed the ceremony, Mr. Best whispering a prayer for both Konkapot and Jacob.

Once the grave was covered, Jacob went over, placed a Ranger bonnet on a stick and drove it into the ground next to the grave. He looked down at Raven, who had laid her head on her paws, not moving. With a heavy sigh, he looked one last time, and then turned to join the rest of the Stockbridge and the Rangers in a clearing where a large fire had been built. The celebration and wake for Konkapot's life had begun.

Mr. Best had brought a few casks of rum and ale with him, and he was pouring, while Abigail watched Jacob and the others. She was intrigued with this Ranger, not only because he had saved her life, but also because she sensed there were layers to this scarred and obviously caring man.

She watched how both the Indians and the others treated him with respect as they drank toasts to Konkapot and his life. Soon more toasts rang out and singing, and then music began to play. Both Rangers and Stockbridge alike started to dance around the fire. Sipping on a mug of rum, its warmth flowing through and relaxing her, Abigail watched Jacob and his two remaining close friends, having learned their names were Peter and Samuel.

Abigail looked in astonishment as Stockbridge Indians came up, removed Samuel's hat revealing the bald spot from when he had survived a scalping, and rubbed it for good luck. Soon the Stockbridge women came up and rubbed his head as well.

Peter still sat in his cart; laughing and speaking in a strange language that was similar to the Dutch she had heard from shop owners near Albany. Then there was Jacob, sitting, drinking, and finally laughing, his emotions freed at last. There was some light now in his piercing blue eyes, a different side from the fighter and savior she had first met.

More Rangers arrived along with other Provincials, all stopping by to talk to Jacob before heading over to Mr. Best and his cask. Major Rogers made a quick call to pass his best to Jacob and the others and made a toast to Konkapot and to all their fallen, to which the Rangers and the Indians responded with a loud cheer. Then he returned to his duties on the island, squeezing Jacob's shoulder as he departed. Music continued to play, and men and women began to dance, or to dance as best as they could, seeing how drunk they were becoming.

Jacob continued to sit and drink, speaking to Rangers and Stockbridge in animated conversations, sometimes spilling his mug of rum as he pushed a point. Abigail looked over to Mr. Best. He looked at her, smiled, nodded his head, winked, and returned to filling empty cups.

Standing up, Abigail, feeling a little tipsy from the rum, settled her skirts into place and asked herself if she knew what she was doing. She thought for a second, answered "no," and strode across the field towards Jacob. He was laughing at a joke a Ranger had told him when he spotted her approach.

"Do you dance, Ranger Clarke?" asked Abigail.

Jacob looked up and replied, "No, not very well."

Acting quickly before her courage wore off, Abigail grabbed Jacob's arms and pulled him to his feet, spilling his rum, and dragged him towards the other dancers.

She said, "Good, neither can I."

Joining the whirling and spinning dancers, Abigail took Jacobs hands, and they began to spin and twirl with the others. Seeing Jacob and Abigail dancing together caused both the Stockbridge and the Rangers to hoot, holler, and clap in time with the music.

Jacob had been coming to terms with the loss of Konkapot when the woman he had rescued at the massacre came up and dragged him into the dance. Perhaps it was the rum having an effect, or the fact that it had been a while since Maggie's death, but he began to feel an attraction to this woman, though he didn't know her name.

She stood only as tall as his chin, with reddish-blonde hair that fell upon her shoulders from under her bonnet. She had a strong grip as she man-handled Jacob about, spinning one way and another. Jacob looked into her hazel eyes and saw a spark he had not seen since the death of Maggie, and finally he just released himself to the moment and flowed with it, letting go of the sorrow and embracing happiness for a short period. War could make life short, so he'd better start enjoying it for a change before his time came up.

As they both danced and laughed, passing near a clapping Mr. Best who handed them both mugs of rum, they were joined by other Rangers and Stockbridge Indians in a celebration of life, not only Konkapot's, but of being alive in general.

In time, the rum had its effect, and the Rangers and Stockbridge Indians began to return to their camps or to just fall to the ground and start snoring loudly. Several Rangers were pushing the cart as Peter sang German songs off-key, while once again it seemed that Samuel had been captured by a few of the Stockbridge women.

***

Jacob, sweaty from the dancing, escorted Abigail towards Mr. Best's home where she was staying for now. From the shadows, watching all of the activity was Big Harpe, especially intrigued by this pretty young thing who had taken an interest in the big Ranger, who had stood up to him and Maclane. "Well, well now, isn't that interesting?" Harpe whispered to himself as he watched the two stumble off towards the sutler shop.

A snap of a branch alerted Harpe who turned to see a rather tipsy Mohawk woman enter a bush nearby and squat down. Harpe smiled to himself. This was turning into a rather good evening, he thought as he stalked towards the Indian. She was completely unaware as she stood up weaving from her squat, until Harpe's big hand closed around her mouth, his other arm going around her throat until she passed out. Lifting her easily over his shoulders, Harpe headed out to his favorite play area at the abandoned farm, softly whistling to himself.

***

Abigail's left arm was linked through Jacob's right, stumbling from time to time, as they entered Mr. Best's storage yard. As

Jacob turned to wish Abigail a good night, she boldly reached up and, taking his head in both hands, kissed him fiercely.

Surprised, Jacob actually began to resist, until the floodgate of pent-up emotions cracked open, and he closed his eyes and returned Abigail's kisses fiercely and passionately. She pulled him close, and they crashed into the wall of one of the storage sheds, their kisses becoming wilder and more intense. Without any care in the world, Jacob pulled Abigail into the shed and their passion burst into a roaring flame that burned his sorrow and regret away.

The next morning, Jacob awoke as the sun rose and streamed into the storage shed where he and Abigail had fallen asleep on soft supply bales. Abigail had curled up and was sleeping soundly on Jacob's chest, but she woke as soon as he began to move.

Jacob slowly stood, stretched, and began to dress, Abigail admiring the rugged physique, but aware also of the numerous scars including the fresh bullet gouge from the recent fight. Dressing and straightening out her hair, Abigail went over and embraced Jacob, then rested her head on his chest.

"By the way, I never did get your name miss," remarked Jacob as he looked down at her.

"It's Abigail, Abigail Schuyler from Saratoga."

Jacob nodded and kissed her once more

"Planning on staying around here long?"

Squeezing Jacob hard, Abigail shrugged her shoulders and once more rested her head on his chest.

"I would like to, but I am sure my father and mother will become worried and may send their people to find me. But until then…" She looked up and kissed Jacob. "… I plan on staying around."

Jacob, making sure the area was clear, led Abigail from the shed and walked her around to the front of Mr. Best's shop.

Abigail stepped up onto the porch so she could look into Jacob's eyes, commenting that he had the sharpest blue eyes she had ever seen.

"Thank you for an enjoyable evening, Miss Schuyler. I would like to call again if possible," said Jacob as he gave her a half bow like a proper gentlemen.

Giggling, Abigail curtsied and replied, "Why Mr. Clarke, I would be honored if you would call upon me again."

Snatching a quick kiss, Abigail turned and entered Mr. Best's store, and Jacob turned the other way to return to the island. As he passed the fort, he observed General Abercrombie and some of his staff officers ride out and head down the road towards Albany.

Jacob walked out onto the footbridge, thinking to himself. While he did mourn the loss of Konkapot and would always mourn the friends he had lost, it was if an old piece of his heart had reawakened for the first time since the death of Maggie, and it felt all right. He did not believe that he was insulting her memory; she would have wanted him to love again, to live life to the fullest.

CHAPTER 9

THE REVENGE OF THE 44TH

Jacob stopped and looked into their hut, where the sound of Peter's snoring was loud enough to be heard from outside. Poking his head in, he saw Peter sprawled out on his back, leg propped up on some packs, and mouth open, letting out snoring worse than a bear with a cold. On the other side of the cabin was Samuel, but with a rather slim feminine arm over his chest, and he was softly snoring.

Shaking his head but smiling, Jacob turned and walked over to Major Rogers's hut. Inside, Rogers and some of the company commanders were going over a plan, and Jacob waited until they were finished.

"Have your companies ready to move by mid-day," commanded Rogers before the captains turned and headed out of the hut. Captain Stark was walking by when he stopped and placed his hand on Jacob's shoulder, squeezed, nodded to him, and then left.

"Something I can do for you Sergeant Clarke?" asked Rogers.

Jacob approached and asked, "Is there anything I need to be aware of sir?" Rogers shook his head. "I am sending as many companies as I can out to locate our missing men and Major Putnam. I want you to stay here and take care of your men."

Jacob nodded. "Sir, I have been doing some thinking, and I have made my decision. You're right. We need good leaders," said Jacob.

Pointing out over his shoulder to the camp, he said, "They need good leaders. I want to volunteer and become a lieutenant, sir. I will still follow you into hell to scalp Lucifer and return if need be."

Rogers smiled, nodded, and shook Jacob's hand. At least it seemed to Rogers that Jacob wasn't holding a grudge against him for Konkapot's loss, and that was a relief.

"When was the last time you were paid?" Rogers asked.

Jacob recalled that it had been some time.

Nodding, Rogers walked over to his desk, took out a quill, a parchment, and some ink. After some quick scratching, he handed the note to Jacob, and said, "I found out those wagons that were attacked were carrying most of the British payroll, but ours is still here."

For some reason the paymaster had taken the entire British payroll with him on the way to Lake George instead of leaving behind the portion that would go to the soldiers at Fort Edward. Some thought he had just wanted to keep a close eye on the money. He would never be able to explain, because he had been killed in the massacre.

"See the new paymaster for what is owed, plus a little extra which I authorized. Go to Saratoga or Albany and get a proper Ranger officer's uniform. I wrote down a merchant who has good materials in Saratoga."

Rogers scratched out another document and handed it to Jacob.

"This is a pass to allow you to go to either Saratoga or Albany to get uniformed or just to go and get some time away from here. I know you have no family, but it can't hurt to take a break to get a fresh perspective on why we're fighting."

Shaking Jacob's hand one last time, Rogers returned to his work, and Jacob returned to his hut. Reading the orders, Rogers

177

had listed a Philip Schuyler Mercantile as the place to get his new uniform from.

At least the snoring had stopped, and when he entered, Peter was leaning up against the wall, eyes bloodshot, and holding his head, swearing softly in German under his breath. Whoever had spent the night with Samuel was gone, and he was sitting up on his bunk, a slight grin on his face when Jacob entered.

Jacob came in, sat down, and told them what he had done, agreeing to become a lieutenant.

"That's nice, but what happened with the woman you were dancing with?" asked Samuel with a twinkle in his eye.

Jacob snorted and said, "Probably the same thing you did with those two Mohican girls," and all three began laughing.

Peter shuffled and hopped to reach under his bunk, and he pulled out a long box that he kept his things in.

"Well, if you're going to be an officer, you need to have one of these," grunted Peter as he pulled a short, thick bladed Jaeger Sword out. It was the one he had found during the fighting around Fort William Henry when they had rescued Konkapot. He handed it to Jacob.

"Yeah, that's right," commented Samuel, who reached under his bunk and pulled out his box, removing a nicely engraved pistol that he had found during the same battle. Samuel had actually found two, but he figured one was enough for Jacob.

"What about you?" Jacob asked Peter, pointing to his splinted leg. Filling his pipe and snorting, Peter shrugged. "At least they didn't cut it off," he said from around his pipe stem. "Dat is a good sign." He puffed then blew a stream of smoke. "But I may not be any good to you if I can't run. My time may be up."

Jacob nodded, and said, "Hopefully, I can keep you around my old friend." Then he looked down at the wolves staring up at him, their tongues hanging out. "And you two as well."

Thanking them both, Jacob told them to take it easy and rest up so they could heal up, and he made his way to the fort. As he moved through the central yard of the fort, the Provincials nodded to him while the regular British soldiers, with the exception of some from the 80th who also nodded, still looked at him with disdain.

Jacob ignored them and made his way to the paymaster. There were some regular British lieutenants and one captain from the 44th in there arguing with the paymaster about their pay. Sitting in the back at a small table were Big Harpe and William Maclane, watching all that was going on around them.

"There is nothing here for you. General Abercrombie has ridden to Albany to secure the pay that was lost in the recent attack. Now move aside." The British officer looked aghast at being so summerly dismissed by the paymaster.

The paymaster waved Jacob forward and accepted the document from Major Rogers. Looking in his ledger, the paymaster whistled and agreed that it had been some time since Jacob had last been paid. Moving into the strong room, the paymaster came out with three bags of coins to the astonishment of the British officers.

"Here is your pay," he said as he dropped the first bag. "Here is the pay from New York," he said as he dropped the second. "And here is the extra pay as instructed by Major Rogers. Please sign the ledger."

He handed Jacob a dipped quill.

"Now hold on one bloody minute!" demanded the captain from the 44th as he grabbed Jacob's arm before he could sign. "This ruddy Provincial, and an enlisted man to boot, is getting paid and I, a commissioned officer of his Royal Majesty's forces, am not?"

The paymaster looked at the captain and simply said, "Yes."

The captain let Jacob's arm go and walked out in a huff.

"Sorry about that," the paymaster apologized. "They're a little testy having found out their pay was captured by the enemy."

Jacob nodded, signed his name in the ledger, and then gathered up his three bags of coins. He could feel the angry eyes upon him as he stepped out and saw the same captain and lieutenants from the 44th talking among themselves with a few other officers and looking at him.

Big Harpe watched with sadistic glee as the British officers stormed out of the office, while Maclane was determining how it would affect his profit margins if the regulars had no pay with which to purchase items. Both were thinking how they could use this situation to their advantage.

Jacob paid them no mind and looked at the other document that Major Rogers had given him. The merchant's name was Philip Schuyler. Jacob stopped and thought about it. What were the chances that this was Abigail's father?

Returning to his hut, Jacob grabbed his rifle, shooting bag, and haversack.

"Going off on an adventure or a knight's errand?" asked Peter.

Jacob shook his head. "Major Rogers instructed me to go purchase an officer's uniform."

Looking down at his well-worn, frayed clothes, he had to agree. Maybe Major Rogers was right. Smoke and Otto looked up from where they were lying, and Jacob scratched them both behind their ears.

"Raven never came back?" Jacob asked, and Samuel shook his head. In fact, they never saw her again. In her grief, she had left the Rangers and gone off into the wild.

Looking down at Smoke, Jacob said, "Well, if I get promoted so do you, Corporal Smoke."

Smoke looked up at Jacob, not understanding anything he had said, head cocked to the side and tongue lolling out in the manner of wolves.

"Look after Smoke while I am away," said Jacob, and both Samuel and Peter nodded. Jacob headed over to Mr. Best's shop and pulled Abigail off to the side, asking if she knew Philip Schuyler.

With a heavy sigh, she nodded. "He's my father."

Jacob explained that Philip Schuyler had been recommended to him for the purchase of his new uniform.

"Do you wish to still stay here?" asked Jacob.

Abigail, looking into his eyes and quickly kissing him, said, "Yes."

Jacob nodded. "Then if he asks, I haven't seen you. I'll be back soon."

Jacob kissed her, turned, and nodded to Mr. and Mrs. Best. They both smiled, Mr. Best winked, and Jacob headed out and began his journey along the Albany Road to Saratoga.

The journey took a couple of days. Jacob walked with his rifle cradled in his arm. It was always ready because he wasn't going to take any chances. It was one of his more relaxing journeys, but he didn't let his guard down. War parties had raided this far south below Fort Edward before.

It had been some time since Jacob had come this way when he had run the Ranger School for the first batch of British officers, who had had him court-martialed for hurting their feelings. It felt odd not heading north into the familiar mountains, passing through farms that were occupied, and seeing other travelers on the road. It almost was if the war had not touched here, and perhaps with all of the blood and death, he and his fellow Rangers' sacrifices had allowed no war to set foot here, at least not yet.

On the morning of the third day, Jacob entered Saratoga, and after asking for directions to the Schuyler Mercantile shop, made his way there. Mr. Best had a nice shop, but it could not compare to this large mercantile store with all types of goods and services available for the town folks.

Knocking the dust off his bonnet, Jacob approached a young woman and asked for Philip Schuyler. Mr. Schuyler came out from a back room and asked what Jacob wanted, and Jacob showed him the letter from Major Rogers.

"Ah, a new lieutenant, I see. Congratulations!" said Mr. Schuyler. "Elizabeth, go fetch Mr. Reynolds and let him know we have a new Ranger officer in need of a uniform."

As Elizabeth ran off to get Mr. Reynolds, Mr. Schuyler looked at Jacob.

"If I may, could I ask you some questions?"

Jacob nodded.

"How bad is it up there? Will the French break through?" he asked.

Jacob talked about the fighting but said he did not believe the French were going to break through. Mr. Schuyler nodded.

"I was a captain. Raised a company in 1755 and was involved in the fighting during the early years. I take it, it hasn't changed much."

Jacob again nodded his agreement. "We may have fought in some of the same actions," Jacob replied, and the two spoke, as soldiers would, of battles and action. Once more Mr. Schuyler looked pensive, and then looked at Jacob directly.

"Are you from Fort Edward, per chance?"

Jacob nodded.

"My daughter Abigail, foolish and headstrong girl that she is, volunteered to help the wounded and went to Fort Edward. Is there a chance you may have seen her? We have had no news."

Jacob looked at Mr. Schuyler and shook his head.

"I'm sorry, sir. I have been out on numerous scouts to Saint Frederic and Fort Carillon. I don't spend much time at Fort Edward," Jacob replied.

Mr. Schuyler understood and started talking again about his military life and experience until Mr. Reynolds arrived. Mr. Reynolds was a tailor, and he began to take Jacob's measurements, who didn't know quite what to do. As the tailor stretched lines with even spaced knots and measured the length of his arms and chest, Jacob felt awkward.

Once the measurements were taken, Elizabeth and another shop worker pulled out the rolls of wool and linen, and Mr. Reynolds began cutting the amount he would need of the dark green and black materials.

"Your uniform will be ready in about five days. Please return then with payment," instructed Mr. Reynolds, who bundled up the cloth and departed for his own shop.

Mr. Schuyler looked at Jacob's dusty and worn bonnet, shaking his head.

"That won't do for an officer. Go see Patrick Finny, our hatter, and get a true Ranger hat such as the one I have seen Major Rogers wear."

Thanking Mr. Schuyler, Jacob found the hatter, who understood what Jacob needed, took measurements of his head, and also told him to come back in five days.

Jacob went over to Shield's Tavern for a warm meal, some rum, and a place for the night. Finding a table in the corner, he leaned his rifle against the wall, took off his bags and haversack, and took a seat.

A bar maid came up, giving a dubious look at Jacob's worn clothing. He simply dropped several New York shillings on the table. The bar maid quickly brightened up and asked what he wanted.

"Warm food and rum," replied Jacob, as he pulled out his pipe and filled the bowl with tobacco, using a candle to light the pipe.

Jacob looked about the room, which was starting to fill as the day was ending. A group of farmers was in a far corner, drinking and talking about the weather. Some merchants were playing cards.

A group of men, pipes in hands and smoke surrounding their heads, were in a deep discussion about politics. They were all finely dressed, and their hands appeared to have never seen a day of hard work. It seemed their conversation was focused around the politics of supporting England, and some of the men were concerned that the English Government was beginning to overstep its bounds.

The bar maid returned with a plate of roast beef, potatoes, and warm bread that she set down in front of Jacob. She winked, and then turned and walked away, her buttocks swishing. Jacob snorted, shook his head, and began to eat his meal. It was amazing how a few coins could change a person.

As Jacob chewed on his roast beef, savoring the flavors of a real meal instead of a field meal, he couldn't help but overhear the political conversation. There seemed to be three distinct ideas. One group argued that they were loyal subjects and should follow faithfully any edict that the crown presented. Another group argued that the colonies were not getting a fair representation as laws and edicts were made without their consent.

It was the third group that caught Jacob's attention. These men were arguing that New York should sue for peace with the French and stop the war. If the war went away, so would the British, and everyone would simply get along. They said the other two groups didn't know what they were talking about. The group that supported peace with the French reminded them how good for business peace would be. Besides, Canada was closer than England and, therefore, it would be cheaper to send their wares to Canada.

Jacob couldn't help himself, some of his pent up frustrations boiled over, and he blurted out, "You have no idea, any of you, what is going on, do you? Do you think you can solve this war here in a tavern?"

The group stopped talking and turned in Jacob's direction, silent.

"What sir, would you know about war?" asked the member of the group who thought peace with France would solve everything.

Jacob slowly stood up, and approached the group, having been hidden in the shadows of the corner.

"I know more about war than all of you put together. I have seen it, lived it, and lost many a friend to it. What have you done?"

The group of finely dressed men was taken aback by Jacob's fearsome visage, scarred face, smoldering icy blue eyes, and deeply stained Ranger uniform, stained from the blood, sweat and powder of fighting. Jacob walked up to the group and stared at all of the men, who remained silent.

"It's easy to sit here where it's safe and sound, away from the blood and gore of battle, and second guess the fighting from your comfortable chairs sipping on spirits. Many of us have died to keep these French you want to negotiate with from coming down here and burning and killing. They and their Indians will not stop until New York and the other colonies are conquered and under their control. There is no negotiating with them. Only killing them will work."

Jacob stared hard at each of them, and they all coughed and looked away. Jacob tossed some coins next to his plate, turned to grab his bags and his rifle, and make his way to a different inn for the night, having lost his appetite. These gentlemen watched in silence. Some of the patrons nodded their heads in agreement with Jacob as he left the tavern, knowing full well what was happening on the frontier to the north.

In the morning, Jacob decided to travel westward to visit the Mohawks and spend time with them while the uniform was being made. Though it had been only one night, he had had enough of this civilized, town living and would feel more comfortable with the Mohawks. Cradling his rifle, Jacob headed westward and found one of the major trails that would lead to one of the Mohawk villages, the sun rising over the eastern mountains, welcoming him.

Jacob enjoyed his time with the Mohawks, finally relaxing for a few days, the longest he had done so in a while. He went out and hunted with the warriors, sat in council, and spoke with the sachems, the war and clan chiefs, on what was occurring in the north. Some of the war chiefs had been up north, fighting the French and their Indian Allies, and they nodded their heads as Jacob recounted the fighting and the battles the French had won.

Sitting in council, Jacob recognized Molly Brandt from his time with Sir William Johnson, and her brother, Joseph. Sitting next to Joseph was Akiatonharónkwen, to whom Jacob had been introduced as Joseph Cook, using his English name. Both Josephs were in discussion, and then Brandt asked Jacob, "We have heard a story of how the French defeated the great English Army at the Carillon. Is this true?"

Jacob nodded, "Yes, it's true. They fought us hard, and the army was forced to return to the southern shore of the lake." Jacob knew he had to choose his words carefully, especially with young war chiefs like Brandt and Cook. Brandt, Cook, and the other war chiefs talked amongst themselves, and Jacob waited for the next questions.

Tekarihoga stood and raised his hand for silence. Tekarihoga, whose English name was Johannes, waited for the chiefs' murmurs to quiet. He looked at Jacob. "What do you think? Can the English beat the French? You have been on the warpath as long as our war chiefs, perhaps longer."

Thinking before he answered Jacob looked around the room at the chiefs, all of whom were watching him. "Yes, I do, if the English leaders change how they make war, I do think we will beat them."

Jacob understood their concerns about the war, knowing they wondered if the enemy would come into their valleys and attack their villages. Jacob recounted their fights and victories, and this satisfied their questions about achieving a victory.

When not in council, Jacob spent a day playing lacrosse against another village, which left him feeling bruised, but alive. Jacob was presented new wampum belts, showing his status as a warrior amongst the Mohawks, in recognition of his deeds as a Ranger.

"Spirit of Okwao," the Mohawk name that had been given to Jacob, the spirit of the wolves, "may the Great Spirit watch over you, guide your hand and make your rifle shoot true. Show these English how warriors truly fight."

When the time came, he departed the Mohawks and returned to Mr. Schuyler's Mercantile in Saratoga. There, his new Ranger uniform was waiting. There was a short, dark green wool coat faced and trimmed in black, with silver buttons and a lieutenant's epaulet on the shoulder. He also had two new dark green breaches, and from the hatter, a new Ranger "jockey" hat, with a black feather attached to it.

He paid Mr. Schuyler and bundled his new uniform, but wore the new hat.

"You're not going to wear it now?" asked Mr. Schuyler.

Jacob shook his head.

"I still have to get back up to the fort, and then I'll wear it."

Mr. Schuyler nodded, shook Jacob's hand, and wished him luck.

Jacob shouldered the bundle of his new uniform and began his trek northward towards Fort Edward. As soon as he was away from the town, he quickly transformed into an alert Ranger, rifle at the ready, watching the woods. The trip was uneventful and after three days, Jacob arrived at Fort Edward, first stopping at Mr. Best's shop where Abigail came out and gave him a big hug and kiss.

"Did you see my father?" she asked.

Jacob replied, "Yes, he did ask about you, but I told him I had been away and had not seen you."

Abigail squeezed his hand, told him to stop by later, and returned into the shop.

Jacob went out to his hut and placed his new uniform on his bunk. Peter was sitting there, leg still splinted and bandaged.

"What's wrong Peter?" asked Jacob.

Peter looked up and sighed. "The surgeon says da war is over for me. My leg may not work right again."

Jacob nodded that he understood.

"Still, I stay here as long as I can to help out where I can."

Jacob reached out, helped Peter to his feet, and handed him his crutch.

"Come on, let's find Samuel and head over to Mr. Best's and get a drink. I'm buying."

Peter's eyes lit up, and he hobbled out after Jacob. Finding Samuel, they slowly trudged over to the shop. When Jacob walked in, there were some Provincials, some Rangers, and even some British regulars in the shop.

Jacob yelled out, "Drinks are on me lads. Mr. Best, pour us some rum!"

Jacob tossed one of his bags that still had coins in it on the bar. The Rangers and Provincials rushed up, and even one of the British regulars from the 80th bellied up to the bar as Mr. Best began to pour.

Abigail came from around back. Jacob motioned for her to come around where he put his arm around her and handed her a mug.

Hoisting his mug, Jacob turned and toasted, "To our comrades, those who were, those who are, and those who will be. Cheers!"

As Jacob was about to take a swallow of his drink, a voice boomed out, "You sir, stop where you are!"

Lowering his mug, Jacob looked around the room, which went deathly silent. Jacob saw a British officer pointing at him.

"Where did you get those coins from?" demanded the officer.

Jacob looked around in confusion, pointed at himself, and asked, "Me, sir?"

The officer replied, "Yes, you sir!"

Jacob shrugged, "My back pay."

"Unlikely story. No one has been paid since the attack," growled the officer, who took the bag and looked at it.

"I am arresting you in the theft of Major Christie's personal money, believed stolen by a Provincial, like you," he sneered.

Jacob stood dumbfounded as British regulars ran in, and two of them grabbed him and began dragging him outside. Samuel looked at Abigail.

"Take care of Peter. I am going to get help!" Samuel said, as he ran out behind the guards and sprinted towards the island. Abigale watched as Jacob was dragged off.

In the back of the shop, pretending to look at wares, Big Harpe smiled to himself; his little game was working out as planned. He had made arrangements with Major Christie's orderly to watch the room when he had to use the latrine. It was easy to pilfer the coins while the orderly was away, then he helped with the spreading of rumors within the fort and amongst the British troops about "overhearing stories from the Rangers of getting even with the British, stealing their coins" and general chaos.

It had taken some time for Harpe to plan out his little game. Of course Maclane had approved, thinking that if Harpe could take the starch out of those Rangers who had stood up for that sutler, then all the better. Now Harpe was going to sit back and enjoy the fun as he watched the chaos unfold. Then he'll make it look like the orderly did it later.

Jacob was pushed and prodded by the British soldiers, their uniforms indicating they were from the 44th. "What the hell happened while I was away?" thought Jacob. He was driven into the fort and locked in a small wooden cell in the fort's guardhouse.

Jacob sat down on the ground and placed his head in his hands, trying to figure out what was going on. A few hours later, Samuel and Lieutenant Daniels arrived.

"Samuel, what the hell is going on?" Jacob asked.

It was Lieutenant Daniels who spoke.

"It doesn't look good. While you were away, someone broke into Major Christie's room and stole several bags of coins. They thought it was a Provincial. Sergeant, er Lieutenant Clarke, no one is here. Major Rogers and all of the officers are still out, and General Abercrombie and his staff are still out as well."

"Then who is in command here?" asked Jacob.

Lieutenant Daniels replied, "Major Christie."

Jacob leaned his head back against the wall and sighed.

"They are going to court-martial you in the morning, and I am the only one here from the corps who can defend you," explained Lieutenant Daniels.

Muttering "great" under his breath, Jacob instructed Samuel to go find his haversack and look for the documents from Major Rogers that showed he had been paid.

Samuel and Lieutenant Daniels left, and Jacob was left to his own thoughts. Things had been going so well after Konkapot's death, and now this.

"Why won't fate just leave me alone for a change," whispered Jacob to himself, "and go bother someone else."

Towards sundown, a guard commanded Jacob to stand back as he opened the cell door. Jacob was surprised to see Abigail with a tray of food and a canteen. He saw that the guard was from the 80th and motioned her inside.

"What's going on?" whispered Jacob to the soldier.

Looking to make sure no one was close by; the soldier from the 80th turned and replied, "It's all bullocks, I think. These bastards are out to prove a point or simply get back at you Rangers for something, I don't really know. I am truly sorry, Sergeant Clarke. I remember you from training us, and your skills have saved my life and the lives of my mates a few times. It doesn't look good."

Jacob nodded and thanked him, and then the guard closed the door and left him and Abigail alone.

Abigail sat down next to Jacob on the ground and leaned against his shoulder as Jacob chewed on some warm corn bread.

"Do you like it?" Abigail asked, and Jacob nodded that he did though it was a bit burned and crunchy.

"Mrs. Best is showing me how to cook. This is so different from being back at home."

Jacob nodded and took a long pull from the canteen.

"What's going to happen in the morning?" she asked as she wiggled closer to Jacob, putting her arms around his waist.

"A trial, and it's probably going to be only for show," replied Jacob, who finished the meal, and then sat there, feeling the closeness of Abigail and enjoying the scent of her.

"Psst, miss, it's time to go," whispered the guard.

Jacob bent down and kissed Abigail deeply, then stood her up.

"I'll be all right," he told her.

She turned and left him, and the cell door was locked behind her.

It was a tough night for Jacob. He couldn't sleep as he thought about what would occur. It was mid-morning when the guard detail came for him, and once again he noticed they were all from the 44th.

Jacob was marched to one of the command barracks and up to the second floor. He entered the room where the court martial would occur. Sitting behind a table in the center was Major Christie himself, and then Jacob noticed the captain and two lieutenants who had been unhappy the day he had been paid. Everyone in the room was from the 44th, and no other unit, Ranger, regular or Provincial alike, was represented.

"Oh, this is not good," thought Jacob as he was brought forward.

Another captain from the 44th stood next to the one who had arrested him at Mr. Best's, and he announced that the prisoner was present for court martial. Major Christie looked up from the document and fixed his eyes upon Jacob.

"Read the charges," Major Christie commanded in a tired voice.

"The accused was found in possession of personal property belonging to Major Christie of the 44th Regiment of Foot.

He is accused of wanton thievery, undisciplined nature, and unbecoming of a soldier. How do you plead?"

Jacob looked up and stated, "I didn't do it. I was not here."

Major Christie with a bored look on his face remarked, "A likely story. Present your case, Captain Hopkins."

Jacob stood in amazement as he heard the tale of how someone had broken into the major's room and stolen his money. Captain Hopkins insisted it had been a Ranger. "Word around the fort has a Ranger bragging about stealing coin and getting back at the loyal subjects of the crown."

Captain Hopkins stopped and looked directly at Jacob, "Are you that Ranger? The evidence clearly shows that you have the coins in your procession, and we all know how you Provincials look down at your betters."

"That is lie. I have said no such things," replied Jacob. But Captain Hopkins waved his hand and replied, "Likely story. So how did you get paid? Any witnesses to support this?"

Jacob saw across the room the same British officers who were present when he had been paid.

"Yes, I have witnesses," Jacob countered. "These officers were present when I was issued and signed for my back pay."

Captain Hopkins turned and looked at the three. "Is this true, Captain Parker? Did you and your fellow gentlemen witness this man getting paid?"

Captain Parker stood and faced Jacob, who recognized him as the member of the 44th who had argued with him and the Quartermaster. "I did not witness this man getting paid. We were denied payment and so was this man who was very cheeky about it, and turned and departed in an ungentlemanly huff."

"You're a damn liar!" growled Jacob, but he was quickly silenced.

Major Christie stated, "I would believe these fine gentlemen of the Royal Army before I would believe the word of an undisciplined Provincial. Still, captain, are there any other witnesses that can confirm the suspicion?"

Captain Hopkins nodded, and motioned to the side of the room. "You there, tell the major what you saw."

Holding his hat in his hand, shuffling forward, was Big Harpe, playing for all his worth the big workman with no brains.

"Yes, yes, me lords. I saw what happened that night," Harpe stammered, looking at his feet.

"Was it this man that you saw?" asked Captain Hopkins.

Shuffling his feet, Harpe looked up trying hard not to break his false face when he looked at Jacob, and then he shrugged. "It was dark, and I saw what looked like this large fellow here, sneaking around the fort."

Jacob again yelled, "Liar!" which resulted in his getting hit in the back by the butt of a musket by a guard, followed by "Silence!" from the major.

Jacob gritted his teeth, and then demanded, "Bring the ledger. It will show I was paid and when." But the major responded that the paymaster was away paying the troops at the lake and was unavailable.

When Jacob demanded he be allowed to show his documents from Major Rogers, he was again summarily silenced.

"Who would believe the word of a Provincial? They all lie and cover for one another," said Captain Hopkins.

Jacob looked at him in astonishment, knowing this was a fight he would not win. Major Christie raised his hand.

"I have heard enough and am ready to pass judgment. This court martial finds this man, whatever his name is, guilty of theft. I sentence you to two hundred lashes to be carried our immediately. The court is dismissed."

Jacob stood in stunned silence as the guards from the 44th grabbed him by his arms and began to march him outside and into the central yard of the fort. Jacob's suspicion that this was all for show was confirmed as a perimeter around the whipping post had already been established by the 44th with bayonet-tipped muskets to keep the few Rangers and Provincials who were present from interfering.

Jacob was marched into the center of the drill yard, his arms were tied to the crossbar of the post, and his frock shirt ripped from his back. While Jacob could not see him, he could hear Captain Hopkins.

"This man was found guilty of theft and sentenced to two hundred lashes; let this be a lesson to anyone contemplating thievery. Carry out the orders of the court martial!"

Jacob's world began to slow down. The sound of the yelling around him become muted as a sergeant from the 44th stepped out and unwound the whip and pulled it back.

The first strike was like a burning, white-hot iron crossing his back, causing Jacob to clench his arms and back as it snapped. Then the second lash cracked, the pain burning into his soul. Jacob refused to yell out, clenching his teeth in anger, his rage boiling up from within. By the tenth lash, Jacob's back felt like molten fire, and he could feel the blood trickle from the wounds. Blood was leaking from where he bit his lips to keep from crying out. He would not give these bastards the satisfaction.

"What is the meaning of this?" demanded a loud voice, and Jacob opened his eyes to see General Abercrombie, Major Rogers, and several Rangers filling the yard.

The sergeant stopped the whip and stood as Captain Hopkins explained that Jacob had been found guilty of theft.

"That's a bold-faced lie, you bloody idiot!" yelled Major Rogers, who was moving up to face Captain Hopkins.

"Who ordered this?" demanded the general.

Captain Hopkins responded, "Major Christie."

"I want Major Christie here, now. Release that Ranger immediately!"

Jacob, who was still blotting out much of the pain, felt his arms being released and several strong hands holding him. Jacob shrugged them off and stood on his own, turning around to face Captain Hopkins. He was soon joined by Major Christie, who asserted that he was justified in ordering the lashing.

"You're a bigger fool than I thought. This man was away, and he had been paid. You sir have been lied to!" shouted an enraged General Abercrombie.

"You know these Provincials can't be trusted sir," was the only excuse Major Christie had.

Reaching into his pocket and pulling out a dispatch, he pointed it at Major Christie.

"This dispatch is from William Pitt himself, who places more trust and confidence in the performance of this Provincial officer," pointing at Major Rogers, "than he does in you, which means I trust him more than I do you! Captain Lee, see that that the orderly book is annotated to show that Lieutenant Clarke of the Independent Company of Rangers was found innocent and all charges dropped."

Then General Abercrombie approached closer to Major Christie, who was looking in disbelief at this man in a now torn and ragged green uniform, shocked to hear he was a lieutenant. He had thought him to be a common soldier.

"Do you know who is the only person responsible for the disciplinary actions of the Independent Company of Rangers?" asked the general.

Major Christie coughed and stuttered, "No, sir."

"That, sir, is I or that man right there." He pointed to Rogers. "Not you."

Jacob walked up and stared directly into the eyes of Major Christie. If looks could kill, then Major Christie would have died a violent and horrible death. Jacob did everything to control the rage welling inside him as he stared at the major.

"I believe you owe this man an apology, major," instructed General Abercrombie.

As Major Christie began to mumble, Jacob raised his hand. In a deathly quiet voice, he said, "You don't owe me anything," he leaned in close so the major could look into his eyes, then finished with "Sir," and walked away.

Standing erect even though his back felt it was aflame, Jacob walked out of the fort head held high, his torn shirt flapping in the breeze, and his blood leaving a trail of droplets behind him. His face was that of smoldering death, and the British regulars quickly got out of his way as Jacob moved through them, followed by the Rangers.

He continued to walk until he got to the island, and once he felt he was well away from the British, he stopped and yelled out, "Damn, this bloody hurts!"

Jacob still had a sense of humor. The Rangers cheered, one of them handed him a mug of rum which helped to dull the pain a little. Jacob then walked over to the surgeon, who had begun to treat the wounds when Samuel came in.

"I'm sorry, Jacob. I tried, but they wouldn't let me in the court-martial, so as soon as Major Rogers arrived, I told him."

Jacob reached up and patted Samuel's shoulder. "You did fine. Thanks."

The surgeon continued working on Jacob's wounds, applying bandages covered with a thick salve. After he was bandaged, the surgeon nodded, and Samuel walked Jacob back to their hut. He sat on his bunk and shifted around to settle the bandages so they were more comfortable.

Major Rogers checked on Jacob a little later.

"Just wanted you to know that Major Christie found his thief. It was a member of his own regiment who had been the orderly that evening."

Jacob snorted and shook his head in understanding.

"It was all a set-up from the beginning, sir, and I have a bad feeling it's only going to get worse before it gets better."

Rogers nodded, and then looked at Jacob with deep respect.

"You faced that extremely well. You showed your sheer toughness, and I am proud of you."

Jacob was not used to praise like that, and he simply nodded his appreciation. "Wasn't going to give those bastards the satisfaction," remarked Jacob as he winced.

Rogers left and soon Peter hobbled into the hut with Abigail. "Now, here is what the doctor should have ordered. This will make him feel better!"

Abigail sat next to Jacob and carefully put her arm around him, amazed at the toughness this man had shown while being lashed. Peter pulled out a bottle, and Samuel brought some cups as Peter pulled the cork and poured. They all drank, and with the exception of Jacob, they all began to spit and sputter.

"What the bloody hell is this and where did you get it, off a dead man?" demanded Samuel.

"This is Enzian, a very special Bavarian Schnapps. Prost!" said Peter as he drank down another gulp. After a few swallows, the taste got better, and Jacob's back no longer hurt as much. After the bottle was empty, Peter was snoring loudly once again, Samuel had fallen asleep, and Jacob and Abigail were asleep in each other's arms.

After a few days, Jacob's back was healed enough, and he decided it was time. Pulling out his bundle from Saratoga, he put on his lieutenant's uniform, slid the sword carrier across his shoulder, and placed his new Ranger hat on. It was time for Lieutenant Clarke to report for duty.

CHAPTER 10

NEW MISSIONS AND RESPONSIBILITIES

Jacob made his way over to Major Rogers's hut. The walk took longer than usual, because so many Rangers stopped him to congratulate him on his promotion or to praise him for how he had faced the senseless flogging. Jacob thanked them and entered Rogers's hut.

Rogers said, "Ah, great timing as usual Sergeant, ah, Lieutenant Clarke. Do you feel up for a mission, I have one for you."

Jacob nodded and came up to the table where Rogers had a large map spread out, replying with "Been through worse."

"As you know, we're spread pretty thin right now. Four companies are supporting the siege on Louisburg, and another company is out west at Fort Schuyler."

Jacob thought to himself, "Here was that name again. How large was Abigail's family?"

"My task for you is two-fold. First, I want you to train some volunteers in our way of fighting, and second, I want you to start positioning whale boats at key points along the lakes. If they can take Louisburg, the Royal Navy will be able to sail up the Saint Lawrence and we will attack Quebec, so I want whale boats positioned where we can get to them fast, like we did back in '56."

Jacob understood what was required, and Rogers showed him on his large map where he wanted the boats placed. Jacob would spend about a week training the volunteers before he began to transport the boats.

Putting his cap on, Major Rogers led Jacob to the area where the volunteers were living. Most of the men who had volunteered were from the New York Provincials, and there were some British regulars mixed in.

"I would like to meet with the sergeants first before I meet the rest of the men," said Jacob, and Rogers called for Sergeants Anderson and Philips. Jacob knew both men, having served alongside them before.

Anderson and Philips came out of their huts and were visibly beaming as soon as they saw who their new lieutenant would be. Rogers smiled and left Jacob to take charge of his volunteers.

After Jacob shook both men's hands, Philips said how great it was that they had gotten someone with experience and not a new gentleman officer.

"Then you know what I expect. These men will be trained to the same standard as we were. I will not accept anyone who won't pull their weight. How are these men?" Jacob asked.

Anderson replied that some of the men had seen action, but not many. They were mostly farmers and villagers who had joined the Provincial regiment, but all in all, they were decent men.

"How is the discipline?" asked Jacob.

Philips gave a sigh and said it was a work in progress. There were some minor problems.

"Not when I'm done with them. Assemble the men with their gear," Jacob ordered.

The volunteers were assembled, about twenty-four men divided in half, with Anderson in charge of the first half and

Philips in charge of the second. From what Jacob could see, most carried themselves like true soldiers, but he could see what Philips meant by some minor issues. A couple of the men were joking in the ranks and moving about while the others were standing correctly.

Jacob positioned himself in front of his new platoon.

"My name is Lieutenant Clarke. You have been given to me so I can train you, and we have tasks to perform. You will perform them correctly, or you will find another line of work. We survive by relying on one another. If I can't rely on you, then no one can."

While most of the men seemed to understand, those few who had been talking among themselves in the ranks were snickering.

Jacob came up to the three men who were snickering with whispered comments about new "louies" and how he would train them. The snickering stopped when they saw Jacob standing before them.

"Something funny?" Jacob asked in a cold, quiet voice.

The man who seemed to be the ring leader, a Matthew Dunning, coughed and replied, "Ah, no…sir."

"How long have you been fighting?" asked Jacob, and Dunning replied, "About a year."

"I've been doing this since well before the beginning of this current fight and have seen more death and fighting than any man deserves. You will listen and follow my orders or else."

As Jacob turned, Dunning snapped off, "Or else what?"

In a flash, Jacob spun and punched the man in the face with his right, and as he fell, Jacob jumped on top of him and held his knife at Dunning's throat.

"You'll be dead!"

Jacob pulled Dunning to his feet and stared at the two other trouble makers. Then he turned and addressed all of them.

"In case you haven't heard, I am not like these other gentlemen officers. I started with Rogers in the beginning and have been fighting most of my life. If you don't follow my orders or if you violate how we operate, …" said Jacob as he got within a nose breadth of the two other men while Dunning tried to stop the blood running from his nose, "… I will kill you myself to save these men from your mistakes. Understand?"

All three nodded quickly with shocked looks on their faces. Anderson and Philips looked at each other, winked, and smiled. This was going to work out just fine. The rest of the platoon also seemed to understand and nodded.

The first day was spent on marksmanship, on accuracy, and on working as a team. Jacob led by example, showing the volunteers how to improve their aim, how to load quickly, and how to cover while the other Ranger shoots. They practiced moving and shooting, how to use cover, and how to withdraw under pressure as a team.

Jacob led the new platoon out into the woods south of the fort to work on their skills. He taught them how to move, how to cover one another, and how to keep a steady eye on the woods around them. Smoke padded silently along with them, watching with a wolf's interest as these men listened and followed Jacob and his sergeants. When they returned to the island, he instructed them on their priorities of work. First was cleaning their muskets and then their gear.

He taught them the importance of "stand to," the daily drill to protect the platoon from an early morning attack by the French or their Indian allies. Each morning, before breakfast or any other activity, they packed their gear as they watched the woods for enemies so they would be ready to fight or flee if there was an attack, unlike the British, who might have to abandon their gear if it was necessary to run.

These were important skills that Jacob had learned over time, but these men had only a few short days to learn them before they headed out on their mission. After several more days of intensive training, Jacob took them out at night to go over how to camp on a mission and how to take turns pulling the watch while the others rested.

During the night, Jacob moved silently among them to see how they were doing. He came across Dunning, who had continued to fall short of what was expected, asleep, leaning up against a tree.

Jacob clamped his hand over Dunning's mouth, and the startled man woke to hear Jacob's quiet voice, "You're dead."

Jacob woke the entire platoon and gathered them around. Pointing to Dunning, Jacob started by saying, "This man just cost you all your lives by falling asleep. The French and their Allies watch and wait for an opportunity to get into our camps, and if they are undetected, to kill everyone. We work as a team or we'll die out there, and I do mean 'we' because I am trusting you with my life as well."

Jacob looked at the assembled men and turned towards Dunning. "Except you. Return to your old unit, now!"

Shrugging his shoulders, Dunning went over to his gear and packed it up, mumbling that he could do a better job by himself than with these people.

By morning, Jacob had returned to Fort Edward with his platoon, making sure Dunning had departed.

Once more, Jacob assembled the men and looked at every one of them.

"You understand that you all volunteered for this. You know the dangers we all face. Because you volunteered, you have the responsibility to act like Rangers, to behave like Rangers, to bring us nothing but honor and prestige."

He stared at them all, making sure their eyes were on him. "We're not like them," Jacob stated, pointing at some other Provincials walking by. "We have our code and rules we live and, if needed, die by." Jacob continued to look into their eyes to make sure they understood what he meant, what it was to be a Ranger.

"Being a Ranger means you have to be better than you were with your old unit, whether Provincial, militia, or even British regulars. Everyone will expect you to be better, to move faster, and to fight harder because that's what we have done for the past couple of years. We are a team. We take care of one another, both here and out there. I expect, and Major Rogers expects, you to be the best, to be Rangers who are better than all others."

Jacob paused to look at the assembled men who seemed to be standing a little taller, a little straighter in formation.

"You will show the world why you volunteered to be the best, to fight the hardest, and to go places where the others won't go. You will carry yourself well and keep your equipment in the best condition possible, especially your weapons. You will live or die based on how well you keep your rifles and muskets clean and ready, your knives and tomahawks sharpened.

"You will use them. We will drive these bastards back up north, and they will fear us as we hunt them and scalp them. They have been winning way too long. That ends today! You will accomplish your mission, even when you're cold, tired, hungry, or hurt. We will be victorious!"

Jacob stopped and looked at them one more time, satisfied they now knew where he stood and what he expected of them.

"Sergeants, see to the men. See that they have clean weapons and their gear is in good shape."

Both sergeants turned, saluted, and took charge of their sections as Jacob went over to Rogers's hut to inform him they were ready to move the boats. Rogers asked if he was satisfied with the volunteers, and Jacob said he was now that he had removed Dunning from the ranks.

Jacob returned to the platoon and told Anderson and Phillips to take details to draw rations for a week and to start cooking. They would depart in the morning for the lake to get the boats. When Anderson and Phillips returned, Jacob helped cook the rations with Smoke padding quietly alongside him, doing his part by supervising and eating scraps.

Once all of the rations had been cooked and placed in the haversacks, Jacob called the platoon together to go over their task.

"In the morning, we march to the southern end of the lake to the encampment where the whaleboats are located. How many of you have experience in boats?" Jacob asked as he looked around and saw only two of the privates raise their hands.

"We'll spend a day learning how to paddle the boats before we head up-lake. Once I feel we're ready, we're heading to this bay," Jacob explained as he used a large stick to draw the outline of the lake and the bay. "From there we're dragging the boats overland to where we'll hide them before returning for another batch of boats and hiding them a little ways more north than the first boats."

Jacob looked around to make sure everyone understood before dismissing them. He returned to his hut, where Peter and Samuel were playing a game with marbles on a board.

"How did the training go?" asked Samuel.

"No different than training you lot, except there are a bunch more of them," Jacob answered.

With a twinkle in his eye, Samuel looked up from the game and asked if Jacob was going to go see Abigail before he left on his task. Jacob raised his eyebrows and simply stated that the thought had crossed his mind. Samuel snorted and returned to the game, winking at Peter as Jacob departed the hut.

He did in fact go to see Abigail, and he spent the night with her, enjoying the peace before heading out once more to war. Abigail watched the next morning as Jacob assembled the platoon, inspected them, and led them into the woods towards the lake encampment. Jacob paused for a second and looked at her before turning and leading his men off.

Jacob made sure everyone spread out as soon as they entered the woods, with Corporal Smoke running ahead of them, and the trip north to the encampment was uneventful. Still, Jacob wanted to get these men into good habits and to stop any bad ones from forming.

No time for complacency, Jacob thought, recalling how many times Rangers, regulars, and Provincials alike had been shot by the enemy just entering the woods north of Fort Edward. While they were securing the southern shore, the British were still having difficulties keeping the area under control and restricting the French freedom of movement.

They stopped at the blockhouse and stockade at Halfway Brook, Jacob observing they were improving the stockade and the gate, perhaps because of the Indian raid. Along with both Provincials and British regulars, there were also civilians, and Jacob noticed a small sutlery had been established.

***

The sutler, Jeffrey Cowper, was in conversation with William Maclane, paying his "union fees" to establish a post there at the brook, which Maclane agreed would make him wealthy with all of the army traffic between Fort Edward and the lake. Standing behind him was Big Harpe, who spotted the Rangers and Jacob taking their break.

"This is just for now Mr. Cowper," Maclane said. "In time I do see a need for something of an inn or tavern at the lake. Would that be of interest to you?" Mr. Cowper nodded his head energetically, and Maclane smiled. "Thought so. You are our company representative here, do well, pay your dues, and once things settle down a bit, we will look to move you to bigger and better business opportunities at the lake."

Once their business was concluded, Maclane and Harpe walked off to the side, and Maclane pointed towards the Rangers. "Wasn't that your last game?" Maclane asked, and Harpe nodded.

Harpe grinned when he responded, "Yes, it was great fun, and worked out better than I thought."

Maclane looked at the heavily armed Rangers. "Are those men someone you want to anger?"

Harpe just shrugged. "Only if I get caught, and I am too careful for that to happen."

***

Once their break was over, Jacob led the Rangers back into the woods and continued along the path towards the lake, passing French Mountain and Bloody Pond, and they entered the encampment with no contact with the enemy.

Jacob had Sergeants Anderson and Phillips move the men over into the tree line, and then had them get food from the encampment's quartermaster so they could save their cooked rations for when they were on the march.

After checking on the men and setting the watch for the night, Jacob settled down with Smoke lying next to him and looked pensively at this piece of land on which so many of his friends had spilled their blood.

Not much remained from the old Fort William Henry or from their old encampment, which had both been replaced by growing stockpiles of supplies and by the men whose camps now covered the entire southern shore. Wherever the ground wasn't covered by the new encampment, Mother Nature had done her part, hiding the remains under a layer of thick grass and wild flowers.

Jacob shook his head, looking at the extensive supplies and the size of the encampment. Even a new French scout would be able to see the British were up to something, given the amount of men and materials here at the lake. It already felt like Jacob had spent a lifetime here.

In the morning, Jacob led his platoon down to the lake and the armada of whaleboats and bateaux assembled along the shore. As he had done in the past, Jacob first instructed the Rangers on how to man and operate the boats and then led them out into the lake where they practiced rowing as a team. After about half a day, the Rangers had finally gotten the hang of operating the boats, and Jacob was satisfied that they were ready for the next part.

It was a tired and sore platoon that returned to their camp that evening. Jacob sent Anderson and Phillips with a detail of men to draw food for their evening meal, while he reported to the quartermaster to finalize the boats for morning.

Once done, he procured a small cask of rum and returned to their camp as the men lay about eating their meals, talking, and joking about their "sailor" training and about how many different muscles were sore from the rowing.

"Well lads, this should help the soreness," Jacob commented as he placed the cask down in the center of the camp.

The men grabbed their cups, and Jacob poured the rum. After everyone had a mug, Jacob raised his and gave a toast to a successful mission. Everyone echoed his toast, and then they all drank.

As Jacob watched his men, he thought, "Wait until the next couple of days and you will really have sore muscles," remembering how he had felt after the last time he had dragged boats.

In the morning, after stand to and their inspection, Jacob and Smoke led the platoon to the shore, and they loaded the boats with their gear. After they pushed off from the shore, the oars came out, making the boats look like giant water bugs. Jacob's boat led the way with Smoke sitting in the bow, nose and eyes pointing to the north. Jacob had to admit he missed Samuel with his normally present wall or swivel gun in the bow. He would have to rely on Smoke's keen senses for early warning.

The small flotilla of boats arrived at the narrows with no sign of any enemy patrol, and Jacob pointed to the east shore to land. Once on the beach, the platoon began to take turns carrying the boats while rotating out to pull security. Jacob led by example and took his turns at shouldering the boats around and through the mountains.

Like turtles, the upside down boats and the legs of the Rangers carrying them slowly made their way through the woods, getting caught between tress from time to time. They rotated duties, attempting to keep the men rested in case they made contact with the enemy and had to fight. Jacob didn't like the idea of a fight; it would more than likely force them to lose the boats and tip off the French about what they were up to.

They stopped once it was too dark to see, Jacob forming a perimeter around the boats and setting the watch. After giving instructions to Sergeants Anderson and Phillips, Jacob and Smoke checked on how the men were doing, with most of the men commenting that they were sore.

The platoon took turns eating, sleeping, and pulling guard, including Jacob and Smoke. Jacob woke before sunrise, his body attuned to the early hour from the many years of scouting, and he had everyone perform stand to. Once he felt sure they were alone, the platoon reformed to continue their journey. The Rangers moved a little bit more stiffly and groaned quietly as they shouldered the boats and began their slow but steady journey towards Lake Champlain.

The spot Rogers had indicated to Jacob was just north of South Bay in a small stream inlet where the boats could easily be concealed. Jacob remembered it from their previous expeditions in the area, and it was where he led the platoon, which arrived at the spot just before sundown.

Taking advantage of the remaining light, Jacob had the platoon place all of the oars under the boats, which were turned over so their hulls were up. He then had the platoon cover the boats with dirt, mud, and branches to conceal them from any prying eyes. The platoon spent an uneventful night nearby with the sounds of owls and whippoorwills serenading them.

In the morning, Jacob led the platoon overland back to the encampment at the southern end of Lake George. Jacob spent the day resting the men and restocking their rations, allowing them time to cook food to replace the rations they had used. The men's sore muscles left them just in time for the second group of boats to be transported.

The second trip went more smoothly then the first, the platoon now experienced and performing well. Paddling up to the narrows as before, the platoon disembarked, and they carried the boats through a series of trails and passes located more northeasterly than the ones they had followed on their first trip. Once they had arrived at a spot near the South River portion of Lake Champlain, they concealed this second group of boats before heading overland back to the encampment.

Recognizing key features in the terrain, Jacob knew they were getting close to the southern shore when Smoke suddenly froze, his ears lying back and a low growl coming from deep within him. Jacob quickly raised his hand to halt, and the platoon froze, slowly sinking to their knees.

In the distance, he could hear voices heading towards them. Jacob motioned the platoon to come up in a line and lay down. Two French officers in their white uniforms were leading a column of Indians and Canadians and speculating about English plans with some of the Canadians.

Jacob looked to his left and right for Anderson and Phillips, and seeing he had their attention, drew his finger across his throat and pointed towards the approaching enemy. Both Anderson and Phillips smiled and nodded, readying the hasty ambush.

***

Ensign La Sarre had followed his instructions, coming down through the South Bay from Carillon to avoid any contact with the enemy. The engineer, Ensign Reinne, having observed the large encampment at the southern end of Lake du Sacrament, was seriously concerned. The English and their Provincials were stocking up for what must be preparations for another attack against them at Fort Carillon.

Sergeant Barre of the Canadian Militia scoffed, saying they would crush the English as they had done the last time. Nodding, La Sarre was about to comment that they should not be overconfident when the woods in front of him exploded and balls began to whistle and whiz by him, something hitting him hard in the leg and causing him to fall over.

***

Jacob had waited until the enemy was less then twenty-five yards away before giving the order to fire. Once the platoon fired, Jacob stood up and shouted, "At them boys!" as he ran forward, Smoke charging into the carnage ahead of him.

La Sarre had rolled over on his side in time to see the green-clad men rush through the cloud of smoke, two of them coming to a halt as they saw him move. One was reaching down to grab him when a large man who appeared to be an officer told them to take him prisoner. One of the green-clad men began to bandage the wound in his leg as the other man loaded his rifle and then stood over him, allowing the man who had bandaged him to load his rifle.

The ambush was quick, efficient, and bloody, having caught the enemy by complete surprise. Sergeant Barre had been shot between the eyes and killed instantly, while Ensign Reinne was wounded. The rest of the Indians and Canadians had been killed with the exception of two Canadians who had been captured.

Sergeants Anderson and Phillips saw to the grisly task of supervising the men as they collected scalps, while Jacob searched the pockets of the dead for anything that could be used for information.

Pleased both with the outcome of the ambush and with the successful completion of the task they had been assigned, Jacob reformed the platoon and led them to Fort Edward where the prisoners were handed over to Major Rogers. Jacob praised the platoon for a job well done before releasing them to clean their gear.

The remainder of the year saw Jacob and his platoon being sent out on a few other tasks by Rogers, which included moving more boats in preparation for the coming campaign. Jacob led his platoon on several scouting expeditions, including a return to Carillon where they were successful in conducting an ambush that netted a captured French captain. He provided a wealth of information concerning the strength of the French, Canadians, and Indians at Fort Carillon and Saint Frederic.

In the meantime, concern was growing around the fort about the reports of missing people, mostly camp followers or traders, who appeared to be vanishing. While the British command attributed it to either "the savages got them" or "they found their senses and went home," worry spread around the camp.

***

Maclane had heard the rumors, and he approached Big Harpe, and asked, "You wouldn't happen to know anything about these tales?" Harpe put on an innocent face and asked, "Who me? Why no, not at all." Then he laid his finger along his nose, and said, "Though I have been helping with the spreading of the rumors."

Maclane nodded and then warned Harpe, "As long as it is not any of our paying members. Just don't draw any attention, especially towards us." Harpe nodded and looked crestfallen. Maclane said, "If you have nothing to do today, I do have a few of these new traders who don't seem to understand the benefits of joining our company."

Harpe's eyes lit up, and he looked at Maclane, who nodded. "Would be a shame if something was to happen to them, or to members of their families." Harpe nodded excitedly, and rubbed his hands together.

After letting Harpe go to play with the traders, Maclane made his way to Saratoga and met with Pierre du Mons in the corner of a small tavern. They sat in a back corner, away from prying eyes and ears, and sipped from their tankards.

"How's business?" asked Pierre.

Maclane shrugged and simply replied, "Well, or mostly well. And you?"

Pierre also shrugged. "As expected. I have heard that you, er… your company holds the monopoly on all supply routes up to the lake." He raised his tankard. "Nicely done."

Maclane nodded and raised his tankard. "I have heard you have secured the supply routes along all the water routes from Quebec and Montreal, and even some of the shipping lanes back to France. Nicely done."

Pierre nodded in return, and then frowned. "Yes, but your damned Royal Navy makes sea trade very difficult. We have to focus on river trade for now. War can be very bad for business."

"Yes," replied Maclane, "but it also can be good for business. I assume your army is getting ready for winter quarters, like ours. That should be profitable?"

Pierre nodded. "Yes, just like your great encampment at the southern end of the lake. That must make it easier for business. Your wagons aren't set upon by warships."

Maclane smiled, "No, but the French and Indians seem to be causing havoc with our wagons." The two men stared at one another, and then Maclane leaned forward. "I have a proposition."

Pierre leaned forward with a raised eyebrow. "I will share information with you, concerning the Royal Navy so it won't cramp your business ventures, for say 10 percent of your profit margin as a business incentive."

Pierre nodded. "What do I have to do for you?"

Maclane smiled. "Influence your military leaders to leave my wagons alone. But they can have free reign on our competition or military wagons. Just good for business, yes?"

Pierre thought about it. "Simple enough. Yes, good for business."

***

As the year moved from summer to fall, the time arrived when the volunteers were going to have to prepare for winter quarters. Most of the time, Jacob's platoon provided security for work details harvesting the gardens around Fort Edward or cutting wood. Rogers did not want another French raid against their work details.

It was a crisp, fall day when a small column of New York volunteers arrived at Fort Edward, led by Major Phillip Schuyler, Abigail's father. Captain Schuyler, having returned to active duty, had been promoted. He had traveled to Fort Edward to check on conditions for the New York Provincial government, when he spotted Abigail on Mr. Best's porch.

Leaping from his horse and rushing over, he hugged Abigail and stammered how he and her mother had been so concerned because they thought she had been killed. While part of Abigail was happy to see her father, she also knew that a part of her life, her time with Jacob, was more than likely over.

As her father met with the New York Provincial officers, he had his men gather up her things and get her a horse. Abigail was sitting on the horse when she spied Jacob in the distance. He stopped when he saw the New York men and Abigail.

Having lied to Phillip Schuyler about Abigail, Jacob knew he could not approach, and he stayed near the wall of the fort. Major Schuyler assured the staff from the 44th Regiment that the New Yorkers would return for the campaign, mounted up and rode to a position next to Abigail.

Looking at Abigail one last time and seeing her eyes looking at him, Jacob placed his hand over his heart, and then raised it in farewell. Slowly, Abigail nodded and slumped in the saddle. She looked one last time as her father turned their horses to lead the men back to Saratoga, and then she turned and rode back to her normal life, leaving the joy of the frontier behind. Jacob accepted it; he didn't like it, but he knew nothing could be done, so he turned around and returned to the island. Life marches on.

CHAPTER 11

RECRUITING DUTY

Jacob was called to see Major Rogers, and when he entered the hut, he didn't like the grin on Rogers's face. Sitting in the room were both Peter, who now worked for Major Rogers as an orderly, and Samuel, who was sitting next to one of the walls.

"Where am I heading sir, and what is the task?" asked Jacob.

Rogers nodded. "Straight to the point, as always. First, good job getting that platoon ready. We're going to need everyone in the spring for the upcoming campaign, at least if what I hear from the generals is true, and we're very much under strength right now. That's where you come in."

Jacob wasn't sure what Major Rogers was getting at, but he waited to see.

"I am sending you out on a very tough assignment. You haven't done this before, and it can be very challenging," Rogers said.

Jacob waited for the hammer to fall – a scout of Saint Frederic, or perhaps a mission as far north as Montreal, or even Quebec, in the fall.

"Now that would be challenging," Jacob thought.

"I am sending you out on a recruiting detail; I want you to travel south to Albany, then over through towns in Massachusetts, the Hampshires, and Connecticut, wherever you can find the men I need. Jacob, you know the type of men we want for volunteers.

I am relying on you to get us quality volunteers, not a bunch of numbers to fill out the roster.

"I am sending Corporal Samuel Penny here to help with the books and the pay, as well as some sergeants who will lead the volunteers back here."

Jacob looked over at Samuel and mouthed "Corporal?" to which Samuel smiled and shrugged his shoulders.

Rogers continued, "Samuel knows what to do with the pay and services. I need you back here no later than the spring. Sergeant Hopkins will report to you tomorrow morning with the men who will be traveling with you. Good luck, and get us some good men."

Rogers reached out and shook Jacob's hand, before returning to his desk and his dispatches.

"Come on corporal, let's go," said Jacob to Samuel.

Peter shook their hands, and the two departed and walked over to their hut. As they walked, Samuel explained his task of keeping the books on the volunteers – paying for their room and board and paying the volunteers, themselves. They would draw the money in the morning before departing.

Jacob nodded as they walked.

"I know this may be a tough question, but are we stopping in Saratoga?" asked Samuel.

After a moment, Jacob nodded, thinking to himself that at least he could say good-bye to Abigail.

Jacob and Samuel prepared their gear, while both Smoke and Otto watched with intent golden eyes from where they lay, ready for the coming adventure.

In the morning, Jacob and Samuel, followed by Smoke and Otto, went over to Fort Edward to sign for the recruiting money. They had been provided with a pack horse to carry the leather satchels holding the books and the bags of coins.

Jacob could feel the tension as British officers, once again from the 44th Regiment, stared at them as they drew the bags of coins. Jacob just stared back, almost challenging them to say something as Samuel counted the bags and placed them in several large leather satchels, which were locked and then loaded onto the pack horse. Once everything was in order, Samuel led the pack horse, and they returned to the island, the two wolves staring back at the officers from the 44th.

Waiting at their hut was Sergeant Hopkins with the recruiting detail, composed of Sergeants Edwards, Carver, and Dobbs; Corporals Stevens, Walker, and Sullivan; and Privates Gill, Johnson, and Henry. Jacob recognized them all and knew they were all veteran Rangers. They had been drawn from the remnants of the companies that were not up at Louisburg.

Jacob shook all of their hands and asked if everything was ready. Each Ranger had his equipment plus either a knapsack or a "snapsack," a large linen sack used to carry their extra gear or rations. Jacob told them their route, explaining that they were heading to Saratoga then down to Albany, stopping at a few towns along the way, before heading east into Massachusetts, then south towards Connecticut, then returning north to Fort Edward before spring.

"Even if we're not out scouting the French, don't let your guard down while we're out," ordered Jacob. "The weather can turn nasty south or east of here, as bad as it can be up here in the fall or winter, and we know the French or their allies have ranged south of here.

"Still, I would recommend that if you can get some time to unwind, take it. We're going to be busy in the spring so enjoy some easy time before things get hard once again."

The Rangers all nodded. No one really liked recruiting detail. It was time-consuming and very boring most of the time.

However, they saw the logic in it: they needed more men to replace their losses. They concluded that they should try to enjoy the boredom as a pleasant change from the constant danger and chance of dying that they normally faced.

After reporting to Major Rogers, they were ready. Jacob led the recruiting detail out and began heading south on the Albany road, waving to Mr. and Mrs. Best as they walked past their shop.

The Rangers carried their rifles easily, but they were ready in case they did run into trouble. Corporal Smoke padded along silently next to Jacob as he led the small column of recruiters. Samuel pulled the pack horse behind him with Otto ranging to their rear and flank, nose sniffing the air and ground.

The Rangers moved easily but still kept a wary eye on the woods around them. They could tell they were getting closer to civilization as more and more active farms could be seen from the Albany Road. They passed some farmers or tradesmen on the road, the Rangers giving them courteous nods, and the tradesmen and farmers returning respectful nods.

Just south of Fort Edward, they passed a large blockhouse surrounded by a palisade wall on some high ground near a stream named Moses Kill and the east side of the Hudson River. Normally the forts were named after the governor or commander who had built them, or royalty like Edward, Anne, or William Henry. But not this fortification, it was simply known locally as Fort Misery, which must not have instilled much confidence in the men assigned to garrison it. Jacob could see men working around the fort and wondered what they thought about garrisoning a place named Misery. The Rangers returned waves from the fort as they crossed a ford across the Hudson to continue south on the western side of the river.

After moving for a few hours, the Rangers stopped at Fort Miller to rest. It was an old fort that had been built back during

Queen Anne's War and had recently been reoccupied. The local militia and Provincial units were busy rebuilding the palisades and blockhouse, perhaps concerned over the French victories and their constant push south of Fort Edward.

The fort was located along both the Hudson River and the Albany Road. Jacob led the Rangers over to a shady grove of trees where they sat, drank from their canteens, and chewed on some dried meat.

After a while, some of the New York Provincials came over and struck up a conversation with the Rangers, mostly asking about the fighting north of Fort Edward and wanting to know if the tales recounting the savagery of the fighting were true. The Rangers confirmed or dispelled the rumors, telling the Provincials the truth about the fighting, the viciousness, and the fact that the enemy was doing a better job at it than they were.

Most of the conversation centered on "soldier talk" about fighting, weapons, and tactics. The Rangers traded some of their extra items for twists of tobacco from the Provincials who sat and smoked their pipes with the Rangers before one of the Provincial officers came over to shoo the men back to work, giving two large wolves an oddly apprehensive look before turning back to his duties.

After the men bid the Rangers farewell and returned to their labors, the officer remained and pulled Jacob off to the side. Making sure they were out of earshot of the enlisted men, the officer asked if he saw tension with the British regulars, especially the officers. Jacob listened and nodded his head, confirming that there was a growing tension between the British and the Provincials.

"Every time they come through here, they look down their noses at us, thinking we are unworthy," commented the officer, a Captain Richard Ellis of the New York Provincials. "They don't seem to understand it's our homes and families we're fighting for, not King and country."

Jacob nodded his head in agreement with Captain Ellis's assessment.

"No matter what, don't lose hope. Keep it firmly set in your mind that we're fighting for our homes and families, and those British officers can be damned for all I care," said Jacob.

Captain Ellis smiled, nodded, shook Jacob's hand, and wished him luck before returning to the work detail at the fort. Jacob watched him go, wondering how bad the situation was south of Fort Edward, when men like Captain Ellis were having the same problems with the British that they were.

Walking over to the reclining Rangers, Jacob commanded, "All right lads, back on the road. I want to be at Fort Hardy by tonight."

Both wolves sat on their haunches, ready to go. Tapping out their pipes and putting their gear away, the Rangers set their packs, their shoulders swimming to settle the straps into place, and they continued on their journey south.

It was towards early evening when the Rangers arrived at Fort Hardy, a major supply point between Fort Edward and Albany. All of their supplies transitioned through Fort Hardy, located at the intersection of a stream called the Fish Kill and the Hudson River, where there were both a ferry and a bridge.

When Jacob and his Rangers arrived, they found the fort surrounded by stacks of barrels and boxes, and large tents for the quartermasters who were busy sorting and inventorying, apparently getting the supplies organized for the coming spring campaign. Jacob led the Rangers to a wooded area near the fort to set up their camp for the night. While the Rangers built a fire and laid out their blankets to sleep on, Jacob went over to speak with the fort's commander, Major Robert Duncan of the New York Provincials.

The fort, originally built by General Lyman to support General Johnson's campaigns in 1755, was still serving as a logistical base for the current army commander. While smaller than Fort Edward, it still had a decent wooden wall with bastions in the corner. It was surrounded by a moat and protected on the north and east sides by the Hudson and the Fish Kill.

In one of the fort's buildings, Jacob found Major Duncan, who was going over supply schedules with a British captain and two lieutenants. Major Duncan looked up and asked, "Yes?"

The three British officers just stared with normal curiosity, probably having never seen a Ranger before.

"Just wanted to report in and let you know that my men and I are camping outside. We're passing through on recruitment duty."

Major Duncan shrugged in indifference, mumbled thanks, and returned to speaking about timetables to the British officers. Having done his duty, Jacob returned to his Rangers.

They had a nice fire crackling, with four chickens, which had already been skewered by metal ramrods and placed over the flames. Smoke and Otto lay nearby, golden eyes watching the food being prepared. Sergeants Edwards and Carver were cutting up potatoes for roasting, and Samuel, Gill, and Henry were making Johnnycakes.

"I see you were all gainfully employed while I was visiting the fort's commander."

Samuel smiled and looked up. "Yup. Went over and spoke with one of the quartermasters. He was one of the few whose hair we managed to save in the Ottawa attack, and he was very appreciative." Samuel spread out his arms to take in their evening meal.

Clapping and rubbing his hands together, Jacob sat down and helped with the Johnnycakes, looking forward to a cooked meal instead of rations. Smoke and Otto never took their eyes off the roasting chickens.

The sun began to set as the Rangers reclined on their blankets and joked or told stories, in true Ranger fashion, trying to outdo one another. The roasting chickens snapped and sizzled as the skin cracked and the grease fell into the fire, causing the flames to lick upward.

As Jacob reclined and enjoyed his pipe, Samuel plopped himself down beside him. He looked earnestly at Jacob, who looked up over his pipe, asking, "Yes?"

"Are you going to stop by and see Abigail since we're here?" Samuel asked.

With a heavy sigh, Jacob responded that he would stop by and see if she was at the store and try to say goodbye without letting her family know he had lied to them about Abigail when he was last there.

Samuel nodded, "Guess it would be considered rather rude letting on that you had lied to her father," commented Samuel, "and a major to boot. What kind of trouble could that lead to, I wonder?"

At the moment, Jacob didn't dwell on it as the chicken was cut up and passed out to the hungry Rangers, who also grabbed up the roasted potatoes and Johnnycakes. The Rangers all pulled out of their haversacks small horns like their powder horns, except these held salt or other spices they had picked up along their journeys. Even Smoke and Otto had their own bowls, which were filled with tasty tidbits that they literally wolfed down.

After enjoying their filling meal, the Rangers settled back. As the stars came out and they relaxed and fell asleep, the snoring soon began. Jacob did lie awake for a bit, tossing about in his mind what he would he do in the morning when he went over to find Abigail. He finally gave up and decided he would just do it and not worry about it anymore, and he settled into sleep.

In the morning, Jacob made sure he looked presentable by removing twigs and leaves from his uniform coat after having used it as a pillow and made sure his sword was hung smartly across his shoulder. He set his hat in place and started for the village of Saratoga, which was just in view from the fort.

Samuel was up. Having restarted the fire, he was boiling coffee. He nodded his head in a good luck gesture as Jacob walked past him into town. It was a cool and comfortable morning, and the farmers and tradesmen were already heading off to their morning chores.

When Jacob approached the Schuyler store, he could see Mrs. Schuyler on the porch sweeping. She looked up and saw Jacob and warmly welcomed him with a, "Good morning, sir. Nice to see you again."

Jacob removed his hat and greeted Mrs. Schuyler. He did not see Mr. Schuyler or Abigail, and he asked if Mr. Schuyler was inside. She indicated that he was and opened the door for Jacob, who thanked her and entered the store.

Mr. Schuyler, who was busy studying a large ledger, looked up when Jacob entered, smiled, and came around to shake Jacob's hand.

"Good to see you, lieutenant. How can I be of service today?"

Still not seeing Abigail and with no real plan, Jacob improvised, saying that he was out on recruiting detail and the Rangers he signed up would be in need of uniforms. He asked if Mr. Schuyler would help the recruits with their uniforms, as he had done for Jacob. As Mr. Schuyler agreed and they were discussing how they could go about requisitioning the uniforms, Abigail came from the back of the store carrying bolts of cloth.

Seeing Jacob, she stopped for a second and stared. Jacob looked over Mr. Schuyler's shoulder and spotted her. As Abigail continued around to the front of the store, her father looked over.

"Ah, Abigail. Let me introduce you to one of the lieutenants who were looking for you. Did you see Lieutenant Clarke while at the fort?"

As Abigail slowly approached, Jacob broke in by bowing and shaking Abigail's hand.

"Like I said before sir, I was gone most of the time either looking for Miss Abigail or hunting her attackers. It's a pleasure to finally meet you, Miss Abigail."

Without breaking stride, Abigail smiled, curtsied, and shook Jacob's hand as if it were the first time they had met.

"Did you find our attackers, Lieutenant Clarke?" Abigail asked breathlessly, trying hard to keep her feelings in check.

"Why yes, miss," replied Jacob. "We found them and punished them for attacking your column."

Mr. Schuyler smiled at answers he seemed to approve of and returned to talking business with Jacob. Abigail went back to stocking items in the store, but she stayed within earshot of the two. Jacob kept sneaking looks at her without drawing Mr. Schuyler's attention as he wrote out the process to procure uniform materials for the Rangers.

Once everything was complete and Jacob had the instructions, it was Mr. Schuyler who asked Abigail to escort Jacob back to the fort, but he said she should return quickly for they had a lot of work to do that day. Shaking Mr. Schuyler's hand and thanking him for his help with the uniforms, Jacob turned to Abigail, who was waiting to escort him and had opened the door for him.

As Abigail and Jacob walked down the road back towards Fort Hardy, Jacob asked how she was doing. Abigail sighed and recounted their journey back from Fort Edward, her mother's tearful welcome home, and her resettling into village life, which was different and boring when compared to living at Fort Edward with Mr. Best and his wife.

Jacob nodded as Abigail looked over her shoulder to make sure they were out of sight of her family store before she moved close and took Jacob's hand and arm, saying how she had missed him as well. They walked a little way quietly, Abigail hanging tightly onto Jacob's hand and arm, not wanting to let go. At the edge of the village, Abigail accepted the reality that this was her life now, and she turned to look at Jacob.

"It was nice while it lasted," Abigail said softly. "But this is the way it must be."

Jacob nodded and, making sure no one was looking, quickly hugged Abigail and kissed her one last time.

"I wanted to at least say good-bye. I didn't have time back at Fort Edward."

Abigail hugged Jacob and rested her head on his chest one last time. Then she let go and, with one last look, turned and headed back to her life in Saratoga while Jacob returned to his life as a Ranger.

Jacob took a few paces, stopped to look back over his shoulder one last time, smiled and with a nod, turned back towards the fort and his waiting Rangers. He didn't linger to watch Abigail leave or study her expression; he would deal with these emotions in his own way, as he had done in the past.

When Jacob returned to Fort Hardy, the Rangers and wolves were up and ready to go. After asking Sergeant Hopkins if everything was ready, Jacob led the Rangers out and back onto the road. The small column of Rangers passed through the middle of Saratoga, the townspeople stopping to wave to the passing Rangers.

As they walked past the Schuyler store, Abigail and her father, who happened to be on the porch, turned and watched the Rangers pass by, Mr. Schuyler waving. Jacob tipped his hat to them and, after a quick glance at Abigail, set his hat firmly in place and led his Rangers through the village and on to their next stop.

This was life and reality as Jacob understood it, knowing it was a risk to have relationships while at war, which could pose dangers to the heart and soul. Jacob thought about it, shrugged, and smiled, determining that it had been worth it in the end. He remembered what Konkapot had told him, that he still had to be reminded he was human and not just a killing machine to have a perspective on why they fought this war.

As the day progressed, a summer shower developed and dumped on the Rangers. Smoke looked accusingly at Jacob as if it was his fault that for some reason they were getting wet. It didn't last long, but the road turned into a muddy mess, so Jacob led his Rangers off the road. They continued their journey walking through the fields along the road, their path not as muddy or churned up as the road.

The terrain changed as they journeyed south, the road leaving the valley and rising to heights overlooking the river and the road. Jacob thought the height of land would make a good defendable position. If they couldn't contain the French at Fort Edward, they could always try to stop them here to keep them from reaching Albany.

The sun returned, and the Rangers dried out as they walked through the next valley. Both sides of the river and the road were covered with farms and fields. They passed more locals, who were making their way between villages or towns. They all nodded or waved to the Rangers as they passed by, seemingly knowing who the green-uniformed men were.

Jacob decided to take a break at the next fort along their way, Fort Winslow. Originally called Fort Ingoldsby, it like Fort

Miller had been built back during Queen Anne's War. Named after General Winslow, it served as a logistical base along the supply route between Albany and Fort Edward.

Finding a nice shady spot to rest, Jacob sat down and leaned back against a tree, placing his hat next to him on the ground. Smoke sat next to him, panting from the heat and trying to cool off.

Like Fort Hardy, Winslow was a hive of activity as stockpiles of supplies were being created and prepared for the coming winter.

"Sure is a lot of supplies being piled up at these forts," remarked Samuel. Having sat down next to Jacob, he was looking out over the activity.

"Hmm...mm," mumbled Jacob from around his pipe stem, "Sure does look like we're in for another adventure come spring," he said.

Samuel nodded and asked, "Think it will be bloody?"

Jacob thought about it, puffing on his pipe. "Yeah, it will be bloody, always is, always will be." Jacob scratched behind Smoke's ears, and Smoke looked at the supplies with wolfish indifference.

The fort was located near a village named Stillwater, the name perhaps derived from the Iroquois or Mohicans, who used to live in the area near the river but now had moved on because of the settlers. As they relaxed, Jacob detailed the next part of their journey.

"We'll make for the Old Dutch area around Ga-ha-oose and spend the night there," Jacob explained.

Some of the younger Rangers gave Jacob a funny look and asked what Ga-ha-oose was? Jacob sometimes forgot that not everyone understood Mohawk.

"Ga-ha-oose means 'place of the falling canoe' because of the waterfall," he said. "Some locals have begun calling it Cohoes because they can't pronounce Ga-ha-oose. We'll camp near the old Manor of Rensselaerswyck for the night, and then we'll turn east, crossing the river there, head towards the Mohawk Trail, and travel into Massachusetts. There we'll start recruiting. We'll hit New York on the way back."

They all nodded, impressed by the senior Ranger's knowledge of the Mohawk Trail that connected the Iroquois with the other tribes to the east. The trail was the main route for trade and movement between the different tribal villages.

After resting for a bit, the Rangers returned to the road and continued south along the now dry road. A column of supply carts and wagons passed them on the road, escorted by New York Provincials. They nodded to Jacob and his Rangers, who stood off to the side of the road to allow the wagons and carts by.

All of the activity they had seen on the road and at the logistic bases definitely pointed to a hard campaign coming in the spring.

Striking up a conversation to pass time, Ranger Gill asked Jacob how he knew so much about the area, and Jacob told him of his youth, hunting with the Mohawks and traveling all across these different trails and towns, trading skins.

It was about midafternoon when the Rangers arrived at Cohoes and the Manor of Rensselaerswyck. The area had been settled by the Dutch back in the late 1600s and developed by two prominent Dutch families, the Van Olohde and the Van Rensselaer families.

The road carried them through the fords across the Mohawk's river at Van Schaick Island, where numerous mills operated. When Jacob had been a long-hunter traveling with the Mohawks, he knew the area as Quehemesicos, the Mohican name for the island, but names like time kept changing.

The Rangers spent a quiet night in view of the large Manor of Rensselaerswyck, built by the Van Rensselaer family, Dutch merchants who had bought up all of the loose land deeds in the area.

It was a humid night, and the Rangers rested on top of their blankets with no need to pull them over themselves. Smoke slept curled up next to Jacob, who stared up at the cloudless sky and the multitude of bright, twinkling stars. Jacob wondered if one of those twinkling stars was Konkapot or Maggie watching over him, as the Mohawk medicine men and shamans believed.

"Hope you are watching over me," thought Jacob. "Might need it."

Something made him feel the upcoming campaign was going to be a bloody one, again. Then Jacob stopped thinking and allowed himself to fall asleep, his Rangers already snoring around him, including Smoke.

After a quick breakfast of rations, the Rangers loaded up and shouldered their gear, Jacob leading them eastward towards the high country. Having walked this trail numerous times in the past, Jacob knew how to reach the Mohawk Trail from the Albany Road.

Soon the road was behind them and the villages and farms disappeared to be replaced by the woods and low hills found near the eastern border of New York. While it had been nice seeing the villages, Jacob and most of the Rangers felt more comfortable in the woods, away from civilization. They didn't fit in with townspeople or farmers.

While they felt more relaxed, they didn't let their guard down and, in fact, once again became a little more wary of the woods around them. They weren't the only ones who knew about the Mohawk Trail. So did the Abenaki and Ottawas, who fought for the French. They had used the trail on raids into Massachusetts before.

Following the trail as it turned and climbed up the rising land, the Rangers crossed the invisible line between the colonies of New York and Massachusetts without incident. The only event of note was when both Smoke and Otto bolted off to chase down rabbits, and both returned triumphantly with dead rabbits held in their mouths.

Jacob guessed that the wolves were either bored or hungry, perhaps a little of both. Jacob thought about it and had to agree about the boredom. He had to admit, even with all of the horror he had experienced, he was actually missing the action. Jacob also had to admit that recruiting duty was boring, but he understood that his was a vital mission, recruiting the right type of men to fill their ranks.

Having worked with the volunteers at their Ranger School, he had seen those types who were in it for the excitement or the bragging rights, but who would more than likely end up getting killed or getting another Ranger killed. Jacob was determined to recruit the right men on this trip. They would have to rely on them for their collective lives soon enough.

CHAPTER 12

THE MOHAWK TRAIL

Jacob and his Rangers climbed up through the low hills into a range of smaller mountains, moving along the Mohawk Trail to the east. Jacob and some of the others had used the trail before the war, either as hunters or trappers. It was the trail that had been first used by the Mohawks in raids, but it soon turned into the main commerce trail to connect the different Indian Nations in New York and Massachusetts.

Signs of the approaching fall were becoming evident. The air was getting cooler both during the day and at night, and the leaves were beginning to change color, which would soon lead to explosions of reds and oranges across the peaks and valleys. The air smelled crisp and clear, and Jacob found it invigorating. Even Smoke seemed to like the change in the temperature. Jacob imagined wolves must not like summer much with their fur coats.

The Rangers began to descend out of the high country into an area that Jacob recalled was an old hunting ground of the Mohicans before they were pushed out, first by the Mohawks and then by the settlers.

Deciding some fresh food would benefit the Rangers, Jacob told Sergeant Hopkins to take a couple of the men and go hunt some deer while they set up camp near a stream. The others would fish.

The task of going hunting and fishing seemed to bolster the morale of the men by breaking up the monotony of marching. The camp was sited in a small clearing next to a babbling stream, and some leaves had already begun to fall and carpet the forest floor.

Jacob and Samuel built a fire for cooking the meat while Sergeant Hopkins and three others departed to hunt. The other Rangers, after setting up their sleeping areas, unwound fishing lines and headed for the stream.

Even Jacob and Samuel sat down on the stream bank, tossing their fishing lines in with those of the other Rangers, who had spread out along the bank. Jacob sat back, just enjoying the peace of the moment. Once they reached their first target, the fort at West Hoosac, they would begin their recruiting efforts.

As he watched his fishing line, puffing on his pipe, Samuel asked Jacob, "So, any plan on how to do this recruiting business?"

Watching his line, Jacob simply replied, "Nope. Just going to be honest with them. Don't want any adventure seekers, just real men."

Samuel nodded, almost hooking a fish but letting his line settle back. "May be easier said than done."

After some time they heard a shot ring out in the distance. Instinctively, all of the Rangers reached over and touched their rifles, which were next to them on the banks, and listened. While it was more than likely their hunting party, the Rangers would not let down their guard. Both Smoke and Otto looked up, ears raised, then settled back down watching the pile of fish to make sure it didn't run away.

They had returned to fishing, adding to the small pile of brook trout they had already caught, when they heard a second shot off in the distance. About an hour later, Sergeant Hopkins and the hunting party returned, each pair of men carrying a swinging a deer between them.

The Rangers got down to the business of cleaning the fish and cutting up the deer, and then they begin to cook them over the fire. Privates Gill and Henry went out with their tomahawks to get firewood to feed the cooking fire, and Johnson went with them as their security.

Jacob took his turn at cooking the deer meat while the fish were skewered on green branches and set over the edges of the fire. As the meat was cooking, Jacob instructed the Rangers to check and clean their equipment to make sure it hadn't rusted or become dull.

As the Rangers took out their gear and inspected it, Jacob pulled out his tomahawk, ran his thumb along the edge, and decided it needed to be sharpened. While he did carry a sword as a symbol of his position, Jacob mostly relied on his tomahawk for close combat, and he began to sharpen its edge.

As the sun set, the Rangers enjoyed the fresh meal of deer meat and roasted trout while they relaxed around the fire. Jacob set the order for the watch, seeing they were on the trail and not near a fort like they had been in the past. A Ranger would stand watch and then rotate after about an hour. While Jacob still had concerns that unfriendly Indians might be using the trail, it was also good to maintain best practices so their skills remained sharp.

Jacob didn't have to stand watch, but he did wake from time to time, Smoke with him, to check on the Rangers and help pass the quiet night. The night air was cooler with a breeze, and the sounds of owls and other night animals echoed through the woods. Before sunrise, Jacob had the Rangers perform stand-to, watching and listening to the woods around them. They packed their gear, and Samuel got their packhorse ready, which he had named Bob.

After only a few hours on the trail, the Rangers came out into a large open area with a stockade blockhouse and a village nearby. The village and stockade blockhouse were known as West Hoosac, and it was the most western stockade in Massachusetts.

The fort had been built in the early years to block any eastern expansion by the Dutch, who had first settled New York, but now the fort was used to protect the inhabitants from the raiding French and their Indian allies. Along with a large central blockhouse, it had two small cannons orientated towards the Mohawk Trail and it was surrounded by a recently improved stockade log wall.

Jacob led his Rangers into the fort and reported to the commander, a Captain Reginald Parker of the Massachusetts Provincials. Captain Parker greeted Jacob warmly and said he had room in his small barracks that the Rangers could use while they were there because there was a small garrison in the stockade. Mostly locals were working on repairing the blockhouse and the walls. Jacob thanked him, gathered the Rangers, and occupied the barracks.

Jacob with Samuel and Sergeant Hopkins walked into the town of West Hoosac while the rest of the Rangers got their small barracks room into order. In the village, they found a suitable tavern near the center, which would serve as a good recruiting place.

Jacob spoke with the tavern keeper and, after paying some rent, received a small table and a couple of chairs, which they placed outside under a large maple tree, and Jacob got down to the business of recruiting. They spent most of the afternoon just watching the villagers pass by, as the villagers watched the Rangers and the two wolves sitting next to them.

Jacob knew it would take time for word of mouth to pass that Rangers were in town recruiting, so he settled in for a long afternoon. The tavern keeper sent out some roasted chicken, a fresh loaf of bread, and some ale for the Rangers.

Some of the locals stopped by and spoke with Jacob, mostly looking for news about the war. They wanted to know what was really going on.

"Stories we hear," asked one townsman, "seem more fantastic than real, and the fighting brutal and bloody. Is it true?"

Jacob nodded, and said that's why they were there, looking for the right men, to spare the settlements from the horrors of war by stopping the French.

Jacob learned that the village was in the process of being renamed after one of the leading families in the area, the Williams family. The new name was to be in honor of Colonel Ephraim Williams, who had been killed at the Battle of Lake George back in 1755, leading one of the Massachusetts Provincial Regiments. Jacob recalled hearing about Colonel Williams at the battle and thought it would be fitting to rename the village Williamstown.

In fact a villager asked Jacob if he had been at that battle, and Jacob answered that he had. A crowd gathered, wanting to hear the tale of the battle and anything else about their town namesake.

Afternoon turned into evening, and there were no takers, only townsfolk who wanted to hear news or tales of battle, so Jacob returned the table and chairs, let the tavern owner know they would be back in the morning, and returned to the fort.

Jacob and the Rangers remained at West Hoosac/Williamstown for five days, and were able to recruit seven men, four long hunters and three men who had served in the Provincials earlier in the war and who wanted to return as Rangers for the next campaign.

After paying them their signing bonuses and enough coins to purchase equipment, Jacob instructed them to meet with Corporal Stevens the next morning, who would lead them back to Fort Edward. Then Jacob and the rest of the Rangers departed for the next village on the trail, which would be North Adams.

Jacob led the Rangers out with Samuel leading Bob, Smoke and Otto ranging ahead and to the flanks. The air was becoming crisper and the leaves were beginning to burst into full color, which meant that fall was there and winter was coming. Jacob and the older Rangers hoped Old Man Winter would hold off for at least a little while longer.

After a day and a half on the trail, the Rangers came out to a large open valley full of farmers' fields. In the town of North Adams there was a village and a large blockhouse fort with a wood palisade wall around it. It was called Fort Massachusetts.

The fort had been around since just before King George's War, when it had been savagely attacked by French and Indians, who had eventually forced the surrender of the ten defenders.

Now the fort, which was being repaired and made ready for the winter, would watch over the Mohawk Trail with about twenty men from the Massachusetts Militia. They were under the command of a local, who called himself Major William Adams. Major Adams, who spoke more like a shopkeeper then a commander, said Jacob and his men could stay in the blockhouse. Most of the men returned home during the night, and he only rotated a few men at the fort. Since Jacob and his Rangers were occupying the blockhouse, he was delegating the responsibility for night security of the fort to them so his men could return to their families.

This didn't bother any of the Rangers, who preferred to do the job themselves, not sure of the capability of the militiamen. They had served with most of the Provincial units from the area, which had performed professionally, but the militias were of a different quality. They would meet to drill maybe once or twice a year. Their main responsibility was to defend their towns unless they were called out for a major crisis.

These militiamen acted like there was no war on. Perhaps to them it was far away and not in their backyard. Yet, their fort had been attacked in 1745 by an enemy force; it could very well happen again. The Rangers would rotate two per watch. They stowed their gear and settled in for the night. They got the fire crackling in the stone fireplace of the blockhouse, and Smoke settled himself near it and, after finishing the rations Jacob had tossed to him, fell asleep.

When morning arrived, the two Rangers who had the last guard watch, Corporal Walker and Private Henry had the fire going with hot water ready and some of their pre-made Johnnycakes warming up. After munching on their rations and washing it down with warm tea, Jacob, Samuel, Sergeant Edwards, and Private Johnson headed into town to start their recruiting day.

The Town of North Adams was of a decent size. It was a farming community with some local businesses. Jacob went to one of the larger taverns near the center of town, the Prancing Pony, and having spoken to Solomon Duncan, the tavern owner, set up a recruiting table outside on the tavern's porch.

For most of the morning, the Rangers watched the community come and go, bringing in produce or shopping. Some of the townsfolk stopped to speak with the Rangers, mostly to ask for news of the war.

Samuel watched the activity, recalling how in his youth he had been in the trading business and thus had been burdened with the responsibility of the books and coin for this detail. "Well," he mused, "at least they're getting the God-given truth from us, and nothing fanciful."

The Rangers were enjoying their lunch when they spotted a large number of long hunters and trappers coming into town leading pack horses loaded with game and skins.

"Now this could be a good sign," said Samuel, who had a mouthful of roasted chicken and was pointing with the chicken leg.

Jacob nodded, appraising the men as they passed by. All looked like consummate professionals, who carried themselves well. After dropping off their game and skins, a few of the long hunters came over to speak with Jacob.

"You Rangers?" asked one of the hunters, and Jacob replied that they were. Then Jacob started up a conversation with the hunters about the local area, recalling his days as a long hunter traveling through the area. By then, more of the hunters and some of the trappers had come over, along with some of the interested young men from the town.

Soon the conversation centered on hunting areas and tales of the hunt, each man trying to out-boast the others. Laughter and general kidding punctuated the conversation. Some of the townsfolks just stood on the fringe, watching and listening to these rough and ready frontiersmen.

When Jacob felt a good number of men had assembled around them and had shared in the stories, he called to the tavern keeper for ale all around, an order that was rewarded with a loud shout of joy from the assembled hunters, trappers, and townsmen alike.

After paying for the mugs with the recruiting fund, Jacob started talking about the war and the battles the Rangers had fought and how they were looking for good men, men like these hunters.

The men listened intently as Jacob described the fighting against the French, the Canadians, and their dreaded Indian allies. While the younger townsmen were enraptured by the tales of battle, the hunters and trappers nodded their heads in understanding, knowing full well what these Indians had done, brutality that most of them had witnessed themselves.

"Are you Rangers as good as you say you are?" asked one of the local men.

Jacob looked at him and replied, "I can sit here and tell you we're the best, but how would I know if you believed me? How about we show you?"

This seemed to pique everyone's interest.

"You fellas up for a little shooting competition? Maybe a little tomahawk throwing?" asked Jacob.

This was met with a loud roar of approval from the gathered men. Jacob smiled and nodded. He had them.

"Put the word out we're holding a shooting and tomahawk competition tomorrow over by the fort. Then you'll see how good we are."

The men all murmured to one another, and then one asked if there would be ale there. Jacob said there would be. That sealed it, and the men left with shouts at one another about who was going to be the best shot. The boasting had begun.

Jacob spoke to Mr. Duncan, and Samuel handed over a small bag of coins. The tavern owner agreed that he would provide the refreshments and maybe even take a crack at the competition. "I may be a little bit past my prime," commented Mr. Duncan, "but I bet I can still hit a target or two."

Jacob smiled and shook the tavern owner's hand. "I look forward to trading shots with you in the morning." he said. The tavern owner loaded up some fresh bread, roasted venison, and stew for the Rangers.

Jacob returned to the fort where, over their evening meal, he told the Rangers about the competition in the morning. The Rangers looked forward to the contest and began to prepare their gear, sharpening their tomahawks and going over their rifle balls to make sure they were smooth with no burs.

The next day dawned clear and bright. The Rangers gathered their gear and headed out to a nearby spot, which was open enough for the competition but which had some shade trees to sit under. The local militiamen who were arriving to work on the fort asked if it was true about the competition. After Jacob confirmed that it was, many decided to take a day off, with Major Adams saying, "Ha, I'll show you all how it's done."

Jacob shook his head, and Samuel turned away and snickered after hearing Major Adams's boast. The Rangers and some of the local militiamen built some wooden tripods to hold blocks of wood that would be the tomahawk targets. Other blocks of wood were marked to be the shooting targets. Sergeants Hopkins and Carver tied these to trees about fifty yards away.

As the targets were being placed, Solomon Duncan arrived with a cart carrying some casks of ale and cups. He was accompanied by some of his helpers and serving girls.

Mr. Duncan, after setting up some tables and the casks, pulled his rifle and shooting bag from the cart and joined the group of locals and hunters who had begun to arrive. Jacob looked them over appraisingly. The hunters and the trappers all had well-maintained rifles and carried them like they knew how to use them.

Even Mr. Duncan's rifle had the look of good care but hard use. It was not a showpiece that sat over a fireplace; it was a gun that had been used. Jacob nodded. This was going to be a good day.

Most of the locals arrived with smooth-bore muskets, although some carried rifles. It also appeared that more people were coming than they had spoken with, so perhaps they'd be able to recruit a decent number of new Rangers.

Jacob called all of the Rangers over.

"Samuel, keep the recruiting book close by. May be a good day," he said, and Samuel nodded.

"Boys, we need to do a good job here, not just for recruiting. Our reputation is on the line. If we get beat by a bunch of locals, the word will spread, and we won't be able to recruit anyone. Let's show these folks why we're the best!"

Jacob determined that a large enough group had gathered, and he called everyone over and got the shooting competition started. Each man approached a line the Rangers had marked and aimed at the targets, taking their shots. Each time someone fired, Jacob and the shooter went down to check the target. A small stick was broken to a length that showed how far from the marked center the shot had hit. It was given to the shooter while Jacob marked the hole with ink.

About thirty men took part in the competition, and as Jacob had expected, the rifle-carrying men did well. Surprisingly, some of the smoothbore musket owners also did well, even Solomon Duncan. The men took the shooting seriously and only a few were sipping on the ale, so Jacob decided to take it to the next level.

Jacob had Sergeants Hopkins and Carver move the targets out to a hundred yards to whistles and "aws" from the group. Then Jacob laid a blanket and called everyone over.

"It seems you men know how to shoot, so I am raising the stakes."

Jacob pointed to the new targets, then pulled out a bag of coins and tossed them on the blanket. One of the men whooped and yelled, "A blanket shoot!"

Jacob nodded. "For those who don't know, we all place something of value on the blanket, and whoever wins the shoot gets first pick of the items. I placed a bag of twenty shillings."

The other Rangers came up and pulled small items from their haversacks, then the hunters followed, and soon the blanket was full. The shooting commenced, now with some of the townspeople coming out to watch and cheer their men on. All of the men with muskets were eliminated, including Solomon

Duncan, who nodded to the Rangers and went over to help pour the ale that the eliminated men were enjoying.

The riflemen were taking the competition very seriously. Their personal reputations were on the line. It had come down to seven men: three Rangers, Jacob, Sergeant Hopkins, and Corporal Walker; two long hunters, Ary White and William Augusta; a trapper named Edwin Parks; and John Carpenter, a local.

Six new targets were made, and Jacob asked Solomon Duncan to be the judge along with Sergeant Dobbs. As the men loaded their rifles, the spectators hooted and shouted, making side bets and boasting. Obviously Solomon was making good ale sales from all of the commotion.

Jacob indicated he would go last. Ary White went first, taking his time aiming and gently pulling the trigger. His shot was only a quarter-inch from center and the crowd clapped and hollered their approval. Then John Carpenter fired, and his shot was just over an inch from the center.

Next up was Sergeant Hopkins, who also took his time but was a half inch from center. More side bets were being made as John Carpenter took friendly ribbing from his friends while drinking a cup of ale.

While the shooting competition was going on, Sergeant Edwards was running the tomahawk throwing contest. Each man stood behind a line and threw his tomahawk at a target ten yards away, trying to sink it in the center marked by a playing card.

Edwin Parks took his turn on the firing line and was just under a half inch from center. Corporal Walker's results were slightly better, just over a quarter inch from center. Ary White was feeling confident when William Augusta went up and in the process of shooting, sneezed and missed the target entirely.

The crowd roared with laughter as William shook his head. "Take another shot," Jacob said to a relieved William, and the crowd voiced its approval by hooting and boasting. William reloaded and fired without incident, but was still about a half inch from center.

It was now Jacob's turn, their reputation as Rangers and his personal reputation on the line. The hunters and trappers had gathered around Ary and were slapping him on the back as he was gulping down ale, believing he had the competition all wrapped up.

Jacob approached the firing line, cradling his trusted rifle in his arm, cocking the hammer all the way back. Looking at the crowd, Jacob asked, "You wanted to know how good we are?"

The spectators hooted and clapped. Without hesitating, Jacob snapped the rifle into his shoulder and aiming quickly, fired. As the smoke cleared from the shot, Solomon and Sergeant Dobbs were spending a long time looking at the target.

"Oh bloody hell, I better not have missed after showing off like this," thought Jacob.

Sergeant Dobbs and Mr. Duncan arrived with the target, a dumbfounded look on Solomon's face as he held the target up for all to see.

Jacob's shot had hit the mark dead center. The crowd erupted into cheers, Ary White spitting his ale in surprise. Jacob was relieved he had not missed; it had been a calculated risk.

The shooters went over to the blanket, Jacob moving up first and reaching down for the bag of coins. He tossed it to Ary White, a gesture which the crowd and a stunned Ary approved. Then the other shooters came up. The Rangers all deferred taking a prize and allowed the locals to choose ahead of them.

The locals came up to congratulate Jacob and pat him on the back, before leading him over to the tomahawk contest. Hoping his luck held, Jacob walked up to the throwing line without hesitating and, still cradling his rifle, he pulled out his tomahawk and threw it smoothly, cutting in half a playing card that had been tacked to the target as the center. Once again the spectators applauded and shouted their approval as they herded Jacob and the other Rangers to the ale for a celebratory drink.

Sitting under the shade trees and drinking ale from cups and mugs, Jacob and the other Rangers told tales of heroism and action in battle. The locals gathered around, listening to Jacob and the other Rangers tell their stories of fighting around Lake George or up against the French near Fort Carillon, with fighting continuing during both the winter and the summer.

They spoke of Major Robert Rogers and Captains Putnam and Stark, explaining how the Provincials and the militia were fighting side by side with them to stop the French from pouring into southern New York.

Jacob said that was why they were looking for good men, men to fill the ranks of the Rangers to help stop the French and their allies before they pushed further south and spread across the colonies.

"It's been some time since they came this way," remarked Jacob. "But if we can't stop them and they pour down the valley to Albany, they'll be here knocking on your doors." The townsfolks and hunters nodded their understanding, pipes and mugs in hand.

Jacob continued, "Many have sacrificed for hearth and home, for loved ones, and we need more if we're going to stop them and stop them cold."

The locals listened intently, many nodding as they smoked pipes. Jacob stood, brushed off the leaves and twigs he had been sitting on, and told them that if they were interested, he would be over there, pointing to a table that Samuel had set up.

Most of the hunters and trappers followed Jacob over. He sat on a box behind the table, and they asked him about serving. Jacob explained that they would serve for a year in one of the independent companies of Rangers, that they would be subject to Ranger and not British discipline, and that they would be paid bounties and other rewards for scalps by New York.

The hunters and trappers looked at each other, commenting that at least they would be in shelters during the winter and would get a crack at the French and their Indian allies with other men like themselves. Why not?

"Besides," one of the hunters commenting as he palmed his coins. "Can't trap and hunt if we're worried about keeping our hair. Bad for business."

They all enrolled as volunteers, Jacob making sure they all signed the ledger as Samuel paid them their enlisting bounty.

As the afternoon turned into early evening, more locals came out and the competition area became an impromptu party site as fiddles and pipes came out, and music and laughter filled the area.

Some of the local men came up. They were mostly younger men who were looking for adventure. Jacob looked them over. A few were just eager greenhorns with no idea of the hardships they would face. He turned them away, but encouraged them to join the local militia or the Provincials.

Some though, as Jacob had seen in the competition, were men who could handle themselves. Some of the militiamen also joined, and even some older men, who had served before in the militia or Provincial forces, signed up. These men, already veterans, were interested in the part about the independent companies being subject only to Ranger, not British, discipline.

"That's correct," Jacob explained. "Only Major Rogers has the authority over us. But make no mistake, he can be a tough taskmaster, and if he feels you are not pulling your weight, you'll be good as gone."

Jacob recounted the farce court-martial he endured, and the lashing. "I was lucky that Major Rogers and the general showed up when they did. Don't know what two hundred lashes would have done to me."

Jacob gave them more tales of harsh punishments they had observed, telling of personal experiences or of witnessing the floggings men received for minor infractions. They told of the tension they had seen between the British officers and the Provincials, who were doing the fighting and dying.

It was becoming dark, and Jacob called out to the new Ranger volunteers, telling them to make sure they arrived by midday tomorrow at this spot with everything they needed to march to Fort Edward. They could purchase whatever gear they need with their bounties.

Jacob was pleased with the results. Twenty men had volunteered. Samuel gave him a knowing wink as he packed up all of the ledgers and bags of money and returned to the blockhouse for the night.

Jacob instructed Sergeant Dobbs and Private Gill to escort these volunteers back to Fort Edward before they got too deep into their ale cups. They nodded and returned to socializing with the locals.

Jacob continued to sit on his box, leaning back against a tree and watching the celebration going on, the music playing, and the locals enjoying themselves. It was as if they had needed to celebrate, even if it was just to celebrate life and enjoy the moment. Both Smoke and Otto watched from where they lay next to Jacob, golden eyes reflecting the fire light.

Jacob nodded and took a drink of ale, wiping the foam from his mouth as Samuel returned with wooden bowls full of stew and bread.

Realizing he was hungry, Jacob took one and thanked Samuel, who pulled up a box and joined him watching the crowd. Smoke sat down as Jacob tossed him some bits of stew meat, Smoke snapping it up before it hit the ground. Samuel did the same with Otto, who never dropped a morsel.

Some of the locals came over and stopped in their tracks when they saw both wolves, but Jacob waved them over, and they sat on the ground, but gave the wolves a wide berth. Ary White came over and handed Jacob another mug of ale, joining them, and also tossing a piece of meat to Smoke, who chomped it before it hit the ground. Soon the others were tossing meat to Smoke and Otto, both enjoying this game of eating tossed meat, but the locals still kept their distance.

"Better be careful," remarked Jacob as both Smoke and Otto snapped meat in mid-air. "You don't want to get fat." Both wolves gave Jacob a dirty look and returned to the game.

As before, the locals asked about tales of the fighting, because they didn't receive much news about the war here in town. Some asked about the life of a Ranger. How did they sleep when in garrison? Did all Rangers have green uniforms? And they wanted to know about the general life of a Ranger while on campaign.

Jacob told them the truth, the hard life of being a Ranger and the commitment and sacrifice it required: the loss of dear friends, the time out on scouts or missions, the strain of being away from loved ones, and the constant danger.

Locals overhearing Jacob's tales joined the group to listen. He continued, saying it took a special breed of man to join the Rangers, and that's why they were the best because they only took the best. They had the responsibility of not just being the eyes and ears of the army, but also of taking the fight to the enemy, not waiting for them to come at them.

Men nodded, pipe stems in the corners of their mouths, the glow of the tobacco shining on their faces. Jacob also told of the rewards of being a Ranger, their well-deserved reputation and the sweet taste of victory when they defeated their enemies at their own game. He told them that in the coming spring, they would be taking the fight to the enemy, and that the new recruits could partake in the glory of victory. He said they would have marvelous tales to tell their friends and family back here when they returned home.

The night was getting late, and some of the locals began to stagger and stumble home. Jacob decided to call it a night. He, Samuel, and the wolves went around and made sure all of their Rangers had returned or were returning to the blockhouse to get some sleep before they departed in the morning.

It was a loud room that evening as many of the Rangers were snoring, tired from the day and the ale they had drunk. Enough so that Jacob grabbed his blanket and, with Smoke found a comfortable space outside to sleep where it was quieter.

In the morning, the Rangers packed their gear and ate their breakfast of rations and any leftovers from the meal that Mr. Duncan had provided. Sergeant Dobbs and Private Gill were packed, and they went over to meet with the volunteers who were beginning to gather.

Jacob returned to Mr. Duncan's tavern to return the bowls and pot that had contained their meal. Jacob paid Mr. Duncan some extra coins for helping with the refreshments. He accepted graciously and wished Jacob and his Rangers Godspeed on their journey.

When Jacob came out of the tavern, five more locals were waiting with their muskets and well-worn bags over their shoulders. These men had the look of men who had experience and were not just looking for adventure.

"Sir, after thinking about it some more, we would like to volunteer as well," said one of the locals. "We're from the local militia company, but want to do more." A second wanted to confirm that they would get the green uniforms, and Jacob nodded, waving them to follow him to the assembly area.

Nodding his head, the volunteer commented, "Good enough for me. Time for me to do my part."

Samuel was pulling the box with the ledger and the bounties off from Bob the packhorse when Jacob arrived, seeing five more men waiting. With a satisfied grin and a nod, Jacob got down to business and signed up the additional ten men and paid them their bounties.

Five of the new volunteers were older veterans who had served in the militia, and their wives were saying their farewells, while mothers and fathers were seeing the younger men off.

After making sure all was in order in the ledger and passing it to Samuel, Jacob called Corporal Sullivan over and had him join the group now that it numbered thirty. Jacob gave some dispatches to Sergeant Dobbs to give to Major Rogers at Fort Edward, detailing their recruiting so far.

He personally shook all of the thirty volunteers' hands, welcoming them to the Rangers and saying he hoped some of them would be assigned to his company. He wished them a speedy journey before Sergeant Dobbs took charge and led them towards the trail for Fort Edward. Family and friends waved and wished them well as the volunteers waved back.

Jacob turned to the rest of his Rangers and led them on to their next stop.

CHAPTER 13

TO THE RESCUE ONCE AGAIN

Jacob was extremely satisfied with the results of the recruiting so far. Getting thirty volunteers would be a windfall for the Rangers. He also hoped that most of the recruits would remain after the training and not change their minds, but he wasn't very worried because from what he had seen, these men were of good quality.

The day was turning grey and cool, the winds blowing the fallen leaves into colorful cyclones on the ground. The Rangers continued along the trail, their recruiting party now reduced to eight men and one pack horse.

Jacob told the Rangers as they walked that they were heading towards Deerfield but would stop at some of the smaller towns along the way to see if their recruiting luck would hold.

"Sometimes, the better recruits come from these smaller towns," commented Sergeant Carver as he chewed on a long stalk of grass. "At least they have skills where these townsfolk wouldn't know which end the ball comes out of a musket."

As they walked, the Rangers joked about the shooting competition, but they still kept wary eyes on the surrounding woods as was their habit, not letting their guard down.

***

Jacob's party was not the only one in the area hoping its luck would hold. L'Kimu and Saqmaw, Mi'kmaq Indians from the small village of Ulustuk, were on the warpath. L'Kimu wanted to prove to the larger tribes allied with the French that they, the Mi'kmaq, could fight and spread terror among the English as well as the Ottawas, Hurons, and Abenakis.

L'Kimu led a small party of twenty personally selected warriors from the Bear Clan, and they had moved deep into English territory without being detected. They had ambushed and taken the scalps of three English hunters the day before. L'Kimu had heard tales of the great raid against the English at Deerfield in times past, and that's where he was leading his band of warriors.

They would find farms, take prisoners to be given as gifts to the French, and enemy scalps, burning the farms after looting them of valuables. These English thought they were safe, away from the warpath. Each warrior had struck the war pole in their village, promising to paint their tomahawks red with English blood. He would bring the warpath to these farmers.

***

Both parties continued on their journeys, unaware of each other as they all headed towards the same general area, Jacob from the west and L'Kimu from the northeast. The Rangers had been on the trail for a few days, only passing a few small parties of Mohawks returning from the east and a group of trappers before they arrived at Charlemont.

A small town originally settled by a man named Moses Rice and his family, Charlemont had begun to grow around the Rice's family farm. Jacob recalled stopping there once as a long hunter, but he didn't recall anything in particular about it.

The Rangers noticed that there were no defensive works in or around the town. It didn't look like a good area to recruit, so the Rangers spent the night on the town's outskirts, having resupplied themselves with some food, sugar, and tobacco. They had talked to some of the locals, getting their news, and the locals in turn had asked them about the war as well as other news from New York and the different towns at which they had stopped.

It was a polite conversation, getting caught up on current events, but from what Jacob observed, there was no one showing any interest in joining them. It didn't surprise Jacob. It seemed to him these people were more interested in the weather and its impact on their crops, then anything outside of their borders.

The Rangers continued along the trail for a few days to the next town, which turned out to be a new township named Greenfield. The Pocumtuck Indians had once fished the local streams and raised field crops until they were wiped out by the Mohawks in the late 1660s. The area had recently been reoccupied by settlers from Deerfield, who wanted more living space than they had had in the old town of Deerfield.

The town had begun back in 1753 and was named after the Green River, which ran close to it. As the Rangers walked into the town, they noticed that there was no fort, stockade, or blockhouse, just as there had been none in Charlemont. This bothered Jacob. Perhaps these townsfolks felt safe and secure so far from the border with Canada, but that seemed foolish to him.

As Jacob entered the town, he noticed approvingly that some of the houses were strong houses, with stout walls and thick shutters which had crosses built into them. Once closed, these shutters could be used for firing at attacking enemies while protecting the shooter. At least these former residents of Deerfield understood the importance of garrison houses in which they could defend themselves.

Jacob and his Rangers stopped at a good-sized inn with the alluring name of the Dancing Wench, and Jacob went inside to speak to the owner. A man came from the kitchen and introduced himself as Thomas Gardner. He shook Jacob's hand and welcomed him and his men to the inn.

Thomas Gardner explained, "I once served in the Massachusetts Provincials, was at the battles at Lake George and Bloody Pond back in 1755 before mustering out. Saw my fair share before I returned to this life as an inn and tavern keeper."

Mr. Gardner took a closer look at Jacob. "You seem familiar to me. Have we met before?" Jacob shook his head but did say that he had been at those battles. Gardner snapped his fingers and pointed at Jacob.

"That bloody morning scout in the rocks. You were there, weren't you?" Jacob nodded, and Mr. Gardner smiled and slapped his knees. "Ha, thought so! Don't know if it was you but I do recall your green uniforms in the middle of the bloody mess. Glad to meet another survivor from that day."

He shook Jacob's hand and settled on a reduced price, and Jacob was able to secure rooms for his men and stable space for Bob, the packhorse. Jacob told his men they didn't have to sleep on the ground or in a blockhouse. He told them to move their gear inside and Mr. Gardner would see them to their rooms.

That seemed to improve the morale of the Rangers as they smiled, shouldering their gear and making their way into the Inn. Jacob even had to admit that perhaps a nice bed would be a welcome change from the hard, cold ground or wooden pallets in a block house.

Samuel and the gear would share a room with Jacob, the room slightly bigger than the ones the rest of his men had. Still, they all looked forward to enjoying the luxury of sleeping in a bed for a change. The wolves looked dubiously at the room, but made burrows under the beds, curled up, and watched.

That night in the common room, Jacob and the Rangers enjoyed a feast of roast duck, venison, bread, and ale. Mr. Gardner from time to time pointed to Jacob and the other Rangers as he spoke with the locals, saying, "Well now, any of you who doubted my stories from the lake, see them Rangers over there, and they will tell you plain and true what really happened!"

Some of the locals took him up on it and stopped by the Rangers' table. They asked about the battles, shaking their heads to learn that Mr. Gardner had actually been telling a watered-down version of the fierce battles. Jacob told them about the bloody morning scout and how the Provincials had held their own against brutal odds.

Mr. Gardner eventually joined them at the end of the meal to swap war stories and hear the news. Locals began to enter the inn, and they made their way over to the Rangers, either because they recognized that they were new people who were in green uniforms or because word had spread about travelers with news from outside of the township.

As in the previous towns, everyone wanted news about the war and the other towns they had visited. Some asked what the Rangers were doing in town, and Jacob explained that they were looking for men to join their ranks. More former Provincials were called over by Mr. Gardner, and they too began to recall their experiences fighting in New York before they were mustered out when their battalion returned to Massachusetts.

Chairs and benches were dragged over and the men sat in a circle, the serving girls moving amongst them as the townsfolks and Provincial veterans bought drinks for the Rangers and continued the conversations about the military campaigns against the French. As Jacob and the Rangers told their tales, the locals sat back and smoked their pipes, the grey of their smoke reminding Jacob of the fog of war when the smoke from hundreds of muskets blanketed the battlefields.

It was a conversation that only those who had shared in the same battles could join, each telling the fight from their own point-of-view, bonding as comrades-in-arms. The veterans asked what had happened after the battles, since rumors of the massacre and destruction of Fort William Henry had made it down to them. Jacob confirmed what had happened, and how there were more fortifications being built on the southern shore and between the lake and Fort Edward. Over pipes and mugs of ale, the men settled down to other "soldier talk," often centered once again on the British and the disparity between them and the colonists.

The veterans said they would talk to their friends and other veterans who had fought back in 1755-56 to see if they wanted to join the Rangers. They liked the incentive of the bounties, the independent command, and the idea of fighting with professionals, but some also made it clear that they had seen enough fighting at the lake, and they wished the Rangers luck.

When Jacob and Samuel entered their room, both Otto and Smoke's heads poked out from under the bed to confirm that it was them before returning to their burrows and falling back asleep.

"Ohhhh...yeah," Samuel groaned as he got into bed, squirming around to get comfortable and enjoying the feeling of not sleeping on the ground.

"I could get used to town life," mumbled Samuel, but Jacob wasn't sure. Most of his life had been spent sleeping on the ground, and he found it strange to be in a bed. However, the comfortable bed won him over, and he was soon fast asleep with a snoring Samuel and Otto next to him and a snoring Smoke under him. At least it sounded right.

***

That same night, L'Kimu and Saqmaw crawled forward to the edge of a farmer's field. In the distance were three farms clustered in the center of recently harvested fields of corn, flickering lights from windows showing the buildings were occupied.

Two groups of scouts quietly joined them, having circled around the field, and they reported what they had found. "Saw some dogs near the houses and nothing near the fields. There was a road nearby, but there were no other farms or dwellings we could see that could alert the English." L'Kimu looked at Saqmaw, who nodded his head in agreement. They had found their target.

"We'll use the fields to approach those farms before the sun is fully up. I will lead half of the warriors to the left while you Saqmaw will take the other half to the right. Kill the men, take their scalps, capture the women and children, and we'll sell them in Quebec to the French. We will show the French father we are as good as the Hurons and Ottawas. The warriors slowly backed into the woods, looking forward to their raid in the early morning.

***

As dawn arrived, the Rangers gathered in the common room and enjoyed a breakfast of fresh warm bread, meat pies, and hot tea. The meal and the fire crackling in the great fireplace at the end of the room warmed the Rangers. Jacob and the others had noticed it was getting colder in the morning now, and they had seen their breath in their cold rooms that morning while dressing for the day.

After finishing his meal, Jacob walked out onto the inn's porch with his mug of tea. It was a gloomy grey day, and a cold breeze stirred the leaves. A flight of geese honked as they flew south over the town. Jacob shook his head. It was going to be a cold, ugly day, and he'd have to set up inside the inn somewhere to recruit. Trying to do this outside would not work. Most of the people were already hurrying by as a few drops of rain splattered on the ground close by. Sipping his tea, Jacob returned inside to ask Mr. Gardner where he could set up a recruiting table.

***

As the Rangers enjoyed their breakfast, L'Kimu and his band of ten warriors moved quietly forward, crouched low, slipping among the bundled corn stalks, slowly making their way towards the farms.

It was a grey day. The absence of sun and shadows helped to conceal the approaching raiding party. While some icy rain splattered on L'Kimu's head, he didn't feel the cold as his blood boiled in anticipation of the attack and the plunder to come. So far, they had made no sound that could tip off the English that they were doomed. The raiding party closed their trap, with Saqmaw's warriors forming the other side of the noose.

The warriors could smell and see smoke rising from the chimneys of the three farms, surprised that they hadn't seen anyone yet and hoping the Great Spirit would continue to favor them. Drawing his tomahawk, L'Kimu looked at Saqmaw, who nodded. Pointing to the second farm and with a chopping motion of his hand, L'Kimu rose up and charged towards the first house, beginning the raid.

***

Back in town, Jacob had spoken to only two townsmen, who were interested only in getting news, not in volunteering. He sat in a chair, looking out one of the windows. Corporal Walker was over at the fireplace to get a light for his pipe. Samuel and Sergeant Hopkins were out on the porch. There had been a quick, cold rain, but now the clouds had parted and the sun was working its way through.

Samuel and Sergeant Hopkins were talking when a rider came galloping into town and stopped quickly in front of one of the shops. The rider leaped from the horse and rushed inside. That got the attention of both Samuel and Sergeant Hopkins. Soon two boys ran from the shop, one heading for the church and the other running through the town and knocking on doors.

"Something's up," said Samuel. He went inside and got Jacob, who came out and joined them on the porch. A church bell began to ring out.

As Samuel was explaining what they just seen, the rider returned and after remounting his horse, he took off out of town. A man came out of the shop, and spotting Jacob and the Rangers, started walking towards them. The man might be a shop owner, but from his grizzled look and the deep scar on his face, Jacob knew this man was not just a common tradesman.

As he approached Jacob, he introduced himself. "My name is Roger Brown, well Major Brown of the Greenfield Militia. We just got a report that some farms close by were raided by Indians, who took prisoners and burned the houses. I've sent my boys out to call the militia, and I could really use your help."

The church bell continued its toll. Responding to the determined look on Major Brown's face, Jacob nodded.

"Samuel, gather the men and grab my gear," commanded Jacob as he walked with Major Brown. Both Smoke and Otto, sensing something afoot, came loping down and were waiting in anticipation.

Major Brown stopped in the middle of the street as men carrying their muskets and shooting bags began to assemble. A boy came running up with a musket, a shooting bag, and a maroon sash for Major Brown, who put the sash over his shoulder followed by his shooting bag and haversack.

"If you don't mind me asking, you were at the lake and Bloody Pond weren't you?" Major Brown asked Jacob, who nodded he had.

"Thought so. You may not have known it, but you saved my life that day when the Indians caught us cold in that ravine. That's how I got this," he said as he pointed to the scar on his face. "These are good men, but against a war party, I could use you and your Rangers' help. About a quarter of them are veterans from that fight, but most are just local militiamen who haven't seen battle yet."

Jacob nodded as Samuel and the Rangers came pouring out of the inn with Samuel handing Jacob's gear to him. Pulling his shooting bag, blanket roll, and haversack over his shoulder and sliding his tomahawk into his belt, Jacob took his sword off and carried it over as Mr. Gardner was coming out with his rifle and shooting bag.

"Can I trust one of your people with this?" asked Jacob

Mr. Gardner yelled inside the inn, and a boy came out.

"Nathan, take care of this sword and make sure no one goes into Ranger Clarke's room!" commanded Mr. Gardner, and his son quickly responded, "Yes Sir!"

He cradled Jacob's sword to his chest as Jacob and Mr. Gardner turned to join the growing militia company. Jacob's seven Rangers were standing off to the side settling their shooting bags, bedrolls, and haversacks as the townsmen assembled.

Jacob could see what Major Brown had been talking about. About a quarter of the men had the look of veterans, gear set about their shoulders correctly. Most though were inexperienced, and Jacob sent his Rangers in to help these men position their gear so it would ride easily on their shoulders.

Major Brown addressed the assembled men.

"John Parker's and the Dawes' places were attacked by a war party this morning. Isaac Davis was riding by when he saw the smoke rising from the farms. He observed several Indians in war paint torching the buildings and at least two women and three children being led off before he rode into town to warn us."

Major Brown watched the reactions of the assembled men, their voices mingling in hushed responses of the news. The veterans had set, determined looks while the inexperienced men had mixed feelings. Some were showing excitement, some fear, and others mostly shock. Major Brown turned to Jacob and asked if his men would lead out, pulling Isaac Davis out of the formation so he could show them the way.

"Isaac knows the trails around here the best," explained Major Brown.

Jacob turned to Isaac.

"They are going to be heading north towards Canada. Where can we intercept them?"

Isaac thought about it and then nodded.

"Breakneck Ford near the falls on the Green is where they'll be heading. It's the only place to cross without being near a town or something."

"We're going to be moving fast. Try to keep up," Jacob instructed the militia members.

He turned to Major Brown, who nodded, and the Rangers took off at a jog with Isaac leading and the rest of the company of about fifty men following. Both wolves took off, ranging to their front as they always did when the Rangers were on the hunt.

After a little while jogging, Jacob could hear the panting and heavy breathing of the men behind them, and he turned to see what their condition was. Major Brown, Mr. Gardner, and the ten veterans were keeping up, even though they were breathing hard and were a little red in the face. Behind them, the column was beginning to stretch out as some of the men were slowing down. Jacob couldn't slow their pace if they wanted to get ahead of the war party. He looked to Major Brown who nodded and waved him onward, and Jacob turned and continued their pace.

"Go do what you…can," panted Mr. Gardner. "We'll be along directly, in no time." Major Brown squeezed his shoulder, and took off after Jacob and his Rangers with the few townsfolk who could keep up.

***

L'Kimu turned to look at his column of prisoners and warriors. Three women, a young man, and five children shuffled behind them. A rope was tied around their necks, and they were being led by one of his warriors who kept tugging on the rope to keep them going at the same pace as the rest of the warriors.

Six bloody scalps hung from his warriors' belts, plus two on his own, showing off their victory. They carried sacks filled with mirrors, tools, and knives, the booty taken from the farms. The sun might be out, but L'Kimu knew the cold of winter was closing in, and he had to reach Canada with his prizes before the snow began to fall.

Saqmaw joined L'Kimu, a happy look on his face, a scalp hanging from his belt, and his bag clanking with booty. Setting his rifle down and leaning on it, Saqmaw commented, "The

Great Spirit has smiled on us, and the great war chiefs of the French and the other tribes will have to recognize our success in battle." L'Kimu nodded and smiled. Perhaps they would make him a war captain when he arrived, bringing great honor to his village and family.

***

The toll of the pace that Jacob had set had started to become apparent. About fifteen men had dropped back, unable to keep up. Jacob couldn't blame them. They were townspeople for the most part, and jogging at a good pace was not normal for them.

Isaac had led them through some twisting game paths and trails that had brought them to a section of the Green River, which wandered lonely through the woods. At least the temperature was cooler, making it easier to keep a quick pace. Isaac had stopped them on a rise overlooking the river, and Jacob halted to allow the men to catch their breath.

Pointing, Isaac showed Jacob the ford in the distance and indicated that the war party should approach from the east. Jacob was hoping the uncanny luck that had accompanied him on this trip was still with him. There could be numerous other trails and directions that the war party might take, and then they would come up empty.

As Jacob was scanning the fields and looking at the ford, he spotted motion to the east. Pulling his telescope from his haversack, he looked at the spot. It was a shiny teapot hanging from a blanket roll on the back of a painted warrior moving through a clearing that they could see from their elevated position.

Major Brown came up and Jacob handed him the telescope and pointed at the clearing.

"Well I'll be," said Major Brown as the first person in the string of prisoners appeared in the clearing. "It's them!"

Jacob nodded and called everyone up.

"It's going to be close, so we have to hit them on the run. Pair up, one fires and the other covers, but keep moving, load on the run, and if you get close, hit them with your muskets or tomahawks. We have to break them up, or they could start killing the prisoners in an attempt to escape," Jacob told the gathered men.

Looking into the assembled militiamen's' eyes, he commanded, "No mercy. They won't show you any."

Major Brown and the veterans nodded, understanding what Jacob meant. The few militiamen who had kept up grasped the meaning, some gulping, but setting a determined look in their eyes, stealing themselves for the job they would have to do. Jacob turned and the men followed him down into the woods.

***

L'Kimu and Saqmaw stood on the bank of the river at the ford, knowing no one was nearby and they could cross the river here and then turn north towards Canada, avoiding the falls just above them. Two of his warriors, holding their muskets and shooting bags over their heads, entered the cold river, sputtering about the temperature, which rose to their waists as they began to cross.

The warrior leading the prisoners stopped to allow the first two to cross, commenting that it was the first time they would be clean in a while and chuckling at their discomfort in the cold water. He hadn't chuckled long before a ball smashed into his head, the sound of his laughing the last thing he heard. Other balls caught two warriors mid-river.

Spinning, L'Kimu saw men in green uniforms burst from the trees along with several Englishmen around them and on the bank of the river. Balls were whistling around the Indians as the men in green shouted war whoops. Then grey blurs moved past him as Smoke tackled Saqmaw, while Otto's strong jaws sank into the man's arms, both wolves dragging him down.

L'Kimu's mind raced. This couldn't be happening to him. He had been victorious. Ignoring the balls that whistled past him, one tugging at his blanket roll as it just missed him, L'Kimu drew his tomahawk and started towards the first women in the line of prisoners, determined that if he couldn't have his prisoners, neither would the English.

With the sound of the woods exploding around them, the women and children were shaken from their stupor, and they instinctively dropped to the ground, mothers holding their children tight to their chests as the rope around their necks went slack.

Their minds still filled with the fog of horror from their ordeal, they witnessed men in green and others in plain clothes burst from the trees, charging into the Indians. One woman shook her head to clear it as she saw the wolves savagely attack and draw an Indian down, and she felt a moment of joy combined with her hatred of her captors. Their salvation was at hand!

Around her, still in the shock of it all, some of the women and younger girls began screaming, pushed beyond the edge of reality.

Bursting from the trees, Jacob saw a warrior turn, draw his tomahawk, and start towards the prisoners. He knew he couldn't get his rifle up in time for a clear shot, so he simply dropped it where Samuel had stopped to take aim at the warrior at the end of the prisoner line, dropping him cold.

With a quick burst of speed, Jacob knocked the warrior over as he raised his tomahawk over the frightened women, who were screaming in terror. Both Jacob and L'Kimu rolled to their feet and faced one another, tomahawks at the ready. Screaming, L'Kimu swiped at Jacob's head, a thrust that was blocked by Jacob's tomahawk, then again at Jacob's midsection. Jacob caught the wrist of L'Kimu in a grip like a vice, and using his own tomahawk as a lever, spun and threw L'Kimu over his shoulder.

Rolling to his feet, L'Kimu was impressed with this Englishman, and he drew his fighting knife in his left hand, beginning to circle Jacob. Jacob stared back at him, drawing his own fighting knife. Finally a worthy opponent to test his skills, L'Kimu thought.

"Your scalp will bring me great power, Englishman," taunted L'Kimu in Algonquin.

"So will yours," replied Jacob in Algonquin, surprising L'Kimu. Clanging his knife and tomahawk together, Jacob asked, "Shall we dance?"

Jacob's tomahawk and knife swayed as he moved sideways, facing L'Kimu, focusing only on him and ignoring the fighting around them.

Major Brown and some of the militiamen formed a wall around the rescued prisoners while the others fired on the remaining warriors. The wolves continued to tear into the screaming Saqmaw until finally Smoke clamped his jaws on the warrior's throat, ending his screaming.

Samuel came up and brought Jacob's rifle to his shoulder, covering him as he fought L'Kimu. "Give him what for!" yelled Samuel as Jacob circled his opponent.

"Show them how it's done Jacob," yelled Samuel as he sighted along the rifle's barrel. "Tear that savage's heart out."

Another warrior, intent on getting a scalp or two before the English chased them off, started towards a mother and the small child cradled in her arms, eyes closed and both screaming. Believing she would be too scared to stop him and would be an easy kill, the Indian reached out to take her head and give her the killing stroke when a large grey blur knocked him back.

Rolling to his feet, the Mi'kmaq found his "easy" kill blocked by two large and growling wolves, teeth bared and snapping, who had placed themselves between the woman and him. Smoke, blood already dripping from his jaws, lips pealed back to show his bloody teeth and a low growl coming from his throat, stared down the Indian as Otto began to circle, the two wolves working as a team.

Before the warrior could react, Smoke leaped, his jaws quickly tearing out the Indian's throat and killing him, as Otto swept in, hamstringing the Indian, all before the woman and child opened their eyes. When they did, all they saw was the dead Indian as the wolves moved on, once more hunting their enemies.

L'Kimu continued to move sideways, and then quickly slashed in with his tomahawk followed by his knife. Jacob's tomahawk clanked as he blocked L'Kimu's tomahawk, quickly side stepping to just avoid the knife swipe, but he caught L'Kimu's arm with his own knife, slicing the wrist and arm open, spilling blood and forcing L'Kimu to drop his knife.

L'Kimu's confidence began to wane as the cold blue eyes of Jacob looked almost into his soul, and he felt like death was staring at him. Growling, L'Kimu made two quick overhead chops at Jacob, who deftly deflected them. Fear, something L'Kimu had not felt in a long time, was rising up in him, and his attacks became more erratic. L'Kimu overextended one of his chops, and he felt a burning sensation across his midsection as Jacob's knife sliced across his abdomen.

In a desperate move, L'Kimu charged at Jacob with his tomahawk over his head. Calmly, Jacob dropped his tomahawk and caught L'Kimu's tomahawk in his iron grip as it was descending. Slashing his knife across L'Kimu's arm, which forced him to drop the tomahawk, Jacob twisted, turned, and threw L'Kimu over his shoulder.

Jacob didn't let go of L'Kimu's arm, forcing him to land almost sitting on the ground at Jacob's feet. Then using his leg as a lever, he pulled L'Kimu over his leg, stretching his neck and chest out. Panting heavily, L'Kimu heard Jacob whisper in his ear, "You lose," as he slid his knife against L'Kimu's throat. The last sensation he felt was his warm blood spilling before the world went black.

Without pausing, Jacob grabbed the top of L'Kimu's hair and in one swift practiced motion, scalped him before kicking his corpse forward to join his blood on the ground. Wiping his knife on L'Kimu's clothes, Jacob sheathed it and turned to face Major Brown, who handed him his tomahawk.

"Impressive, very impressive," Major Brown said. Jacob just shrugged and thanked the major for his tomahawk, then wiped it on L'Kimu's clothes.

Samuel came up and handed Jacob's rifle to him, and both Smoke and Otto joined them, muzzles bloody and sporting a wolf's satisfied expression. Jacob smiled and scratched Smoke's ears. "Been busy I see."

Major Brown and the militiamen were helping the rescued prisoners; some still in shock, but all looked at Jacob with respect and nodded their approval, including his Rangers, who joined him.

"Well done, lads," Jacob said to his men, then turned and repeated, "Well done," to the militiamen.

Major Brown and the rest of militiamen joined Jacob after scouring the ford, making sure all of the Indians were dead.

"We won't make it back to town before nightfall," said Major Brown, and Mr. Gardner concurred. "Sun is already setting."

Jacob pointed to the rise from which they had spotted the enemy.

"We can camp there. It's defendable, and then we'll travel back to town in the morning."

As the men were forming up around the rescued prisoners, they heard motion and crashing through the woods.

Everyone turned to face the woods, rifles and muskets coming up, when Mr. Gardner and the militiamen who had fallen behind burst onto the scene of battle. Major Brown yelled out for everyone to hold their fire, and the weapons were lowered.

Huffing and puffing, the men had disappointed looks on their faces, having arrived at the scene after all of the fighting was done. Still, Major Brown was glad to see they hadn't quit and returned to the town and that they had found them.

With Jacob, the Rangers, and the wolves leading the way and the militiamen forming a protective circle around the rescued prisoners, they returned to the top of the rise. They found a suitable spot and built some warming fires for the former prisoners while Jacob and Major Brown discussed who would take turns on watch. Major Brown said the Rangers had done enough and didn't need to stand watch. Jacob explained that the Rangers would stand watch anyway, so he might as well include them.

As night fell and the cold crept in, Jacob and his Rangers shared their blankets with the rescued women and children, and everyone shared their rations and water with them. The women and children sat huddled together around the fire, still shocked by what had happened to them. Jacob knew it would take time to heal their hearts and move on from their loss.

"Always a terrible sight, to see poor families caught in the middle," commented Major Brown. He joined Jacob, who was watching the area of the ford. Jacob nodded.

"You're good at what you do. Haven't lost your touch since the lake, I see," said the major. "You must have been doing this a long time."

Jacob nodded, quickly telling of the loss of his family in a similar Indian raid and then serving since 1755 with Rogers and his Rangers. Major Brown whistled and nodded his head, then move closer to Jacob.

"Do you think it will ever end?" asked Major Brown, "Do you think there will ever be peace?"

Jacob thought about it, and answered, "I don't know. I hope so. If we don't stop them next spring, you can expect more of this."

Major Brown nodded, shook Jacob's hand, and left to go check on his men.

Jacob was continuing his rounds, rifle cradled in his arm, when Samuel with Otto and Smoke joined him.

"Another close one; we got lucky again. I hope your luck never runs out," said Samuel, and Jacob had to nod his head in agreement. It could have gone real bad for them today, or at least they could have missed the war party at the ford, and the Indians would have been heading north with their prisoners.

"It's nice having you and your strange luck around," continued Samuel. "Please stick around, if you don't mind, for a little while longer, at least until the campaign or the war is over." Then Samuel winked. "Or whichever comes first."

They continued to walk around the perimeter, checking on their Rangers and the militiamen who were on watch. Then Samuel put on a serious face, turned, and faced Jacob.

"Jacob, have you thought about what you will do when the war is over?" asked Samuel.

Jacob stopped and thought about an answer.

"To be perfectly honest, Samuel," Jacob began. "I haven't really thought about it. Been doing this for so long, I can't seem to think of what it would be like without it."

Jacob thought on it for a moment, before continuing his rounds.

"Another war will probably start anyways," Jacob mused. "It always does. Look how many wars have been fought here already between the English and the French. I think they'll keep fighting until one of them is finally defeated or we're all dead, whatever comes first."

Samuel nodded, and responded, "Well, think about it…Sir," before moving off to find a place to sleep next to one of the fires. Jacob continued on his rounds, but he did think about what he would do when the war was over. He really didn't know, so he would wait and see first if the war ended, and then he'd think about it. This was it. Except for hunting or trapping, this was all he knew.

The Rangers shivered in silence through a cold night, but knew the rescued prisoners needed their blankets more than they did, and it would be colder this winter, so they shivered through the night without complaint. In the morning, the Rangers and the militiamen woke stiff from the cold and chewed on cold rations before shouldering their gear and beginning the trip back to Greenfield.

Jacob and his Rangers led the column, at a much slower pace than the one they had taken to get there. The militiamen once more formed a protective circle around the rescued prisoners, Major Brown sending out flankers to make sure there were no other war parties out there who might try to ambush them.

It took most of the morning to return to the town, and there had been no sign of any other war parties in the area. When they reached town, the townsfolk were waiting for them.

The women came out to help the rescued prisoners as best as they could. Major Brown assembled the company one last time and gave them a "well done" speech before releasing them to return home. Many happy mothers and wives greeted the returning men, overjoyed that no one had been lost and there were no injuries, except to the pride of those who had missed the fighting.

Major Brown shook Jacob's hand and once more commented, "Impressive," before returning to his family.

"Come along, lads," said Mr. Gardner. "Let's feast to our victory!" and he led the Rangers towards the inn.

Waiting on the porch were Mr. Gardner's family and workers, including Nathan, who had Jacob's sword hung over his shoulder, the scabbard dragging on the ground. Mr. Gardner approached his son.

"Everything secure, Mr. Nathan?"

His son snapped his heels together and with a not-too-shabby salute and a serious look on his face, he reported that everything was secure. Then Nathan and his dad broke out in grins.

A worried Mrs. Gardner hugged her husband and whispered thanks to God that he was safe and sound.

"Oh Margaret, we had nothing to worry about with these Rangers here. They scared those bloody savages to death."

His wife looked over at a blood-stained Jacob, and tsked at his uniform. "That just won't do," she fussed and demanded Jacob and his Rangers hand over their coats so the maids could wash the blood out.

"Wouldn't be respectable covered in all of this," she said holding up Jacob's smeared coat and blanched. "Blood!" She instructed the serving maids to wash the clothes and be quick about it.

Mr. Gardner entered the inn, and after seeing the uniforms were being taken care of, his wife quickly moved up and joined him. She took Jacob by the arm, thanking him, and asking God to bless him and his Rangers for delivering her husband from those godless heathens. Jacob nodded his thanks and went to his room where Nathan was waiting with his sword.

"No one entered your room, sir. I saw to it myself," Nathan said proudly.

Jacob stood to attention and saluted Nathan for a job well done. After taking his sword from the boy, he smiled and winked at him. Samuel walked past, nodding his head to Jacob as he patted the boy's head.

Mr. Gardner had not been kidding when he spoke of a feast in celebration. The common room soon filled with the smell of roasted chicken, pork, duck, and bread.

The militiamen and some of the townsmen came in to join in the celebration as the Rangers were finishing up their meals. Soon fiddles and pipes came out, and the room filled with music and laughter, the ale flowing like a river as everyone celebrated being alive.

Jacob was surprised when some of the rescued women came by to thank them, which seemed odd because everyone was celebrating being alive while these people had lost loved ones. Jacob and his men graciously accepted their thanks, and hoped the best for the rescued women, knowing full well the pain that they were dealing with and would continue to have to deal with as they came to terms with what had happened.

As the music played, the stories about the fight at the ford began, but it was mostly the retelling of Jacob's fight with the raiding party leader, many commenting that the Rangers had really showed them how it was done. Jacob's and his men's hands were never empty, mugs of ale constantly being placed in them.

Soon the stories were getting bigger and more exaggerated as the ale was taking its effect, and the militiamen were trying to out-boast one another on how accurately they had shot or how well they had fought in the battle. Jacob sat back and allowed the ale to take over, listening to the tales, leaving these men to their moment of glory.

A serving girl was hovering over Samuel, running her hand over his bald spot as he obviously was telling of his scalping and survival. Jacob spotted another serving girl eying him from across the room, and he raised his mug in salute. Perhaps it wouldn't be so cold a night after all, he thought, as the music played and blended with the laughter of many happy people.

CHAPTER 14

BACK ON THE ROAD

Jacob did have a warm and interesting night. When he entered the common room where Samuel and Sergeant Hopkins were already eating breakfast, the smell of fresh bread and bacon was delightful. After eating and with a nice warm mug of tea, Jacob went out on the porch to see what kind of day it would be.

The sun was up and the air cold and crisp, but it looked like a pleasant day. He decided they would once more try recruiting outside on the porch. Mrs. Gardner and some of the serving girls brought their freshly laundered uniforms to them. The young lady, who had helped to entertain Jacob, held his coat, Jacob winking in thanks.

Borrowing a table, Jacob set up his recruiting table as Samuel brought the box with the ledger and the bounties, escorted by Otto and Smoke. They were joined by Sergeant Edwards and Private Johnson. While some of the townsfolk stopped by to talk with the Rangers, no one appeared interested in volunteering.

"Well, can't say I blame them," Sergeant Edwards said. "After what happened yesterday, more of the men will want to stay close to home to protect their families."

Jacob had to nod in agreement. It made sense. Mr. Gardner came out with his son Nathan to talk to Jacob about recent events, while Nathan asked Sergeant Edwards and Private

Johnson hundreds of questions about being a soldier, a Ranger, fighting, everything.

Mr. Gardner chuckled as his son interrogated the two Rangers, only pausing long enough to listen to their answers before asking more questions.

"Interesting times we live in," said Mr. Gardner. "Hopefully Nathan here won't have to see the ugliness of war. What do you think, Lieutenant Clarke?"

Jacob looked at Mr. Gardner and answered seriously. "I don't know, but unfortunately I think he will see war before he's old. Either this one will grow larger or another one will start right after this one ends."

Mr. Gardner nodded. "Yes, you're correct. Always seems another starts when one finishes." He looked at his young son. "Hopefully, he can grow up first. Maybe."

During the afternoon, six of the veterans who were in the militia came over to speak with Jacob. They asked the normal questions: Would they serve only with the Rangers as an independent company? Was it true about the bounties? Did the Rangers discipline their own men?

Jacob answered their questions in the affirmative, and the six men looked at one another. "Will we learn to fight like you?" Again, Jacob nodded. They would learn.

"Well, we've talked among ourselves. Those of us with wives talked it over with them, and we've spoken with Major Brown, and we decided we want to volunteer for the Rangers."

Jacob was happy at their decision and had them sign the ledger as Samuel paid them their joining bounty.

"Get what items you need, especially cold weather items, and meet back here tomorrow. You'll march out with us. Welcome to the Independent Company of Rangers!" Jacob shook each of their hands and watched them head off to gather or purchase gear. At least they had been able to get some volunteers in this town. Six was better than none.

After one last night sleeping in a bed, the Rangers readied their gear, and Samuel loaded Bob the packhorse with the boxes and bags.

"I'll miss that bed," mumbled Samuel as he tugged a strap tight on Bob. "Especially when I am sleeping on a root or something."

Mr. Gardner provided some dried meat, jerky, and biscuits for the Ranger's supplies and wished them well on their journey.

The six new volunteers arrived, carrying mostly muskets with their shooting bags, haversacks, and snapsacks. Jacob asked if they had all been privates or if any of them had been corporals or sergeants. One man, Moses Little, raised his hand and said he had been a corporal.

"Corporal Little, you're in charge of your section. While we're on the trail, Sergeants Edwards and Hopkins here are going to instruct you in our ways. Your Ranger training starts now," said Jacob, who pointed to Sergeants Edwards and Hopkins.

Major Brown, Mr. Gardner, and some of the townsfolk came out to wish both the Rangers and the new Ranger volunteers luck on their journey as Jacob led the column out of town and back onto the trail. He turned the column south instead of continuing east.

"We're not heading towards Boston?" Samuel asked at which Jacob shook his head.

"No, we'll follow the river south towards Springfield, then on to Rhode Island. From what I've seen the few times I have been to the Boston area, I don't think they'll have the type of men we're looking for."

Samuel who had been a trader before the war nodded, having also been to Boston. "Yeah, I see your point," he said. "They seemed a bit soft in the hand when I knew them. Not what we're looking for, though some of those sailors I met were cut from the same tough cloth as us."

Jacob shrugged as he led them southward. The type of men they wanted lived out here on the frontier, so this is where they would look for quality volunteers. Most of the city or townsfolk they had met would not make good Rangers.

The journey south was uneventful. More of the land opened up to farmer's fields with small forested areas separating the farms. Most of the fields had been harvested or were in the process of being harvested, mostly corn and grain.

The Rangers passed a few carts and wagons bringing the harvested crops to the mills that were dotted along the river. While some of the farmers nodded or waved, most kept to themselves and simply ignored the Rangers as they passed by. By late afternoon, Jacob and his men arrived at the outskirts of Deerfield, a good-sized town that thrived on agriculture, keeping Massachusetts and the other colonies supplied with corn, flour, and bread.

Deerfield, known for the Indian raid that had nearly destroyed the town back in 1704 during Queen Anne's War, had grown significantly now that Greenfield was settled. There was also a new township known as Deerfield Northwest. Both towns continued to expand as more people came from Boston and other more urban areas to start their lives anew.

With the weather getting colder and wetter, Jacob paid a small fee for the Rangers to occupy an empty floor in a local miller's barn. He also paid for some straw for them to lie on instead of the hard, dusty floor.

That evening, as a cold rain began to fall, Jacob led the Rangers and the new volunteers over to a place called Shield's Tavern for a warm meal. Most of the other people in the tavern were locals or a few travelers, who seemed to pay the Rangers no attention and kept to themselves.

It was a nice meal of stew and warm biscuits. Jacob went over to speak with the tavern owner, a Mr. Peter Hotchkiss. Most of the conversation was spent on news, Mr. Hotchkiss asking about the war and New York while Jacob asked about the town and local area. As Mr. Hotchkiss wiped the bar with a cloth, Jacob asked about potential volunteers. Mr. Hotchkiss snorted.

"Maybe some younger men from the outer farms," he said. "Most of the townsmen here are either farmers or millers, with some coopers, and none have any experience fighting except with their livestock."

Then he snorted again as he continued to wipe the bar. "Or their wives."

Jacob nodded and asked about the local militia, which caused Mr. Hotchkiss to chortle even louder.

"The local militia is mostly in name only, not much what I would call a fighting force. They hold their summer drill, but most of the time they're busy stumping and politicking. That's good business for me and the other tavern owners with the amount of ale they buy. While there are a handful of good men, mostly farmers who can shoot and live out near the woods, most of the militia, including their commander, Colonel Erikson, can barely move as a unit and fire their muskets."

Again, Jacob nodded. "Sounds like you have experience with this."

Mr. Hotchkiss nodded. "Served in that trouble I guess they call Pometacomet's Rebellion, when those Wampanoag went all crazy and attacked the towns. I was younger then, and our militia was better back then too. Now, I hope no trouble comes our way."

Jacob told him about the recent attack on the farms up at Greenfield which made Mr. Hotchkiss look concerned.

"Haven't heard about that. Thanks for the news," he replied and thought hard for a moment. Then he shrugged and went back to cleaning the bar.

Thanking him for his information, Jacob joined Samuel and the Rangers, who were finishing up their meals and smoking their pipes. Pointing over his shoulder at Mr. Hotchkiss, Jacob recounted what he had been told about potential volunteers and the local militia.

"This may be a dry hole, but we'll spend a few days here and see what we can get, and this will give Sergeant Edwards some time to work with the Greenfield volunteers," Jacob said as he lit his pipe, his grey smoke mixing with the smoke coming from the other pipes. The rest of the evening, most of the Rangers sat in the common room, just talking and relaxing before heading to the barn for the night.

It was still raining when Jacob and the others who had stayed latest in the tavern returned to the barn and climbed up to the second floor where other Rangers were already curled up asleep or playing cards in candlelight.

Jacob went over and told Sergeant Edwards and Corporal Little that they would have a few days to work on training while they set up here to see if they could get some volunteers. They both nodded. Jacob left and went over to his straw pile, while Sergeant Edwards began going over ideas with Corporal Little on training.

As Jacob approached, Smoke, already curled up, watched over his bushy tail, which was wrapped over his nose. Scratching Smoke's ears, Jacob pulled a wool cap on his head before wrapping up in his blanket. The nights were definitely getting colder, and Jacob could see his breath hanging in the air.

As Mr. Hotchkiss had warned, there was little interest in volunteering for the Rangers. The ones who stopped at the recruiting table were mainly townsfolk stopping by to ask for news.

"Well, at least we are still providing a service, even if it's just news," griped Samuel, then he thought about it for a moment, "perhaps one can make money from this."

Jacob even turned away some younger men whose heads were full of heroic stories and who wanted to bathe themselves in glory and become heroes themselves. They would have been liabilities, and Jacob politely thanked them for their interest, but said no.

Sergeant Edwards took the Greenfield volunteers out on scouts around the area for training, but also to see if there were signs of Indian activity in the area. Jacob stayed in Deerfield for three days and was only able to recruit four volunteers who were the type of men they were looking for. They joined Sergeant Edward's volunteers and would also learn on the march.

Jacob and the Rangers continued south, following the river to the next town, which was Huntstown, named after Captain Ephraim Hunt. He had been killed during King William's War, and his family had inherited the land for his service.

Like Deerfield, the town's primary industry was agriculture with large farms and supporting millers, coopers, and shop owners. The area was known for the large number of ash trees growing there, so there was some woodworking business as well.

Jacob noticed that there was a fortification being completed, a central blockhouse surrounded by a twelve-foot tall palisade wall. He talked to the tavern owner and secured permission to recruit at the tavern. The owner told him that the town had a local militia, but he couldn't describe their abilities.

"I don't get out much," he explained as he wiped his hands on his stained apron. "My responsibilities here keep me busy." Then he leaned in so only Jacob could hear and whispered, "Also the wife won't let me associate with the militia. Says it's bad for my health."

Jacob nodded and looked over the innkeeper's shoulder at the large woman to whom he was pointing. A very stout woman, wearing a firm and serious expression, was running a rather tight ship with the serving girls and boys. "I see what you mean," Jacob replied.

The Rangers only spent two days in Huntstown; most of the townsfolk were more interested in preparing their farms for the coming winter than in volunteering for service. From what Jacob observed, the townsmen were not of the quality they were seeking anyway, as suspected.

He was becoming worried that as they moved further east, away from the frontier and towards the more settled areas, men of the type they wanted would become scarcer. However, he was able to recruit three long hunters, who had thought about wintering there in Huntstown. The lure of bounties was a good incentive for them.

While they appeared to be hardy, rugged men, their strong interest in pay concerned Jacob. But he accepted them and assigned them to the growing volunteer section under Sergeant Edwards and Corporal Little. Depending on how well they did in the next couple of towns, Jacob might send Sergeant Edwards and the volunteers back to Fort Edward while the remainder of his small troop moved into Rhode Island.

Jacob led the Rangers northward and back onto the Mohawk trail, before turning east and continuing on their recruiting mission. They traveled for two days, with the weather offering colder days and definitely colder nights.

The new recruits were shouldering their learning tasks well and were dealing with the cold weather, which was important for when they arrived at Fort Edward. It would be winter then, and they would have already been exposed and conditioned to help them acclimate quickly when they arrived. They still looked miserable, but soldiered on.

The Rangers spent a night in the area that was part of the Pocumtuck Indian Nation, whose old villages nearby included Squawkeag, and Peskeompscus. These villages were abandoned with most of the native population displaced and/or sold into slavery as a result of Pometacomet's Rebellion, or as some have began calling it, King Philips War, and a series of massacres of local Indian villages.

The Rangers spent a cold night in the ruins of the old village of Squawkeag. When not on watch, they slept around their fire, which was kept burning all night to keep the cold off. In the morning, they warmed their rations over the fire and heated water for tea before continuing their trip eastward.

Jacob watched the huddled volunteers eating their meals. "Don't get too used to having fires," he warned. "Most of the time on scouts, its cold camps, even in the winter. Fires draw the attention of the enemy, which we try to avoid."

The new volunteers nodded as they chewed on their biscuits or dried beef. "Much rather be cold and alive and with my hair, then cold and buried," remarked one of the recruits.

During the next day, the Rangers passed through the town of Orange, a small, agricultural town that Jacob determined did not look like a suitable place to try recruiting. They continued on through the day and arrived at the next town, Westminster.

They passed a two-story garrison house situated on a hill just outside of the town, whose purpose was to defend the local residents from Indian attacks. With numerous ponds fed by a meandering stream, several mills, including both grist and sawmills, were busy grinding corn and grain or producing boards.

Jacob also spotted three long hunters/trappers pass by with a packhorse laden with skins. Nodding his head and thinking this could be a good place to recruit, Jacob headed over to what appeared to be a decent-looking inn/tavern with the name, The Traveling Goodman.

Jacob was able to secure all of the inn's rooms since no one else was traveling at the time. It would be a little tight, but better than sleeping out in the cold. The inn owner, a Mr. John Parker, was happy to rent out all of his rooms, and he was looking forward to the revenue that the Rangers would bring by purchasing food and drink. He was especially happy that Jacob had the coin to pay for all of this, and he went out of his way to make sure the Rangers had everything that they needed.

After getting settled into their rooms, Jacob sharing his with Samuel and the wolves as usual, the Rangers headed down to the common room for a well-cooked meal of pork, chicken, and duck with fresh bread and strong ale. Soon, the room filled with conversation and laughter as the Rangers spoke with local farmers and hunters, sharing news and war stories. A cold wind blew outside, but the common room was filled with warmth and pipe smoke as the Rangers mingled with the locals.

With the following dawn and after a good breakfast of warm bread, bacon, and pork pies, Jacob set up a table near one of the large stone fireplaces, and he didn't have to wait long before two trappers and three long hunters came in to talk about volunteering. It seemed that the word had spread that the Rangers were recruiting, especially the news about pay and bounties.

"We heard about the trouble near Deerfield," one of the hunters remarked. "If they're ranging this far south, it won't be safe for anyone."

While Jacob was uneasy about men whose motivation was based on coins, but he did understand, so he answered their questions about the volunteering bonus and what New York was paying for scalps and other bounties. When Jacob was busy, Sergeant Carver and Private Johnson also answered questions. The trappers and hunters asked about the shooting competition they had heard about and wondered if their shooting was really that good.

Those five men, plus two locals who had previously served in a militia unit, volunteered, signed the ledger, and were paid their bounties to buy extra equipment. They were instructed to be ready to march in two days. They also attracted interest from other younger men, mostly farmers or millers who came seeking adventure but who had no skills in muskets or woodcraft. Stories and legends were their motivation, and they wanted to become heroes like the men in the stories.

They weren't happy when Jacob turned them away. He told them that while the Rangers would not accept them, they should join the local militia or Provincial forces, which he was sure, would start recruiting soon for the upcoming spring campaign. These youths walked away grumbling, telling Jacob to wait and see when they came to rescue him during the next military campaign. Jacob hoped they survived long enough to try and make that boast come true.

During the evening, Jacob had an interesting talk with Mr. Parker over a good bottle of port. Along with the typical questions about news and the war, Mr. Parker was very interested in the relationship between the Provincials and the British. He described how some of the local political leaders of the community were becoming dissatisfied with British rule and believed they should have the ability to rule themselves.

Jacob nodded his head over his pipe stem as he listened. "I'm a simple fighting man," commented Jacob from around his pipe.

"Too busy fighting the war to worry about politics." He blew smoke out in a long stream, "Seems to me its politics that causes all of these messes."

He did confirm that he had seen growing tension between the British and the Provincials, but he hadn't heard or seen anyone else discussing the idea of the colonies ruling themselves. "Times be a'changing," remarked Mr. Parker. "These be strange times indeed."

The second day also turned out to be good for recruiting. Another five men who appeared to be the right types volunteered. After the ledger was signed and bounties were paid, these men were told to be there in the morning, ready to travel and ready for cold weather.

Jacob called Sergeant Edwards, Corporal Little, and Private Johnson over during dinner and told them they were taking all of the new volunteers back to Fort Edward in the morning. He also instructed Sergeant Edwards to continue training the new volunteers on the march.

"As you pass through the towns, pass the word, if it hasn't reached them already, about the raid," instructed Jacob, and Sergeant Edwards nodded. "Keep your eyes and ears open. Report everything we've seen to Major Rogers."

Samuel gave Sergeant Edwards some bags of coins for any supplies they would need on their return trip. Nodding their understanding, the three men went back to their table to have one last big meal and some ale before their journey back in the morning.

As the remaining Rangers and Samuel prepared to continue their recruiting trip, Jacob saw Sergeant Edwards and the small platoon of volunteers off on their return trip. He told the new volunteers to follow the instructions of Sergeant Edwards, Corporal Little, and Private Johnson; their lives might very well depend on their learning to fight the Ranger way.

Nodding to Sergeant Edwards, who turned and led the platoon westward, Jacob and the remaining five Rangers headed east with Smoke and Otto trotting alongside. They only journeyed east until they came to the Blackstone River at which Jacob turned south and followed a trail along the river.

The next town the Rangers came to that looked like a good area for possible recruits was Worcester. Jacob recalled that the area had once belonged to the Pakachoag tribe of the Nipmuc Nation. Jacob knew the area by the Indian name of Quinsigamond, meaning "fishing place for pickerel." Nearby was Lake Quinsigamond, which provided fine hunting and fishing grounds a short distance from the Pakachoag's main village near a spring on Pakachoag Hill.

Like the previous Indian villages, they were empty. The Pakachoags no longer lived in the area, having been driven out by raids by other tribes, King Phillips War, Queen Anne's War, and other conflicts. Even the English settlers had been driven away, and the current Worcester was the third attempt at establishing a working town in that location. Jacob secured rooms for his Rangers in a small tavern named the Crimson Grape.

Jacob, with Samuel and Sergeant Hopkins, sat at their recruiting table, but they only spoke to a few locals. No one seemed interested in volunteering. As Jacob, Sergeant Hopkins, and Samuel were discussing where they should head next, a finely dressed man in a red militia uniform walked into the tavern and spoke with the owner.

The man appeared agitated and in a hurry with a frustrated scowl on his face, all of which Jacob observed from his chair. Turning, the man spotted the Rangers and quickly approached them.

"If I could trouble you, my name is Lieutenant Benjamin Lincoln of the 3rd Regiment of the Suffolk County Militia as

A Fury of Wolves

well as their constable. Could you men help me out of a sticky situation?"

Jacob looked at both Samuel, who shrugged, and Sergeant Hopkins, who also shrugged, and nodded, motioning Lieutenant Lincoln to go on. Samuel and Sergeant Hopkins looked on; wanting to know what had this man all flustered.

"I am in pursuit of a renegade named John Frances and a Nipmuc named Metacomet, who are robbing travelers and are reportedly heading in this direction. I have been tasked by the court to bring these brigands to justice," explained Lieutenant Lincoln, whose face then fell.

"Though it seems I am having difficulties in finding these reprobates and bringing them to justice," he added. Lincoln looked expectantly at Jacob, Samuel, and Sergeant Hopkins.

"I could really use some good trackers. Am I safe in assuming you men are Rangers? I have heard you can track anyone, at any time, through any place, and I could really use some help."

Jacob looked over to Sergeant Hopkins who shrugged and nodded. Looking over at Samuel, who also shrugged, Jacob said, "We don't seem to be occupied at the moment. Why not? Besides it could be good for recruiting if word gets out."

Jacob looked up into the eyes of Lieutenant Lincoln. "We would be glad to assist the local constabulary in bringing these criminals to justice."

A broad smile broke out on the lieutenant's face.

"Sergeant, grab Carver and Walker and meet me out front. Samuel, I leave the recruiting to you and Private Henry," Jacob said as he stood up, knocking the tobacco ash out of his pipe on the heel of his moccasins. Smoke and Otto looked up, and Jacob nodded. "Yes, boys. Going to need your keen sense of smell. You're coming too."

Both wolves cocked their heads to the side, and then smiled in their own wolfish way, tongues hanging out.

He turning to Lieutenant Lincoln and said, "We'll meet you in front in a few minutes after we grab our gear."

Lieutenant Lincoln nodded and headed outside. After grabbing his rifle, dropping his sword on his bed, and picking up his shooting bags and haversack, Jacob joined Lieutenant Lincoln in front of the tavern.

Along with the lieutenant, there were three other men in militia uniforms and two constables in civilian clothes. As Jacob and the other three Rangers joined them, they were clearly relieved though they looked dubiously at the two trotting wolves.

"What do you know about these two wanted men?" asked Jacob.

Lieutenant Lincoln explained, "These two brigands began robbing good people on the road just outside of Boston, and they were believed to be heading in this direction. They have known acquaintances in the area, and thus I have been looking for them here, but haven't seen them for the past two days."

Lieutenant Lincoln had a committed expression on his face. "I have been tasked to capture these men to answer for their crimes by the high court of Boston, and it's on my shoulders to bring them in."

Then once more the lieutenant's face fell into an almost mournful expression. "Though it seemed I may have been a little too sure of myself when I told the justices I would have them by sundown." Lincoln looked at Jacob, "That was two days ago, and I think the justices may be holding me accountable if I don't apprehend them by today."

Jacob looked to his men, who nodded, and he turned back to the abashed Lieutenant Lincoln.

"Do you know which way or road they are traveling or where they may be heading to?" asked Jacob.

Lieutenant Lincoln thought about it and recalled, "John Frances has family near the town of Orange. There are some roads and trails that run there that are close by." Nodding, Jacob turned to speak with his Rangers while Lieutenant Lincoln talked to his men.

"What do you think Sergeant Hopkins?" asked Jacob.

Sergeant Hopkins thought about it for a moment, rubbing his face, and then he snorted. "Well, it's going to be just like chasing down that war party a few days back, trying to find the right trail and not lose them in the woods. It's going to be a gamble, but why not?"

Jacob and the others nodded. They were going to hope that Jacob's luck along with the keen senses of the wolves would help them to be on the right trail to intercept these two men. It was still gamble; the brigands could take trails that no one knew about. At least it was something different, breaking up the monotony of recruiting duty.

Jacob turned to explain what must be done to intercept the men. "We're going to have to set an area ambush, watch a couple roads at a time, not knowing exactly which one they are traveling on, but we must be close enough to support one another. I would suspect they will use a trail or a road not often used."

Lieutenant Lincoln agreed, "I'll position my men on the turnpike while you watch a fork coming off the river road." Telling his men to form up as he mounted his horse, Lieutenant Lincoln led them out of town to the east. The Rangers trotted alongside as the local militiamen and constables tried to keep up. Smoke and Otto trotted alongside, anticipating the coming hunt.

Just as the lieutenant indicated, they moved to an area a little east of Worcester near the river where a smaller trail branched off from the main road. As Lieutenant Lincoln turned his horse to travel down the track, Jacob stopped him. "If these men are as experienced as you say they are, your tracks will alert them that you and your men are in the area."

Jacob pointed towards the woodline, "Move through the woods and avoid the trail. Find a suitable place to set up an ambush, and wait for your quarry." Jacob looked into the expectant eyes of the lieutenant. "Be patient, and you'll bag your highwaymen."

Lieutenant Lincoln nodded and dismounted from his horse as he followed Jacob and his men into the woods. Jacob looked back at the militiamen moving through the trees, Lincoln's red coat easy to see amongst the branches. "I hope he doesn't get killed," Jacob muttered under his breath. "Or get us killed."

The Rangers led the way until they came to a place where the trail split into a fork. Jacob stopped, motioned Lieutenant Lincoln over, and pointed to the two trails.

"We're going to have to split into two groups and set up on these trails. Then we'll hope luck smiles on us and we can bag these two."

Smiling and nodding, Lieutenant Lincoln wished Jacob and the Rangers luck, before turning and leading his men off to cover the fork on the left, while Jacob and his Rangers went to cover the right-hand trail. Jacob watched the militiamen head off and take cover behind some bushes and trees, before he and the Rangers moved deeper into the woods to a point where they were concealed but could still observe the trail.

After some time, Jacob was becoming concerned about the red militia uniforms and the noise the militiamen and constables were making whispering to one another. He could hear and sometimes see flashes of their red uniforms through the brush. He looked over to Sergeant Hopkins, who simply shrugged and continued to watch the trail. Both wolves lay silently, ears perked, ignoring the militiamen and watching the trail.

Time progressed and afternoon moved into early evening, shadows starting to help conceal both the Rangers and even their red-coated militia counterparts. As the Rangers waited, their quarry approached, unaware they were being hunted.

***

John Frances was deep in thought, remembering that he had never lived a normal, upstanding life. Abandoned as a child when his family died from the smallpox, John had made his living by stealing and surviving. Meeting Metacomet had just made it better. He was an Indian with a grudge against Englishmen, who enjoyed inflicting pain and taking prized possessions from the people they robbed.

Walking along the dusty turnpike, having robbed a family in a cart early that morning, John was enjoying his freedom, not answering to anyone, not a care in the world. Growing up an orphan had soured his resentment toward the townsfolk, who had chased him away when all he wanted was food and some clothes. Now it was payback, and he was enjoying it.

John was heading towards his cousin's farm near Orange, where they could hole up and divide their recent loot. He traveled with Metacomet, who was also satisfied with his life, considering what grudges he had towards townsfolks.

Along their journey, they had added more men to their merry band of brigands. Two were Nipmuc Indians and another was a highwayman, Joshua Curtis, whom John Frances had met in jail in Boston. He and his band of highwaymen were starting to make names for themselves, and he, Joshua, liked that. He had even heard the constable was out hunting him,

"Must have made an impact somewhere to stir up this constable Lincoln fella to come after me," Joshua thought. He started to whistle, thinking how his fame, or infamy, could be used to his benefit.

They were all using a small trail that was hardly traveled, though it was called a turnpike, whatever that meant. Looking over to Metacomet, John asked, "Well, my friend, where to next?" Metacomet thought about it for a moment before replying with an evil smirk.

"Hmm, I think we need to find a farm with women. Kill and scalp the men, then take the women, use them and, when done with them, kill and scalp them too."

John thought about it, brutal but effective, and he had to agree because it had been some time since he had had a woman. He looked back at the other three, who were hanging back, looking through the sack of goods they had taken off the cart they had robbed.

***

He was thinking about where the nearest isolated farm was located, when John heard a cough and saw a flash of red from the bushes close by. He realized they were being watched. "Damn," growled John, Metacomet looking at the movement as well.

Crashing from the woods was Lieutenant Lincoln on his horse, demanding "Hold there!" Having seen their quarry approaching, believing providence had finally smiling on them, Lieutenant Lincoln's pulse began to race, and he quickly mounted his horse and, with his five men, charged out of the bushes to bag their prize.

When they broke out onto the road, the men froze as they aimed their muskets at John and Metacomet, when the other two constables yelled and pointed at Joshua Curtis and the two other Indians a few paces back. They had been flanked.

As Lincoln and the militiamen paused and turned towards these three, Joshua dropped his loot bag and whipped up a small blunderbuss, which he fired from the hip at the militiamen at close range with a thunderous boom.

Having loaded it with a handful of buckshot, pistol balls, and some odds and ends, he caught the militiamen in the flank, the projectiles tearing into the men and the horse, which fell screaming and kicking, pinning the rider under him.

As the smoke cleared, two militiamen were down, the third was crawling away wounded, and the other two could not be seen, having run back into the woods. John had a satisfied smile on his face, his heart pumping, as he looked through the grey smoke and saw the horse and its pinned rider. "Now this is interesting," remarked John as he looked over to Metacomet who was pulling out his scalping knife, a wicked grin on his face.

Lieutenant Lincoln struggled to get himself out from under his fallen horse, using his free leg to try and push his dead horse off of his pinned leg. His heart was racing. *How did everything go so wrong?*

John walked over the fallen militiamen, kicked to make sure they were both dead, eyed the wounded militiaman dragging himself towards the woods, and nodded to Metacomet, who smiled in return and moved towards the wounded man.

John then turned his attention to the fallen rider, approaching the horse, and moving around to look down on the officer pushing and kicking with his one free leg, trying to get out from under the horse.

Whistling softly, John reached down, pulled a pistol from the saddle holster, admired it with a nod, smiled, and then cocked it. The sound caused Lieutenant Lincoln to stop struggling and stare up at him. Kneeling down, John moved close, admired the pistol once more, and then looked down at a pinned Lincoln.

"I'll wager you didn't think about this when you woke this morning, did you?" smirked John as he slowly pointed the pistol at Lincoln's forehead. "Guess it's not your lucky day."

Breathing heavily, Lieutenant Lincoln just stared back defiantly. Shaking his head and taking a deep breath, John shrugged. "Nothing personal you know," he said as he placed the end of the barrel against Lincoln's forehead. "I have a reputation to uphold." As he was about to pull the trigger, John froze as he heard distinct growls of wolves, causing him to look up quickly.

***

Jacob and the other Rangers, having heard the yell of "Hold there!" from the direction of the militia and realized that the militia had found their target, or the target had found the militiamen, increased their pace as his gut told him something bad was about to happen.

"Ah damn," muttered Jacob when the large boom from the location of the militiamen echoed off of the trees.

"Of all of the bloody luck," Jacob groaned as he motioned for the Rangers to follow him, and they took off to render what aid they could, the wolves loping alongside. They were moving quickly through the trees and soon came upon the scene of the fight. Jacob assessed the situation and could clearly see that Lincoln and the wounded man were in grave danger.

When the Rangers arrived, they quickly spread out, Jacob heading towards the man standing over Lincoln. Smoke and Otto burst into a sprint and headed towards the Indian stalking a wounded militiaman, and Sergeant Hopkins, Carver, and Walker flanked around to intercept the other three.

The wolves worked as a team, Otto's jaws clamping on Metacomet's leg as Smoke leaped, snagging his knife-holding arm and pulling him down. As Metacomet fell, Smoke released his bite on the arm, and clamped on Metacomet's throat, issuing a low growl and looking into Metacomet's frightened eyes.

The sound caused John to look up just in time to see Sergeant Hopkins and the two Rangers crash into Joshua Curtis and the two other Indians, who were now down, having been knocked down by the flat side of the Rangers' tomahawks. The Rangers placed the muzzles of their rifles on the three heads, holding the men in place.

Immediately to his right, John could feel the muzzle of a rifle against the back of his head, and he turned to look at Jacob's rifle and into his cold, blue eyes. He had not heard Jacob's approach.

"Easy friend, easy now," said John, slowly raising his hands, the pistol spinning under on his finger. "Now, don't do anything rash. We can all be friends. Just a misunderstanding, that's all."

As Jacob covered John, Sergeant Carver came up, took the pistol, and roughly bound his arms together. Once he was satisfied their quarry was secure, Jacob moved around and helped free Lieutenant Lincoln from under his horse, handing his pistol back to him.

"Believe this belongs to you?" remarked Jacob, and Lincoln nodded in acceptance, looking venomously at the bound John.

As Lieutenant Lincoln caught his breath, Jacob moved around to check on the men who had been killed. Seeing the blunderbuss lying on the ground, he picked it up. "Hmm, I know of someone who would appreciate this."

Metacomet had been released by the wolves and bound by Sergeant Hopkins, when the two constables who had run off returned sheepishly to be met with an ugly look from Lieutenant Lincoln. Trying to avoid Lincoln's gaze, they went about assisting Jacob and the Rangers. Smoke and Otto growled at the detained highwaymen, keeping their golden eyes on them.

The Rangers helped to build a travois to carry the injured and dead militiamen back to the town, as they escorted the captured highwaymen. Jacob tied a rope around the necks of the captured men, with John in front, and led the prisoners back to town. Sergeant Hopkins was in the rear of the row of prisoners, and the two wolves walked alongside.

Even a bound John kept bantering with Jacob, a smirk on his face, already knowing his fate. "You boys are pretty good to get this famous highwayman," he quipped. Looking at Lincoln, he said, "I guess the constable had to hire out for good help."

The smirk quickly left John's face as Jacob with a dark, ominous look, walked over and whispered in his ear. "Lucky he found you before we did," Jacob warned. "If we had got there first, you wouldn't have known what hit you until you woke up in Hell with your scalp hanging from my belt."

It still didn't seem to bother John, who had resigned himself to his fate, commenting, "It was good while it lasted." John kept talking, but Jacob ignored him and just pulled the prisoners along.

Once they arrived at town, Lieutenant Lincoln was able to get some support from more of the Worcester constables to help take their prisoners back to Boston for trial. The injured militiaman was passed to a local doctor, while the dead were given to the gravediggers to be buried.

Jacob and the Rangers sat on the porch of the tavern, watching the column get ready to move. Lieutenant Lincoln came over and shook the hands of Jacob and the other Rangers.

"You saved my life; I owe you a debt that I don't know if I can ever repay."

Jacob and the other Rangers nodded. "Best of luck with your travels," Jacob said, then loud enough for John to hear, added, "If an accident would happen to this riffraff along the way, I'm sure the courts would see it as providence."

Lincoln turned and looked at John, who didn't seem shocked or frightened by Jacob's comment. He had already accepted that his fate would be at the end of a hangman's noose. Looking back at Jacob, Lincoln started to say, "You think I can," then stopped before he could finish the sentence. He thanked the Rangers once more, and then led the column of prisoners towards Boston.

Samuel and Private Henry rose up from the table when Jacob and the others entered. Jacob handed the blunderbuss to Samuel.

"Thought you would like one of these."

Samuel's eyes lit up, and he nodded in approval, cavorting around in joy with his new toy. Looking at Jacob, Samuel said with a twinkle in his eye, "Still liked that old swivel gun though, but this one is easier to carry."

Jacob and the others took their gear to their rooms before returning to the common room. Feeling hungry from doing their civic duty by helping the lieutenant, Jacob called for ale and warm meals for his men. Soon a steaming platter of roasted venison, pork, potatoes, and fresh bread arrived with large mugs of ale.

Jacob turned to his men, raised his mug, and toasted them on a job well done. They returned the toast and took large swallows of their ale. Jacob was happy that they had been able to assist and that all of his men were uninjured.

Word that the Rangers had saved the lieutenant and the militiamen and had captured the wanted men had already spread around town. The following morning, the Rangers were able to recruit four more volunteers before heading on to the next town on their way south.

In a day, they arrived just outside of Oxford and set up camp in the old Huguenot Fort, which had protected the original Huguenot settlers. It was not well-maintained and much of it was falling down. There was one old building that was still intact and had a working fireplace. The Rangers occupied this building and set up camp while Jacob went into town to find a place to recruit, settling on a small tavern.

They spent three days in Oxford, during which Jacob secured new food, which the Rangers cooked for rations. While in Oxford, they were able to recruit four more volunteers. Jacob and the Rangers, along with the eight new Ranger volunteers, moved on. Jacob had assigned Sergeant Carver to train the new volunteers as he had done with the others while they were moving.

They passed through the town of Webster, which had produced no volunteers after two days. Jacob was becoming concerned that the farther south they went, the scarcer the type of men they were seeking would become.

CHAPTER 15

FINAL LEG OF THE JOURNEY

It was cold and windy when Jacob and his Rangers crossed into the colony of Rhode Island. A light snow was mixed into the biting wind, and the Rangers and their new volunteers were bundled either in blankets or capotes.

Jacob and Sergeant Hopkins told the volunteers that this would seem like a warm day when they got to experience the full weight of Old Man Winter in the north along the lakes and mountains. The volunteers nodded, and they all shivered a little harder for a second as that thought penetrated their minds.

While the little bit of snow began to ease up, the cold wind continued to blow as the Rangers entered the town of Gloucester and took up rooms in a decent-sized tavern and inn. The weather appeared to get worse as the night fell, and Jacob decided to try their luck here for a few days, at least until the bad weather blew through.

When Jacob went into the common room for breakfast, the weather was still miserable outside. A wet sleet and blowing wind seemed to keep most of the town residents inside. Still, he was able to set up a recruiting table near the fire while Sergeant Hopkins and Carver took the volunteers out in the bad weather to show them how to survive in the cold.

As Jacob had feared, no one really showed any interest during the day in volunteering. He spent most of his time speaking with the tavern owner, trading news. This tavern owner was also concerned about talk of the colonies wanting self-rule apart from England.

To help warm up their bodies, Jacob had some warm mulled wine waiting for the volunteers when they came in from their cold training.

The weather was still cold the following day, but it was not raining. Jacob decided to continue on and try to complete their recruiting trip so they could get back to Fort Edward before winter really started to set in.

He led the Rangers southeast, heading to one of the larger colonial towns in the area, Providence. This large community was based on the agriculture, fishing and maritime industries, and the area was heavily settled by Quakers who were pacifists and by other people looking for religious freedom. This could be an issue when looking for volunteers who would fight as Rangers.

Both Jacob and Samuel had dealt with Quakers before in their youth. Samuel asked, "You think we are going to have any luck with this lot?" steam rising as he spoke. "You know that fighting is not their way."

Jacob shrugged. "We'll see, won't we?" Then looking at the sky, raising his nose and smelling the wind, he said, "In either case, I think our recruiting duty will need to end soon before we get snowed in and can't make it back to Fort Edward."

By evening, the Rangers had arrived in Providence, and Jacob secured lodging for them in a good-sized tavern and inn with the name, the Dancing Fish. The Rangers had warm fish stew and roasted potatoes to help warm their bodies up after their long walk on the cold road.

The following morning was bright and sunny, if a little cold and Jacob hoped it would be a decent day for recruiting. He set up his recruiting table and chairs out on the porch and was joined there by Samuel and Sergeant Carver.

After a short period of time, Jacob was surprised to be approached by several men who were former sailors. They asked what was happening in the war, what it would be like to serve in the Rangers, and how they would be able to fit in. Most of these men had grown up as farmers or woodsmen, but they also had taken up the trades of fishing and sailing.

Jacob saw an opportunity because these men not only understood some woodcraft, but they also were experts in whale boats and bateaux. They were surprised when Jacob told then about the Rangers' use of these boats for scouting expeditions and raids against the French. They talked briefly among themselves and agreed to join.

"No one is hiring abled-bodied seamen in the area," commented one of the new volunteers. "And I think we can lend a hand with those boats."

The new volunteers, seven in all, began to sign the ledger, and Samuel paid them their joining bounty. Two asked about muskets because they had none. Jacob told them that there were muskets up at the fort that they could be issued once they were there, and that satisfied them.

Jacob told them to be back in the morning, ready to travel to Fort Edward. Once they nodded and walked away, a young man about 16 years old approached Jacob and asked if he could talk to him about the war.

He introduced himself as *Nathanael* Greene, a resident of Warwick, which was just south of Providence, and said he was very interested in learning about warfare. Jacob asked, "You seem stout enough. Why not join them and find out for yourself?"

Nathanael shrugged his shoulders, looked down and replied, "Easier said than done. My family are Quakers and are strongly against my joining the militia or fighting in this war." He looked at Jacob. "Still, I am interested, and even though my family may not see it, there will come a time when we can't avoid the fight and must get involved. Better to be ready than lambs to a slaughter."

Jacob sat and spoke with the young man about the fighting and tactics employed, amazed at the depth of his knowledge, which *Nathanael* explained he had acquired by reading and studying. Jacob was really impressed by *Nathanael's* thoughts on warfare. He was very interested in the non-traditional way the Rangers fought, which was different from the militia drill he had observed.

"Doesn't that go against your family's beliefs and ideals?" asked Jacob from around the stem of his pipe.

Nathanael nodded.

"The pursuit of knowledge is also not looked upon favorably in our community, but if we don't do something, we may not have a community. If the French win, we will have to leave again to be free. Sometimes you just have to take a stand."

While Jacob was discussing these issues with Nathanael, three more woodsmen, with rifles and cold weather clothing, volunteered, motivated by bounties. After signing them up and giving them their bonuses and instructions to be ready in the morning, Jacob once again tried to convince Nathanael to volunteer. He politely declined, but thanked Jacob for the discussion on tactics and fighting.

"I wish you all the best of luck, lieutenant," Nathanael simply stated as he rose and shook Jacob's hand. "All the best on your journey."

Sergeant Carver and Corporal Walker were tasked by Jacob to leave in the morning to lead the eighteen new volunteers back to Fort Edward.

Jacob's recruiting party now consisted of Sergeant Hopkins, Private Henry, and Samuel, with Bob the packhorse and the wolves. After he shook the hands of all of the new volunteers and wished them a safe journey, Jacob led his small party west towards Connecticut, the home province of many of their previous volunteers.

All of the leaves were gone from the trees except for the evergreens, and there was a constant cool breeze blowing, whispering, "Winter is coming." It was an uneventful march westward, passing through Warwick, where Nathanael Greene had said he was from. As they passed through, Jacob thought of the interesting youth with the quick mind and hoped for the best for him.

Jacob and his small party of Rangers crossed into Connecticut and stopped for the night in a town called Plainfield. From what Jacob had observed, it was mostly a mill town with two rivers running through it. They spent the night in an inn, where Jacob spoke with Sergeant Hopkins and Samuel to see what they thought about their recruiting chances in the town. They confirmed Jacob's impression that the town probably wouldn't produce many volunteers, if any.

So Jacob decided that they would just spend the night, get some food, and continue their journey westward. The next stop on their journey was another textile town known as Willimantic Falls. While the Rangers spent the day there attempting to recruit, no one showed any interest.

When Jacob and his men entered the next major town of Hartford, there were numerous people such as traders and woodsmen who would make good volunteers. Jacob spotted an Inn known as the Wandering Rose, and after securing rooms and permission to recruit from the owner, Jacob got down to business.

Hartford was located close to the center of the colony in the Connecticut Valley along the Connecticut River. There was a mix of farmers, tradesmen, millers, and woodsmen in the town. Since Major Rogers had come from this region, Jacob thought it might be a fruitful stop. He hoped the word of mouth would spread that the Rangers were in town recruiting and that that message would draw interest. Jacob decided to try for a few days to see if they would get lucky.

The first day, only a few interested townsfolk and locals stopped at the recruiting table to ask the Rangers for news, but soon the word started to get out. On the second day, five local men who were experienced woodsmen volunteered.

On the third day, seven long hunters and trappers volunteered to join, the stories of Major Rogers's exploits having spread to the Connecticut Valley. On the fourth, four more woodsmen arrived to sign up to volunteer. All of these volunteers carried their own rifles and muskets, cold weather clothes, packs, and even snow shoes with them, which made it easier for Jacob to accept them as volunteers.

As Samuel finished handing out the bounties for volunteers, Jacob asked how they were on funds. Samuel looked through the strong box and indicated that they were getting low, but they still had enough to support room and board along with payments for a few more recruits.

Sergeant Hopkins and Private Henry were tasked to lead these sixteen new volunteers back to Fort Edward. Shaking their hands, Jacob told Sergeant Hopkins that he and Samuel would continue on to New Haven and then make their way over to New York and return back to Fort Edward.

Jacob also handed some dispatches to Sergeant Hopkins to bring to Major Rogers.

"Hope to serve with you again, Jacob. You're a good man. See you back at Fort Edward," Sergeant Hopkins said as he finished shaking Jacob's hand, and Private Henry nodded in agreement.

Jacob and Samuel watched them turn and head northwest, bundled against the chilling wind.

"Well Samuel, ready to go?" asked Jacob.

Samuel, who was tightening a strap on Bob and securing his new blunderbuss close at hand on the horse, nodded and took the reins of the pack horse. Smoke and Otto moved ahead and ranged in front of the two as they journeyed west.

Jacob and Samuel stopped in Wallingford for the night, and after speaking with the tavern owner they were staying with, determined they wouldn't find any volunteers there. The town was mostly pewter and silver smiths, tradesmen, and craftsmen, he said, and Jacob thanked him for the information.

Jacob and Samuel pushed on through a stormy day to reach the coastal town of New Haven. Jacob and Samuel set up a recruiting table and chair in The King's Champion Inn, the inn where they were staying. Mostly seafaring men were in the inn drinking and talking, and they were not remotely interested in joining anything except a game of cards.

As day turned to afternoon, another group of men entered the inn from Yale College, intellectuals and academics who seemed to split off into groups for discussions over glasses of port.

Jacob and Samuel were sitting at a corner table, smoking their pipes after enjoying a good meal of roasted vegetables and pork. "Damn Jacob," remarked Samuel, "I hate to say this but I am looking forward to getting back up north and back into the fight. This is so boring!" Both men were ready to finish up this trip and return to just being normal Rangers again.

Samuel continued as he lit his pipe from a candle. "I almost miss going out on wintery scouts and fighting the French." He spoke from around his pipe stem, puffing and getting the ember to glow. "Well, almost."

Jacob nodded and snorted, and then a loud discussion erupted nearby from a group of young men who were in a heated debate concerning personal liberty. Both Jacob and Samuel turned to watch the group as their voices rose and fell, depending on the passion of the speaker, who was either for liberty or who stressed loyalty to the English crown and government.

Jacob watched with concern, smoking his pipe. "This is the same insanity I have been hearing all along this trip." Samuel nodded somberly. "Just proves my point. Let's be done with this and get back to where we belong before this insanity takes us," he said. Both continued to watch the growing debate.

"You are completely fooling yourself if you believe the crown will ever allow the colonies the ability of self-rule," said one man.

Another quickly retorted, "Self-rule? Why would we want to rule ourselves? We are loyal subjects of England. They have been ruling over us for years and are doing a bloody good job at it. I don't see the need for self-rule."

The heated debate continued and became more aggressive as the amount of port consumed had increased, and the men were emboldened by the spirits. Jacob and Samuel just observed and shook their heads.

One of the young men, tipsy from the drink, looked over and saw them shaking their heads and yelled out, "You, Sir! Where do your loyalties lie?"

Jacob looked at the young man, not believing he had said something directly to him. Jacob lowered his pipe.

"Are you talking to me?"

The young man nodded, staggered a few steps around his table and came around to face Jacob, his colleagues turning to see what was occurring.

The young man continued pointing at Jacob's uniform with his glass, sloshing port onto their table.

"Yes. Are you so dense you can't understand what I was saying? I can tell by your uniform, you must not be that enlightened since you serve in this senseless war."

Samuel lowered his pipe and mumbled, "Ah damn, stupid kid, go away," and thought, "I hope Jacob doesn't kill him."

Jacob slowly placed his pipe down on the table, stood up from his chair, and came around and faced the insulting young man. As Jacob approached and his cold blue eyes stared deep into the befuddled young man's soul, the scholar's mouth clicked shut. Jacob approached him and stopped when only an inch separated him from the young man's chest.

In a low voice, Jacob asked, "What do you truly know of loyalty?"

The young man looked to his friends for encouragement, saw there was none, and then turned back to Jacob.

"There is a movement afoot, a desire for peace, and, without the English ruling over us, we can make our own decisions. We wouldn't be in this conflict with the French."

"Are you so sure that we would have done better than the English have?" asked Jacob in return. "I may not directly approve of their methods and sometimes their arrogance," continued Jacob, "but they are fighting and dying to keep you safe. What have you done to help keep your home and family safe?"

The young man's confidence began to wane, and he took a deep drink of his wine.

"What have I done?" the young man replied, his voice rising. "I have seen the coming storm and heard from other scholars across the colonies the need to stand up to tyranny and stand for freedom and justice!"

Unfortunately, the young man once again caught up in his fervor, punctuated his points concerning freedom and justice by poking Jacob in the chest as he said the words. Even the young man's friends thought that was a bad thing to have done, and Samuel was seriously worried.

"Ah, bloody hell," Samuel whispered. "Please Jacob, don't kill him. Please don't kill him." Then looking at the youth, he uttered a deep sigh. "Or at least just hurt him a little bit, but don't kill him. He doesn't know what he is talking about."

Jacob was beginning to lose his patience with this young hothead, as he continued to rant about the need for self-rule and for independence, trying to talk over Jacob by using scholarly words. Samuel watched as Jacob tried to remain calm, but starting in his neck and slowly moving up his face, Jacob was turning red as he clenched his mouth shut.

The final straw came when the young man once more poked Jacob in his chest to punctuate a point, at which point Jacob grabbed the hand that had poked him, and using his other arm, drove the young man to the ground onto his knees.

All of the debating scholars groaned in horror and were stammering for Jacob to not hurt their colleague.

"What do you know of loyalty? What have you done to earn loyalty?" growled Jacob.

The scholar began to groan as Jacob applied pressure to his arm, and he stammered, "Ah…well…in class we discussed the need for …," but Jacob stopped him in mid-sentence.

"In class! I trust that man over there with more than my life because I have earned his loyalty, and he has earned mine!" Jacob growled as he pointed at Samuel. "Our loyalty means life: We stay alive to fight another day. To fight to keep you free to go to class and 'discuss' the need for loyalty, for if the French and their Indians win, you won't have that freedom. You'll be dead."

Jacob paused and looked at the other young scholars.

"The French would have attacked us anyway, even if we were ruling ourselves. They want these lands and will do anything to take them. I may not agree with the British, and I definitely hate the politics both from us and from them, but at least we're trying to make a difference, not just sit in class and 'discuss' it."

Jacob let the young man go and turned to look at the others.

"What have you all done with your lives that meant anything? At least we have tried to save lives, the lives of those who are innocent, who are just caught in the middle and are trying to get by. People who don't have opportunities like you all have. I have seen more in my life, knew more honorable men than you ever will, and have learned more about being alive than any of you will learn here in this college."

"If you want to make a difference, other than figuring out where everyone's loyalties lie, help the common man. Use this knowledge you're gaining here to help people, not to sit in taverns and discuss politics. Make a difference."

The young men nodded quickly, and Jacob pushed through and went up to his room. Samuel let out the breath that he had been holding in case Jacob had decided to educate these men with his fists. Samuel stood up and, moving around the now quiet group of scholars, smiled and shrugged his shoulders before he went up to his room and settled in for the night.

Jacob was seething and grumbling, both wolves watching from under the beds. "That's it, I've had enough!" growled Jacob as he turned to look at Samuel. "I have had enough of these civilized towns. We're heading home, now!"

The following morning reflected Jacob's mood, dawning grey and blustery. He led them away from New Haven and decided to push westward, Samuel, Otto and Smoke following along. They traveled northwest and stopped at the town of Danbury. They spent a day there and were successful in recruiting three volunteers.

The group crossed into New York on a ferry during a light snowstorm and moved on to their next stop, the town of

Newburgh. Jacob and his men stopped at an inn to thaw out and see how their luck would hold for volunteers. Jacob was able to recruit four more men there, all of whom had previously served in the New York Provincials.

Jacob began to lead their group northward along the Hudson River, instructing the new men on their tactics and cold-weather skills as they traveled. They stopped at Fort Deyo's Hill, a stockade blockhouse overlooking the river and the road following the river. While there, Jacob was able to recruit three more former Provincials as volunteers, giving him ten new volunteers.

They continued northward, and already the tops of the mountains were showing snow. As they marched, Jacob realized Old Man Winter was beginning to settle in, but they had luckily reached New York before the worse of it began.

Jacob's small group of would-be Rangers traveled through Albany and was back on familiar ground, though that ground was beginning to be covered in a light dusting of snow. Both Jacob's and Samuel's spirits rose as they moved along the Mohawk Valley and back into areas that they considered home. They stopped at the blockhouses along the way before crossing over the Hudson to the eastern side, and then they made their way along the Albany road to Fort Edward.

Even the wolves seemed to be happy as they entered the valley and could see Fort Edward in the distance, columns of smoke rising into the grey sky as snow mingled with the blowing wind.

As Jacob, Samuel, and the volunteers passed by Mr. Best's shop, he came out and called out to Jacob, welcoming him and Samuel back. They waved back in return. The new volunteers followed Jacob as he passed by the fort and led them across the footbridge to the island. Jacob noticed that at least the river hadn't frozen over yet, so their hut should be safe from flooding.

A Fury of Wolves

What really drew his attention was the completed, large and long barracks that had smoke rising from some of its chimneys. There were a few soldiers moving around and between the barracks and the old hospital, but everyone else appeared to be inside the log building.

In contrast, Jacob noticed that there were only a few columns of smoke rising from the Ranger huts, and many of them were standing empty when Jacob led his volunteers over to Major Rogers's hut. The only one there was Peter, who limped out and warmly shook Jacob's and Samuel's hands, welcoming them back.

"Where is everyone?" asked Jacob as he stood in front of the fire in the hut, warming his hands.

Peter told him that Major Rogers and most of the Rangers were out on a scout to the north, thinking the weather would give them an advantage over the French.

Peter also explained that most of the companies were still lacking in numbers, even with all of the volunteers they had recruited. He recounted the different scouting expeditions and said there had been no change with the British leadership over at the fort while they were away.

"So nothing has really changed?" asked Jacob, and Peter slowly shook his head "no."

Then Peter thought for a moment, and replied, "Well, there have been some strange things afoot."

Jacob looked at his old friend. "Strange, how?"

Peter puffed on his pipe for a short while, then answered, "Been some folks disappearing, both civilians and military. Some think the soldiers are deserting, but the civilians? No one knows." He then leaned in close and whispered, "Even been talk about some monster stealing people in the night, a devil."

Jacob thought on it for a moment. "So why does this have you concerned. We have seen soldiers desert or just walk off, especially towards winter."

"Ya, but it's not da same," Peter continued. "Soldiers, yes, I can see dat. It's the civilians. Most are women, camp followers and cleaning girls, but some were wives. About every other week or so, someone disappears."

Samuel asked, "What have the scouts seen? Any sign of a raiding party?"

Peter shook his head. "No tracks, nothing. Why would a raiding party just take one, and not stir up trouble?"

Samuel shrugged. "Lonely maybe. Need someone to keep him warm in the winter?"

Both Peter and Jacob gave Samuel a hard look, at which he held his hands up and quickly replied, "Just joking, just joking." But it did make Jacob think. These were very strange events indeed.

Peter took charge of the new men and led them to their platoons while Jacob, Samuel, and the wolves returned to their hut. Peter still lived there and had kept it neat and clean. Fresh wood was in the fireplace, and it didn't take long for Jacob to get a fire going.

Samuel led the pack horse over to the fort to return the strong boxes and what was left of their funds to the quartermaster. After patting Bob on the nose, he turned him over to the quartermaster, picked up some rations and some rum, and returned to a now warm hut.

Jacob looked up from his bunk and helped to start cooking the rations that Samuel had brought as well as to share in the bottle of rum.

"We're going to have to put some new chinking in the logs. I can still feel a few drafts," pointed out Jacob.

Samuel nodded. "Yeah!" Then he looked up with a smile and raised a mug of warm rum. "Damn, I hate to admit it, but it's bloody good to be home and off the trail!"

Jacob nodded and, holding his cup up, toasted to being home. Samuel clinked his cup with Jacob's, and the two gulped down their rum. From under Jacob's bed, Smoke peered out with his golden eyes and looked over at Otto. In their own wolfish way, they seemed happy to be home as well.

CHAPTER 16

1759: THE NEW WINTER CAMPAIGN

Old Man Winter arrived in true form, cold winds and icy snow blowing through the valleys and covering the mountains in a thick blanket. The bears had retreated into their dens to sleep through the winter until spring when the sun would return. Only wolves prowled amongst the trees, some on four legs, and some on two.

While most of the frontier settled in for the winter, some were busy getting ready for the coming spring. It was a time of change as 1758 transitioned to 1759, even though it was a bitterly cold winter. Major Rogers and his Ranger companies were still short of full strength despite all of the new recruits that Jacob and the other recruiters had been able to convince to volunteer. The heavy attrition they were facing was still making it hard to keep up their numbers.

Over the past couple of years, the British had grudgingly learned the value of the Rangers, and they needed them back to full strength for the looming spring campaign.

Brigadier General Gage, overall British commander for the forts and garrisons across New York, instructed the new British commander for Fort Edward, Colonel Haldimand, to provide two hundred British regulars to augment the Ranger companies. Major Rogers had worked with British regulars in the past for this very same purpose, but he had never been successful at it. A few British regulars had adapted, as shown by the 80th Regiment of Foot under Lord Howe, but that regiment was the exception, not the rule. The regimented British system was too ingrained in most regulars for them to adapt the Ranger style of fighting.

Due to the British failures in 1758, General Abercrombie was replaced by General Jeffery Amherst, who had recently taken Louisburg, and now was the newly appointed British commander-in-chief for the colonies.

While most military operations were on hold until spring, Major Rogers, having returned from his scouting, was instructed to continue gathering intelligence on the French and their activities around Fort Carillon. Since just about all of the Provincials and militia forces had been allowed to go home for the winter, the need for scouting the French fell on those Rangers who were still on the island, supported by the British regulars who were still garrisoning Fort Edward.

Getting right back into action, Jacob began leading patrols around the fort, in part as training of new personnel, but also as a way to maintain vigilance in case the French or their allies made another winter raid. Along with weekly patrols around the area, Jacob also escorted wood-cutting parties or resupply sleds going to the different outposts around Fort Edward.

***

Big Harpe had been a busy man as well, securing the support and loyalty of the different sutlers and tradesmen who joined the South Sea Company. For the moment, they had the total monopoly of all non-military support to Fort Edward and the new garrison at the southern end of the lake. His employers were pleased, that flop Aislabie was happy, and William Maclane who allowed his little entertainments, was very pleased.

Support was easy, as William recruited the sutlers by arguing how membership in the company also meant security, as the people disappearing from the fort were not from the company. "I can guarantee," William would exult. "You sign on with the company, and you will be safe. There is safety in numbers, and the South Sea Company has the numbers." No one seemed to notice that the people who were vanishing had refused to join the company, or were acquaintances of those who had refused, but now had joined.

Harpe had to be cautious though. He was doing a better job of disposing of or hiding the remains of his "hobby," having found an abandoned farm's well into which he dumped the bodies. He was making his way back to the fort early one morning, having disposed of a frail camp follower, who had surprisingly put up a fight. He was cherishing that final moment as she fought for her life when he was almost spotted by one of those damnable Ranger scouts.

Nearly walking into them, Harpe was able to crouch in a large blackberry bush thick with ice and snow and watch the Ranger section walk by. He recognized Jacob, who was giving instructions to some men who Harpe assumed were new recruits.

"Well, look who's back," Harpe whispered to himself. He patiently waited for the Rangers to move further away before continuing back to the fort.

"I bet that big bastard would put up one hell of a fight," thought Harpe as he watched the Rangers disappear into the woods. Then he shook his head. "Wouldn't be as much fun as that last one, whatever her name was."

Once he was sure the Rangers were out of sight, Harpe stood back up and continued on his way back to the fort, again fondly recalling the girl's last moment of fight as he squeezed her life away and the light went out of her eyes. Harpe even began to whistle to himself as he trudged through the snow. He had started the tale of the "Devil in the woods," and wondered how he could expand the story.

***

The following morning, as Jacob was getting ready to lead a local scout out again, word had been passed to the Ranger encampment of a missing girl, a servant for Major Dunbar's wife. "The commander is asking for the Rangers to search the surrounding area for any signs of this girl, who is a relative of some important politician back in England," briefed Captain Bishop, who had been sent over from the fort to inform the Rangers.

Rogers nodded then turned to Jacob. "Lieutenant Clarke, take your section and conduct a sweep around the fort and see if you can find any sign of this young girl." Jacob nodded, and then went out to the company street to assemble his section and lead them out.

***

As all of this commotion was going on in and around the fort, Robert Aislabie, who was having a small get-together with some tradesmen over mulled wine, excused himself and approached Maclane, who had been standing in the corner, nursing his cup.

"All of this excitement, all over a young girl. Is there anything we in the company can do?" Robert actually looked sincere and may have wanted to help or at least, to become a hero in the eyes of the officers at the fort.

"I believe the army has it well in hand my lord," Maclane replied. "I saw several groups going out, including those Rangers out on the island. If anyone can find her, it will be those Rangers."

Robert looked crestfallen. "Oh, I see," he said disappointedly. "Even your man Harpe can't help? He seems resourceful enough to find a lost girl."

Maclane gave Robert an odd look. "Are you getting into the hero business, my lord?" he asked. Robert laughed and waved the thought away with his hand. "Oh, most certainly not," Robert said with a chuckle. "But I am in the making money business. Just think of the reward we would get for rescuing this lass, and how it would endear these military men to me."

Maclane bowed his head to Robert. "I'll see what my man can do, but I can't make any promises."

Maclane left the room in the fort that had become Aislabie's office and entertainment area, and headed over to a corner of the fort where Harpe was dicing with some of the waggoneers. Harpe saw him and collected up his coins and joked how he would clean them out next time, and then he walked with Maclane as they moved away from anyone who could overhear them.

"Something I can do for you?" Harpe asked expectantly. Making sure no one could hear what he said, Maclane replied in a low voice, "Did you know the other night who your plaything was?"

Harpe thought about it for a moment and shrugged. "You mean that scrawny strumpet of a serving girl from the other night? No idea who she was."

Maclane turned on Harpe. "She was a daughter of Lord Perrymore in England, a member of Parliament with connections. She wasn't a simple strumpet." Maclane looked into the uncaring eyes of Harpe, who again shrugged and said, "So?"

Again making sure no one would overhear them, Maclane whispered, "So? Is her body at least out of sight so no one can find it?"

Harpe just smiled. "Don't worry your pretty little head. She won't be found."

Maclane countered, "Tell me she can't be found by those Rangers, who seem to find everything?"

Harpe again smiled and nodded. "Even those Rangers won't find her. Relax." Then Harpe took a deep breath and sighed. "If it will make you feel better, I'll take a little break for a while, until all of this commotion blows over and we can get back to business."

Maclane knew he had to tread carefully with Harpe. He didn't want to lose his unique abilities. "Yes, that will be fine," he answered and then smiled. "I will have work for you soon enough, don't worry. You'll only have to stop playing for a short while."

***

True to his orders, Jacob and his section circled around the area near the fort. While they found tracks of numerous men moving through the snow, they could not find any sign of the missing girl. In fact, Jacob had moved through the very farm where Harpe was dumping the bodies during the scout, not knowing how close he actually was to the girl's body.

The search was called off, and the fort returned to its normal routine of winter garrison duties. The few British regulars and local Provincials who were being integrated into the Ranger sections were going through an impromptu winter Ranger school. Jacob trained a group in winter tactics and in how Rangers did their scouts.

He watched these new Rangers, who were mixed with some of the veteran Rangers, having given them the same speech he had given his first platoon about learning or suffering the consequences. So far, the scouts around the fort and up the valley had been uneventful and made Jacob wonder where the French were, especially their old adversary Langy and his Indians. As they scouted between the fort and the lake, Jacob noticed that there had been new military improvements since he had left on the recruiting trail.

Halfway Brook blockhouse and wooden stockade had been built up into a formidable position. Perhaps the bloody massacre from the summer before had helped influence its construction. He learned that the British had renamed it Seven Mile Post, as it was truly seven miles from Fort Edward, but to Jacob and the veteran Rangers, it would always be Halfway Brook.

Continuing on towards the lake, Jacob pointed out to the recruits French Mountain, their other landmark between Halfway Brook and the lake. It was comforting seeing the old lonely mountain, like seeing an old friend. The mountain was silent, looking down on the Rangers as they made their way through the woods, following the military road.

The southern shore of Lake George remained a fortified camp, though much larger than he recalled, as it still served as a supply base for the upcoming spring campaign. In honor of General Gage, the fortified camp had been named Fort Gage. Supporting the camp was a large blockhouse surrounded by a palisade wall and a dirt wall/moat.

Jacob had his Ranger trainees took a break at what had been the old compound from 1755, but no sign of it remained. It had been consumed and integrated into this sprawling logistical base and military outpost.

As the Rangers were resting before heading back to the fort, Samuel nodded his head at the stacks of snow mounds, hiding the piles of supplies. "Must be the supplies we saw on the trail," he said, and Jacob nodded. "Definitely looks like one hell of a campaign coming," Samuel added.

Jacob nodded and thought for a moment. "A bloody one at that if what I am seeing is true," he said. Taking up his rifle, Jacob motioned for his Rangers to fall in and follow him into the woods as they made their sweep back towards Fort Edward.

Along the route between the lake and Fort Edward, the British and New York Provincials had been working on other fortified camps. Four Mile Post was a new fortified camp located four miles from Fort Edward on the road to the lake. Jacob thought that at least it seemed the British leaders were starting to learn and prevent their enemy freedom of movement. These new posts could reinforce one another in case of an attack.

This year's cold winter was brutal, and harsh winds and blowing snow made it difficult to do much of anything except stay warm. Luckily, the river did not freeze and force ice floes onto the island, creating a return of flooding to the Ranger huts. Jacob and the other Rangers continued to make repairs to the huts that were occupied, as well as to the commanders' huts and the hospital. Jacob remained in his original hut with Samuel, Peter, and the wolves.

The winter continued, with Jacob going out on local patrols until March arrived and Major Rogers began planning the next major scout of Carillon. Due to the limited forces, it was planned to be a combined scout, using both Rangers and British regulars.

Jacob had been called into the command hut as Major Rogers and the assembled officers discussed the up-coming scout. Major Rogers would lead the gathered Rangers, which only numbered around ninety, the fifty-man Mohawk Company under the command of Captain Lottridge, and two hundred or so British regulars who would be under the command of

Captain Williams. An engineer, Lieutenant Brehme from the Royal Americans, would accompany them to draw detailed maps of the enemy's positions.

Major Rogers was discussing the route the expedition would take when a debate started about who would be in command. Jacob, who was standing in the background, rolled his eyes and groaned to himself, "Here we go again," as Captain Williams challenged Rogers's authority to lead the expedition. "It never changes."

Captain Williams, looking at Rogers demanded, "I will lead this expedition. I am a royally commissioned officer in his Majesty's Army and have the largest force."

Jacob gave Major Rogers credit for listening to the captain and not saying a word, though an expression of "Here we go again" played across his face. Once the captain had finished, believing he had made his point, Rogers gave his rebuttal.

"Captain, this is a scouting expedition, and I am in command of the scouts, and I too hold a royal commission that outranks yours." Rogers stared back at the captain whose mouth was opening and closing.

It was finally settled by Colonel Haldimand, who had been observing from the other side of the room. "Captain," the colonel softly said, "Major Rogers will be in command of the expedition because of the importance of this scout and the intelligence it will provide."

Outranked by the colonel, the captain grudgingly gave in and nodded, and Rogers returned to planning the expedition. Jacob was amazed. Normally, the British would bully or browbeat any Provincials. The Colonel supporting Rogers was a first. Jacob nodded. "Perhaps things are getting better, finally," he mused.

The scouting expedition departed Fort Edward on March 3. Jacob was placed in charge of a section of Rangers, once

A Fury of Wolves

again paired up with Sergeants Hopkins and Dobbs. Since the Independent Companies were still being reorganized, Jacob had not been given a permanent company and was assigned to whoever needed him. The Rangers assigned to his section included some of the men he had recruited from West Hoosac and North Adams, Massachusetts, including Corporal Little. Jacob did not recognize a few of the new men, but they seemed to recognize him, having heard about him from the others.

He immediately went to work getting his section ready for a cold expedition in the short time they had before the mission began.

***

Harpe was feeling frustrated, having not been allowed to go play due to the weather and Maclane not wanting to draw attention. As much as he said he could control it, Harpe's murderous desires were starting to control him. He stalked around the fort and headed towards the back of Mr. Best's shop where he spotted Mrs. Best with a young girl in the back and alone.

Licking his lips in anticipation, he growled, "Damn Maclane and want he wants. What matters is what I want."

Staying in the trees that stood behind the shop, Harpe was slowly making his way towards the two women. The sun was setting, there were long shadows, and no one would see or hear him. He was close enough to hear Mrs. Best speaking with the young girl who kept answering, "Yes, ma'am," when he spotted Jacob with another Ranger and two wolves.

Harpe froze, staying in the shadows of the trees, and slowly sank down to a knee.

Jacob and Samuel approached Mrs. Best, Otto and Smoke trotting along with them.

"Oh hello, Lieutenant Clarke. What can I do for you?"

Harpe watched from the shadows as Jacob asked Mrs. Best if she or someone there could sew up Samuel's shirt, which was beyond his skills.

Mrs. Best lifted the shirt to look at the numerous patches and zig-zagged repairs when Smoke gave a low growl, looking in Harpe's direction. Mrs. Best looked down at Smoke and Jacob turned to see what he was growling at.

"You see something?" Jacob asked as Smoke looked towards where Harpe was concealed in the shadows. Jacob started to look around to see if he could pick up what Smoke was growling at.

Grimacing, Harpe slowly backed away and when he was deep enough in the shadows, he slowly turned and made his way away from the growling wolf and curious Ranger. "Damn!" he fumed to himself. "That man is ruining my fun. I am going to have to do something about this."

Jacob looked around and when Smoke stopped growling, returned to speaking with Mrs. Best. Once she agreed to try to salvage what she could of Samuel's shirt, the Rangers returned to the island.

"What got Smoke all riled up?" Samuel asked, and Jacob shook his head. "Don't know, but it seems to be nothing," he said as they crossed over the bridge and returned to their camp. But he did wonder what had gotten Smoke's attention this close to the fort.

The following morning, the Rangers and regulars assembled. The air smelled of a coming storm as the column snaked away from Fort Edward. The expedition stopped at the fortified encampment at Halfway Brook until night fell. Major Rogers wanted to avoid any enemy detection and planned to move only at night.

Along with the challenge of leading the mixed group of new Rangers and regulars through the woods in the dark, the weather added to their problems when the temperature plummeted. Jacob began to watch the men and spotted several who were showing signs that the cold was affecting them.

Pulling Major Rogers off to the side, he whispered, "The cold is getting to them." He pointed out the regulars who were showing signs and symptoms of cold. Rogers looked to where Jacob had pointed and could see the shivering and the waxy look on the faces of the British regulars.

"This isn't good," said Rogers, agreeing with Jacob's assessment. "And we're only at Halfway Brook. What's going to happen when we start heading up north?"

Jacob looked at the shivering men and simply replied, "Nothing good."

Jacob's fear came true only two days into the scout, when twenty-three men came down with frost bite and could no longer continue. Most were British regulars, but what bothered Jacob was that those suffering from frost bite included a few of the new Ranger volunteers.

Having no choice, Major Rogers called for Sergeant Edwards and a small detail of Rangers to lead the twenty-three men back to Fort Edward.

"This damnable weather," growled Rogers, and Jacob had to nod in agreement. It was not supposed to be this cold so late in the season.

With the weather staying nasty, blustery and cold, Major Rogers called for Jacob. "Take your section, lead out towards Carillon, and I'll bring the rest of the column up," he instructed. "You know what to look and listen for. Find them before they find us."

Jacob, bundled in his thick capote and fur-lined hat, was covered in a thin sheet of white ice and snow as Old Man Winter made the trip northward extremely difficult. While the blowing snow and sub-zero temperatures kept any enemy eyes blind to their movements, the weather was continuing to cause cold weather injuries to expedition members.

As they trudged through the frozen grip of Old Man Winter, Samuel quipped through his chattering teeth, "I've...changed... my mind. Warmer...climate might be...better."

When the remaining men stopped at Sabbath Day Point to rest, many of the regulars and even some of the Rangers were suffering from the cold. Jacob and a few of the other officers checked on the men and helped where they could to assist the men to cope.

Jacob shook his head; it wasn't good. Many of the men, including the Ranger veterans, were showing signs of cold injuries, while the British regulars appeared to be suffering the most. Old Man Winter had a death grip on the expedition, and Jacob wondered if the major would call a halt and return, or if he would keep pressing on to the enemy fort.

After resting a few hours, Jacob had his answer when Rogers instructed the expedition to continue through the night, with Jacob leading them through woods he knew well after all of the years he had scouted in this area.

The stormy weather finally broke, Old Man Winter deciding to have some mercy on the men, and the night became clear and cold. Through the wisps of his breath, Jacob spotted their landmark, Old Baldy, which had helped guide the expedition through the fighting ground the previous winter when they had battled the French and their allies on snowshoes.

As Jacob watched the silent trees and snow drifts around him, he could hear the echoes of the fighting from a year ago whispering from the pines of the forest. But if the spirits of the dead were watching them, they didn't interfere as the column trudged through the snow drifts and wound their way towards Fort Carillon. Perhaps it was even too cold for ghosts.

Jacob led the column to Rattlesnake Mountain, the large high ground southwest of Fort Carillon that overlooked both Lake George and Champlain. The Rangers had used this mountain on numerous scouts before to observe the French, and Major Rogers planned to spy on the French once again from its heights.

Jacob led the column to a depression full of thick brush that would serve as their camp, and everyone settled in for a cold night. They only rested for a short time before Rogers assembled the first scouting party to head up and take a position before the sun rose.

Major Rogers headed out followed by Jacob, who led the security detail of Rangers, followed by Lieutenant Brehme, who would assess the enemy fortifications for strengths and weaknesses. Rogers led them to the lofty heights of the mountain, where they could look down on the bloodied field where the British expedition the summer before had been broken on the French defensive line.

The French abatis were still apparent through the clear air of the dawn, as well as the bastioned-tipped square outline of Fort Carillon. Jacob checked on the Rangers he had positioned around the observation spot, watching out for any French movement, and he was surprised that there had been no activity seen around Fort Carillon.

As the sun rose higher over the Rangers, Major Rogers and Lieutenant Brehme determined the best way to attack the French positions, including the most logical place for the British commander to place artillery. Rogers pointed out how devastating artillery would be if the guns were placed on the mountain to rain shot and shells on the French fort below.

"It didn't work from those bloody barges," Rogers told the engineer. "Not to mention the devastating effect of the fort's guns." Jacob snorted to himself at the memory of Captain Reynolds losing his head to one of those cannon balls.

Lieutenant Brehme agreed. "We can fire with impunity from here, using mortars to drop right in the middle of their works." Though they had a good vantage point, the lieutenant desired more detailed information on the French position. Understanding what he needed, Major Rogers sent one of his Rangers and five Mohawks to watch the main trail to Fort Carillon for any sleighs.

Then Major Rogers called for Jacob. "The lieutenant needs more information on the enemy works," Rogers instructed. "Take him to the outer works, collect what information you can, and bring him back in one piece."

Jacob had suspected this tasking would come, and he nodded his understanding and led the lieutenant back to his Rangers.

Jacob selected Sergeant Hopkins, Corporal Little, and eight former long hunters who knew how to move quietly through the woods in snow. "Boys, the major wants us to take the lieutenant down to the outer works so he can get a better look at them," he whispered. "And he wants the lieutenant back in one piece."

Using a stick to draw his plan in the snow, Jacob traced the route for their approach to the works. Basically, they would be following the same route they had taken the previous summer during the battle.

Once he was sure everyone understood what they were doing, Jacob had the men go and prepare their gear. "We're traveling light, but bring gear to stay warm." Jacob did not plan to stay out longer than a day, and he wanted to move as quickly and quietly through the snow as possible, relying on stealth.

Once the Rangers were ready, Jacob did a quick inspection, including Lieutenant Brehme, and was satisfied with their preparations. He informed Major Rogers they were departing, and Rogers wished them luck. Returning to the section, Jacob motioned for Sergeant Hopkins to lead them out, Jacob took his position in the middle with the lieutenant next to him, and Corporal Little brought up the rear.

The day was clear and the sky blue and the snow had an icy crust that crunched under their snowshoes, attesting to the extreme cold. Still, Jacob felt at home as they moved through the familiar woods he had traveled through on so many scouts over the past couple of years.

As he watched the woods around them, Jacob was again concerned that he saw no French activity, either patrols or work details, as they approached the outer French defensive lines. He gave steering directions to Sergeant Hopkins, which took them through the woods that were south of the summer's killing fields.

Moving cautiously, the Rangers broke from the woods and began to weave through the snow-covered and ice-hanging abatis, stopping frequently to listen for any French patrols. Hearing none, Jacob motioned for Sergeant Hopkins to continue on as they made their way to the French earthworks.

Jacob and the Rangers stopped, kneeling and leaning against the wooden redoubt, again listening for any sound of French patrols. Sergeant Hopkins and the others looked at Jacob, who shrugged and whispered, "Fate favors the bold."

He stood and pulled himself over the redoubt to the French side of the line. The other Rangers quickly followed suit and joined Jacob on the other side.

Looking all around them, they noticed no tracks or any indicators that the French had been in the area in the past two days. Remaining crouched and constantly scanning the area, Jacob and his men scouted the entire French defensive line without running into a living soul. While rather wide-eyed, the lieutenant kept up with Jacob and stayed relatively quiet for a non-Ranger.

"Take a look around lieutenant," whispered Jacob. We'll keep our eyes and ears open."

Nodding, the engineer looked with experienced eyes at the construction of the works, studying how the log redoubt was built, the use of fascines for support, and the firing step for the infantry. As the lieutenant measured and probed with his hands, Jacob and the Rangers kept a wary eye out for the enemy.

It was bothering Jacob that here they were, inside the French position, and yet they saw or heard no one. There was no smell of smoke or cooking, just the crisp, cold breeze caressing the Rangers' faces and cheeks.

Believing that all of the French had withdrawn into Fort Carillon, Jacob checked on the lieutenant who nodded that he was finished gathering information concerning the defensive positions. Satisfied everyone was ready, he gave the signal to move out. Jacob knew he was ready to go. Being this close to the enemy in their field was eerie. He led his men back to the base camp and reported to Major Rogers.

"As directed sir," Jacob reported, "I return the lieutenant as I found him, in one piece." Major Rogers nodded his appreciation. "Any sign of the enemy?" Jacob reported that they saw, heard, or smelled no one." Rogers accepted the report, and then spoke with the engineer on his findings.

Jacob noticed there were fewer men in the camp. Mostly, it was the British regulars who were gone. "Did we miss something?" Jacob asked Samuel as he resumed his position in the camp. "Where is everyone?"

Samuel said that while Jacob was out on the scout, Major Rogers had seen that more men were showing severe cases of frostbite. "He sent Captain Williams with the injured, escorted by a company of Rangers, to Sabbath Day Point to build bonfires and try to thaw out."

Looking around the smaller perimeter of the camp, he noticed it was mostly all Ranger veterans, and even they were looking worse for wear from the cold. After his consultation with Lieutenant Brehme, Rogers called in all of the remaining officers.

"Boys, it seems we have an opportunity here," Rogers announced. "So I decided we'll get more information for the generals if we can take a few prisoners back with us." Jacob nodded. He had expected this, that Rogers would go on the attack, which was true to form. The expedition was now down to ninety-two men, mostly seasoned Rangers and the Mohawks. Only one British regular remained.

Jacob, two other lieutenants, and Captain Lottridge were all that remained of the original officers who had departed from Fort Edward. Rogers planned to move around Fort Carillon and attack woodcutting parties on the western shore of the lake to get his prisoners.

Major Rogers laid out his plan. Jacob and his section would lead the way and move towards where they had observed woodcutters from their vantage point. There, they would encircle, take as many prisoners as they could, and then head back to Fort Edward. Using a stick, Rogers sketched out his plan in the snow, pointing out the positions for his men with his stick. Once everyone understood, he released the officers to gather their men.

"On another turkey hunt?" asked Samuel as Jacob approached, and Sergeant Hopkins came over and knelt down next to Jacob, who motioned Corporal Little over to join them.

"Yeah, the major wants prisoners, so we'll lead the column down and follow almost the same track we took to the field positions, but more north so as not to follow the same track twice. There is a spot where they're cutting wood. We'll take our section to the left, Captain Lottridge will take the right, and we'll bag the lot of them in between us, then beat feet back to Edward."

They all nodded, went back to their positions, tightened up their gear, and were ready to go in a short period of time. Having shouldered his own gear, Jacob looked to see if everyone was ready, nodded, and then led them to the head of the forming column. Rogers was waiting, and with a nod, motioned for Jacob to lead them out.

Just as the sun was slowly creeping up in the cold morning, the Rangers began their steady pace towards their target area. As they were moving towards the woodcutters, Jacob came across a large group of tracks moving south. He halted the column and took a look at the tracks as Major Rogers and Captain Lottridge joined him.

Looking at the tracks and the outline of the footprints, Rogers asked, "What do you think?" Jacob, tracing the outline of the print responded, "Abenaki, or maybe Canadian winter moccasins." They looked at the trail and the direction they were heading, which was generally south.

Rogers, face concerned, looked back at Jacob and Captain Lottridge. "Well, they're heading south, so that means either the encampment on the southern shore, or Fort Edward." Jacob and Captain Lottridge nodded in agreement, and looked at the trail. It was a decent-sized force, perhaps forty to sixty warriors, but they had already moved through the area about a day before. Major Roger nodded. "Nothing we can do now. Let's bag our game," he said, and Jacob continued to lead the expedition to their objective.

Moving through the woods, everyone wearing snowshoes because the snow was four feet deep in some places, the Ranger column had traveled for about eight miles when they arrived at the Little Mary River. There they spotted their objective, a French woodcutting party hard at work in the clearing just ahead of them.

Jacob had halted the column and then slowly moved in a crouch to the edge of the woodline, joined by Major Rogers and Captain Lottridge. They observed about forty men, about a third of them providing security while the rest chopped and stacked firewood. Rogers nodded and led the officers back to the waiting Rangers.

"Have your men strip down. We're going to hit them fast and hard. Get everyone ready!" Rogers commanded.

Jacob went over to his section and briefed them on their objective as they took off their capotes and packs, piling up the packs with their capotes tied to them. The men checked their rifles, making sure they were primed, and settled their knives and tomahawks in their belts.

Once everyone was ready, Jacob returned to Rogers and nodded. Major Rogers brought everyone up on line, and after looking to his left and right to make sure the Rangers were ready, he waved them forward. As the Rangers churned the snow into a white mist charging forward, they heard the signal cannon fired from the direction of Fort Carillon.

"Damn!" Jacob yelled as Rogers and the Rangers burst from the trees, yelling their war cries, which mixed with the war cries of the Mohawks.

The Frenchmen, frozen by the signal gun, burst into a run, and the Rangers began to fire on them from the woods. The Frenchmen had a head start, but the Rangers were in close pursuit of their quarry. Jacob brought his rifle up to his shoulder, drew a bead, and led one of the running Frenchmen before pulling his trigger, dropping the runner into the snow face first.

Loading on the run, Jacob joined the pursuit as the other Rangers fired at the running Frenchmen. Along with the man Jacob had killed, there were three other dead bodies that they ran past, but the Rangers and Mohawks grabbed seven men alive and took them as prisoners.

Rogers continued the pursuit, forming the point of the wedge of Rangers and Mohawks who chased the Frenchmen, all the way to Fort Carillon until they entered the fort. The Rangers brought their pursuit as close as they dared and then stopped. The sound of the long roll was coming from the fort, and Rogers decided it was time for them to withdraw.

Samuel turned and waved at the growing number of faces staring at them from the walls of the fort, before turning back into the woods. "Au revoir!" he yelled before following close behind Jacob as they ran back towards the prisoners. Jacob looked over at Samuel, who responded, "Just being neighborly."

Moving back to where they had dropped their gear, Jacob and his men quickly threw their packs on their backs and prepared to move. Major Rogers had already sent the prisoners and their escort ahead. The rest of the Rangers and Mohawks moved back in an orderly fashion.

Rogers expected that the French would soon be in pursuit, and he knew they would have to find a defensive position from which to delay the pursuit while the prisoners and their escort made it to Sabbath Day Point.

After traveling for only about an hour, Rogers spotted a small hill that would serve as a good defensive position in case their pursuers caught up with them. Jacob and his men fanned out and took cover behind trees and rocks, watching back the way they had come as Rogers deployed the rest of the Rangers and Mohawks.

***

Colonel Hebecourt, the current commander of Fort Carillon, had been informed of the tracks made by Jacob and his men inside the French defensive lines, and he ordered the signal cannon fired to recall the woodcutting party.

A Fury of Wolves

Now receiving confirmation of the Rangers' presence, Hebecourt assembled a force of eighty Canadians and Indians to send after the Rangers while he assembled a second force of French regulars. The Canadians and the Abenakis ran from the fort, war whoops echoing from the walls as they charged after the Rangers.

***

Jacob and his men could hear the war whoops in the distance as they readied their rifles. "Here they come, boys. Make ready," commanded Rogers, and all of the Rangers made sure they had a good firing position. Their elevated position was looking down on the route from which the enemy would more than likely approach.

The pursuing Canadians and Abenakis did not expect the Rangers and the Mohawks to be waiting so near for them, and they were stunned when the hill in front of them exploded with gunshots. Several Canadians and Abenakis fell dead, and a like number were wounded.

Rogers ordered, "Fall back by sections!" The Rangers leapfrogged back, covering one another. Jacob and his men loaded on the run as they passed the covering section, which fired another volley into the staggered pursuers.

Without having to think, Jacob loaded his rifle automatically while keeping watch on his Rangers. They moved through the snow, spinning around and taking up good firing positions, using what cover of trees and rocks they could find. Samuel knelt, taking a steady bead on an approaching Canadian. He pulled his trigger as Jacob spun and took up a kneeling firing position.

Jacob could see the progress of the enemy advance and their withdrawal, by the line of fallen white capotes of the Canadians and Abenakis. He was impressed. There was a good space between the lines of fallen enemies, showing when the Rangers turned and fired. So far, no one had been hit, and Jacob hoped their luck would hold. Vivid memories of the fight on snowshoes and the losses they had suffered still haunted him.

As Jacob and his Rangers moved back, they could see Rogers, who was standing and pointing to his left and then to his right, with Rangers falling into line with Rogers in the middle. Jacob and his Rangers skidded to a halt, snow flying up in the air as they spun around and prepared to fire on the pursuing enemies. "They're still coming," said Jacob as he looked over his sights at the approaching targets.

Waiting until they were about fifty yards away, Rogers gave the order to fire, and the line erupted in fire and smoke once again. Jacob sighted down his rifle barrel and centered on the chest of the Canadian who had just broken out of the woods. The Canadian had about a second to realize he was in Jacob's line of sight before his chest exploded and Jacob's rifle ball tore his life away.

That volley was all the Canadians and the Abenakis could take, and they turned and ran away from the Rangers and the Mohawks. Rogers ordered them up, and Jacob and his men, who had quickly reloaded their rifles, fell in line with the other Rangers and continued south towards Sabbath Day Point.

Jacob checked on his Rangers They all had the post-battle "we survived" grins on their faces, steam rising as they breathed hard from the exertion. No one was hurt, and that was good with Jacob as he settled into a distance-burning rhythm, moving through the woods.

Rogers believed that the French would not give up so easily in their backyard, and he found a long ridge, where he deployed his men once more in a defensive line facing the direction from which their enemies would come.

"Get a breather lads," Rogers ordered as he walked along the staggered line of Rangers. "Let's see if these bloody bastards are still out there."

While waiting to see if they were being pursued, Jacob told his men to grab something to eat and drink quickly. He pulled some cooked rations from his own haversack and chewed on the dry meat, watching for the enemy. A sip of water from his canteen helped to loosen the dried meat, making it easier to chew. As he ate, Jacob watched the woods in front of him, trying to detect the approach of the enemy.

After only a short wait, they picked up the sound of approaching men, and the Rangers and Mohawks brought their rifles up and took aim, getting back to serious business and making sure they had good firing positions as the sound of approaching men grew steadily louder.

"Fire by sections, pick your targets, no volleys!" commanded Rogers. Swallowing his dried meat, Jacob brought his rifle up and looked along his sites, taking a deep breath, and then letting it out slowly.

"Half of you fire on the first command," Jacob ordered. "You other half, cover and be ready."

Jacob could see some of the Canadians leading a line of French regulars who had now caught up and joined them. They were moving through the woods towards the Rangers, their feet kicking up puffs of powdery snow. Taking another deep breath and slowly letting it out, Jacob waited for the order to open fire, at which he and half of his men pulled their triggers. As the smoke cleared, Jacob could see several of the enemy bloodied and fallen to the ground.

Spinning his rifle around, Jacob began loading while keeping an eye on the enemy. The other half of the section took aim, and then fired at the now halted French regulars. Recovering from their shock, the French dove behind trees and began to return ineffective fire.

The French balls whizzed harmlessly by and smacked into trees as Jacob and the Rangers took careful aim at any exposed Frenchmen and fired. The fire broke the French pursuit, and they withdrew.

Jacob looked over at Samuel, who was lowering his rifle, the smoke wreathing his face, and disappointment showing on his face. "What's wrong with you?" Jacob asked, and Samuel simply replied, "Not much of a fight. Thought it would be more."

Waiting to make sure the French didn't return, Rogers and the Rangers watched and listened, but there was no other sound than the wind in the trees. Satisfied they were on their own, Rogers ordered the Rangers and Mohawks back into column, and they continued their journey to Sabbath Day Point.

The sun had fallen behind the mountains, with the cold once more becoming severe. Jacob was leading the column when he spotted the glow of the bonfires that Captain Williams had built. The Rangers and Mohawks stumbled into the camp around midnight, exhausted and shaking from the cold and exertion.

Major Rogers, who was beginning to suffer from early signs of frostbite himself, took stock of the situation. The raid against the woodcutters and the French had forced them to move more than fifty miles in one harsh day before ending there at the camp at Sabbath Day Point. While the fires had saved some of the men from severe frostbite, over two-thirds still had some frostbite in one fashion or another.

Going against their very principles, Jacob and his Rangers collected around one of the bonfires to thaw out their clothes and gear and warm up. "Don't know if I'll ever thaw out," grumbled Samuel, but then Sergeant Hopkins handed him a mug of warm rum. "Well," Samuel said, smacking his lips. "That could do it."

The rest of the Rangers joined in on a good laugh as the mug was passed around.

By daybreak, Rogers, who was still shivering from the effects of frostbite, dispatched Lieutenant Tute and some of his Rangers to move ahead to Fort Edward to gather sleighs and sleds to recover the frost-bitten men at the encampment at Lake George.

Jacob was also feeling the effects of the bitter cold, with the tip of his nose, portions of his cheeks, and the top of ears slightly frost-bitten, evidenced by a waxy white area that was numb. Jacob pulled his hat over his ears, and tried to wrap a scarf around his face to at least prevent his cheeks and nose from getting worse. Rogers had Jacob lead the column out of Sabbath Day Point and down to the southern shore of the lake.

Jacob and his men kept the pace slow because the British regulars and some of the Rangers hugged themselves as they stumbled through the woods, suffering from cold weather injuries. "Was this price worth it?" Jacob asked himself as he led the broken column through the woods. "I hope the information we got was worth it."

It took them all day at a slow, measured pace to reach the encampment at the southern end of the lake. Lieutenant Tute was waiting, having made good time to Fort Edward. He had returned with sleds and sleighs, into which the most severely injured were loaded and quickly moved to Fort Edward.

Some of the men who could not be loaded into the already full sleds and sleighs were placed in huts there at the encampment waiting for the sleds and sleighs to return. Jacob and his men found a patch of ground where the snow was thin, and built a large fire to warm themselves.

They were tired, so Jacob decided they would not continue the rest of the way home until morning. Sergeant Hopkins and some of the men visited the quartermaster at the encampment for fresh meat and rum. Jacob, having made his bed of pine boughs, sat atop his ground cloth and helped cook the fresh meat. His nose and cheeks were beginning to sting and burn as they thawed out and feeling returned. After taking a sip of rum from a communal cup that was being passed around, Jacob handed it to the next man sitting around the fire.

Soon, the freshly cooked meat and fresh biscuits, which had been warmed by the fire, were passed out to the men. Jacob savored the meat, allowing the warmth to spread from his stomach.

Satisfied "oohs and ahhs" were coming from his gathered Rangers, Jacob joining in as the rum and food warmed his insides and made life bearable.

"Boys, you did well out there," Jacob said to the gathered men. "You did a good job."

The men nodded and smiled at the praise as they enjoyed the fresh meal. Samuel raised a toast to "thawing out and warming up," and everyone replied with "here…here!" They talked and joked among themselves, the stress of the expedition washing over them.

Jacob wrapped himself up in his blanket, covering his head in a wool cap and allowing the fire to warm his body. Instead of standing a watch, the men took turns keeping the fire burning. When it died down and got cold, one of them would go fetch an armful of wood to feed it and stoke it back up again while the others continued to sleep, mostly with their backs to the fire to stay warm.

As the sun was beginning to rise, one of the men placed a pot of water on the fire to heat so they could have hot tea to help warm their insides as they ate their breakfast of leftover biscuits and meat. They rolled up their ground cloths and blankets, repacked their packs, and prepared to march the rest of the way back to Fort

Edward. They left the fire burning as sleds returned for the rest of the injured. Jacob and his men accompanied the line of sleds to Fort Edward, which was a welcome sight when it came into view.

Jacob led his section out to the island. He shook the hands of the men he had led and told them he was proud to have served with them and he looked forward to conducting other missions with them.

Jacob watched the men break up and head to their huts before he and Samuel turned and walked towards their cabin. He was almost to the hut when Smoke came running out and knocked him over. Samuel, who had started to laugh, was knocked over by Otto, who had followed Smoke out of the hut.

"Well, that's a homecoming for ya," he said as he fought Smoke. Meanwhile, Samuel was losing his battle with Otto's wet tongue. The wolves finally let them up and bounced into the hut as Jacob and Samuel entered their old home.

After taking care of his gear and hanging it on pegs, Jacob sat on his bunk with a groan and began to clean his rifle. Samuel also cleaned his while the warmth of the cabin relaxed their muscles.

Later, Peter hobbled into the hut and welcomed Jacob and Samuel home. He told them that Major Rogers was bundled up in his hut, trying to recover from the exertion and the frostbite he had suffered on the expedition. Jacob could relate. His ears, the tip of his nose, and his cheeks were finally thawing out.

Soon the exhaustion of the trip was having its effect on Jacob, and his eyelids were constantly closing on him.

"Stop fighting it, and just go to sleep," advised Peter. Samuel had already slumped over and was snoring loudly.

Jacob nodded and after pulling his blanket over himself, wrapped up and fell quickly asleep.

Major Rogers was so tired from the expedition that it was a few days after they had all arrived back at Fort Edward before he was able to complete his report on what they had found at Fort Carillon. The report, which was sent to General Gage in Albany and then on to General Amherst in New York, said that the French had been cleared from the area along Lake George, and they were now only at Fort Carillon.

As the Rangers recovered from the harsh expedition, General Amherst began to set in motion the spring campaign.

The winter was losing its grip on the valley as spring melted away the snow and ice. Jacob went out from time to time on scouts around the area, along with other Ranger patrols, because he still wasn't permanently assigned to a platoon. He wondered if Rogers did this on purpose so he could call on Jacob for unique assignments.

The spring also brought the enemy back to their area. A small patrol of four Rangers was ambushed, and one man was killed and two captured. The lone survivor made it back to report to Major Rogers. Later in the spring, a thirty-man platoon under the command of Captain Burbank was wiped out by an Indian ambush.

Spring allowed work to continue on the British fortifications. General Amherst wanted to make sure as he launched his campaign against the French that his rear lines were secure from enemy attacks.

A new construction, which was begun near the fort, was a welcome surprise. General Amherst had authorized the building of a spruce beer brewery. Spruce beer was normally a staple of the rations, and as the number of men grew at the fort, the demand had grown for more. As most of the logistics focused on the coming campaign and not beer, it made logistical sense to build a brewery there to directly support the army.

While this was welcome news that quickly spread throughout the fort and the camps, Jacob was less enthusiastic when he found out that the main developer of the brewery was none other than Robert Aislabie and the South Sea Company. When Jacob passed on what he had learned about the brewery, Samuel remarked, "Ah no! Not a company brewery. Damn!"

Jacob shrugged, "We'll have to wait and see. Maybe, it will be good having a brewery right here." Jacob was more doubtful once he saw his "favorite" company men again, Maclane and Harpe. They were accompanying this Robert Aislabie and Mr. Pommery, whose sutler shop, and not Mr. Best's, would be the main distributor of the beer.

Samuel watched the company men walk around the brewery construction site and shook his head. "Damnable luck! It had to be these men." Then he looked at Jacob. "Don't think it is going to be as good as we hoped."

Jacob shrugged and replied, "Still too early to tell," but to himself he admitted he didn't like these company men, and he was starting to have big doubts.

The encampment at Halfway Brook continued to be expanded and strengthened to secure the military road there. They also changed the name of the fortified encampment at the southern end of the lake to Fort Amherst in honor of the overall British commander.

Just outside of Fort Edward and across the river on the western shore, the British built the Royal Blockhouse to provide early warning and security for the fort. In addition to strengthening the encampment on the shore of Lake George and the continued stockpiling of supplies, they began building a new fort opposite of where the old Fort William Henry had stood on the southern shore. They named it Fort George. Another new construction, Fort Gage, named after General Gage, was also built on the southern shore, just below the ruins of Fort William Henry.

Men and equipment began moving to the encampment in preparation for the campaign. Columns of wagons from Albany and supply bases in the south arrived regularly at both Forts Gage and Amherst.

As the leaves grew and the warmth returned, Jacob was finally permanently assigned to a Ranger company when Major Rogers began organizing his seven companies, mixing his experienced and veteran Rangers with the new volunteers and the augmentees from the British regulars. Jacob was assigned to a brand new company under the command of Lieutenant David Brewer, who had not yet received his captaincy because he had not been able to recruit all of the men he needed for his company. Two companies of Stockbridge Indians arrived, and with Lt Brewer's new company, Major Rogers once again had ten companies. Men and equipment were distributed, all in preparation for the campaign that was about to begin.

Lieutenant Brewer warmly welcomed Jacob into the company, knowing Jacob's reputation, and he had already decided that Jacob would serve as his second-in-command. Jacob was able to get Samuel assigned to Lieutenant Brewer's company, and he and Samuel were leading a training scout when both Smoke and Otto smelled something, let out a low growl, and laid their ears back. Seeing this, Jacob halted the company and began scanning the woods. They were not far from the fort and were concerned they might have come across an enemy scout.

Lieutenant Brewer made his way to Jacob and whispered, "What is it? What do you see?"

Jacob shook his head. "Not what we saw. What they smelled," he said pointing to Smoke and Otto. Jacob studied where the wolves were looking, and decided to lead the company in that direction.

"Keep your eyes and ears open. We may have company," Jacob warned, and the Rangers nodded, scanning the woods with their eyes and their rifles. They were moving slowly in the direction the wolves' noses were pointing when Jacob picked up the scent, the very distinct scent of dead bodies.

"You smell it too?" Samuel asked, and Jacob nodded. "Anything close by?" Samuel asked, and Jacob thought about it. "No, nothing but that old farmstead is in the area," Jacob responded. Moving cautiously, Jacob led the company as Lieutenant Brewer watched.

The rest of the company could smell it now, the distinct smell of rotting flesh, and it was coming from the old farm. Jacob halted the company and brought the Rangers on-line. Jacob looked at Lieutenant Brewer, who nodded, "You take them."

Jacob addressed the company. "Don't know what we have, but considering what we can smell, it can't be good. Break into sections, search the farm, and be ready for anything." He motioned them forward with his hand, and the Rangers broke into sections and began searching the farm.

It didn't take them long to find the source of the smell, the old well. All of the Rangers were wrinkling their noses, and even the wolves were staying away. Some of the newer Rangers could be heard retching.

Jacob steeled himself and looked into the well. The smell was overpowering, and it was too dark to see what was down there. Samuel, holding his nose asked, "Could it be a dead animal, a very dead, big animal?"

Jacob shook his head. This scent was very particular, and it didn't smell of a dead animal. It smelled of a dead human. "Samuel, take a section and return to the fort and tell them we found something out here that needs investigating. We'll secure the area."

Samuel nearly jumped for joy at the thought of getting away from the smell, and the men he picked to go with him were delighted as well. As they quickly headed back to Fort Edward, Jacob and Brewer pushed the company out in a perimeter that spared them from most of the smell while securing the site.

After a short while, Samuel returned with a detail from the fort, including the provost and the fort's deputy commander. The regulars held perfumed handkerchiefs to their noses and were turning green from the smell. A rope was tied around a small man with a lantern and, he was lowered into the well.

Soon the sound of retching could be heard, with a yell of, "Oh my God, pull me up, pull me up!" The detail pulled the unfortunate man back up and as he fell out of the well, the lantern crashing to the ground as he violently threw up everything in his stomach.

"Bodies! It's…full…of…bodies," he panted before dry heaving because there was nothing left in him to throw up. The Rangers were sent back, and a detail from the fort secured the site and began retrieving the bodies from the well.

The following day, Jacob with Lieutenant Brewer, Samuel, and Major Rogers returned to the farm where the work detail had lined the remains up near the well. Most of the bodies were only skeletons; some had pieces of clothing left, but nothing substantial. Lieutenant Colonel Perkins motioned for them to come over.

"This is perplexing. Can you determine how these poor souls were killed? Would those savages or the French do this? Their partisans?" asked Perkins. Rogers and Jacob went over, and Jacob, taking a knee, looked at the remains. It was evident all of the heads had hair still on them, and they had not been mutilated.

Rogers knelt down next to Jacob and asked, "Thoughts?"

"They all have their scalps. No mutilations," said Jacob as he looked at the heads and the bodies. "And they're mostly women." Rogers nodded. "I agree."

A Fury of Wolves

Jacob stood up and looked at Rogers. "This was done by someone here. There is a killer amongst us." Rogers nodded. "That body you found up at the lake … do you think it's connected?"

Jacob thought for a moment, and then nodded. "I think it might be, plus all of these disappearances we've been having, I don't think it's a coincidence."

Jacob and Rogers approached Lieutenant Colonel Perkins who was keeping his distance from the bodies. "Sir," Rogers began, "it's our belief that no Indian, no partisan did this, that these are victims of murder."

Perkins, looking shocked, asked, "What are you saying?"

Jacob replied, "Sir, you have a killer in the fort."

***

Word quickly spread to the fort as the carts with the remains arrived to be buried in the fort's cemetery. Whispers of murders in the night and a killer or killers on the loose, and even a devil in the woods spread like wildfire through the fort and the camps. Maclane excused himself from a meeting with Aislabie when Aislabie mentioned the rumors, and he sought out Harpe.

He found Harpe in a corner of the fort behind some bales and boxes, dicing once more with a few waggoneers. "Gentlemen, hate to break up your game, but I need Mr. Harpe here for business. You understand?" The men nodded and took up their earnings and dice and left Harpe alone with Maclane.

Once they were alone, Maclane's anger took the best of him and he actually pushed Harpe up against the wall with a crash and pulled his knife, placing it against Harpe's throat. "You fool! You bloody fool and your damn games!" Maclane roared at Harpe, not concerned if he drew attention, his anger was so severe.

Harpe grabbed Maclane's wrist but was amazed how strong he was, and the knife never moved from his throat. "Do you realize your little game could cost us this venture? I told you to control it, and sure enough, those damn Rangers found your dumping area."

Harpe didn't say anything, just shrugged. Maclane continued, "What am I supposed to do with you if you can't control yourself? You're going to ruin everything we have created here!"

Harpe just stood there, with no care or concern in his eyes.

With a heavy sigh and a loud "Damn!" Maclane released Harpe, who rubbed his throat where the knife had been. "It was bound to happen sometime. So what? They still don't know I did it," Harpe justified himself.

Maclane looked venomously at him, and then sighed once more. "You have to leave, get away until all of this settles down." Harpe shrugged and waited. "I know I might regret this," Maclane grumbled, "but I do have a task to your liking, and it will take you away from here."

Harpe smiled and patiently waited as Maclane continued. "We are having difficulties with the competition up at Louisburg, which will soon be under our control. I am sending you there to fix the situation."

Again Harpe just smiled, but this time, he responded. "By whatever means I see fit?" Maclane glowered, and then nodded. "Yes, by whatever means you see fit. Just secure our monopoly, and I'll join you later to finish the deal."

Harpe smiled even more broadly. "I'll pack immediately and be on my way."

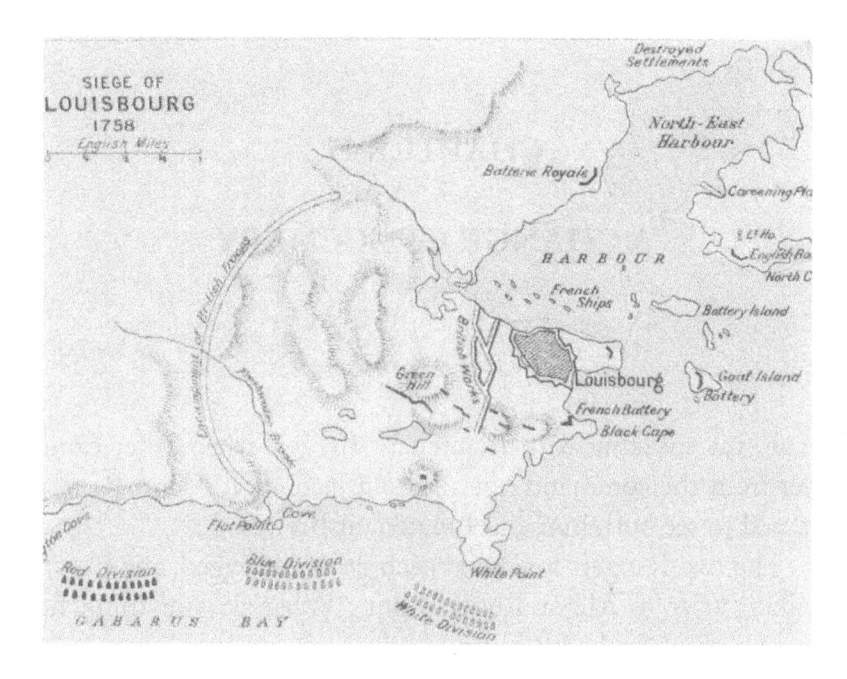

Map of the Siege of Louisburg

CHAPTER 17

A CHANGE OF SCENERY

Jacob was speaking with Lieutenant Brewer, when Peter came over from the command hut and told Jacob that Major Rogers wanted to see both him and Lieutenant Brewer.

The two Rangers looked at each other, shrugged, and began walking over to Major Rogers's hut. "What do you think he wants with us?" asked Brewer. Jacob simply replied, "More than likely, we're training the company on the march, or at least a platoon. I'm sure the Major has an operation for us."

Both men entered the hut and removed their hats as Rogers finished reading a letter. Looking up, Major Rogers gave a heavy sigh and said, "Lieutenant Brewer, I am going to have to take Jacob from you."

Jacob's heart sank. He had finally been assigned to a company and was getting into the swing of things training and preparing the Rangers. Jacob chased the feeling away. This meant the major had something very important for him, and his disappointment was quickly replaced with a feeling of excitement as he waited to hear what the major had for him.

Rogers looked at Jacob, and said, "I have another tough assignment for you, and it's not by choice."

Jacob nodded and waited for Major Rogers to drop the hammer on what he would be doing now. "Perhaps I am going somewhere new, perhaps a scout up in Canada," thought Jacob as he waited for the details.

Holding up the letter he had been reading, Rogers said, "This is a dispatch from General Amherst concerning his plans for the spring. He is launching a campaign to take Quebec, and we are returning to take Fort Carillon and Crown Point."

As soon as Jacob heard "Fort Carillon," the horrible vision returned to his mind of the killing fields in the Fort Carillon abatis last summer.

"Jacob, I need you to go to Halifax. I received a request from Captain Hazen for an experienced officer to help mold and lead his company of ...," Rogers looked at a second letter on his desk and read, "... very inexperienced and not the best quality men thrust upon me to lead."

Looking up at Jacob, Major Rogers said to the two officers, "Sorry to do this to you, Lieutenant Brewer, but I need to send Jacob to Captain Hazen."

Nodding his head, Brewer turned to Jacob, shook his hand, and said, "Well, it was nice while it lasted. Best of luck!"

Lieutenant Brewer was dismissed, and he departed to return to his company.

Jacob awaited his specific instructions from Major Rogers.

"You'll travel to Albany where you will board a schooner that will take you to Halifax. There you are to join the army and Captain Hazen."

Major Rogers stood and came around to hand Jacob his orders and documents as well as dispatches for the Rangers supporting the campaign. Then he reached out and shook Jacob's hand.

"Best of luck, Lieutenant Clarke. Your orders also state that once the campaign is over, you will be released to return here and rejoin this command."

Jacob nodded, relieved that he would be returning, and shook Rogers's hand. After pocketing his orders and dispatches, he headed to his hut and packed his gear. As he was packing, Samuel came into the hut, and Jacob told him of his assignment to Halifax.

Looking down at Smoke, Jacob scratched his ears and told him that he would be staying with Samuel and his wolf, Otto, and that he probably wouldn't like the trip on the schooner over to Halifax anyway. Samuel nodded and said he would take care of Smoke for Jacob while he was away.

"You are planning to come back, right?" asked Samuel.

Jacob nodded and patted his uniform pocket where the orders were.

"I am instructed to return to this command once our operations are done."

Samuel watched as Jacob shouldered his pack and grabbed his rifle, leaving his sword behind. He followed Jacob over to the command hut where he reported that he was departing. Peter was there and logged in the orderly book that Jacob was reassigned and was *en route* to his new posting. Shaking both Peter's and Samuel's hands, Jacob wished them luck in their campaign against Fort Carillon, and they in return wished him luck in his campaign against Quebec.

Jacob traveled south to Albany, stopping at the same forts and blockhouses that he had stayed at during his recruiting trip during the fall. At Fort Hardy, Jacob avoided going into the town of Saratoga. He had said his farewell to Abigail, and that part of his life had come to an end like the others. He bypassed the town and continued on to Albany. Along the route, he passed numerous lines of wagons and carts heading north, carrying supplies to Fort Gage at Lake George.

As Jacob watched the columns of men and materials head north, he wondered about the looming campaign. "Hope these bloody generals have their act together," mumbled Jacob to himself. "Lost too many good friends already due to their stupidity."

At least the weather was pleasant, cool but comfortable, as Jacob moved past farmers out planting their fields. At Albany, Jacob reported to General Gage's headquarters. The orderly checked Jacob's orders and confirmed that he was to take the Schooner Marble Head, which was carrying dispatches to the army assembling at Halifax.

It would be two days before the schooner sailed, so Jacob went over to an inn near the port called the White Horse Tavern. Settling into a table with a mug of ale, Jacob had just brought it up for a swallow when an orderly from General Gage's office arrived.

"Ah, Lieutenant Clarke of the Rangers?" the orderly asked, and Jacob nodded. "Sir, you are to return to the commander's orderly office."

As the orderly waited, not wanting to waste the good ale, Jacob sighed, drank the entire mug before putting it on the table, wiped his mouth with the sleeve of his uniform, and then stood and told the orderly, "Lead on."

Jacob followed the orderly through Albany back to General Gage's headquarters, where he was directed to a different officer sitting at a desk writing orders, a Major Meyers.

As Jacob approached, the officer looked up and said, "Ah, the Provincial heading to Halifax." Jacob nodded in the affirmative.

Reaching behind his desk, Major Meyer produced a satchel and handed it to Jacob.

In a tired tone, the major ordered, "Take this to General Wolfe in Halifax. It contains dispatches from both General Gage and General Amherst. These dispatches are for the general and the general alone."

Jacob took the satchel, and rendered a salute, which was summarily ignored by Major Meyer, who returned to writing a new dispatch. Jacob dropped his salute, spun, and departed. None of the orderlies or other officers seemed to notice him, as if he were invisible.

As Jacob left the orderly room with the satchel, he wasn't much bothered by the major's disrespect. It had become an almost expected response now from British officers.

Jacob returned to the inn and added the satchel to his pack, then returned to the common room to enjoy a warm meal and a drink and to watch the comings and goings of the people. He enjoyed the peace and quiet for the two days he waited to sail, knowing full well that once he arrived at Halifax, he wouldn't have much time to rest.

As he thought about his trip, Jacob began to contemplate the sights and sounds that would be different from what he had experienced so far. It would be something new and different, and it excited him. Jacob raised his mug and made a toast to his coming adventures, to the spirits of his old friends and comrades, and to lady luck, hoping she would keep smiling on him.

The morning arrived for Jacob to board the schooner. He shouldered his pack, insuring the satchel and other dispatches were secure. The morning was grey and misty as Jacob made his way to where the schooner was moored. Jacob had never been on a ship before, and he was looking forward to the experience.

Walking down the dock, Jacob reported to the first mate at the bottom of the gang plank, who asked to see Jacob's orders. Satisfied, the mate motioned for Jacob to follow him, and he showed Jacob where he could stow his gear in a small cabin below deck.

The schooner was the standard two-mast type, with large foresails and main sails, as well as top sails. Jacob estimated that the schooner was about thirty feet long and in good shape. His enthusiasm about the coming trip began to subside; he had never sailed before, and the small cramped cabin he had been given made him uncomfortable. He preferred the open spaces of the woods to this close, cramped room with only a slight breeze moving through the small porthole.

After securing his gear and rifle in his cabin, Jacob climbed up on deck and while staying out of the way, watched the crew make ready to sail. Orders were yelled out, the lines cast off, and the great canvas sails were hauled into position and tied off by the crew. The wind caught the sails, which snapped and flapped in the breeze, and the schooner began making her way down the Hudson. Jacob enjoyed the smell of the breeze, mixed with the odors of the schooner, which included dried wood, pitch, tar, and the hemp of the ropes.

After the schooner got under way, the lines had been stowed, and the crew had gone about their normal duties, Jacob found a place to sit in the bow to watch the land pass by. "Well, it's better than walking," he thought.

The schooner rocked with the motion of the river, and Jacob was soothed by a strong breeze and the warm sun that was shining down. He made himself comfortable against some coiled rope and fell asleep.

After napping, Jacob went below to where the schooner's cook was ladling out beef stew and biscuits. Once lunch was finished, Jacob joined the first mate and the schooner's captain, John Goodwin, on the aft deck.

Jacob knew nothing of sailing, and he watched the various seamen at their jobs while carrying on a pleasant conversation with Captain Goodwin. Mostly, the captain wanted to know about the war to the north, while he told Jacob about the threat of French privateers roaming along the coast. Jacob noticed that several swivel guns were being brought out and mounted on the bulwarks.

The trip down the Hudson was uneventful, and when the schooner arrived at New York, Jacob was impressed by the number and different types of boats and ships in the harbor. Everything from schooners and sloops, to massive three-masted warships and merchant ships either rode their anchors or were sailing into or out of the harbor.

The river emptied into the large harbor, which was composed of the lower bay and the upper bay and opened into the Atlantic Ocean. Jacob noticed that the schooner had begun to rock more as the waves became bigger than they had been on the river.

Jacob began to get a queasy feeling in his stomach, and it must have shown because the captain began to chuckle.

"Aye lad," the captain consoled. "Give it some time; you'll get yer sea legs." Then he looked at Jacob, and added, "Though I would suggest heading over to the side there until you get them."

Standing next to the bulwarks, Jacob rode out the slight rise and fall of the schooner, unfortunately losing his lunch in the process. As Jacob recovered and fought to gain his sea legs, he noticed the large wooded islands that the schooner was passing.

Leaning on the bulwark, Jacob asked a sailor who was coiling lines, "Do they have names?" Looking up from his rope, the sailor pointed. "That there is called Manhattan." Then he turned to point at a large island they were heading towards, and said, "That one is called Long Island."

The waves became even bigger, and soon the schooner was slicing through them, the sea spray washing over the bow. Jacob watched the setting sun to the west as the shore line shrank and was folded into the shadow of the coming night, the schooner creaking and groaning as the wind blew her along.

Along with dealing with the rise and fall of the schooner and his stomach, Jacob had to learn the other portion of gaining his sea legs, how to walk on a pitching ship. He noticed that most of the sailors were barefoot, which he guessed helped with their footing.

After an evening meal of fish stew and biscuits, Jacob sat with the crew, who were playing cards by the light of a swinging lamp. He was still trying to get his stomach to settle despite the rolling of the schooner, and he seemed to be winning his wrestling match.

Sleep was difficult because Jacob was not used to the motion of the schooner. He also needed to feel the wind on his face. The cabin was stuffy, and he wasn't used to it. Even their hut back on the island was bigger than his cabin on the schooner. He decided to go up on deck. Finding the spot on the bow where he had napped earlier, he wrapped himself in a blanket and fell asleep, lulled by the creak of the schooner's planks and the wind.

However, by morning, the wind had picked up, and the schooner was rolling more than the day before. The bow rose and crashed through rising waves. The clouds were grey and thick above and on the ocean, creating a thick fog. Rain began to pelt Jacob as he slept on the foredeck, which forced him below deck.

As the ship heaved and rolled with the waves, Jacob was knocked about in his small cabin. He moved to a covered area on the main deck where he could stay out of the way of the crewmen, who were taking in sails and moving lines based on the commands of the captain.

The roll and pitch of the schooner finally beat Jacob, and with his stomach unable to tolerate the constant rise and fall, he vomited again over the side of the schooner

"This has got to end," groaned Jacob as he fought with his stomach. He was glad he hadn't brought Smoke. How would a wolf handle this?

Wrapped in a ground cloth to protect himself from the rain, Jacob rode out the storm on the deck, grimacing and clenching his teeth as his stomach slowly began to adjust to the pitch and roll of the schooner. The captain began steering the schooner with the waves so that the ship was just rising and falling with the waves, not rolling side-to-side against them.

The rain began to dissipate, and the wind lessened, but the grey clouds and fog remained. Sailors moved to change the sail configuration now that the weather was improving.

Wrapped in his ground cloth, Jacob climbed up on the quarter deck and stood near the captain and first mate. The first mate looked him over and with a twinkle in his eye, asked how Jacob was doing. Jacob replied, "Getting the hang of it." However, Jacob thought that the cold bitter winter of the north was better than being tossed about on the ocean with no control. At least when it was cold you could do things to warm up.

His thoughts were cut off when the sailor up in the crow's nest yelled out, "Sail Ho!" The captain and first mate looked up in the direction the sailor was pointing. The first mate took the wheel as the captain moved over and pulled out his telescope.

Jacob fished into his ground cloth for his haversack, pulled his own telescope out, and looked in the same direction. In the distance, another ship the size of the schooner, was angling towards them, sails billowing to catch the wind. Jacob could see crewmen running about, and then small black tubes began to appear as small cannons were run out.

"Oh, bloody hell. A French privateer," growled the captain.

Shutting his telescope with a loud click, the captain yelled out, "Privateer! Man the swivel guns, run the canvas out, and give us some speed!"

The crew was spilling out of the foredeck and from wherever else they had been on the schooner, and they began to run out sails or to move to the bulwark facing the approaching privateer and load the swivel guns.

No longer worrying about his stomach, Jacob went quickly to his cabin, threw his ground cloth off, and grabbed his tomahawk and knife, which he put behind his back in his belt. He grabbed his rifle and shooting bag and rushed back up on deck,

The First Mate saw an armed Jacob come up on deck, and he nodded in appreciation. "Where should I go?" asked Jacob, and the First Mate pointed to a spot on the quarter deck.

"You good with that?" the First Mate asked. Not knowing if he meant his rifle, his tomahawk, or his knife, Jacob nodded "yes" with a set expression on his face and made his way to the spot the First Mate had indicated.

Nodding his head again, the First Mate returned to issuing orders as Jacob found a space near the quarter deck. The approaching privateer now was flying a large French flag and was quickly closing on them.

Jacob began loading his rifle as crewmen passed out muskets, axes, and cutlasses. The swivel gun crewmen were blowing on their slow matches in preparation for firing. The captain came over to Jacob.

"If you could pick off some of their gunners, or, and I hate to say this, their captain, I would be deeply grateful."

Nodding again, Jacob began to estimate the closing distance of the French privateer. The crewmen were becoming more visible and easier to pick out. Jacob was concerned about the rise and fall of the two boats; he would have to time his shots with the schooners.

The French privateer's bow was mostly facing them now, trying to catch up and overtake them. Bringing his rifle to his shoulder, getting the feel for the rise and fall of the ship, Jacob took aim at one of the lead gunners looking over their bulwark. Trying to aim from a moving ship against a moving ship was as challenging as leading a deer running through the mountains, he thought.

Jacob settled into a good shooting position. This new challenge of hitting a bobbing target on a ship was something he would have to deal with. The wind was a factor, but that was no different from shooting in the mountains. Jacob's heart began to beat faster, the adrenalin coursing through his blood.

Breathing in and slowly releasing his breath, Jacob waited for the ship to pause for a second in the rise and fall, and he pulled his trigger. Jacob's ball tore through the chest of a gunner, who fell back out of sight.

"Nice shot!" boomed the captain.

Jacob nodded as he reloaded, muttering to himself, "I was aiming for his head. I need to figure out the rise and fall of this ship."

The shot and the fact that it had hit someone startled the privateers, who had believed they were out of range of muskets and had not realized that someone had a rifle.

Jacob loaded as fast as he could and brought the rifle up as the privateer was about two hundred yards away. Waiting for the schooner to just finish its rise, he fired his second shot. He was rewarded with seeing another privateer fall.

The privateer ship was slowly closing in, but it was still far enough for Jacob to get a few more shots off, dropping several privateers, which must have made an impact because the privateer ship all of a sudden turned away so they could fire their small cannons at the English schooner, but from more than a hundred yards away.

"Take cover!" yelled the First Mate as the privateer fired four small cannons, about three-pounders, at their schooner. Jacob ducked below the bulwark as one ball flew over the schooner, one tore through a sail, a third hit the side of the schooner with a thud, and a forth fell into the ocean.

Rising up, Jacob took a snap shot at the privateer's quarterdeck, aiming at what he thought was the captain. But his ball caught another privateer, who had moved in front of his target, and the captain was sprayed with the unlucky sailor's brains and blood.

The privateer began to crab, pointing its bow at the English schooner to close the distance, turning to fire its cannons, and then returning to the bow-forward position to gain distance. Every time the privateer turned to fire its cannons, the First Mate yelled to "take cover."

The privateer was closer now, less than a hundred yards, and its cannon balls were tearing up the sails or hitting the bulwark hard enough that large splinters were flying out and injuring some of the crewmen. The English schooner's swivel guns now returned fire with chain shot, which was two small balls with a chain between them, or bar shot, two small half-balls with a bar between them, all designed to tear up the privateer's rigging and sails.

The privateer was also close enough to fire both its cannons and its swivel guns. Jacob stayed low, looking over the bulwark to watch the privateer and pick his targets. He could see that there were a lot more privateers than there were English crewmen.

Time seemed to slow as Jacob became caught up in the battle, the sounds of cannons booming and screeching shot, orders being yelled, and the cries of the crew. Battle sounded the same, whether on ground or out at sea.

"There is no way in bloody hell I am going to be killed or captured by these Frenchmen after surviving all of these years!" growled Jacob as he brought his rifle up to his shoulder, aimed and fired. His target spun around and fell into the ocean.

"And I'll bloody well not die out here seasick!" he growled as he quickly rammed another ball into place before spinning his rifle around to prime. He looked over the bulwark, trying to spot his next target.

Both ships were close enough now that the crews fired muskets at each other, along with the swivel guns and cannons. The air was filled with the smoke of battle, musket balls and splinters flying through the air, along with the screams and groans of the men they hit.

Jacob felt a stab of pain across his head as he was aiming; a splinter had nicked the right side of his head across his temple. Shaking it off, he re-aimed and fired, satisfied when another privateer gunner fell.

Jacob had to accept that as a single rifleman, even though he was doing damage, his skill with the rifle might not be enough. He could see the privateer closing now to within twenty-five yards. Across the distance, privateers were yelling and hooting, and men with grappling hooks could be seen getting them ready.

"Load double grape, load with balls, scrap anything, get ready to repel boarders!" commanded the captain. He was pacing the deck, his cutlass out, swishing before him.

As the two ships closed, Jacob looked over and saw a blunderbuss on the deck near him. Staying low, he grabbed it and moved it next to him, then looked across the way at the enemy. Jacob could clearly see the privateer's captain, and he brought his rifle up and over the bulwark. He aimed, centering on the privateer captain's chest to be sure.

Time seemed to slow as the privateer captain ordered the grappling hooks to be thrown, and Jacob pulled the trigger. The captain had just got the order out when Jacob's ball tore his life away, and he crumbled to the deck.

As the grappling hooks began to clank onto their ship, Captain Goodwin gave the order to fire the swivel guns at the privateers who were beginning to swarm over the side of their ship. Three of the four swivel guns fired. At the fourth one next to Jacob, the gunner took a musket ball and fell. He threw the slow match, which Jacob caught in midair. Dropping his rifle, Jacob turned the swivel gun to face the screaming privateers and lowered the slow match, firing the swivel gun, which shredded some of the charging privateers.

Dropping the slow match, Jacob ducked under a jumping privateer, dove and rolled on the deck, picking up the blunderbuss. Turning and firing from the hip, he blasted three privateers who had just landed on the schooner.

The crew crashed into the French privateers with clubbed muskets, cutlasses, and pikes, the French and the English stabbing and jabbing at one another. Pulling his tomahawk and knife from behind his back, Jacob gave a war cry and charged into the melee. Catching a privateer's sweeping cutlass with his tomahawk, Jacob followed through with his knife, slicing his throat open and spraying blood on his fellow privateers.

Following through and spinning around, Jacob buried his tomahawk in the back of a privateer who was struggling with one of the crewmen. As the privateer fell, Jacob spotted one of the grappling hooks and chopped it with his tomahawk.

As the rope separated from the grappling hook, a privateer tackled Jacob and drove him to the ground. As he fell, Jacob spun while holding his attacker, and he landed on top of the privateer, knocking the wind out of him. As the privateer tried to catch his breath, he released Jacob which allowed him to bury his knife in the chest of his enemy.

Rising up, Jacob raced along the bulwark and chopped more grappling hooks. The captain, seeing what Jacob was doing, pushed his crew to drive back the privateers who were beginning to jump back across to their ship as it pulled away because it was no longer connected to the schooner.

When Jacob arrived at the last grappling hook, he just got his tomahawk up in time to defend himself against a determined privateer and his cutlass. Sparks flew as tomahawk and cutlass clanged together repeatedly.

The privateer had a crazed look in his eyes as he beat his cutlass against Jacob's tomahawk. The privateer's swings got bigger and bigger, until Jacob was quick enough to catch the sword on the down swing. He spun to his left and locked his left arm and tomahawk under his opponent's arm pit. He brought his right arm up, and pulled the surprised privateer over his shoulder, over the bulwark, and into the ocean. The he chopped through the ropes of the last grappling hook.

Spinning the wheel, Captain Goodwin heeled the schooner over, and it began to pull away from the privateer. Jacob's killing of the privateer's captain might have taken the fight out of them, as well as the number of injuries they had sustained from what they had thought would be an easy prize. The privateer did not turn to pursue and in fact turned away and moved in a different direction.

The crew cheered as the privateer shrank in the distance, and then they got busy collecting the injured or dead and making repairs to critical parts of the schooner. Jacob helped where he could, assisting with bandaging the injured. The captain stopped by to shake Jacob's hand.

"I have heard tales of you Rangers and your shooting; thought they be tall tales. Now I see it's all true."

Jacob nodded, and the captain continued on his rounds, checking on the condition of his ship and crew. As Jacob continued to help, he realized he didn't feel seasick anymore. "Hmm," Jacob thought, "perhaps fighting is a cure for seasickness."

The day after the attack, Jacob attended a quick ceremony at which the captain committed to the sea the four crewmen who had lost their lives. The captain spoke at the ceremony, recalling the men's deeds and evoking the tradition of sailors returning to Mother Ocean.

The dead sailors had been sewn into their hammocks, weighted down, and then slid into the ocean, where they sank below the waves. Jacob helped the crew sew sails that had been torn by the privateer's cannon shots and worked with the carpenter to repair or plane the splintered wood smooth.

The weather remained nice, and Jacob finally had his sea legs. The schooner had favorable winds that quickly pushed it up past Massachusetts. With no other excitement, Jacob decided he wanted to pass the time by learning more about their craft of sailing.

Making sure not to be in the way, he talked to the captain, the first mate, and other crewmen on how a sailing ship worked. They seemed happy to share their knowledge of sailing and their love of the sea. To help himself learn, Jacob followed some of the sailors doing their duties, and he tried his hand at various skills. He even took a turn on the ship's wheel under the eyes of the first mate.

He learned that every rope, every sail, every part of the ship had a name and purpose, and he learned how to use them. Jacob took turns with the crew, raising and lowering sails, moving the sails to better use the wind, and tying the right knots so the ropes wouldn't get loose. It was a good way to kill time, but Jacob determined the sailor's life was not for him. Give him his mountains any time.

They traveled for two more days before finally arriving at Halifax and the recently captured fortress city of Louisburg. Jacob had just begun to get the hang of being a sailor when they arrived at their destination.

Located on the northeast side of Halifax, Louisburg was swarming with vessels and activity as the British gathered the army for the coming campaign against Quebec. The small schooner made its way between large vessels, including the ninety-gun ship of the line HMS Neptune that was sailing into the port.

Jacob whistled to himself as he looked up the side of the warship, much taller than their little schooner, and he admired the rows of large cannons poking out from the side of the ship.

"Aye," commented the captain, seeing Jacob's appreciation of the warship. "Not as fast as me little darling here, but boy can that pack a punch."

The fortress sat on the west side of the harbor, where several large warships and merchant ships rode at anchor. On the ground and hills surrounding the harbor and the fortress was a sea of the army's white canvas tents. Jacob, having shouldered all of his gear, waited on deck as the schooner made its way through the larger ships to a dock where it tied up.

The captain and first mate saw Jacob off, thanking him once more for his assistance in repelling the privateer. "Yur pretty good with that rifle there," the captain commented as he shook Jacob's hand. "You ever get sick of this land-lubbing, come look us up."

Making his away along one of the many battalion streets, Jacob asked for and received directions to General Wolfe's headquarters. He observed British companies and battalions drilling, either marching or going through loading and firing drills.

Jacob snorted and laughed to himself, remembering the first time he had arrived at Fort Edward and how the sea of tents surrounding the walls made it the largest place he had ever seen. Now looking out over this new camp, Jacob nodded to himself and returned to doing his duty.

***

Harpe was walking along the road to the docks, when he spotted Jacob and quickly moved behind a pile of old casks. "Well now, what has fortune brought me?" he whispered. Jacob walked past, unaware of Harpe's evil eyes watching and following him.

"You are one of those damn do-gooders that ruined my fun back in New York and got me sent here," Harpe muttered. "Well my old friend, revenge can be bloody." Harpe watched Jacob continue on his way before he stepped out from behind the casks and made his way to the shop of the sutler he was supposed to recruit.

***

General Wolfe was headquartered in a small house near the fields where the army was encamped, the door flanked by two grenadiers in their tall, bearskin hats. They watched as Jacob approached, following him with their eyes, and seeing Jacob's epaulette, they stood a little straighter but didn't salute.

Jacob didn't really notice the discourtesy and entered the headquarters. After removing his hat and waiting to be recognized, Jacob was directed to an orderly sitting behind a large desk.

"Dispatches for the general from Generals Amherst and Gage in New York," Jacob informed the orderly, who accepted the satchel.

"If I may ask sir, where would I find the Ranger encampment?"

The orderly gave him directions. "Their camp is on the far side of the field there; look for the ones uniformed in green, and you'll find them." Jacob thanked him, saluted, and headed off to join the Rangers. Jacob was chuckling to himself at the direction to look for the ones in green.

After a short journey across the field, he arrived at a mix of tents and lean-tos and was directed to Captain Moses Hazen's company area. Captain Hazen was speaking with two of his sergeants when Jacob found him and waited for him to finish.

Jacob remembered Captain Hazen from when he had served during the fighting around Lake George and Fort William Henry, but Captain Hazen hadn't been an officer then. He had been a sergeant, like Jacob. Major Rogers had personally recommended Hazen for promotion to lieutenant in one of the companies at Fort Edward, and then he was promoted again and placed in command of one of the companies here in Louisburg. When he was finished, Captain Hazen turned and, seeing Jacob, smiled and extended his hand.

"When I sent that dispatch to Major Rogers, I didn't expect him to send you, but damn I am glad he did!"

Shaking his hand, Jacob handed his orders to Captain Hazen, who simply stuffed them in his haversack. As he followed the captain to the command hut, Jacob was asked to bring him up to date on the fighting and the campaigns against Fort Carillon and Crown Point.

"Has it been as bad as we have heard?" Captain Hazen asked. "The British command here only seems to inform us about the fighting when we have lost. Have we been losing that much?"

Jacob shook his head no, though there had been some setbacks. He told Captain Hazen of their expeditions and scouts, and Major Rogers's raids. Then Jacob told him about his adventure fighting off the privateers to get there.

"Aye, that is true. We have definitely been hearing of those attacks," said Captain Hazen. He led Jacob to his command hut, placed Jacob's orders on his desk, and then began telling him about their company.

"I'll be blunt and to the point. These are not the same quality of men as we had in Lake George. We had difficulties in recruiting the quality men we needed. Instead we got the scraps from the bottom of the barrel."

"Are they local volunteers?" asked Jacob, and Captain Hazen answered, "Some yes, and some are from the British regiments, mostly trouble makers they don't want in their ranks. So we get them as volunteers."

Captain Hazen showed Jacob to his tent, explaining that he planned for Jacob to serve as his second in command. After Jacob dropped off his gear, Captain Hazen took him around and began introducing him to the rest of the company.

There were two other lieutenants, Baker Hatch and Charles Frost, new lieutenants who were still learning their jobs. Jacob also met First Sergeant David Heard, an experienced Ranger whom Jacob also remembered from the early actions around Lake George and Fort Edward. First Sergeant Heard also voiced his approval of Jacob being assigned to them.

"We have a lot of work to do to get these men ready for the campaign. Some of them are decent, but a good majority of them are here for the wrong reasons, mostly greed," he said.

Jacob nodded. He had seen this all before.

First Sergeant Heard called for the other sergeants, David Dolby, Robert Foley, and Andre Howard, and introduced them to Jacob, who looked them over. All were grizzled and seasoned veterans who carried themselves as Rangers should, and Jacob nodded his head in approval.

Captain Hazen left Jacob with the sergeants. "I'll leave you to it," he said and returned to his command hut to continue his work. Jacob introduced himself, explained how he had risen through the ranks from enlisted man, to sergeant, to lieutenant. He also stressed how he would rely on them to assist him to get the company ready.

"I have a simple policy," explained Jacob. "Everyone fights, and everyone does their job. Anyone who can't handle it or pull their weight is gone. I will not risk your lives or the lives of these men over one person, period!" The sergeants nodded and smiled, liking how Jacob did his business. "Well, you know where I stand. Time to meet the company. Form the men," he instructed.

It was a company of about eighty men, and each of the sergeants was in charge of one of the platoons of about twenty men. Looking at the assembled Rangers, he saw a mix of emotions. Some of the more professional and seasoned Rangers looked confident, others looked as though they were still figuring out the Ranger life, and then Jacob saw the troublemakers who were smirking and whispering to one another.

Jacob eyed these men. This was the same problem they had faced in New York when men like this were forced onto the companies to quickly grow their size. "Quantity over quality," Jacob growled under his voice as he looked the company over. Standing erect, he walked up to the company and muttered, "To hell with quantity, give me quality." He stood before the assembled Rangers, looking into their eyes and reading their faces.

"I know what you are thinking, another dumb lieutenant for the company," Jacob began, and received the expected snorts and laughs from the rank. Jacob smiled, and then hardened his face. "I am not one of those," he growled as he planted his fists on his hips and faced the company. "I've been fighting this war from the beginning, starting out as a private, then corporal and sergeant, and now as a bloody lieutenant. I have seen more than my fair share of action, almost lost my hair a few times, and took many more scalps from the enemy."

Jacob stopped to allow his words to sink in. The veterans nodded in approval, the unsure Rangers still didn't know what to expect, and unfortunately, the riff-raff Rangers still snickered and spoke behind their hands, not taking him serious. Jacob approached the trouble maker, and stared death into his eye.

"Did I say something, amusing?" asked Jacob in a low voice. The smirk fell from the face of the Ranger, who swallowed and shook his head no. Jacob closed to within inches from the offenders face, stared into his eyes, and then into the eyes of his neighbors, who had been sharing in the laugh.

"Don't do your job, and I'll kill you myself. I will not lose a Ranger because someone didn't do their job." Jacob spoke softly as he closed within fractions of an inch from the offender's nose. "Because someone thought this was a joke." The man actually shivered looking into Jacob's icy expression. "Do you understand?"

Jacob stood back and addressed the company once more. "Does everyone here understand? Everyone will do his duty or else!" Most of the company yelled in agreement, while some still looked confused, and some actually looked scared. "Those who don't, I recommend you find a new job with someone else today, for tomorrow I am going to see what kind of Rangers you truly are!"

After releasing the company, Jacob looked around and met some of the Rangers one-on-one, before returning to his tent to fix it up. He was impressed to see that he had a wood and canvas cot to sleep on off the ground, a small stool and table, and a lantern. "Hmm, guess rank does have its privileges." After getting everything settled, Jacob went over to the quartermaster to get new powder and lead to replace what he had used in the fight against the privateers.

This was by far the largest encampment Jacob had ever seen, even larger than the tent city that grew around Fort Edward. As the sun set, the sea of white tents began to glow and flicker from lanterns and the thousands of fires, which caused a small cloudbank of smoke to hang over the encampment.

As with other camps, the sound of thousands of voices filled the evening air mixed with the various tunes from musical instruments, all accompanied by the songs of the night birds and insects. Heading over to the company's field kitchen, Jacob filled his wooden bowl with a thick stew, grabbed a couple of warm, thick biscuits, and found a place to sit and eat. Some of the Rangers came over to ask Jacob to confirm the stories they had heard about his saving Major Rogers's life or about the fighting down in New York.

Jacob snorted and smiled, and responded, "Which time? I have pulled the major's bacon out of the fire so many times I have lost count." Jacob recounted rescues on the lake, outside of Fort Saint Frederick, and in the Battle on Snowshoes.

"Did they really kill everyone at William Henry?" was what most of the Rangers asked. Jacob recounted what he had observed. "It was an ugly fight," he recalled. "No one was spared. The French were slow to respond, and in the end, everyone suffered."

In the silence as the Rangers reflected on what he had told them, Jacob's mind raced back to those gore-filled days and the horrors he had experienced.

The company quickly learned Jacob was a man of his word as he began running them through their paces. While the regular

British companies drilled in the European style of warfare, Jacob led the company through Ranger drills, retraining them on Ranger tactics and techniques that they had improved on back on the island. Captain Hazen watched with an approving eye as Jacob worked not just the men, but the lieutenants and sergeants as well.

Some of the enlisted "riff-raff," those who were strictly there for the money and the plunder, were either quickly weeded out or they simply left in the night. First Sergeant Heard reported that ten men had decided to leave. Captain Hazen was not surprised. "Good riddance to bad trash," he said. "This is working out nicely," he thought.

Replacing these men was not a problem. Once the word spread around the camp that Jacob had arrived and had begun training the Rangers, many requested transfers to Captain Hazen's company. Most of these men had also been at Lake George and/or Fort William Henry in the early years, and they remembered then Sergeant Clarke training them at Ranger school.

Captain Hazen was pleased as more experienced men joined his company, and the weaker men left. He again mentally thanked Major Rogers for sending him Jacob. He no longer felt so unsure about the looming campaign. In fact, Captain Hazen felt more confident every day that not only he, but most of his men, might even survive.

CHAPTER 18

THE RIVER CAMPAIGN

May led into June, the temperatures warmed, and the sky cleared into a bright blue, which meant that the campaign season was upon them. The army continued to prepare itself for the coming battle, and the commanders and their men were waiting for the order to march. The army was composed of three brigades, all manned with regular British regiments. The only Provincial soldiers were the six companies of Rangers, and even they were placed under the command of a regular British officer, Major George Scott of the 40th Regiment of Foot.

Along with Captain Hazen, the other Ranger captains included Jonathan Brewer, Benonie Dank, Joseph Gorham, James Rogers, and William Stark. Jacob recognized some of the officers as he went around and was introduced, men he recalled from the early days at Fort Edward. James Rogers was Major Rogers's younger brother, and he asked how the major was doing up in New York.

"As expected," Jacob replied. "He continues to develop strategies for fighting the French, and sometimes the English."

James snorted and nodded in agreement, "Sounds like him. Glad to hear he still has his hair." Jacob smiled and nodded, answering, "Barely," and he continued to meet the other officers.

Captain Gorham was considered the senior commander, having led the Ranger detachment during the Louisburg campaign, but now he had been replaced by Major Scott.

"We're in a tight spot here," explained Captain Gorham. "We are constantly fighting for supplies, justifying why we're here, and insisting that we're not a sacrificial lamb to be led to the slaughter."

Jacob nodded. "Do we get any support from the British officers?"

Gorham raised his eyebrows, thought for a minute, and replied, "From some, but not many. Some are accepting what they call the 'light infantry' concept that you all started in New York. Some accept it, and others fight it tooth and nail. We do have a few supporters who almost treat us as equals, but mostly no, not really. At least not amongst the senior staff, though Major Scott seems to be coming around."

General Wolfe had instructed that the army was to drill and rehearse before the campaign began. Officers were to inspect their men and equipment, insuring both were in good condition. General Wolfe ordered that all infantrymen were to be sure they had thirty-six rounds of ammunition per man. The quartermasters issued casks of musket balls to the Rangers who shrugged their shoulders and shook their heads.

"Once again they don't seem to grasp the concept that we don't carry their beloved Brown Besses," grumbled Captain Hazen.

Jacob nodded. "Have the men break out their pots and melt the balls down. We'll cast our own. The Rangers poured the balls into the small iron pots until they melted, then ladled them into their bullet molds.

Jacob watched in satisfaction as the Rangers took it in stride. They didn't complain, but sat in small groups, working together to cast and file the balls while talking and laughing. This was a good sign. It showed the morale was good, and the men were able to adapt, which might come in handy in the looming campaign. This was one of the same problems he had faced in New York. In a way, it was refreshing to see these logistical issues here as well.

These logistical issues were perplexing General Wolfe, who was facing the daunting and unique challenge of gathering all of the supporting materials he would need and figuring out how to transport them to Quebec. As part of the preparations, a large number of flat-bottom boats, whaleboats, and cutters were being assembled. The army was instructed to practice loading and unloading from these boats, because they would be needed in Quebec, and the soldiers had to be ready for amphibious operations.

Having received his order to prepare his men for boat operations, Captain Hazen went looking for Jacob, who he assumed was a lot more experienced in training men in boats than he was. He found Jacob, who was puffing on his pipe and overseeing the casting of rifle balls, and pulled him off to the side.

"You're familiar with small boats like whaleboats?" asked Captain Hazen.

Jacob nodded. "Major Rogers had us learn to use whaleboats for operations on both lakes. Why?" Captain Hazen told him of their instructions to have watercraft training.

"Is it just us or all of the Ranger companies?" asked Jacob, and Captain Hazen answered that they were all required to learn. Nodding and knocking the burnt ash from his pipe, Jacob said, "Have the officers and sergeants meet me at the boats tomorrow, and I'll train them to be cadre so they can train their own men. Once they're trained, then I'll start with our company, if that is good with you and Captain Gorham."

Captain Gorham readily agreed to Jacob's plan to build training cadre. He passed the word and in the early morning after formation, Jacob was waiting next to the shore where several whaleboats sat with their oars readied. The Rangers gathered around Jacob, looking at the boats and then out into the mist-shrouded bay.

First, Jacob explained the basic principles of the boats, how the men would sit, where they would store their gear, and how they would work as a crew. Once the men seemed to grasp the basics, Jacob assigned officers and sergeants from the same company to a boat. "Right. Let's start working on those blisters and sore backs!" he ordered, and he had the new crews man their boats and push out into the bay.

Just as he had done with the Rangers in New York, he began teaching them how to use the oars as a team. As with the previous lessons, it took some trial and error for the crews to begin working together to row and to steer the boats. In the beginning, some of the boats mostly spun in circles, and two even collided and bounced off one another. Spectators, who had come to observe the training, lined the shore, slapping their knees and laughing at the plight of the Rangers.

Some of the frustrated Rangers turned to say something to the British regulars who were watching at laughing at their expense, but Jacob grabbed them and turned them back to their lessons of loading and unloading the boats from the shore. "Don't let them see you sweat," whispered Jacob with a stern look, "let our actions speak louder than our words. Remember, it will be their turns soon."

By lunch, the crews had the hang of it. Jacob gave them a break to eat their cooked rations sitting on bales and boxes of supplies on the shore. As Jacob predicted, the British regulars were attempting to load and unload the flat bottomed boats, assisted by crews from the Royal Navy. Many a fine red-coated soldier splashed into the water, jumping up spitting and sputtering after loosing their footing or falling overboard when the boat jerked in the waves.

Some of the sergeants and lieutenants asked Jacob questions about the actions in New York, especially the ones where they had used the boats for scouting or fighting. Jacob recalled the ugly fight at Sabbath Bay Point and the landings on the northern shore of Lake George, the bloody fighting with the French and their Indian allies in canoes.

When lunch was over, Jacob decided to capitalized from the conversation, and spoke about how to use the boats in action. He showed where on the whaleboats swivel guns could be mounted and how to use them. "One of my men named Samuel," recounted Jacob, "loved his swivel gun and was very effective with it, only be sure what you're aiming at. Who ever is in front of them, be they friend or foe, will catch hell."

As the day ended, Jacob explained how to best train their men in boat procedures and discussed tactics for employing all of the boats, working as a unit, and how to effectively land and withdraw from the beach. "In the morning, it's all going to be you doing the training, so look to your men, guide them and mold them, but be ready for some wet Rangers."

The following day, Jacob led his company to the shore, and with three whaleboats, he assigned one sergeant and lieutenant with their section to each boat, and he began running them through their paces while Captain Hazen observed next to him.

The other Ranger companies were down at the harbor as well. Whale boats were all over the place, like a multitude of white water bugs skittering around the harbor. Along with the Rangers, the British regulars were still working with the Royal Navy, were having their turns, and from what Jacob observed, the

Rangers grasped the concept quicker than their regular counterparts.

By afternoon, the companies were practicing boat tactics, including how to approach a shore, one section covering while the others made their landings and the Rangers splashed to shore. Then they practiced how to withdraw with the boats.

From the shore, jealous eyes observed and the frustrated voices of British officers could be heard as they berated their men for not performing well. "The bloody Provincials have figured it out," Jacob could hear a very loud major yelling at his junior officers. "How is it we, the pride of His Majesty's forces, can't bloody well load and bloody well unload these boats without drowning ourselves!"

Jacob, wanting to make a point, decided to bring it all together and make sure everyone understood his role with the small boats. He decided to run a full, live-fire rehearsal of a landing by having the entire Ranger battalion of six companies, carrying their arms and equipment and with swivel guns in the bows of the boats, conduct a landing. He selected a safe area on the shore as their landing zone and even placed white painted wooden targets to check the Rangers' accuracy under pressure.

Captain Gorham notified Major Scott and invited him and his staff to observe. On the morning of the landing, Major Scott watched from the shore with some of the other regular British officers, including Colonel Howe of the 58th Regiment of Foot and Major Hussey of the 47th Regiment of Foot, along with their staffs. These regiments had been designated light infantry by General Wolfe for the army. Alongside were other officers from the army who, having learned of the exercise, were interested to see how these Provincial Rangers would do.

The Rangers loaded into their small fleet of armed whaleboats, and pushed out into the bay, the captains all pleased that not a single Ranger had slipped or fallen into the water. Captain Gorham led the Ranger flotilla out to the harbor entrance, turned them around, and began approaching an empty piece of shore where they could conduct the live-fire exercise. Jacob and Captain Hazen manned their boat, the other two boats from the company on either side of them, as they made their way towards the shore.

The boats deployed into line, and the oars lifted and fell in unison as they approached the shore. To make a dramatic entrance, Jacob gave the command for the swivel guns to commence fire, blasting his wooden targets. The wind carried the smoke forward, serving as a screen as the bows of the whaleboats bit into the shore.

The first Rangers went over the sides and held the boats steady as the rest of the Rangers splashed ashore, carrying their rifles and shooting bags over their heads. They then deployed into their skirmish lines. Luck smiled on them, and not a single Ranger fell as they landed on the shore. The Rangers commenced firing at the wooden targets.

Once he had landed and taken up his central position, Captain Gorham directed the "raid" as the Ranger sections moved to their assigned areas. Jacob and Captain Hazen led their Rangers towards their objective, their white wooden targets riddled with holes from the swivel guns and from their own rifles. Some of the Rangers even drew their tomahawks and threw them, the wooden targets falling over, "dead."

Pleased with their performance, Jacob looked back out on the shore and watched Captain Gorham point out targets to the covering whaleboats. Satisfied, Captain Gorham gave the order to withdraw by sections, the Rangers firing their rifles and the swivel guns covering until all the men were back in the boats and rowing away. Jacob held the bow as his men scrambled in and pushed out into the bay. The exercise appeared to be a success.

With a satisfied smile on his face, Jacob turned to look up at the assembled light infantry officers and Major Scott, who were also nodding their heads in approval and clapping their hands. Major Scott himself tipped his hat to Jacob and the Rangers. Jacob also observed payments of wagers, either for or against his men, being exchanged by the junior officers.

From a short distance away, General Wolfe also nodded his head in approval. These Rangers were living up to their reputations and his expectations. "Make a note, gentlemen," General Wolfe instructed his staff. "I expect our men to be as proficient, if not more. See to it." General Wolfe looked back out to the Rangers. "Yes," he said to himself. "I will have some work for you to do soon."

EPILOGUE

The thunder crashed and the rain beat down on the cloaked form of Maclane as he made his way through the muddy streets to the tavern in Saratoga. The tavern's sign swayed and creaked in the wind, thunder rattling the wooden shingles as he opened the door and stepped into the dry main room.

Shaking the rain from his cloak, Maclane allowed his eyes to adjust to the dim light, candles flickering and the fire at the end of the room throwing a dancing glow, punctuated by the lightning seen through the tall windows, the rumble of thunder outside. Maclane spotted the table in the corner where Pierre sat with two mugs before him, nodding towards Maclane.

He took a seat across from Pierre, who welcomed him by saying, "Ah my friend, so good to see you. The weather is not fit for man or beast, no?"

Taking a long pull from the tankard, Maclane looked over the top of the tankard and replied simply, "No." Then after finishing the tankard, he placed it back on the table.

Pierre waited until the serving girl deposited two more tankards and departed before starting their conversation.

"So my friend," Pierre began. "Has business been as good for you as it has been for me? I have heard that with the exception of a few independent owners, the South Sea Company is the main provider of goods and services from New York City to what you call …," Pierre thought for a moment, "…Fort Amherst?"

Maclane kept a poker face, but nodded. "Your information is quite good, monsieur. I need to know your sources and make them an offer."

Pierre raised his tankard in salute and then took a drink.

"I have heard that the Company of New France has also been doing well," Maclane said. "My sources say you have the entire network of goods and services along the Saint Lawrence through the Richelieu, controlling Quebec, and Montreal ..." Maclane paused. "... all the way down to Carillon."

Again Pierre raised his tankard in salute. "Your sources seem to be as good as mine. Perhaps I can buy them away from you?"

Maclane snorted as he took a drink from his tankard. "Not likely."

Pierre countered, asking, "Oh, they are that loyal?"

Maclane snorted once again and replied, "No, they're greedy. Don't think even you could afford them."

It was Pierre's turn to laugh. "So it seems your company and my company have locked up the northeast in a nice, tight bow, no?"

Maclane looked seriously at Pierre and again replied, "No."

Pierre's eyebrows rose in surprise. "And why do you say this?" he asked.

"I imagine that seeing we now control Louisburg and the mouth of the river, it may be more difficult for your wares to make it downriver to Quebec or Montreal."

Pierre waved his hands and snorted, "Pah!"

He seemed disturbed. "So your English friends have the city, but they will not for long. The bane of your very existence, the Marquis Montcalm, will do to Louisburg as he did to your precious Fort William Henry!"

Pierre took an angry pull from his tankard and slammed it back on the table, rattling it. With the commotion of the thunderstorm around the tavern, no one noticed but Maclane. He sat back and smiled to himself but kept a stony, blank look on his face.

"We can move goods when we need to," Pierre said. We have received orders to supply the reinforcements that are on their way here from France! Thousands are coming, and these are our finest from the best regiments, who will sweep your pitiful army aside easily!"

Then Pierre loomed close to Maclane, leaning on the table and said more softly, "You should take care my friend, before I buy you out as we take back everything, and then move swiftly to Albany. You may be working for me sooner than you think."

Maclane kept his face as blank as possible. The news concerning the French reinforcements would reward him handsomely, once he passed it to his benefactor. Pierre looked angry, and he was breathing heavily, so Maclane decided to smooth his ruffled feathers.

"That may be. You would not be a bad person to work for, as long as it's profitable," soothed Maclane, which seemed to take some of the edge off Pierre's anger, and he returned to his near jovial self. Maclane added, "I meant nothing of it. Here, let me make amends."

He called the serving girl over and purchased drinks for Pierre and himself. The conversation returned to normal, and once again Pierre clanked his tankard with Maclane's. "Yes my friend. It's nothing personal. It's simply business. We should remain friends, and not hard competitors," Maclane continued.

"Yes, my friend," Pierre replied. "It's only business." Then he raised his tankard once more. "May your business and my business be profitable and our competitors go poor!"

Maclane saluted this toast, and the two businessmen finished their drinks and slammed them on the table. Pierre wiped his mouth on the sleeve of his shirt, and then looked seriously at Maclane.

"You know my friend, pretty soon it may come down to just you and I as the competition. I would hate to see that. I enjoy our conversations and the game, but there will be no independent businessmen soon, if you and I keep up our pace of acquisitions."

Maclane returned the serious look, nodding. "That may be true my friend. That may be very true ..." Looking into his tankard and draining the small amount that was left at the bottom, he added, "... and very unfortunate." Maclane motioned to the serving girl for another round, and then turned back to Pierre.

"I truly think of you as a friend. I would hate to have to go up against you. We should be working together, not against one another."

Maclane paused as the serving girl returned with two full tankards and placed them on the table. Maclane raised his tankard to Pierre, "I propose we work together and combine our assets and rule the world through commerce!"

Pierre smiled and clanked his tankard against Maclane's. "You know, that's not a bad idea! I think between the two of us, we could own the world and all of these damn kings and queens would answer to us for we would have the gold, all of the gold."

Pierre drained his tankard in one long pull, and then smiled. "For those who have the gold make the rules. It's only business, yes?"

For the rest of the evening, the two men drank and bragged of their exploits, trying to outdo one another. Maclane made sure that Pierre was drinking twice as much as he, of course. He made sure Pierre's tankard was always full. Maclane was able to glean more information about French naval and troop movements, based on Pierre's business holdings and involvements. As Pierre kept talking, Maclane stored the information away to be used later.

It was near midnight when a very drunk and happy Pierre was helped by holding a giggling serving girl under his arm as he lurched and staggered towards his room, singing a very off-key French song. Perhaps because it was late and the rest of the patrons of the tavern were drunk, no one noticed that Pierre was singing in French, although Maclane believed the townsfolk of Saratoga didn't really care.

Pulling his cloak on over his shoulder, Maclane left the tavern and made his way out into the damp darkness. While it was still raining, there were only a few flashes of lightning off in the distance and no thunder. Maclane's boots squished along the muddy road as he headed to the small house the company used in Saratoga, his mind deep in thought.

Maclane entered a dark room that served as a company office and froze. He could sense that he was not alone in the dark. His ears strained to hear any tell-tale sound from whomever he had sensed. He gently closed the door and was slowly reaching under his cloak for his concealed pistol, when a voice called out from the dark.

"Come now, captain. There is no need for that. Just an old friend in from this foul weather."

A well-made lantern door opened, revealing a man sitting at a clerk's desk, his fingers resting on the lantern. Maclane released the handle of his pistol and allowed it to remain hidden in his cloak, which he took off and hung on a wall peg.

The man's face and some of his upper body were illuminated by the light from the small lantern. "How is our friend from up north? Well, I presume."

Maclane sat in a chair across from the man and replied, "As well as can be expected. He was very forthcoming with information today."

Of average height and unassuming visage, Richard Bedlow waited until Maclane settled himself in the chair across from him. While also a businessman like Maclane, he went by Major Richard Bedlow, chief of intelligence for his Majesty's Army in the colonies, or simply the spymaster that Maclane answered to and also his benefactor.

"Well captain, what news do you have for me?" Bedlow asked as he opened the other small lantern door, adding some more light to the room. Maclane arranged his thoughts in order, weighing how much to give to Bedlow and how much to keep to himself in case he might need the information at a later time.

"Pierre strongly believes that the reinforcements sailing from France will be enough to stop our spring campaign," Maclane reported. Bedlow asked, "Do you think he is right?" Maclane thought about it and shook his head.

"I believe he is overestimating their chances based on Abercrombie's amateurish assault against Fort Carillon."

Bedlow nodded and asked, "Even knowing we now control the mouth of the Saint Lawrence and Louisburg, he still feels confident?"

Maclane nodded, "Pierre believes that they can maintain their lines of supply from other locations until they retake Louisburg, then it will be smooth sailing all the way to Albany and beyond."

Bedlow nodded, taking in all of this information. He would have to send a message to General Wolfe and stop by and speak with General Amherst. Bedlow looked at Maclane and asked, "Your thoughts on this?"

Maclane again chose his words carefully before replying. "I believe Pierre is full of hot air and full of himself."

Letting out a loud laugh and slapping the table, Bedlow replied, "Please captain, continue with your line of thinking. What else do you believe?"

Shrugging, Maclane said, "I truly believe the French are overestimating their abilities, and underestimated ours. Luck may have been on their side, but I truly believe their luck has run its course, and soon we will benefit greatly from the coming campaign."

"We will benefit, or you?" asked Bedlow.

Maclane raised his hands in defense and answered, "Both. Our King will reap the rewards when Canada is securely in his grasp, and I will reap the rewards when I, or I should say the company acquires Pierre's holdings and controls the entire northeast trade."

"Auspicious, if I do say so myself," replied Bedlow. "As long as I, on behalf of the Crown, continue to receive our percentage. How goes your acquisition of Louisburg and establishing your foothold in Canada?"

It did not surprise Maclane that Bedlow was aware of his operations in Louisburg; he wouldn't be the spymaster he was supposed to be if he was unaware, although Maclane still hoped that Bedlow did not know about the unique problem of Harpe and his late-night hobby.

"Yes, our company man is there and working on securing the logistical requirements with General Wolfe's Quartermaster-General. So far everything is in order and the company's merchantmen, protected by the Royal Navy, …" He paused and bowed to Bedlow, who had made arrangements for the Royal Navy to protect their convoys from French warships and privateers. Bedlow bowed back and smiled. Maclane continued, "… have begun stockpiling and preparing to move with the army as it sails for Quebec and Montreal."

"And how goes the supplying of Amherst's campaign?" asked Bedlow. Maclane replied, "Well, the company ships are making it up to Albany, the road up through Fort Edward and on to the staging camp is now well-protected, and the French have been kept at bay. All is in motion and should be ready for the campaign to begin. Unless the generals make some critical mistakes, this campaign will see our King victorious!"

Bedlow nodded and what Maclane had said matched his own assessment of the coming campaign. He was impressed by how Maclane balanced his roles of mercantilism and gathering information, and he couldn't fault him for making himself rich. Of course, he was getting his cut of the action, which was setting up a nice retirement for when this war was over.

"I may have need of you in Charles Town down in South Carolina. There seem to be new issues growing there with the Cherokee, the French, and the Spanish, who are sticking their noses into business that does not require them," Bedlow continued. "Your man in Louisburg appears to be very efficient."

Maclane nodded as Bedlow sketched out his new plan. "Once we have secured the northeast, we will need to expand into the old French territory of the Ohio Valley and southward. I have plans to see if I can obtain the services of this Major Robert Rogers to secure all of the French holdings to the west. He has been harassing the general staff for a regular commission in the Royal Army. Perhaps I can secure him one and send him out west. He seems to be able to move great distances and to be very effective."

Maclane continued to listen, wondering what his role would be in this plan and how he would profit from it. Bedlow continued, "You and your special man, once you have secured your business between here and Quebec, will need to head to South Carolina to secure His Majesty's interests."

Looking at Bedlow, Maclane asked, "And what are those interests?"

Bedlow smiled. "Once this war is over, more settlers will head to the colonies and will need more room. Down in the Carolinas, the Cherokee Nation has all of the best land to settle and is very resistant to giving it up without a fight," Bedlow said.

Maclane shrugged. "What do you want me to do about it?"

Bedlow looked into Maclane's eyes. "Why get their land of course."

"And if they don't want to give up their land?" Maclane countered. Bedlow simply responded, "Then make them. Either directly or indirectly, make them leave so the Crown will have its new land to settle."

Maclane nodded, believing he understood where Bedlow's line of thought was going. "If they choose to fight?"

Bedlow shrugged his shoulders lightly, looking down at the small flame flickering in the lantern. "The colony's militia will have to fight. If they are as any good as we have seen here, they can do the business of moving the Cherokee or any other Indian Nation further west. If they fail, then that would require the Crown to send the army to stop those heathens. In either case, we win. The Cherokee are gone, the colony must support our army to protect themselves, and we get all of the Cherokee lands."

Bedlow stood up and picked up his cloak, which had been hanging over the back of his chair. Maclane happened to notice the glint of the pistol handle concealed within the cloak. "The Crown can be very receptive to those who serve the King with such fine dedication, and with all of this new land in the Carolinas or westward, the Crown may need some new governors."

Bedlow let that thought hang in the air as he took up his lantern and looked at Maclane, who was already deep in thought as he considered his different options and how he could support the Crown and his profit margins.

"Think about it," Bedlow said, and Maclane looked up from his thoughts. "Once you're ready, I'll provide you with the name of our Indian agent there, and you two can work out the details. Until then, keep me informed on your progress and on anything that could impact the coming campaign. Good night, captain. Or should I say, 'good morning?'"

Realizing it was only a few hours until dawn, Maclane nodded and watched Bedlow make his way to the door and slip out, once more plunging the room into darkness.

Maclane barely realized that Bedlow had left, with the exception of the darkness in the room. His mind was buzzing as he weighed the pros and cons of the different options he could use to expand his holdings and leverage the requirements of the Crown for the Carolinas. Everything was in motion, two major campaigns were about to begin, and they should be the final nail in France's coffin.

Scratching his chin, Maclane recalled the army disposition and the plan for the coming campaigns. "Wolfe should have an easy go of it unless something slows him down, and he gets caught in fall and winter," he mused. He shook his head. That was unrealistic! General Wolfe's army was well-equipped, and due to his efforts, well-supplied for the coming campaign. With the Royal Navy supporting the army and assuming his information from Quebec was accurate, there should not be a major fight for Quebec, even if Montcalm and those reinforcements arrived.

Then Maclane thought about General Amherst's plan to take Fort Carillon, which he thought would be the most challenging of the two. "Why did we ever allow the French to occupy and build that fort on that point of land?" Maclane said to the empty air around him. Even with all of the logistics the company had provided, Maclane's sources couldn't help him to determine what the enemy would do.

"It was a small force that stopped Abercrombie. What will happen if there is a major force there?" Maclane thought, and then slowly nodded his head. "Of course, that means that if they strengthen Carillon, then Quebec will be weak, and if Quebec is strong, then Carillon will be weak. If the generals are patient, they can secure one and destroy the French there, and then combine their forces and take the other."

Maclane sat back in his chair, again going through in his mind the pros and cons, weighing the difficulties and the benefits, the causes and effects of the options. He was still in thought when he saw the pink of the dawn through the window, realizing he hadn't slept.

Snorting to himself, rubbing his eyes, and stretching his arms, he finally realized he was tired. "Well now, how about that?"

Maclane's final estimate was that it was going to be a very profitable year coming up, perhaps two. "It's going to be bloody," he thought as he stood up with a groan, "but that is also good for business."

The coming campaign to take Quebec could be very bad, as the city sat high on looming cliffs, protected by a thick, stone wall and fortifications. Still, General Wolfe had an army of nothing but regulars, although he had heard that there was a small battalion of those green-uniformed Rangers. With the regulars, heavy siege artillery, and the Royal Navy pounding the French resistance into dust, Quebec should fall.

Then Amherst and his army, while a mixed bag of regulars and Provincials, had the numbers if he planned smartly and did not hesitate but maintained good initiative.

He did have this Major Robert Rogers and his Rangers who seemed almost fanatical in taking the fight to the French. "All the better," thought Maclane. "Rogers's dedication will force Amherst to stay on the attack so he looks like he is in charge and not this Ranger. I think Amherst will be victorious, Carillon will fall, and after Quebec falls, Montreal won't last, and Canada will be ours!"

Maclane walked over to a cupboard, and rooted inside until he found what he was looking for, a map showing the southern half of the colonies, the Carolinas. After lighting some candles and using the candlesticks to hold the corners of the map down, Maclane looked at the lines showing the southern Colonies: Virginia, North and South Carolina, and Georgia.

What really grabbed his attention was the expanse of land west of the Appalachian and Allegheny Mountains, all ripe for settlement once the Indians were either chased off or killed off. In his mind, Maclane saw the large green expanse of the thick forests, the blue shimmering lakes and rivers, and all of the game to be had.

His jaw creaked as he yawned, and he stood up from his map. He blew out the candles, and the room was now grey with the dawn. Maclane made his way upstairs to finally go to sleep and wondered what it would be like to be a governor.

"Hmm, Royal Governor William Maclane has a better ring to it than just Captain Maclane," he thought as he clumped up the stairs to his bed. He climbed into bed and started snoring as soon as his head hit the pillow, just as the world was awakening around him.

To the north in Louisburg, Jacob and his fellow Rangers were already up, preparing for their coming campaign. In Louisburg, Harpe was disposing of the body of his latest plaything, a young prostitute. To cover his tracks, he was chopping up her remains and feeding them to the large heard of pigs, which was there to feed the army. This was a great joke to Harpe.

At Fort Edward, Major Rogers and his company commanders were going over their support to Amherst's plan of attack against Fort Carillon. Just as before, the Rangers would screen the army's advance, making sure no French or Indian allies would see the army until it was too late. General Amherst himself was pacing his office, going over the details in his mind to make sure everything was covered for the coming campaign, not wanting to repeat the disaster of the previous assault led by Abercrombie.

The stage was set, the actors in their places, and the music was about to play. Now it was time to see who could truly dance this waltz of war and finally become the masters of this land.

In the audience, the tall grey mountains watched and waited in silence, patiently anticipating the final act on this global stage. The die was cast; all what was left was to see who made the final curtain call.

About the Author

Dr. Erick Nason grew up in the Adirondack Mountains, treading the same woods and lakes that Rogers led his Rangers. After graduating from Glens Falls High School, he began his twenty year career in the Army, serving in the 2nd Ranger Battalion, and with the 10th Special Forces Group. During his career, he deployed on several operations across the globe, to include Europe, Central America, Africa and the Middle East. His education includes a Bachelor of Science degree in World Military History, a Masters of Science Degree in Military Studies-The American Revolution, and a Doctorate in Education, specializing in leadership and military history. He is avid historical reenactor with the 2nd Regiment, South Carolina Continental Line, and a member of the Continental Line establishment. When not reenacting, he is a presenter and supporter of the Campaign 1776 battlefield preservation, a speaker at the Francis Marion Symposium, an Emergency Services Officer and Squadron Historian with the Sumter Composite Squadron of the Civil Air Patrol, and a volunteer firefighter. He works for US Air Forces Central Command as a Personnel Recovery Support Manager on Shaw AFB. His previous works include "From Desert Storm to Iraqi Freedom: One Soldier's Story" and the first book of this series, "In the Presence of Wolves: The Adventures of Ranger Jacob Clarke." He lives in Sumter South Carolina with his wife Karin.

Back page:

As the sun was getting closer to setting, Langy decided to try one more final throw of the dice. He would try and bag Rogers and his surviving Rangers by "coup de main," charging with everyone, and by sheer numbers, overwhelm and finally put this boogey man and his Rangers to rest. Pulling Durantaye and Wolfe close, he quickly pointed out which way he wanted them to go before raising his fusil over his head and giving the command to "Charge!"

With a great surge, the human wave of Indians, Canadians, and Frenchmen broke from the woods and charged up the hill with shouts and yells, some stopping to fire at the Rangers in the purplish grey of the setting sun.

"Every man for themselves. Run for it!" yelled Rogers, as it seemed the very gates of hell itself had opened and released these screaming demons and hellhounds charging up the hill at them.

Breaking up into two- and three-man groups, the Rangers scattered into the growing darkness. Some fell to the accurate French and Canadian fire. The wounded tried to move as best they could, but were quickly overtaken and killed by the charging Indians.

Review Requested:

If you loved this book, would you please provide a review at Amazon.com?